SILVER Player

L.B. DUNBAR

www.lbdunbar.com

ROMANCE. FOR SEXY SILVER FOX LOVERS.

2023 Graphic Cover Design: Blue Moon Creative Studio
Editor: Melissa Shank
Editor: Jenny Sims/Editing4Indies
Proofread: Karen Fischer

Other Books by L.B. Dunbar

<u>Sterling Falls</u>
Sterling Heat
Sterling Brick
Sterling Streak

Parentmoon

<u>Holiday Hotties (Christmas novellas)</u>
Scrooge-ish
Naughty-ish

<u>Road Trips & Romance</u>
Hauling Ashe
Merging Wright
Rhode Trip

<u>Lakeside Cottage</u>
Living at 40
Loving at 40
Learning at 40
Letting Go at 40

<u>The Silver Foxes of Blue Ridge</u>
Silver Brewer
Silver Player
Silver Mayor
Silver Biker

<u>Sexy Silver Fox Collection</u>
After Care
Midlife Crisis
Restored Dreams
Second Chance
Wine&Dine

<u>Collision novellas</u>
Collide
Caught

L.B. DUNBAR

The Sex Education of M.E.

The Heart Collection
Speak from the Heart
Read with your Heart
Look with your Heart
Fight from the Heart
View with your Heart

A Heart Collection Spin-off
The Heart Remembers

BOOKS IN OTHER AUTHOR WORLDS
Smartypants Romance (an imprint of Penny Reid)
Love in Due Time
Love in Deed
Love in a Pickle

The World of True North (an imprint of Sarina Bowen)
Cowboy
Studfinder

THE EARLY YEARS
The Legendary Rock Star Series

Paradise Stories

The Island Duet

Modern Descendants – writing as elda lore

Dedication

Because it takes a village, or in this case a small town,
I'd like to dedicate this one with gratitude to:
Shannon, Melissa, Jenny, Karen.
Thank you for continuing the journey with me into a new year
and a new decade.

L.B. DUNBAR

Chapter 1
Joke's On Me

[Billy]

A young girl walks into a bar…

I'd like to say this is the start of a bad joke, but it isn't really.

It's my life.

It all started as I was giving my sister a pep talk about getting back out there—dating again. Opening herself up to someone new. I practically wrote the book on this cheerleading speech as I've lived by this philosophy for the past sixteen years.

"Hey, boss, there's a girl here to see you," the new busboy addresses me. Blue Ridge Microbrewery and Pub is my pride and joy, and the help is a second family. Our waitstaff has minimal turnover, but with summer ending and college kids going back to school, we lose a few, gain a few, and I don't recognize this kid yet. Our specialty is house beer brewed by my family's business—Giant Beer Company. We've been brewing beer for decades, although my eldest brother is the official Giant in the title. I didn't want to continue working directly under our father, and when Giant returned from the military and Rachel left me…well, let's just say the pub was my gift—happy thirtieth birthday to me.

My youngest sibling, Mati, sits across from me in my office. Her lion-red hair doesn't match the rest of my siblings who have varying shades of gray appearing as we grow older. She's one of the consistent workers as head waitress, human resources of sorts, and event concept coordinator. Basically, a Jill-of-all-trades. Mati's husband died over a year ago, and she isn't sure if she should follow her heart and do the horizontal shuffle with her once best friend from high school who recently returned to Blue Ridge. Their reunion has taken twenty-seven years.

Me? It took me a dozen years to wise up about sex. More like a dozen years of having sex. Random. Wild. Uninhibited. I'd been a blind fool over my high school sweetheart back in the day, but that's a story for another time.

"I'll be there in a minute," I say.

"Always something," my sister mutters under her breath as she stands from the seat opposite my desk. I chuckle, not in the least concerned I just admitted to my sister I'd slept with someone I shouldn't have. Someone clearly stalking me. Mati excuses herself for the kitchen, and I head to the bar. I wasn't in any rush to get out there, but I didn't want to keep anyone waiting, especially if it's a lady.

"What's up?" I address Clyde Bebzene once I stand behind the large counter. Clyde is a slight hot mess with a wild beard and thick sandy brown hair. He's a few years younger than my forty-six, but we're still close enough in age that we get along well. He's a decent guy, coaching baseball for the local peewee team, and an excellent bartender, but I won't admit that to him. He tips his head in the direction of a young black-haired beauty sitting on a barstool—and I mean young, like not legal to sit at the bar, but it's okay because it's the middle of the afternoon. Her light brown eyes pierce me to my core, and there's something familiar about those eyes. She'd be a looker minus the emo shit she has going on. Pasty skin. Kohl eyeliner. Nearly black lips. Midnight-colored fingernails. I immediately dismiss the sensation of recognition. Every woman looks familiar to me.

They have breasts. They have lips. They have fingertips.

Only I don't do the young ones, and regardless of a body looking like a twentysomething, she still has the face of a teen.

"May I help you with something?" I ask, standing behind the bar while Clyde dries some glasses near me. We're prepping for the nightly rush of those appreciating local craft beer and community camaraderie. I opened the bar with the intention of improving our little downtown area, hoping to attract tourists and locals alike to boost our mountain ridge economy.

"I'm looking for Billy Harrington," she states as though she's about to deliver a message. Her voice rings rough as if she's a member of *The Godfather* or something equally mysterious despite being youthful and female. Her eyes scan my body as if she likes what she sees, but she's also sizing me up. I'm over six feet with silver in my hair but dark scruff on my jaw. My brothers tease me, thinking I dye the facial hair for visual contrast. They'll never know the truth. Besides, the ladies are attracted to the dichotomy, so what do I care. *Keep the ladies coming*, and there's a double meaning in that declaration. Only I don't dip lower than thirty years old lately. Those twentysomethings want spankings and baby girl nicknames and have daddy issues. *No thank you.*

"What can I do for you?" My voice teases, and I hear Clyde chuckle next to me.

"You him?" She pauses. "You look different than I thought."

I'm a little surprised she might have thoughts about me one way or another. Her expression clearly tells me she'd eat me up and spit me out, so I don't think when I say, "Not interested in fulfilling some daddy fantasy, honey."

I reach for a rag and begin swiping at the wood bar top although it already shines. Her Tennessee-whiskey gaze makes me nervous all of a sudden, and when her eyes narrow, the sense of familiarity washes over me once again.

"You're sick, and you would be the furthest thing from my fantasy. I'm your daughter."

My hand pauses on the bar. The hint of country music fades in the background. The sound of some afternoon sports competition on the television funnels to silence. The voices around me trip and mutter to a stop.

What did she say?

"Excuse me?" I chuckle while choking and then clear my throat as if the action will open my ears and clear my hearing. I look left and right to see if I'm being punked but find the bar empty minus a couple I don't recognize and Clyde.

"The only daddy issue I have is the issue of you being my dad."

"I…" What. The. Fuuuuuuuu*ck*. My brain wants to say, *impossible*. My dick knocks against my zipper suggesting, *maybe*.

No.

No, this can't be.

I always wrap my shit up. No leaks. No tweaks. No just a dip and I'll pull out. Full coverage. Every damn time.

"I…" I can't seem to find words, so she spears me with a few more.

"Yeah, I can't either," she states as if she read my thoughts. "And an absentee dad on top of that. You win father of the year, Billy Harrington. *Not*."

With that, she raps her knuckles on the bar, hops off the stool, and sashays her black-jeaned ass out of my bar.

No joke.

Chapter 2
No Joke

[Billy]

"Boss, there's a woman here to see you." A déjà vu and a you've-got-to-be-kidding-me moment arrested me as I sit at my desk with my hands over my face, and Clyde gives me a second declaration that someone is looking for me.

I'm your daughter.

It just isn't possible, right? If I'm a baby daddy, she'd be a…baby…not a teenager. That girl looked all of fifteen or sixteen. If I count back in my head to who, when, where—and won't be able to remember any of those answers—I'd certainly know the why and how of sixteen years ago.

My wife left me.

Blue Ridge is a small town. The youth pool is mainly those who go to the local schools, and Rachel and I were like Blue Ridge High School royalty. Blonde hair, blue eyes, and legs for miles, she was every teen's wet dream. Horny and ornery, my high school years were enhanced by her teasing nature and a swollen dick every time she was near me. Look on the internet for erection lasting more than four hours without relief, and there's an image of my lower appendage and my name engraved underneath. I didn't fault Rachel, though. I thought she was just holding out on me.

As high school sweethearts, we went to the same college where we had an up and down relationship but married upon her graduation. I had dropped out. I loved her. She loved me. I never knew we were so disconnected until she left eight years later. Afterward, sex became my sole focus—sex, sex, and more sex—to validate me as a man. It wasn't that women didn't like my dick. It was only my wife who didn't. I didn't mind the reputation I garnered afterward. But sometimes, I wondered if that reputation held me back from something bigger. Something amazing.

When I went on my sex-spree, I was vigilantly protective and preventative, which is why this new development didn't make sense.

"Boss?" Clyde's voice waffles through the room like a haze over hot pavement. He witnessed the conversation with the girl in the bar but graciously ignored me as I walked back to my office. Now, he's holding out for an answer after telling me another woman's waiting to speak with me.

"I'm busy," I say, not recognizing my own voice.

"The hell he is," screeches a female accent I'd know anywhere. Two small hands grip Clyde's bulging bicep and yank him to the side, revealing my nemesis who is pushing her way into my office.

Roxanne McAllister.

Great. She's the last thing I need today.

"Get out," I spitefully snap. Clyde ducks his head, steps back into the hallway, and disappears. Of course, I wasn't speaking to him. I'm addressing Roxie. This is our thing. We hate one another, and we don't mince words when we're around each other. She's the cock-blocking bookstore owner across the street who I was complaining about to my sister only an hour ago.

The first time I met Roxanne McAllister, she called the cops on me.

"Billy Harrington, what did you do?" she snaps at me, placing her hands on her hips, a million bracelets jingling down her bare arm. Roxanne has broad hips, accentuated by the gypsy-looking skirt she's wearing, which looks like an oversized bandana. Her waves of silvery hair flow wildly over her shoulders where she wears a simple white T-shirt that clings to her large breasts. She'd be my curvy fantasy, if the reality wasn't, she's my worst nightmare.

"I don't have time for your hullabaloo today," I bark, wiggling my fingers and flicking my wrist to dismiss her. Roxanne is a bit eccentric, and I can't handle her brand of voodoo on a good day. This woman knows when I'm down on my knees, and that's when she comes out to poke the bear. It's spooky, actually. I stand to my full height, vibrating in irritation at her presence, ready to dismiss her again when she speaks.

"What did you say to her?"

"Who?" I snap, falling into Roxanne's trap. *Don't engage*, I warn myself too late and instead raise a hand. "You know what? Don't answer that. Get out, like I asked." My arm swings outward, and a finger points at the open door. Roxanne crosses her arms, enhancing the swell of her breasts, and narrows her dark eyes at me.

Narrowed glare. Something familiar.

The hand I raised to dismiss her comes to my forehead and rubs in frustration.

"I don't recall you asking." She pauses. "Politely."

My temper flares. "Leave. Please."

Her eyes narrow to near slits, and her fingers dig into her paisley-covered hips. "What did you *do*?"

Staring back at her, I note her eyes for another second. Although she's all of forty-something, the piercing glare matches the younger eyes stabbing me a half hour ago. My knees shake, and I want to lower to my seat, but I won't give Roxanne the satisfaction.

Speaking of satisfaction, she's one woman I can scratch off my list of potential past pleasure-seekers. I wouldn't touch her if my pole was ten feet and—

"William," she barks my given name. "Must I repeat myself? What did you say to Sadie?"

"Who's Sadie?"

I don't think a person can perfect a glare like the one Roxanne gives me, and then her brows slowly rise, and an expression of dawning occurs.

"Didn't she tell you?" Her tone sounds puzzled.

"Did who tell me what?" I think about my question. "You know what, I don't have time for you today." I lower to my seat after all. My eyes drift to my desk as if I'm busy, but there isn't a chance I can read a single invoice before me. Words blur together, and papers blend with other objects. My hands shake as I push around a few items. Then, I scoop together a spread of papers, stack them together, and collectively tap them on the desk hoping to express my disinterest in her.

"Sadie. Your daughter." The disgust in Roxanne's tone makes my blood boil, but her displeasure isn't misplaced.

How did this happen? When? Who?

"I don't know what you're talking about," I lie as Roxanne takes a step toward my desk. But my tongue trips over the truth before I can keep the next words inside. "And how would you know such things anyway? Look into a crystal ball and view my past? I know you're obsessed with me, but that's a bit much even for you," I mock as I roll my hands over themselves mimicking her staring into a glass globe to learn all about me. She isn't really obsessed with me. At least not that I can tell. I seem to repulse her at every encounter we have, but she's darn good at poking the bear in me. And for some reason, I prod right back at her just as eagerly. One way I do that is by flirting with the assumption she has a crush on me, which would never be true.

She seems immune to my charm and has no interest in playing with me. Sexually, that is.

"You aren't that interesting, actually, but I do know a bit about your past. Sadie McAllister is your daughter because you slept with my sister."

"Excuse me?" I stare at those piercing orbs. Roxanne has these dark gray eyes, and I hate to admit I always notice them. Exotic. Rich. Gemlike.

"You." She points at me, distracting me with her own form of sign language. "Slept." She sticks her index finger through the circle made by her thumb and forefinger of her opposite hand. "With my." She points at herself. "Sister." Her hands return to her hips.

"Who's your sister?"

"Theresa McAllister."

"*Trixie* McAllister is your sister?" How did I not know this? *Because you make it your purpose in life not to know anything about Roxanne other than her opening a bookstore across from the pub a few years ago and being a sour beer ever since.* However, Theresa, nicknamed Trixie, I vaguely remember. She had a crush on me back in high school, and I haven't seen her in, gosh…fifteen or sixteen years.

The timeframe rolls through my head like flipping back through an ancient calendar. *Fifteen or sixteen years.* I was thirty back then. Rachel and I had recently divorced. There was some sort of girls' weekend reunion happening here in Blue Ridge. I'd slept with Trixie, fulfilling her high school fantasy of me and firing the starter pistol on my race to screw every woman I could.

The gleam of Roxanne's eyes laser beams into mine, and I see the vague resemblance to her sister.

"What happened to you?" I snark, knowing I don't mean it. Trixie was a looker back in high school and equally as good looking during our night together, but Roxanne and her look nothing alike.

"What do you mean?" Her arms lower to her sides, and she presses her fingers on the edge of my desk.

"Your sister was so pretty." It's a low blow, and I don't miss her flinch at the insult. It's an asshole comment because I'm in a shit mood. I actually think Roxanne is rather stunning. That eye color, with its strange mix of cold steel and sparkling silver, and how her light tan skin enhances the shade. However, as she's the last person I want to see right now, I lash out at her. Then again, she's the first person I need. "How did this happen?"

Roxanne smirks at me. "Well, William," she begins in a mocking game-show announcer voice. "When a man loves a woman…" She stares down at me again, those swirling eyes quickly regaining a mask. "Oh wait, in your case…when a man only wants one thing, and he takes it—"

"Now wait a minute," I seethe, standing back to my full height and leaning my hands on my side of the desk. "I never need to take, darlin'. Your sister gave herself willingly, repeatedly, and in more ways than one."

"You're disgusting," she spits.

"The truth doesn't hurt. I can admit my faults, but disgust wasn't the expression on her face when we finished." I dig the knife deeper, feeling the need to strike at her in my fear—the real fear—that there is a teeny-tiny inkling of possibility her sister and I created a child. "How do I know she's even mine?"

"Did you look at her? She has Harrington written all over her."

Actually, I did look at the girl, but I didn't see a single trace of me in her. Of course, I didn't realize I should be looking for signs, but with the raven-colored hair and the icy brown eyes, she doesn't come remotely close to looking like a Harrington. As I glare back at Roxanne, I realize the eyes burrowing a hole into me from the young thing at the bar match the shape of the woman before me digging just as deeply.

"I don't understand." I hate the tremble in my voice.

"As I already said, William, when a man puts his penis in a woman's vagina, things can—"

"I understand the mechanics of sex, Roxie." When she formally calls me William, it reminds me of the disappointing ring to my father's voice when he addresses me by my full name, and I hate it. I shorten her name to spite her because she hates when I use the nickname. "Please spare me the clinical explanation."

"Oh, do you need the more detailed one called consequences of sex? After ejaculation, a sperm travels up the channel…" Roxanne pauses to ripple her hand as if imitating a fish swimming through water.

"Thank you. Please keep your limited sexpertise to yourself." A shiver slithers down my spine as though the thought of Roxanne having sexual relations revolts me. Who says ejaculation, anyway? I don't ejaculate into anything other than condoms. Always condoms.

"And then, one lucky swimmer wins the race and forces its way into…" Roxanne pauses to shove her index finger into her opposite fisted hand again, working at her visual display. "And at the end of nine months, *voila!*, a baby."

My jaw clenches. What I want to know is how do I know this Sadie girl is mine.

Mine? I have a daughter. Maybe.

I shake the thought and will away the sudden patter inside my chest. I clutch at my BRMP shirt near my heart and then smooth my hand down the front of it to disguise the action.

"I have no reason to believe she's mine," I argue although another pinch occurs inside my rib cage.

"There's also the mechanics of a faulty condom. Then again, that would be considered operator error, so—"

"Roxanne, seriously, shut up." My voice growls at her, and her expression softens for the breadth of a second. She looks away from me, glancing at the open door.

"You can have a paternity test done." She nods all clinical and practical, which contrasts with her overall appearance. She looks like a hippie with her waves of white and silver hair, and armful of bangling bracelets, and I hate that she's the voice of reason. "A swab in your cheek sent to a lab for testing will confirm everything."

Now, I'm the one disgusted, and I don't even know why.

"I'm not swabbing anything or pissing in a cup or..."

"Sorry, pal, but you already did the pissing. On my sister's life. Time to man up." Roxanne stands straighter while she speaks and then blinks at me. Before I can read the expression on her face, she quickly turns and stomps out of my office with the grand exit of slamming the door.

Chapter 3

Men

[Roxanne]

This is all my fault, and I knew it the moment I heard Sadie double-timing up the wooden back stairs to my apartment above the bookstore.

"I hate him," she muttered as she climbed. I surmised who she meant, which sent me on a mission to cross the street.

"I hate that Billy Harrington with a passion myself," I grumble as I march back out of the pub.

The first time I met Billy Harrington was back when we were kids, but he didn't remember me, which was apparent when I met him for the second time upon returning to Blue Ridge. That night, I called the cops on him and some party he was having at his pub.

And as they say, the third time's the charm because the third time I saw him, he was screwing some woman up against the brick wall in the alley behind his pub.

Yep. I hate him.

Although that isn't really true, a vital part of me whines.

"Shut up," I argue with myself as I stomp back to my bookstore. Blue Ridge Microbrewery and Pub faces Main Street as does my place, but our businesses are neighbors by way of Third Avenue cutting between us. BookEnds. That's my little cozy niche in life, and it generally makes me happy.

Grace Eton works today, and I'm so grateful as I made a rather hasty exit from my office in the back of the store with thoughts of maiming Billy. I didn't need to know all the details from Sadie to know what happened.

Billy rejected her.

This whole hullabaloo started when I registered my niece for high school a week ago. I needed to show proof of guardianship, which I don't have yet but have filed for in the local courts. She needed a birth certificate, and like a badly told joke, the name of her father was blank. Of course, I'd always known his identity, but as I loved my older sister, and she swore me to secrecy, I never told another soul, including Sadie. Sadie stared at the empty space as the school registrar filled in my name as guardian instead of her mother and raised a questioning eyebrow at me about the missing father.

During the week, Sadie and I were discussing some of the who's who in the community now that she lives with me, and his name just popped out.

"Then there's Billy Harrington who owns the pub across the street." Once those words escaped, there was no reeling them back in, and for a moment, silence hung in the air like a freshly caught fish stunned by oxygen.

"Billy Harrington, as in William Forrest Harrington?" Sadie repeated his name with dignity and indecision, as if she hoped he was one and the same as much as she worried the names identified the same person. Sadie was smart, though, and within seconds, she'd put two and two together, or should I say, one and one which equaled her.

"How do you know that name?" I asked, holding my breath. Sadie rolled her eyes, admitting she'd heard the name before in reference to her unknown father, and I didn't have the heart to continue the omission from her history. She'd been lied to long enough, but there had been so many hard truths lately, and she was only sixteen. For a moment, I wonder if this was another reason my sister chose me to become her guardian.

With Billy's knowledge of Sadie, everything could change.

"Grace, I'm going to need another minute," I call out after re-entering the shop and pointing at the ceiling, indicating the apartment above the store. Grace instantly understood. She's a military widow and mother of five boys ranging from thirteen to five.

"Take your time." She waves at me with a knowing smile, and I duck through the door labeled *private*, taking the staircase up to the second floor. My place is the entire length of the store from front to back. Narrow and tidy, it's been an adjustment to have a teenager move in, and we're still wading around one another. The bonus is I love my niece and have a special bond with her.

"Sadie." I softly rap on her door before opening it. I remember being her age and want to respect her privacy, but it's strange having a door closed in my apartment. The wooden barrier clearly tells me to stay out, but I enter anyway to find my struggling girl face down on her bed. Her room is smaller than mine, and I assume it had been the original dining room as it's across from the kitchen and missing a closet. It has two large windows taking up most of one wall while her twin bed lines the opposite wall. Every day a new poster covers the plaster, along with angsty poems, inspirational one-liners, and questionable images, turning the wall space into a true teenager's bedroom. The dark motif matches her mood and her clothing.

She's a vision of black lately. Boots, jeans, T-shirt, hair and nails, and against her pale skin it looks dramatic, beautiful, and sad. She is sad. She's done this to herself over the course of a few weeks, but I don't fault her. There have been so many changes.

"He's a pig," she mutters into her pillow. There wasn't much she could bring from her mother's home in Atlanta. The yellow pillowcase and patchwork quilt contrast with her dark appearance.

"Sadie, honey," I say as I lower to sit on the edge of her bed and rub a hand up her spine. I don't hesitate to be affectionate with my niece although it certainly was easier to pull her in my lap when she was six. At sixteen, the lap-holding is hardly appropriate, but we've hugged everyday as I'm hoping to break through to her, hoping she'll understand I'm here for her. My sister was more of a talker and planner while I am more affectionate and quiet. Most of all, I understand her pain.

I continue to stroke over Sadie's back until she rotates to face me. She's been resilient so far, but I'm waiting for a breakdown. It's only been six weeks. Her eye makeup is currently smudged, but I can't decide if she shed tears or if the smear is from pressing her face into her pillow. She continues to twist until her back hits the mattress, and she stares up at the ceiling. I glance up to find a pattern of glow-in-the-dark stars overhead. *When did she put those there?*

"What did he say?" I soften by tone as I question her, being reminded Billy never answered the same question from me.

"He hit on me."

"What?!" I screech, expecting the stars above my head to peel off the ceiling and rain down on us. "Oh my fu….*effing* God." I swallow back the curse, but Sadie's black lips smirk.

"You can say *fucking*. It's not like I haven't heard it before." I should admonish her directness. A mother would do that, but I'm not her mother.

"What did he do?" My hands tremble and my legs twitch, suggesting I stalk back to that god-awful pub and give Billy another what-for and then a swift kick in his wayward balls.

"He told me I was too young for him, and then I told him he disgusts me."

Well, this sounds about right. Billy disgusts me, too, yet despite my opinion of him, I don't honestly believe he'd stoop to hitting on a teenager. He's definitely not hard up or hard on the eyes. As a known player in the community, I can't think of any single women who haven't had a night with him.

Oh wait, yes, I can. *Me.*

I seem to be the one woman in this town who repulses him. I dismiss the thought as I wouldn't want his pole within ten feet of me, but Billy does have this look about him. Charismatic. Charming. Cheeky. Age agrees with him. Salty hair with specks of pepper and a midnight beard make him unique among men. I'd wager my vintage Jane Austen collection he dyes it black in order to look distinct. His best feature, though, are his eyes—a muted brown color—but he prides himself on his body. And Lord knows, he's full of pride, all firm chest and solid legs and thick hands, not that I have any firsthand knowledge of these things.

Never touched him.

Never would.

Yes, you might. I quickly dismiss the cry between my thighs, and I fight with fist and hammer against any attraction to Billy Harrington.

"What did he say about being your father?"

"I didn't give him a chance to respond." Her eyes close, and she swallows hard. I can't tell if she's upset or concerned, as if she's done something to him, like insulted him or set a fire in his bar. I go with option two first. It wouldn't be unlike my niece to speak her mind or act out.

"What did you do?"

"I told him the only daddy issue I had was him being my dad."

Goodness. I exhale because I couldn't agree more, but then I reconsider. Is this a fair assessment? First of all, Billy didn't know he was a dad until an hour ago. I can't fault him for knowledge he didn't have prior to today, unless he did know, and never did anything to claim Sadie. If Theresa eventually hinted to Sadie about her father, did she finally break down and contact Billy? I doubt it. She'd have told me. Then again, she never mentioned having a discussion with Sadie about her father, and it's a reminder that mother and daughter shared things that aunt and niece do not.

On the other hand, if I rule in favor of Billy's ignorance—and let's face it, I consider him ignorant—he definitely should understand condoms are only ninety-four percent effective. Maybe he never should have slept with Theresa in the first place. I understand why she was with him, and why he might have been with her. My sister was the outgoing one, the pretty one, the life of the party one back in high school.

Something wiggles to the forefront of my brain from our brusque conversation earlier.

"What happened to you? Your sister was so pretty." Billy nipped at one of my deepest insecurities. I wasn't pretty like my sister had been. All blonde hair, blue eyes, and trussed up, she looked like a beauty queen. On the other hand, I was heavier when we were younger, round and jovial with dull brown hair and these strange gray eyes. I lost almost seventy-five pounds before returning to Blue Ridge and opening my shop. I'm a healthy one hundred and fifty-five now for my height of five-six. My bone structure is bigger than my sister's, and my wide hips are a sensitive issue for me along with the premature gray hair. Billy's comment struck a nerve, and I don't want to give him the energy of my

anger. He isn't worth it, but still—what he said, implying I'm not pretty—it stung.

This is one of my checks against him. He makes me feel inferior, as if I'm not good enough for him. Not pretty enough, bouncy enough, peppy enough.

"I don't want to give Billy credit where he doesn't deserve it, honey, but it's not like he knew he had a child until today." Damn Theresa for keeping this a secret so long and letting me be the one to unmask the mystery. Sadie had a right to know and a lot sooner than this week, as well as under better circumstances.

"It doesn't matter. I don't need him." Sadie rolls to her side, placing her back to me. Unfortunately, there might be nothing further from the truth.

Chapter 4

Specimens

[Billy]

"Want to talk about it?" Clyde's voice interrupts my thoughts. He lowers himself to the chair opposite my desk while I stare at the computer screen before me. I'd like to tell Clyde I don't know what he's talking about, but I do, and so does he.

"So you heard all that?" I nod in the direction of the door.

"You want me to pretend I heard nothing? I can do that."

I close my eyes and scrub two hands over my face. "I just…I don't need my family to know anything yet." That's the last thing I need.

Do you know how hard it is to be the third son? The fuckup? Giant went into the military, was medically discharged with honor, and returned home a hero. James worked search and rescue for almost twenty years, saving lives daily. Charlie, my younger brother, serves as the town's mayor. Me, I just like to party. *Good times all around and drinks for everyone.* I won't even discuss my sister, Mati, who I love most, but she's the princess as the only girl and baby of the family.

My dad thought I needed the military, and then he called me a mama's boy, as Mama stood against the suggestion. The family business of brewing beer wasn't any more of an attractive offer than the military because it involved working under a man I admired and disappointed. My grandfather Pap was the owner in name only back then. My father was the man in charge and a slave driver as I worked in the brewing facility throughout my teens. But I didn't want to work directly under George Harrington Jr. even if beer drinking is one of my favorite pastimes. When it was decision time—military, family business, or college—I chose college even though I wasn't very studious and nearly flunked out. I quit instead.

Forget that I run a successful business on my own. Forget that Rachel left me through no fault of mine.

Fathering a child out of wedlock and keeping her a secret for sixteen years—forget the fact I didn't know she existed—will be icing on the proverbial *Billy is a fucktard* cake.

"I don't really know what to say," I tell Clyde, feeling his eyes on me.

"Whatcha doing?" Clyde nods at the computer screen, but he can see a good selection of the listings. I tilt the screen in his direction. "Paternity tests?" His eyes squint. "Do they sell those in the pregnancy test aisle?"

He's trying to be funny, but I don't find any humor in this issue.

"She can't be mine," I state.

"Yet you're googling paternity tests." Clyde raises one bushy eyebrow at me.

"I don't know what to do." My first thought was to deny her existence. She can't be my kid, like I said. But this growing uncertainty in my chest, like the root of a tree spreading, makes me wonder. *What if.*

What would I do with her? What does she want with me? Where is Trixie? Why didn't she tell me?

The last question is the one I've been asking myself for the past couple of hours.

"You need an attorney. You have some rights here."

I blink back at Clyde.

"I don't know what to do with a kid," I stammer, and the tree root sensation tightens within me as if clawing at my internal organs, constricting my airway, and squeezing at my heart. I rub at my upper chest as I did earlier in the day when that blasted bookstore owner stood before my desk.

Damn, Roxie is hot when she's pissed.

Which I should not be thinking, considering everything else going on.

"I don't think any father knows what to do before he becomes a father. But dads have rights, Billy. You need to know what yours are in this case." He pauses a moment. "I always thought I'd be a good dad."

I glance up from the computer screen, which I'd been absently staring at, and watch as Clyde gnaws on the corner of his lip. A strange sense of loss fills Clyde's eyes, and he quickly looks away from me. I'm not an emotional guy, but we've reached a sensitive subject for my bartender friend.

"Want to talk about it?" I tease, hoping to lessen the heaviness in the room. I fold my hands before me on the desk and pose myself as if I'm a knowledgeable psychiatrist.

"Now, you're just being cruel," he mocks, but there's another hint of seriousness in his words.

"Sorry, man. I'm just…I'm still in shock."

Clyde nods, dismissing my apology. "What are you going to do?"

I tip my head back to the computer screen. "I guess I'm going to purchase a paternity test and take things one step at a time." Only I don't even know what those steps should be. The root-clutching sensation returns.

"Well, that's how babies learn to walk. One step at a time," Clyde states, sitting taller in his chair and proud of his advice.

"Is that supposed to make me feel better?" I mean, she isn't exactly a baby. She's a teenager, and I'm not certain what would be worse—an infant or a female on the edge of womanhood. My eyes close with the second thought.

I fucking snarked at her, telling her she was too young for me. I'm a sick fuck.

Infant, I decide. Definitely an infant would be easier than accepting I need to interact with a teenager, a girl no less, who I should be teaching to avoid men—*boys*—like me.

"You okay, boss?" Clyde asks as my stomach pitches, and I smooth a hand down my lower belly.

Oh God. She needs to be protected from men like me. She needs to be locked up, not let out of the house, not allowed to date until she's thirty, and even then…

"Boss?"

Bile rises up my throat as reality hits me.

I have a daughter. And one day, she might encounter a man like me.

"I…"

"Billy?" Clyde stands at the same time as I do as though he expects me to spray him with the vomit nearly to my throat. Instead, I rush to the private bathroom off my office and empty the contents of my stomach into the toilet.

I can't be a father. I'd be the worst dad.

+ + +

While I'm no alcoholic, I know all the stages of the twelve-step recovery program. None of those steps fit how I feel, so I'm jumping to a shorter list: the five stages of grief. I'm still in denial but working my way into anger, and it's in full flare when I cross over Third Avenue to one *un*neighborly bookstore before her closing time. BookEnds is one of the last places I'd enter if given a choice.

First off, I don't read. Period. I don't like books or what they stand for or anything about them. Too many words. Not enough pictures. Plus, I have more exciting things to do with my time than stare at letters on a page.

Second, from the moment BookEnds opened, its owner has been a pain in my ass. Within the first few months of her opening, she called the cops with a noise complaint for an outdoor concert on *my* property. It's not my fault she lives above her shop and couldn't handle a little late-night rebel-rousing music. From the moment I confronted her, we've been at each other's throats, so I make it a mission of mine to stay away from her.

Part of the issue is that Roxie's one of the few women in town who seems numb to my flirty personality. She doesn't take my shit, and that pisses me off.

My sister, Mati, is our event's idea person, as I dub her, and one idea she has for improving business is making peace with the bookstore owner and offering a books and brew night to feature popular books with coordinating beers. It's a ridiculous idea, but Mati was rather insistent on it until the permit for our annual Oktoberfest was requested, and we've hit a setback—*again*—because of this damn bookstore. But I'm not here tonight about the permit issue.

"So how do we do this?" I demand, swinging open the door and stepping into the dim lit store. There are just so many books in here. I shiver.

"We're closed," Roxanne mutters, but with the lights still on and the door unlocked, she's lying.

I stalk the few feet to the counter where she lingers over a book under her bent arms. *This woman.* She can feel my glare, I'm certain of it, but she doesn't look up in my direction.

"Roxie," I drone.

"William," she states in that grating tone without glancing up. *Dammit.*

"We need to talk."

"Oh, now you want to speak with me?" She pauses to flip a page of the book under her gaze, still not lifting her eyes. "Well, I'm busy," she repeats my words from earlier.

"The hell you are," I snark, repeating hers, and tug the book toward me.

"Hey," she snaps, reaching over the counter, but I'm holding the book by the cover and dangling it parallel with my shoulder.

"I said, we need to talk," I growl.

"And I said, I'm busy. You're hurting that book." Her arms flail over the counter as if she can reach it while her stomach lays on the flat surface, and I have the strangest thought, wanting to stand behind her in this precarious position and take her. I shake the image from my head along with the book.

"Oh, *ow, ow, ow*, he says." I mock the book, flapping the pages as I yank it up and down.

"William Harrington, that's a limited edition." Roxanne stands and stomps her feet as she marches around her counter, coming for me. I snap the book shut and slip it into the front of my jeans.

I could have held it over her head and made her reach for it, watched her bounce up and down and jiggle those large tits for me, but I'm not interested in flirting with her, or watching her dance, or any other thing. And I'm confident the last place Roxanne McAllister will ever get is in my pants, so here the book sets, daring her to take it from me.

I'm so childish.

Roxanne freezes, her eyes leaping to my zipper region. "How…I…you…"

"Got your attention now, don't I?" I tease. For that matter, I also have the attention of Grace Eton, a worker in the store, but I don't bother removing the book from my jeans. Instead, I knock at my zipper with my knuckles, allowing the sound of something firm underneath the denim to resound around us.

"You are such a pig," Roxanne groans. "I'll never get that—" She points at my jeans, but we both know what she means. "—off my book."

"There are worse things than my junk on your book," I stammer, and we lock eyes on one another. Grace snorts from somewhere to our sides and then disappears behind a shelf of books.

"In my book, your junk is the worst thing," she mumbles, twisting my words. Then she adds, "Your junk, as you so eloquently called it, will never come anywhere near my book."

She's good with all this play on words.

"I wouldn't want to touch your book," I snark back, and Roxanne gasps.

"You don't touch a book, William. You read it. You enjoy it. And this book is closed to you," she states, circling a finger over her body, "as is my store, so get out."

I turn to walk away, but two firm hands grip one of my biceps, and she spins me back to face her.

"Not with my book." She nods down at my zipper and extends her open palm, wiggling her fingers. I'm a little disturbed by how much the motion turns me on, as if she wants to grab my dick, *demands* I give it to her.

"Come and get your book, Roxie." I stand, holding out my hands to the sides.

"Just give it to me, William," Roxanne whines, and my mouth falls open.

Sweet Jesus.

"*Ah.* Words you only wish you could say to me," I mutter, and those steely eyes flare, turning to onyx jewels.

"Never," she hisses. Here's the thing. She's right. I'm not certain what I've done to her to make her so irritated with me, but she'll never have a crush on me, and I'll never touch her unless she begs me. And even then, I'm not so certain.

You're a liar. A lying liar who lies to himself, Billy Harrington.

We stand at an impasse.

"Look." I exhale, scrubbing two hands down my face and noting a sudden discomfort at having a book shoved down my jeans, especially since I've grown hard with our sparring. I lower my hands for my hips and narrow my eyes at her. "Where's Trixie?"

Roxanne's sight has dropped to the front of my pants, but her focus no longer appears to be on what's inside my jeans. Slowly, her lids close as she clasps her hands together before her. Her fingers clench and unclench before she stills.

"Theresa died six weeks ago."

Shit. "Shit, Roxie…I'm so *sor*…" The word fades from my lips as I step forward, lifting a hand for her arm to express my condolences. She flinches back from my anticipated touch before I make actual contact. The movement stings, but I don't fault her. I don't know what I'd do if I lost one of my siblings. Us Harrington brothers are close, well, minus James, and even Mati's treated like a brother by me.

"What happened?" My voice lowers as if I'm speaking to a child, and then I remember there is a child involved, a teenage girl, who recently lost her mother. *Sadie.* Her name feels strange on my tongue, like a mixture of concern and fear I've never felt before.

"Theresa was in an accident. She was hit by a car."

"Car accident?" I parrot until Roxanne corrects me.

"Motorcycle."

Motorcycle. Trixie rode a motorcycle? My brother James owns one and belongs to the local MC, Rebel's Edge. While the idea of looking for adventure and riding down the highway sounds liberating, I've heard so many horror stories about bikes getting clipped by cars, and I shudder with the thought of such a horrific death.

"She was wearing a helmet, but she was thrown off the bike. We were told she didn't suffer."

Didn't suffer? *Jesus.* Then another word stands out.

"We?"

"Sadie and me." Her eyes drift up to me. "She's here to live with me." There's a hesitation in Roxanne's voice.

"Is there anyone else? Her husband or what about your parents?" I don't remember the fine details of the comings and goings in the community. Trixie—*Theresa*—McAllister was my age, but I didn't remember her having a younger sister.

"Trixie never married. My mom died when I was fifteen." Roxanne swallows. "And my dad passed a few years ago."

"What about other siblings?"

"Sadie's an only child." That isn't what I was asking, and it takes Roxanne a moment to understand. "It was only Theresa and me. She was specific; she wanted Sadie with me." The fire returns to Roxanne's eyes, flaming brighter than before.

I nod although I don't know why.

"But if I'm her father, she belongs with me." I swallow back the weight of those words while Roxanne spears me with another glare.

"She belongs with me. I'm the only family she has."

"That might not be true," I defend. She might be a Harrington. She'd have an aunt and tons of uncles, cousins, and a set of grandparents. My father will be so disappointed, but my mother will be elated.

"Well, I guess we won't know." Roxie blinks and then lowers her eyes to her foot, which kicks at nothing on the hardwood floor.

"Why not?"

Her head pops up, and another trace of caution laces her voice. "Did you decide to take a test?"

"I did." Although I hadn't until this moment, standing before Roxie in her store, with a book down my pants, and her challenging glare on me.

"She's suffered a lot of loss, Billy. If it isn't you…" The use of my name in a soft but serious tone makes my heart stammer. I admit, it sounds like Sadie has lost a lot. Her mother. Her grandparents. Moving here means she left behind her friends and her home.

"What do you mean *if it isn't me*? You two are the ones hell-bent on saying I'm the father." I pause as I exhale in frustration. "I can man up to my responsibilities, Roxie."

"Don't act like you're doing us any favors," she snarks. "Sadie doesn't need you." Her eyes widen with the words, and there's a hint of untruth to her statement.

"I'm not doing anybody any favors," I snap.

"Of course not," Roxanne argues.

"What's that supposed to mean?" We're back to square one where all we do is throw jabs. Roxanne sighs and shakes her head again, ignoring my inquiry.

"So you're taking a test." There's still a question in the statement, but I nod in the affirmative. "You'll need Sadie, I think. You'll need something from her to match your DNA."

It's all so clinical, and suddenly, that sick feeling swells in my belly again. The last thing I need to do is puke in front of Auntie Roxie, though. She'll be seeing enough specimens from me soon.

Chapter 5

The Prophet Doesn't Profess to Know Everything

[Roxanne]

When Billy hands my book back to me, I take it with the tips of my fingers near the edge of the spine. I don't want to touch anything that has been near his dick, and Lord knows, there have been plenty of things near it.

His bare ass exposed, him thrusting up into a woman against a brick wall, is burned in my memory, and I try not to recall such things, especially when deep down, in a place I keep locked up tight, I wish it had been me. Just once. Him and me and a wall at my back.

"What is that anyway?" he asks after he passes the book to me. I don't know why he doesn't just read the cover for himself.

"*The Prophet* by Kahlil Gibran."

"The prophet, huh? Because it's a miracle you got in my pants." Billy winks at me.

"Well, I *wasn't* in your pants," I snap.

"Not yet." And with that, he turns on his booted feet and leaves.

He's so full of himself, I think as I step up to the front door and flip the sign to closed. I'll never be in his pants because here's the thing, he never hits on me. Not in earnest. I've watched him flirt and tease and obviously have sex with someone against an exterior wall, but he's never acted remotely interested in me. He jokes. He pokes. But he does it to get *to* me, not get me.

Twisting the lock at the door, I recall the sympathy in his eyes when I mentioned Theresa's death and the determination once he agreed to take a paternity test. I have no doubt in my mind Billy is the father, mainly because Trixie was adamant it was him, but as we later learned, you can't just add a paternal name to a birth certificate without the father's admission or DNA proof, of which Theresa had neither.

"He'll never need to know," my sister said to me while peering down at the new baby in her arms. *"We don't need him."*

One reason my sister didn't need Billy is because she had me, ever the helper—generous and easygoing. My sister, on the other hand, was principled, self-controlled, and a perfectionist, which makes the irony of her unplanned pregnancy even sweeter. She thought she could do it all on her own, but that had never been the case. Single motherhood was the opposite of her practical lifestyle, but then again, so was the motorcycle she owned—a sliver of rebel streak remaining from her younger years. She had been confidently outgoing while I was excessively introverted. I liked to read. She liked to socialize. Her extroverted personality kept her always trying to move forward on the corporate ladder without appreciating what was immediately before her. My sister was strong-willed and determined, hard-working and stubborn for a reason. She constantly worried about Sadie and her future.

The right kindergarten. The right elementary school. The right high school all led to the right college. Theresa wanted no risk of Sadie repeating her history. However, I wasn't convinced all the education in the world could prevent such a thing. In the case of my sister, an unplanned pregnancy was the result of a momentary lapse in judgment and had nothing to do with her smarts.

When Sadie was thirteen, I told my sister about my vision to own my own bookstore. I'd worked for a big chain for years, moving from floor sales to management. I loved being around books, but the large-scale store didn't provide the intimacy I wanted in a shop, and when the Atlanta location closed its doors, it was a sign to move on.

My hardest decision was where to locate a small business. After living near a big city for almost fifteen years, I recalled my love for the simpler feel of Blue Ridge, so opening my store in a town working to build its economy was the obvious choice. However, it meant leaving Sadie behind, and my sister wasn't pleased. This disrupted her plan of me always being present to pick up the slack of raising Sadie.

"You won't be able to do this on your own." It was a projection of my sister's fears. She'd have to step up and be a mother for Sadie as she

reached her teen years. It was a difficult decision, but it had been time for me to do something for myself.

"You okay?" Grace questions as I remain before the front door staring at the pub across the street.

He might have married Theresa, I think before turning to face Grace.

"It's been a long day." I exhale, having no idea where thoughts of Billy and marriage to my sister came from. Grace smiles in response, and a comforting hand comes to my arm. Billy had reached for me earlier, but I pulled away. I didn't trust his touch. Getting so many women to sleep with him made him a master manipulator, and I shiver with the thought.

"It will all work out," Grace assures me. I'd unleashed the basic details to my co-worker and friend after leaving Sadie to stew in her room.

"I don't even know what that means." What do I want *his* responsibility to be? I didn't plan on Billy being part of Sadie's story yet. She came to me after Theresa's death, and that was all the fairy tale I needed. I didn't want to tell her anything about her father until she was older, but in hindsight, I see the trouble this could have led to, and the trouble it's already been. Sadie needs the truth, and like ripping off a Band-Aid, she has it. I just wish so many changes weren't happening all at once for her.

"Billy Harrington is a good man," Grace assures me, and I snort.

"Depends on what kind of *good* we are discussing." I lift a brow. Good in bed, perhaps.

"Well, he's good to look at." She giggles. "But I mean he's a decent person. He'll do the right thing."

Again, I question what I want the right thing to be from him. Billy has questions, just like Sadie, and I'm caught in the crossfire without all the answers. I just want what's best for Sadie. She's my only concern.

+ + +

Two days later, I'm surprised to see Billy standing in my store again, looking sheepish with his hands in his pockets. His jeans hug him just right, and he's wearing a Pub T-shirt with the long sleeves pressed above his elbows. His eyes scan the various shelves and fall decorations in the window, but it's obvious he isn't focused on any one thing.

"Can I help you?" I offer, keeping my tone professional. I must admit, seeing him standing in my bookstore for the second time in less than a week does seem like a miracle. It's also doing things to my girlie parts when it shouldn't be. I don't think he's ever been in here other than after I called the police and he nearly tore off my front door, rushing in here to verbally assault me with his displeasure.

"It was a concert. We had a permit."

"It was loud and late, and I needed sleep." I'd opened the store only a week or so prior, and I remember the exhaustion of doing everything on my own. The issue with being a helper is it isn't always a personality people reciprocate. No one steps up to help me. Theresa was so bitter I left her that she didn't bother to visit the store for three months.

"Sleep when you're dead," he said. *"You're only proving you don't know how to have a good time."*

He wasn't totally wrong. I didn't want to make waves. I only wanted much-needed rest.

"So I've been thinking…" He pauses as his earthy eyes squint at something in the side window. In the bright sunlight, they glow a lighter brown but still rich and deep. There's a reason women are drawn to him, and as I said, his eyes are one of his best features.

"Sounds like a dangerous thing," I tease.

He scrubs a hand down his face and cups under his jaw. The scruff on his chin is dark but thin, not thick like his older brother Giant who owns the official brewery supporting the town.

"It usually is." He's silent after the comment, and a quiet Billy makes me nervous. His mouth opens, snaps shut, and then pops open again. "I thought maybe before I swap bodily fluids with Sadie, we should meet under better conditions."

My mouth falls open with the suggestion, and my hands slowly lower to my hips. "You are so—"

"That's not what I mean. That came out wrong." He closes his eyes, and it might be the first time I've ever seen Billy Harrington struggle for words. It unnerves me. Where's his fire? Where are his biting comments? Where's his displeasure with my presence? Then again, *he* came into *my* store. "I mean before we exchange blood or swabs or whatever we need to do to test our DNA. Maybe we should meet where I'm not thrown off guard and she isn't insulting me."

I stiffly chuckle. "Well, I can't guarantee she won't insult you again, but you might be right. It might be best to give your first impressions a second chance." I'm uncomfortable with the suggestion. I don't want Sadie getting her hopes up about Billy and fatherhood.

"Do you think he'll want to know me?" she whispered two nights ago while we ate dinner. Before I could answer, she sat straighter, squaring her shoulders. *"Never mind. I don't want to see him anyway."*

Even though she hasn't mentioned him again, he's weighing on her mind. She wants to meet him, if for no other reason than out of curiosity, and I have no doubt Billy will grow to love her.

"What do you suggest?" I can't believe I'm asking his opinion, but I admit he looks kind of cute with the fluster on his face. Billy Harrington is attractive, too attractive for his own good.

"I was hoping you'd have a suggestion."

"Why me?"

Billy's eyes roam up and down my body before he scrunches his nose. "You're a woman, like a mother figure, and I thought you'd have an idea." Well, nice of him to notice I'm female, but somehow, the motherly comment strikes a nerve. I'm not Sadie's mother, and with his roaming eye, it's as if Billy suggests I'm matronly.

"Ask your own mother," I snap.

"I can't." His eyes close, and he inhales. My eyes narrow at him. He's moved from cute-frustration to ugly-exasperation.

"Why?" I growl, already concerned about his answer.

"I..." He swallows the rest of the words.

"You don't want your family to know about Sadie," I deduce. The precious Harringtons are like royalty in this small town along with a few other names. The Chances and the Conrads come to mind. This scandal could rattle their world. Then again, each of his siblings isn't without their own story. It's amazing what I've learned from Dolores at the diner down the street. It's a reminder that no family is perfect.

"I'm not ready yet."

"What does that mean?" I ask as soon as the words are a thought. "You've had sixteen years."

Billy blinks at me. "Actually, I haven't even had seventy-two hours." His jaw tightens, and a finger points in my direction. "You're just as guilty as she is. *Was*. In keeping this from me."

I grip the finger pointed at me. Dammit, he's right that he hasn't known as long as I have, but I won't fully acquiesce to him. "I'm not guilty of anything. I did what my sister wished, and it's not like you and I are even friendly." By crooking the finger within my grasp, he tugs me toward him, and I stumble. His other hand comes forward, settling on my hip before I crash into him. This is the closest I've ever been to Billy, and he smells divine. Like cloves and cinnamon and another spice I can't identify but that makes my mouth water.

"Well, whose fault is that?" he snaps.

"Certainly not mine," I hiss.

"You and that damn complaint."

"You and your screeching noise." My chest lifts and lowers with the irritation of him.

"You and your attitude."

"You and your…your women," I snap. It's the lamest comeback, and Billy's eyes widen.

"What's that supposed to mean?"

"You sleep around, William Harrington, so this is more your fault than it will ever be mine." It's a low blow even if true. I'll never admit to seeing him with that woman, watching him a few minutes when I shouldn't have been watching. It shouldn't be my concern if he can't keep it in his pants, but for a moment, I wonder if he has other children he doesn't know about somewhere else in Georgia. My heart crashes at the possibility. I don't really think he has a hundred children out there. It's more the probability of him sleeping with a hundred women and none of them have been me. I'm the one woman he hasn't tried to sleep with, and I don't know why, but it bothers me.

"Sometimes I hate you, Roxie."

"The feeling is mutual, William."

However, I'm conscious of how that isn't how I feel, and I'm equally aware of how close we stand. My hand is still wrapped around his thick finger, callused against my palm, and although I thought it was me grabbing him, it suddenly feels like he's holding onto me. My breasts nearly brush his heaving chest, and our breaths mix with weighty tension. Our eyes lock for the briefest of seconds, and then he tugs his finger free from my grasp, shaking his hand toward the floor as though he's discarding a piece of trash, as if my touch was filth, and I understand why he's never legitimately hit on me.

I repulse him.

He steps back, still holding my eyes.

"It's always my fault," he murmurs and spins away from me without another word.

Chapter 6
Blame and Shame Are Not Good Bedfellows

[Billy]

When Rachel left me, my family blamed me. I was too much of a flirt. Everyone thought the divorce was my fault. They didn't know the truth or even half of it, and I really wanted to keep it a secret for Rachel. She isn't ashamed of who she is, and neither am I. I just wish we had both recognized the signs sooner, but life can sometimes be deceiving and difficult.

Like asking Roxie for her help.

It took courage to approach her and ask her advice about a second introduction with Sadie. I'd been thinking about our first meeting for two full days, and the scenario played out in a million different ways. But my motto is not to live in the past. I can't change it. I'd like to consider the future instead, which seems equally as dangerous.

"I hope you aren't getting your hopes up, boss," Clyde warns when I return to the pub, huffing in frustration. Damn Roxie and her words. And those eyes. Her silvery orbs remind me of the color of an antiquated bracelet my mother owns. When she focuses on me, looking me right in the eyes, something happens like she's put a spell on me and all I want to do is kiss her damn mouth.

"What hopes?" I snap at my bartender.

"Hopes that you might be her father."

"I don't—" I stop myself. It's not that I don't wish to be Sadie's dad. I don't know what I want, and damn Clyde for being so observant and thinking he knows something I don't.

"It's a strange feeling, isn't it? Hoping that it's true. Wishing it to be." He smiles to himself, and I stare at my friend. *What are we, a Hallmark movie?* Clyde shakes his head as if ridding his thoughts as he pulls the tap and fills a glass with our fall blend. His expression hardens from his easy smile as he passes the pint to a customer.

"I don't know what I want," I lie because deep down, like way down, I do want to be Sadie's dad. Not that I know Sadie or think she's anything special yet. I just think—*I don't know*—I might be okay at being a dad. I'd certainly try to do better than my old man, who is a great guy by most people's standards but didn't have the same connection with me as he seems to have with my three brothers. And forget about my baby sister, Mati. She's his princess.

"So what did you decide?" Clyde asks, turning his back to the bar to ring up a tab.

"I'm doing the test. I just don't know how or when or what to do." I scrub at my face in frustration. I can't ask my family for help, and when I mentioned that fun fact to Roxanne, she looked as though she wanted to skewer me. She doesn't understand. It's not that I'm ashamed of Sadie—although there will be plenty of blame and reprimand—it's that I'm afraid if it isn't true, then there will be plenty of blame and reprimand. My mother will be crushed she doesn't have another grandchild, especially as I seem the least likely to produce one. My father will shake his head, implying the thousands of lectures about keeping it in my pants.

I don't know why he even bothered with us boys.

"You need a lawyer."

A lawyer. My youngest brother is one, but he's also the town mayor and doesn't need more scandal. Then again, it's my life, not his.

"I do, but I can't ask my brother."

"What about his partner?"

Jordan? "He's still family. I don't want any of them involved yet." I sigh. Jordan is my nephew. My sister, Mati, has twins. Jaxson followed in her footsteps as a wild child, and he's currently the sales director for Giant Beer Company with a baby on the way from his baby mama. *Ah, the one-night stand pregnancy might run in the family.* For a moment, I want to high-five myself, but then I reconsider. Mati's other son is Jordan. He followed his father's path and became a lawyer. Responsible, organized, and a bit anal, Jordan studied under his father and uncle until Chris died. He took his father's place as partner to my brother Charlie.

"Yeah, but there's such a thing as attorney-client confidentiality, and it's not like he's a direct sibling."

Clyde has a point. One I'm greatly considering. After googling paternity tests and rights of the father, I've found all kinds of things I don't quite understand, so as much as I hate to admit it, I do need advice and legal guidance.

"True, true," I mutter, patting Clyde on the shoulder and excusing myself for my office. Maybe a little bit of family will be okay.

+ + +

"You got a girl pregnant?" My twenty-seven-year-old nephew stares at me over the edge of his tortoiseshell glasses like he's the judge and jury on my sex life.

"Yeah, well, maybe. *Sixteen* years ago," I emphasize with a smirk, failing to find humor in the situation which matches the gaze he's giving me. Suddenly, his shoulders fall, and he glances in the direction of a picture on his desk. His wife, Maggie, is a pretty brunette with sad eyes. Jordan shakes his head and then squeezes his forehead, pressing his thumb and forefinger into his skin. "It's raining babies," he mutters, and I question what he means. His brother's having one, but I'm certainly not.

"She's sixteen, so that hardly qualifies as an infant."

Jordan releases his forehead and presses his glasses up the center of his nose. "And you don't want anyone to know?"

"I don't even know for certain. That's why I'm here. I need a paternity test."

Jordan turns to his computer and taps away at the keys. "I can order something at the local clinic that will need to be sent to Atlanta. If you test positive, we go from there. Where's the mother?"

"She passed away." It's difficult to consider Trixie kept the truth from me. *She should have told me.* I've struggled with my anger for the past few days, but I can't do anything about what I didn't know. There's no way to confront her now, so I'm equally sad to be swimming through this mess alone. I just need the truth.

"Right. So we file a Paternity Acknowledgment Form and then file for custodial rights."

"What does that mean?" I question. I'm sketchy on family law, but the word *custody* has me bristling.

"Meaning, as her father, you have the right for visitation or, in this case, for her to reside with you. But you'll also have some financial responsibility."

Whoa, whoa, whoa. Stop the scenic train. Live with me? I swallow loud enough Jordan gives me another judge-y glare.

"That's what you want, right? To see her? Have her live with you?"

"What about Roxanne?" I'm a little surprised she's my first thought, but it's evident she's close to her niece, not to mention Sadie knows her aunt better than she knows me.

"Roxanne is her aunt and has no legal claim to her unless specified in a will. Was there a will? Did she file for guardianship? Was CPS involved?"

Child Protective Services. "I have no idea." I sigh, growing frustrated with my lack of legal knowledge. "Look, I don't want her going to some random home or something. She has family."

Jordan sighs, ignoring my rant. "Even if a will specifies Roxanne as guardian, you trump her. You have rights as her father."

"*If* I'm her father."

"Do you want to be her father?" The question doesn't stump me since Clyde's already asked me. I've been asking myself the same thing, but I still pause before I answer.

"I want to do what's right." I nod, as if I'm making a grown-up decision as a grown-up.

"You know, Uncle Billy, there are people who desperately want children and can't have them. A case like yours makes people almost envious." He glares at me once again, acting as if he's the only adult in the room.

"Meaning?"

"Maggie and I have been trying to have children for years. Jaxson has a one-night stand and gets a girl pregnant, and still isn't certain he wants to marry her. You…" He waves a hand toward me. "Practically the same thing happened. My mother when she first had sex—"

I hold up a hand to stop him. I don't need the sexual history of my younger sister although I've overshared mine with her plenty of times. Still, I already know Mati got pregnant on one of the first few times she had sex with Chris, who had the sense to wait until they graduated high school before doing the deed with her.

"It just isn't fair." Jordan's words bring me up short, and I sit taller in my seat.

"I'm not shirking my responsibility or treating this lightly. I just don't want to get ahead of myself. I'm not certain I'm the father, and I think it's important to establish one thing at a time."

Jordan nods in agreement, his shoulders falling in relief as he returns to his computer. "I'll need to schedule an appointment for Sadie, too."

I exhale in relief myself but need to break the tension between us.

"Looks like I'll be having my first father-daughter date." At a medical clinic for a paternity test.

+ + +

I'm back at Roxanne's bookstore. Only this time, I'm at the back entrance staring up the outside staircase to the apartment above the shop. Most of the buildings down Main Street have a second floor, several of which are residential rentals. Over the brew pub, we had to overcome all kinds of zoning issues when we turned the second floor into a private party room.

"See anything interesting up there?" The gravelly feminine voice behind me sends a shiver down my spine.

Roxanne. My, how this woman can grate on my nerves, but I admit for the second time this week, I need her. I close my eyes and inhale, steeling my resolve as I spin to face her.

"Roxanne," I drag out her name. "How wonderful to see you again."

She stares at me a long moment, those piercing eyes doing things to my belly at the same time as they make me want to cover the family jewels.

Should have covered them before because she might be family. The thought strikes me as inappropriate and possible. Roxanne wouldn't be direct family, though. More like baby mama's sister. And as for coverage, it had to have been faulty prophylactics because I haven't been uncovered with someone since my ex-wife.

"Cut the bullshit, William. What are you doing creeping on my staircase?" She carries a grocery bag in each hand, and I reach for them, not allowing her to refuse me. We struggle for a moment as I slip the bags from her wrists, and she slaps at my quick reflexes.

"What the…?" She stops swatting at me and puts her hands on her hips. "Are you going to try to shove my groceries down your pants this time?" Her eyes lower for my zipper region, and then they leap upward, meeting mine. I wiggle one brow, making my eye dance, until she says, "I suppose zucchini might be an improvement."

My mouth falls open. *Is she kidding me?* "More like an eggplant." I snort.

Her lips separate, a soft gasp escaping. *Why is that making my belly flip?* Then she starts to laugh.

"I mean, I'm more comparable to an eggplant," I explain, my face heating.

Her nose scrunches up, and her lips sneer. "Ouch."

It's my turn to chuckle. Why are we comparing my junk to vegetables? I'm all protein down there.

"Anyway," I draw out and tip my head in the direction of her stairs.

"What are you doing?" she questions.

"Inviting myself to dinner," I say, lifting the bags I now hold in my hands. "Truce, Roxie. For five minutes, I'm waving a white flag." I give her my best pouty face and puppy dog eyes, and Roxanne shakes her head while I hold my ground. Finally, she acquiesces and passes me. I follow her, taking my time, telling myself I shouldn't be admiring her backside as she climbs ahead of me, but my eyes have a will of their own. Roxanne's ass is perfectly tight under another flowing skirt in a swirling pattern which hits above her knees. Her hips sashay in this sexy way, side to side, with each step she takes. If I pause a few steps below her, I might get a peek up her skirt, and that makes me feel like a pervert. It reminds me of my twelve-year-old self hoping to catch a glimpse under the uniform of Tara Lou Perry.

"It's red," Roxanne says, while my eyes roam up the back of her knee-high boots and swallow at the exposed skin behind her knees.

"What?" I choke.

"My underwear. It's red." Her monotone voice is dry, even bored sounding. Did she just tell me what color her underwear is? "I know you're looking."

I snort, trying to cover the lie. "You wish."

"I wish you'd see my underwear?" she questions, and it's just too much of an opening.

"So, you admit you *do wish* I would see it?" I tease. She stops short, and I practically run into her from a step below her. This means my face comes level with her fine ass, except she abruptly turns to me and now I'm eye level with …

"Eyes up here, William."

"Roxie," I breathe against her skirt near my face. Her hand cups my chin and tugs my attention upward. Narrowed eyes glare down at me.

"What are you staring at?"

Damn, her hand on my jaw feels good. Why does that feel good? What's happening to me?

I swallow under her gaze. *Is her thumb stroking my jaw?* It takes a moment for me to realize that it is. As my chin rests in the palm of her hand, the pad of her thumb slowly glides over the edge of my face, scraping against the scruff.

"What are you staring at?" I ask, my voice cracking like the twelve-year-old me as I drag my eyes up her body. She's bent forward and more than a hint of cleavage presses against the V-neck of her shirt.

"It's soft," she mutters, her voice dropping as the pressure of her thumb increases. Is her head lowering? My eyes fall to her lips, and she rolls them inward, then out before her tongue slips along the seam.

"I'm soft," I stutter although I'm anything but. With her tender touch on me, my body is overreacting, and I'm hard. *So hard.* I lift a hand, going for her cheek in hopes to bring her mouth to mine, forgetting about the grocery bag in my fingers until it rattles something inside, and Roxanne instantly releases my face. Standing to her full height, she returns her hands to her hips. I blink.

What the hell was happening?

I…*I almost kissed her.* Kissed *Roxanne.*

But the way she touched my jaw, the unexpected tenderness after years of snapping at each other, I just…wasn't thinking.

"Dinner?" I question, jiggling the bag in my hand, reminding us both why we're standing on these steps when I want to forget dinner and just kiss the daylights out of her.

"Dinner," she whispers, turning around and hustling up the final steps, which only makes my mouth water more and it's not for a meal.

Chapter 7

Dinner Plans

[Roxanne]

I don't know why I touched his face, but that stubble…my fingers twitched, and I had to know if it was soft or prickly. The direction of my thumb determined the texture. Soft. Prickly. Soft.

I'm soft, he said. *Did he mean his…* Is sex the only thing this man thinks about? Then again, was he not affected by me? Is this why he's never hit on me? Not that I want to be another one of many—I definitely do not want to be a notch on his bedpost—but I want to understand. Am I that unattractive to him?

What happened to you? The question returns to my mind. *Your sister was so pretty.* Meaning, I'm not. I'd like to think I'm woman enough to accept that not every man will be attracted to me, and I do accept that knowledge, but when a known player seems turned on by every freaking woman in the town, what is it about me that turns him off?

With these thoughts rattling around in my head, I enter the back door into my kitchen, and meet Sadie's eyes in greeting until hers drift to the man behind me.

"What's he doing here?" she spits.

"Sadie," I warn. "Manners."

Sadie clamps her lips closed while Billy puts the bags on the counter. He swipes his hands down his jeans-covered thighs and then rubs a hand along his throat. My mouth waters, and I lick my lips like I did while looking down at him. When his face was near my…

"Aunt Roxie, what's going on?" Sadie's suspicious eyes narrow, and for a moment, I see her mother, the uptight boss woman she became after having a child.

"Billy would like to join us for dinner."

Billy hastily steps forward, offering a hand to my niece who stares at his palm. "Billy Harrington," he states as if he's at a business meeting instead of making the acquaintance of his child.

"Sadie McAllister," Sadie huffs, crossing her arms and refusing to touch Billy. Billy flinches at her full name, and I suppose if he gets his name on the certificate, he might want her last name changed to Harrington. Something about that makes me sad until I notice the stance of my sister's daughter.

"Sadie," I drone, tipping my head in the direction of Billy. She reaches out for his hand and shakes it once.

"It's nice to see you again," Billy offers, his tone scratchy as he withdraws his hand. The three of us stand in awkward silence for a moment, and then Billy claps his hands so loudly Sadie and I both jump. "So what's for dinner?"

"Since you invited yourself, I thought you were cooking," I mutter under my breath, stepping over to the counter and removing the contents of my bags. "Spaghetti is on the menu this evening."

"Spaghetti," Billy moans, his smile tight. "My favorite."

I sigh as my eyes leap to Sadie. This is one of her favorites as well.

I make quick work of filling a pot with water and turning on the oven for garlic toast. "I don't have beer," I mutter to Billy as I don't drink it. "But I have sweet tea, lemonade, water…"

"Water works," Billy says still remaining statue-still behind me near the opposite counter. Sadie continues to stand as well, returning her arms to her chest.

"Why don't you tell Billy about your new school?"

"School sucks," Sadie says, and I close my eyes, taking a deep breath. It hasn't been ideal for Sadie to lose her mother, leave her home, and go to a new school, but my store is here, and owning a business isn't like transferring jobs.

"Yeah, I wasn't always a fan of school either," Billy says, his voice curt and sharp. He's suddenly talking too loud.

"Why don't you both sit down?" *You're each making me nervous.* I'm struggling with the spaghetti jar, straining and grunting in my attempts to twist the lid. I even have it clutched between my breasts, hoping the placement will give me additional leverage. Billy reaches for the jar, tugging the container forward, and pops the lid with one flick of his wrist. *Men.*

"I loosened it up for you," I mumble.

"I'd like to loosen something else," he mutters under his breath, and my eyes leap to his and then over his shoulder to Sadie. Billy straightens as if he's quickly forgotten a teenager stands among us. His eyes lower, and he bows his head a second. Turning on his heels, he faces Sadie.

"Tell me more of what you don't like about school." He pulls out a chair and helps himself to a seat at the table. Sadie's struggling. I can see the hesitation in her eyes, like a deer trapped in headlights. She wants to plop down across from him and open up while at the same time she's keeping her walls securely in place. I don't blame her. Having Billy Harrington in my kitchen is a bit unnerving.

Sadie speaks but with minimal word answers until she mentions Mrs. Pritchard.

"She's still teaching?" Billy snorts. "She must be a hundred. She used to let me copy off Katlyn Reiss although she didn't know she was doing it. *Here Billy, look at Katlyn's paper for help,*" he mocks in feminine imitation. "Help it was. Got an A in her class thanks to Katlyn."

I bet that's not all he scored with Katlyn Reiss near him, but Sadie smiles, just a little, enough so her eyes sparkle a rich deep golden tone.

"I think she single-handedly made me hate reading," Billy adds, and I gasp.

"You hate to read? Blasphemy," I mock, placing a hand on my chest.

"That just proves we can't be related, as I love to read," Sadie states, the wall returning to its full height.

"I'm glad to hear it. Reading's important; I just couldn't do it." Billy sits a little straighter, staring down at his hands clenched together on my wooden table. "I have dyslexia, which wasn't diagnosed until I was out of high school." He inhales, and adds, "Do you have anything like that?"

My brows pinch at the genuine concern in his voice. He's worried she struggles because he has dyslexia, and as his child, she might as well. But he owns a business where he must be able to read, and he's proven he's successful despite any challenges to him.

"I'm not dumb, if that's what you're asking," Sadie says, her tone defiant, and I glare at my niece. Admitting this struggle must have taken courage from Billy, and the least she can do is be sensitive. She doesn't have any learning disabilities like he's just admitted, but she doesn't need to be a little snot about it.

"Sadie Wilhelmina. That's enough." She's just being rude. She has enough sense to blink down at the table, her body language the only sign of her chagrin.

"Wilhelmina? What kind of name is that?" Billy chuckles softly.

"Apparently, my father's name in feminine form." With that, Sadie stands and leaves the room.

"Shit," Billy mumbles into his hand which covers his mouth. "I'm doing so bad at this."

My heart skips another beat of compassion. It's difficult for all of us, and I've known this secret for sixteen years.

"It takes time. You'll get the hang of it."

"She hates me." Billy sighs.

"She doesn't hate you. She just doesn't know you. Once she does, then she'll really hate you," I tease.

Billy's lips part as if he has a retort, but when he sees the crooked smile on my face, he relaxes back in his seat.

"I'm an acquired taste."

"I bet," I huff as my face heats. I turn back to the stove, adding the pasta to the boiling water. I shouldn't think about tasting Billy. Not those lips that look like they wanted a sip of me on the back stairs. Not his neck just under the hairline of that soft scruff. And definitely not any other parts of his anatomy.

Eggplant? I internally snort.

"What about you? Are you an acquired taste?" His voice is at my ear, and his presence behind me sends more heat rushing through my entire body, forcing latent parts to ignite into long-suppressed flames.

This is not good. I cannot be turned on by him.

"You'll never know," I mock while stirring the pot of spaghetti before me.

"We'll see," Billy hisses, his hand coming to my hip for a second. My body trembles at the intimate touch. He's playing with me, but I'm not about to be played. The oven beeps for the garlic bread, and I step back, forcing Billy to release me. He chuckles as he returns to his seat.

"How am I going to win her over?" he asks, his tone turning serious.

"She isn't a prize, William. She's a gift. They aren't the same thing."

When he's silent a moment, I crane my neck to look at him over my shoulder. His head is lowered once again as he stares at his feet.

"Should I bring her presents?" He's concentrating on his scuffed boots.

"You can't buy her either. For now, just *be* present. Be here. She's struggling with everything. Losing her mom. The move. Leaving her friends. She needs all the support we can offer."

"*We?*" His head springs upward.

"Well, yes. I'm her aunt. Her family. But you're her father, and while she gets to know you, I think we should present a united front."

His eyes shift to the front of my T-shirt and linger a second. "Not that front."

"I'd still like to unite fronts," he flirts.

Good God, he's impossible, but I laugh all the same.

Eventually, I call Sadie back to the kitchen. Dinner passes with the same unease as when Sadie was present earlier, only this time awkward silence fills the spaces between. It's awful. And then Billy drops the bomb.

"So I made a date for us. An appointment to be tested."

Holy what?

"What?" I stammer while Sadie looks from Billy to me.

"I have school," Sadie adds.

"We can go afterward," Billy continues. "There's a lab right here in Blue Ridge that will do a legal test. They are open until five. In roughly three days, we'll know for sure."

"*For sure,* that you're the sperm donor?"

"Hey," Billy snaps. Sadie's really pushing it tonight, and I admit her comment crosses another line, but he can't raise his voice to her. He doesn't have the right. Not yet.

"William," I hiss under my breath.

"Look, this isn't easy for me either," he states, his voice still louder than necessary. "And I'm trying to do the right thing here."

"Well, don't do me any favors," Sadie yells again, setting her fork down with a clatter.

"Maybe I'm doing this for me," he retorts, and instantly, I can see he's lost Sadie. She shuts down completely and turns to me.

"May I be excused?"

"Sure, baby." My heart aches for her, and I'm ready to spout off at Billy until I turn to him and read the horror on his cheeks.

"How am I the bad guy?" he questions. "This is new to me."

"It's new to her, too," I offer, sympathizing with both of them.

"I went too far." His voice lowers as his shoulders sink.

"You did." I want to reach out and comfort him, touch him, but I don't think it's best.

"I didn't mean it how it sounded."

"You never do," I say, keeping my voice steady.

"Meaning?"

I only shake my head. I don't have the energy to keep sparring with Billy, and I can't coach him on parenting. He needs to figure out this minefield on his own.

My phone rings, and I reach for it on the kitchen counter. It's Grace, reminding me she needs to leave early, which means I need to get down to the store.

"I need to head downstairs," I tell Billy, standing from the table although his plate remains relatively full. He hasn't eaten much I notice.

I'm not a gourmet cook, but I've been trying to incorporate kid-friendly foods into my menu and keep a scheduled dinnertime for Sadie. She needs stability and repetition.

"I'll clean up," he says standing briskly to the point we almost collide in my small kitchen. His hands grip my upper arms to catch me.

"I can't leave you here with Sadie." My brows lift, emphasizing my concern.

"Nothing's going to happen. I'll keep to the kitchen, hide the knives, and make sure she doesn't ignite the stove to set me on fire."

I shouldn't laugh, and I don't, actually. It's more of a nervous chuckle.

"Do you even know how to wash dishes?" I snort.

"Barkeep, remember? Glassware is my specialty. I take care of delicate things." His eyes meet mine, and I hesitantly scoff again.

"I'll be downstairs. Just let Sadie be, okay?"

"Scout's honor," he swears, holding up four fingers, and I know right then he's a liar because the Boy Scouts only use three.

Chapter 8

A Date

[Billy]

My mother would have never let us stew after she cooked a meal. Cleanup was on those who didn't cook, and if I am Sadie's father, the same rules will apply in my house, so I help myself to wander Roxie's apartment until I find a door marked with a wooden cutout of Sadie's name painted yellow and hanging on the doorknob.

"Sadie, Roxie had to go down to the bookstore. We need to do the dishes."

Silence.

"Look, house rules. If you didn't cook, you clean up. Roxie made us a nice dinner, and we repay her by cleaning the kitchen."

More silence.

Man, this kid is tough, but then again, I don't know what I expected.

"And I'm sorry I raised my voice," I say softly to the door and then turn back for the kitchen. I'm not known for my apologies, but I'm trying here. As I walk back down the hallway, my eyes wander for Roxie's bedroom, but I don't have the energy to snoop. Instead, I veer left for the kitchen and stopper the sink to wash the dishes. The basin fills with suds and water while I scrape the plates, and then I scrub the silverware and set it on a dish towel. Suddenly, the utensils move, and I peer over my shoulder with my hands deep in dishwater. Sadie stands next to me with another dish towel, wiping the forks dry. We work quietly in tandem for a while before she speaks.

"What do we need to do for the test?"

I've read up on a few possibilities, but I'd come to the consensus it is rather simple. "We each swab the inside of our cheeks, and a lab analyzes the results to see if we match."

"Like ancestry dot com?"

"Something like that."

A question still lingers between us—*what happens after?*—but neither of us asks.

"It takes about three days for the results," I add. She nods, and I take this as acceptance. "So, it's a date?" I tease, handing her the bowls I've cleaned.

"Do you want to date my aunt?" she blurts out, and I slowly grin.

"What? No. *Ew.* Dating is just yucky." I wiggle my entire body as though I'm repulsed by the idea, which isn't a total lie. I don't date. I'm more a pick-up man. Pick-her-up and another word which comes close to rhyming. I keep things casual, up front, and no commitment, and none of this is information I'll be sharing with a sixteen-year-old.

"No one says yucky," she snarks, glaring at me with those eyes that match the shape of her aunt and must have matched her mother's. I don't see a single trace of myself in her.

"Okay, well, dating is gross, like I want to hurl." I'm definitely pulling out vocabulary from a past era and showing my age here, but I don't know what the kids say. "And you shouldn't do it until you're thirty...five."

"This isn't the eighties," she states, shaking her head like I'm an idiot, but when I laugh, I catch the corner of her mouth curling upward— just a teeny bit—but it's more than the straight-line frown she's been wearing in that deep, dark lipstick. Her clothing ensemble matches the jet-black hair that's obviously a dye job. I wonder what her natural coloring is. Does she have brown hair like me, or lion-red like my sister, or is it blonde like I remember her mother having?

"Besides, I've already been on dates."

"What?" The pot I'm scouring slips from my hands and suds splash up on my shirt. "You're only sixteen."

"Exactly. I'm sixteen, and I've been on dates."

What the...? I can't be a father. I won't be able to handle these things.

"So spaghetti is your favorite, huh?" I ask, attempting to shift the conversation. I normally don't struggle with things to talk about. I'm good with women as long as they are over thirty, but teens, not so much my speed, and I don't want to discuss her dating history.

"Not really but Aunt Roxie makes salads all the time, and I don't love vegetables."

Huh, maybe we do have something in common.

"Right, who needs foods that are good for you?" Of course, I should talk. I'm more of a protein man. "Can I tell you a secret?"

She shrugs.

"I don't like vegetables much either, but I don't like spaghetti at all. Those noodles look like worms, and just *ew.*" I force a full-body tremble and leave out the part where I was hungover once as a teen and my mother made pasta. My dad knew I wasn't feeling great, and he knew why, and he made me eat the entire plate. Scarred for life from revisiting that dinner shortly after eating it.

"Then why'd you eat it?" Sadie asks, taking a pot off the soaked towel on the counter.

"I didn't want to hurt Roxanne's feelings, and I was trying to impress you."

"Maybe you just wanted to impress Aunt Roxie?" *What is this kid getting at?* Sadie tweaks up a brow at me, giving me a knowing look, but she knows nothing. There's nothing to know.

"Think it worked?" I tease. I mean Sadie, not Roxanne. I don't care what Roxanne thinks of me.

Lying liar who lies…

"No." Sadie snorts like only a teenager can pull off.

"I meant with you." I try to keep my tone light, but my voice catches on the seriousness of what I'm asking. I want to impress this girl. I want her to like me.

"The jury is still out on that," she states, sounding wise beyond her years, but I have to agree with her.

The jury is still out on a lot of things, kid.

+ + +

The next day, I meet Roxanne and Sadie at the clinic for the swab test. True to his word, Jordan hasn't said anything to my brother, and I am relieved even though I really need someone to speak with about the next step, and I'm not only thinking legally.

What am I going to do with a teenage daughter?

"Are you nervous?" I ask Sadie as she sits next to me in the orange plastic seats of the waiting room. I rub my hands down my jeans-covered thighs.

"Are you?" Sadie sits with her hands under her upper legs, dragging the toe of her black Converse absentmindedly back and forth over the tile floor. Roxanne sits on the other side of Sadie, acting like she's interested in some magazine, but her hand shoots out and covers Sadie's knee, halting her from the slide of her feet.

"Yes," I admit. "But it isn't the test that's making me nervous."

"If you aren't my dad, you're off the hook, you know?" I turn my head to look over at her, but her eyes remain on her now still feet. Roxanne peers at me over Sadie's head. Her eyes soften. The silver sparkles like well-polished candlesticks, and my chest does that strange clenching thing.

"Maybe I don't want to be *off the hook*," I say, keeping my eyes on Roxanne who quickly looks away. I glance down at Sadie to find her peering over at me. "But if I am your dad, you're stuck with me." I bump her shoulder to lighten the mood, but she reacts like my touch electrifies her. She covers her shoulder with a hand and shifts away from me.

"Yeah, that would be yucky," she mutters but another hint of a smile like the one from the other evening appears. I'll take it.

+ + +

The three-day waiting period might end up being the longest three days of my life. I'm still on edge about Roxanne putting in for a permit for the same weekend as our Oktoberfest, and I'm ready to explode.

"What is the meaning of this?" I snap, holding up a printed email from the permit office telling me there's another permit request for the same street for the same weekend. My wrist flicks in the direction of Roxanne who calmly sits behind her desk in her office.

"I want to have a book sale. I'm calling it Booktober. Cute, right?"

"Cute?" *Is she kidding me?* "That's the same weekend as our Oktoberfest. We need the street."

"So? I need the sidewalk." She stares up at me, blinking from behind a set of reading glasses which make her look teacher-y, and I suddenly want to take a ruler and spank her perfect backside.

"You can't have the sidewalk. We need the street," I repeat.

She continues to look up at me, and my arms wave for visual emphasis. "Big tent. Lots of tables. Beer. Entertainment." I pause as my arms flail out to my sides. "Loud music," I growl, warning her. *Don't you dare report me again for a noise violation.*

Roxanne stands and rounds her desk, which is piled with books and stacks of papers. She stalks toward me like a predator, and strangely, I feel preyed upon. I'm frozen as those silvery eyes narrow on mine, and she stops toe-to-toe with me.

"Did you hear something?"

I'm so worked up over the permits I don't catch her meaning.

"I *heard* you're trying to sabotage my party," I bark. Roxanne's eyes flick back and forth between mine, and then her damn hand reaches for the scruff on my jaw. Why is she touching me again? And why do I like it when she does this?

"Did you hear about Sadie?"

Anger washes out of me, and my shoulders sag, but my heart rate skyrockets, misinterpreting again. "Did something happen to her? Is she okay?" Concern laces my questions.

The change in my tone startles Roxie, who removes her hand, holding it away from my cheek as if she might slap me. Instead, she examines her palm, almost contemplating why she touched me. Quickly, she lowers her hand to her side.

"Sadie is fine. I meant the results."

"Oh." I let out another breath, calming at the explanation. "No, nothing yet."

Roxie weakly smiles, her eyes expressing almost…understanding. As if she understands I'm on edge and possibly overreacting about the permit because everything is setting me off while we wait out the paternity results. That look in her eyes does something to me, and I can't help myself. I reach for her cheeks, paper still in my grasp, and draw her closer to me until we are almost nose to nose.

This is the second time I've been this close to her, and she smells divine. Like fresh rain and springtime and a naked roll in a meadow.

Dammit, don't think of such things.

"Why are you so damn infuriating?" I hiss, my voice without my previous irritation as my eyes drop to her mouth where her lips have parted. A slight wisp of her breath crosses my own. It's as if she's kissed me by air, and I suck in the invisible heat. She rolls her lips together and then the tip of her tongue peeks out to lick the seam.

"Roxie," I groan, straining in more ways than one as her lips beg me to kiss her, and my dick leaps to life.

"William," she exhales, breathy and sultry. I'm a hair's breadth away from doing something that will change everything.

"Roxanne, honey. I don't mean to interrupt…" Grace's voice restores my senses, and I release Roxie's face. Taking a giant step back, I exaggerate the distance between us, making us look guilty of something that didn't happen.

"But you did," I think I hear Roxie say under her breath as she turns to give Grace a full-wattage smile. "What did you need?"

"The supplier is on line one."

"Thank you," she states before turning back to me. Out of the corner of my eye, I see the broad smile of Grace before she steps back for the main store.

"More books for your Booktober thingy?" I snark, recalling my earlier agitation.

"Just more books *to read*. I even upped my stock on parenting books, especially fatherhood."

My back straightens. Does she think I'd make a poor father? Admittedly, the past forty-eight hours have been stressful while we wait, and I don't know how to proceed with Sadie. Do I call her? Do I encourage more communication? Do I come to see her? It's not like I haven't thought of these things, like a father might think, but I don't know what to do. And I won't admit that to Roxanne, not after she blasted me the last time I asked for help.

"I don't need help parenting," I snip. Not to mention, reading some damn book about it when I told her the other evening reading takes effort for me.

"We all need help, William." Her tone in that name restores my negative energy toward her.

"Not me," I assure her, standing taller and crossing my arms, crushing the email against my chest. "I'm a one-man show."

"You're *all* show, that's for sure," she says, a chuckle lilting with her words.

"Meaning?"

"Oh." Roxie holds her fingers up to her throat. "Don't ask me for help explaining. You're the one who's got it all figured out, Mr. One-Man Show. More like a one-hit wonder," she mutters.

"I am *not* a one-hit wonder."

"I..." Roxanne closes those lips I wanted to savor moments ago but now want to vanquish in my anger. "I have no interest in discussing your sex life."

I stare at her a second, slow to interpret what I think she's saying. "Are you implying I'm a one-hit wonder *in bed*?" My voice rises an octave or two and practically cracks on the last words.

"Given your track record of women, and the misfortunate way Sadie came to be, I'd say one hit might be your thing."

"And what else do you think you know about me and my sex life?"

"I know you like to pound into women up against the alley wall outside your pub."

I stare at her. *What in tarnation?* "What the hell?"

"Exactly, it was hell watching your bare ass and you doing..." She points her finger at my zipper region. "...with whoever she was."

"I..." I have no fucking idea what she's talking about.

"In my limited *sexpertise*, as you call it, most women like more than *one showing*, William, more than a *one*-night stand, but since you know everything, I guess you don't need me to *mansplain* these things."

I'm so startled by her words, I'm tongue-tied, but I don't get the chance to think, to speak. Roxanne steps back and reaches for her landline, pressing a button and answering the call waiting for her. It's clear she's dismissing me, no explanation needed.

Chapter 9
Close Calls Aren't Close Enough

[Roxanne]

"Roxanne?" A familiar voice carries through the line when I pick up the handset. I'm visibly shaking from the near miss—*near kiss*—with Billy Harrington. I watch him leave before I speak into the phone.

"Grace?" I question as her voice registers.

"It sounded pretty heated in there, and I thought I'd rescue you."

My shoulders relax as I realize Grace did rescue me.

Then why do I feel deflated about being saved?

"Thanks, Grace," I say. "Everything's okay back here."

I can't believe I admitted to seeing him. His *I know what I'm doing* attitude, and I just blurted out what I saw because he had to act all uppity about his sex life.

I hate that he has a sex life.

And I hate that I feel like he was about to kiss me.

I shouldn't want him to kiss me. I'm the last person Billy wants to kiss, and that's the crux. He's probably kissed most of the eligible women in this town and, I don't doubt a handful of women before they were ineligible, but not me. It's like I'm the only woman he *hasn't* kissed, and I should be grateful, but some days, I wonder what's wrong with me. He flirts. He teases. I don't understand why I'm not good enough.

But maybe that's the crossroad. I don't want to just flirt and tease and to be some one-time wonder to Billy. I'd want a little more—like all of him—which would mean Billy being monogamous, for one thing, and that's definitely *not* one of his character traits.

I've heard the rumors about his marriage. What he did and how it ended.

The other night, I heard Kristy Moseley was hot on his trail, and I can only assume he's been on her trail a time or two to warrant her chase.

She's the former wife of Denton Chance, a famous rock star from Blue Ridge who left before I was a teenager. Denton's older sister, Dolores, owns the diner down the street. She's a good source of gossip although she doesn't spread it; she simply knows it all.

I heard she's after Billy Harrington in hopes to make Denton jealous, one nosy Nelly stated.

Heard she's going to be the future Mrs. Harrington if she has her way, another replied.

One look from Dolores stopped both women from talking, but the rumors had been cast. If Billy did take a wife, that woman would be Sadie's stepmother, and where would that leave me? What will Billy do once he finds out the truth? Once he knows from a scientific test that he's the sperm donor, as Sadie called him. I will not be squeezed out of Sadie's life. She is practically my child for all the raising I did of her before she was thirteen. Leaving her behind had been difficult for me, but the reality is: *she wasn't my child.* She was my sister's. I am the only living relative on her mother's side, minus some distant cousins, and I wouldn't let anyone take Sadie from me, including Billy Harrington.

+ + +

Within another day, we receive the results we already knew. As I read through the chart, analyzing numbers that make no sense to me, I find the only percentages we need. Billy needed a combined parent index of over one hundred percent with a probability of paternity over ninety-nine point zero. Billy has passed with both a one hundred and fifty-two and a ninety-nine point three. There wasn't any doubt, but this confirms everything. I stare at the numbers, uncertain what they mean. Well, I know what they mean, but I'm waiting for emotion to hit me. Should I be relieved, appeased, or something between? I don't know how to feel about these results, and I believe I should feel something. Instead, I'm numb as my mind races.

"So, he's my dad," Sadie states after I interpret what I can of the results with her. I emphasize the bottom-line percentages, and Sadie stares at the numbers as I do. "Does this mean I have to live with him?"

It's a question I've been asking myself but avoiding an answer.

"Do you want to live with him?"

"I don't know him," she states, looking up at me from where we sit at my kitchen table. I brush wisps of hair behind her ear. I hate the black color, but I won't mention it to her. She needs to work through her own emotions, and I can't imagine being in her position: dealing with the death of her mother, making new friends here, and finding out who her dad is. It's too much, and I've considered finding her someone to talk to about everything.

"Can I still live with you?"

"Of course, baby. If that's what you want."

"Do you want me to be here?" The question startles me.

"Absolutely." I cup her cheeks, holding her face so she's forced to look at me. "This is where you should be. With me. But I can't deny Billy his right as your father, and if he wants you to live with him…well, we'll just have to work something out."

"Like every other weekend or something?" Sadie's question turns sharper, disappointment and disapproval in her tone.

"I don't know what's next." I do know I should talk to my lawyer, the one I hired for the petition for temporary custody until full custody could be guaranteed. She's back in Atlanta because in a small town, there aren't many choices. It's either one Harrington or another, and I already know Billy secured his nephew Jordan Rathstone as he is who ordered the legal DNA testing. I want to ask Billy if we can just settle things between us. He doesn't need to file for custody. I'll take full responsibility for Sadie. Ideally, we could work out visitation or whatever else among ourselves, but the logical side of me knows it's in Sadie's best interest to go through legal channels. Her mother would definitely not approve of some kind of gentleman's agreement or a handshake on schedules and finances. She didn't want to bother Billy with being the father out of fear he'd want half of Sadie's time. Theresa didn't want to share.

He's already given me this unwarranted gift. I don't need to divide her with him.

Yes, the one-hit wonder, king of the one-night stand was perfect for my sister's independent spirit, not to mention, being with him—as her unending high school crush—was fantasy fulfillment. I've heard that's a heavy aphrodisiac. Theresa couldn't have made a better plan for becoming a parent. As far as planning goes, though, Theresa never saw herself as a parent.

I did. I was the one who wanted children and didn't have any. Instead, I have a niece.

A small part of me wants to do right by Billy. It would never be fair to ask him to deny his knowledge of Sadie, for her or him, and he doesn't seem to be balking at the idea of fatherhood. As always, he seems overconfident, as though he can fall into parenting without assistance. No man, or woman, falls into parenting *with* experience, but most people have a support system. When I think of the Harrington clan, Billy will have more than his share, which leaves me wondering, once again, where I'll fit into things.

When we don't hear anything from Billy or a lawyer, as I expected, Sadie grows quieter in asking questions, and I become irritated. His child isn't some floozy he can dismiss or play games with. I'm sure Billy has a checklist regarding the number of days before he can call a woman, if he even calls at all. But Sadie is his kid, and I won't let him blow her off. These thoughts fuel my ire as I stalk across the street late one evening and enter the Blue Ridge Microbrewery and Pub to confront the father of my niece.

When I enter, Billy is intervening in an altercation near the bar between a wasted Denton Chance, the newly returned prodigal rock star, and his ex-wife, Kristy Moseley. I'm quick to assume Billy's interference is to protect Kristy as Denton is holding her waist, and my fears of Billy excluding me from Sadie's life with a potential wife double. When Mati Harrington arrives, Denton leaves with the aid of Billy but not before he makes another small scene.

I shouldn't be staring, but the flame of my anger dulls a little as Billy escorts Denton out of the bar. I help myself to a stool and smile at Clyde Bebzene, who's bartending. I don't typically frequent the pub. It's not my scene nor do I drink much but tonight feels like a night for some wine.

"I'll take a Moscato," I say to Clyde. He's a rumbled mess. His jeans don't quite zip and his flannel could use an iron, but his smile is sweet. He isn't married, and he doesn't have kids, but he coaches Little League baseball, and one of Grace's sons is on his team. I've gotten to know Clyde over the years as his reading interests include superhero comics and fan fiction retellings.

"It's a brew pub. We only serve beer," a deep masculine voice states from behind me. Clyde's eyes widen, and I don't need to turn around to know who spoke to me in such a manner. Clyde shifts his large body to rest his hip against the bar and side-eyes the array of liquor bottles on the back wall. Then he turns back to me and lifts an eyebrow. I shake my head, attempting to ignore the man behind me even though he's the reason I'm here.

"Billy," Kristy Moseley squeals. "You're my hero tonight."

I don't want to acknowledge them, but their presence is close, and the ear-splitting squeak of Kristy leads me to remember her cheerleading days with my sister. In the reflection of the mirror behind the alcohol bottles, I watch Kristy make a short leap for Billy who catches her on her sides near her breasts while Kristy's arms wrap around his neck.

"I've been looking for you for days," Kristy purrs, and Clyde's head shakes. A huffed-chuckle comes from his mouth, and he reaches under the bar for a cooler. A bottle of wine mysteriously appears, and he fills a glass to the brim for me.

"That's more than a pour," Billy snaps behind me, but Clyde ignores him and slides me the glass.

"On me," he states with a wink.

"Why haven't you called me?" Kristy whines, and I can only imagine the pout of her puffy lips. She's bleach-blonde and big boobed, and probably everything Billy looks for in a woman. My sister certainly matched the description, but I never did. Being overweight as a teenager, my breasts were uncomfortably large. Once I started eating better and working out, I liked myself better, but the extra frontal baggage had to go. I had a breast reduction so guys would stop noticing my triple Ds before looking up at me. And I was never a blonde but a brunette before the pre-maturing gray. Now I sport a full head of wispy silver and dark chrome.

Nope, I'm definitely not Billy Harrington's type.

"Have you been avoiding me, Billy Harrington?" Kristy drones, and I catch her fiddling with the collar of his shirt through the reflection in the mirror. Suddenly, I've abandoned my purpose for being here this evening, and all I want to do is disappear. I turn enough to see I'm blocked in my seat by the Krist-illy embrace behind me, and I don't know how to escape them. Twisting back for my wine, I take too large a sip, as I rush to finish the glass, and choke on the fizziness.

"Now, why would I avoid you?" Billy responds. Clyde has walked down the bar to help another customer, but he looks up at Billy's comment. I close my eyes, willing them all away. When I open, Clyde stands before me. He tilts his head to the side, keeping his eyes on me.

"Want to get out of here?" he mutters, and if I didn't know better, the proposition would sound clandestine and appealing, but I have a sneaky suspicion Clyde has a crush on my employee. Still, I'm happy for his intervention due to the scene behind me. "I get a break in…" He looks at his wrist, which is missing a watch. "Now."

"The hell you do," Billy snaps from behind me.

"I'm taking five," Clyde states, speaking up to his boss, and I watch him step to the end of the bar and then circle around for me. Clyde wedges his big body between Krist-illy and extends his elbow for me. I slip my hand into the crook, silently thanking him with a glance.

"I'm so relieved chivalry isn't dead." I giggle as I slip from the stool, and Clyde walks me to the door. Once we step outside, I slip my hand from his elbow and stop him on the corner.

"Thank you. That was…" I turn in the direction of the front window to the pub. I don't know how to explain myself, but my heart races, and I'm grateful to be out in the fresh fall mountain air.

"Let me walk you across the street," Clyde offers, but I chuckle.

"The store is closed, Clyde. Grace went home."

"What? I…I was keeping up the chivalry act." He winks at me again, but he's teasing. I pat his thick forearm.

"I can handle myself from here," I state and press up on my toes to kiss his cheek. He's a sweet man, and if Grace would ever open her eyes, she'd see someone looking for her.

I turn for the crosswalk, abiding by the rules as I cross straight across the street, then turn left to walk the length of my building for the back entrance to the apartment above. I've almost made it to the staircase when I hear heavy boots thundering behind me, and I spin in time to have my mouth covered before I can scream.

"Don't scream. It's me," Billy says as a thick palm covers my lips, and I'm pressed against the brick building. Immediately, I swat at his broad shoulders, telling him with my body language to get off me. His free hand captures my wrist and holds it near the side of my head.

"Calm down. I just don't want you freaking out the neighborhood." He withdraws his hand and quickly captures my other hand, pressing it to the wall near my head as well. For some reason, his fingers spread, forcing mine to link with his.

"Oh, and like you didn't freak me out by running up after me, slamming me into this wall, and covering my mouth, telling me not to scream."

His pelvis leans against my lower belly, holding me in place, and a rush flutters up my middle. "Are you hurt? Did I hurt you?" Concern fills his eyes although his body has not moved back from mine.

"No," I whisper. He's so close. His breath on my face. His hands holding mine. His lower half pinning mine to the wall at my back.

It's just like her. The woman I saw him with.

"Why were you at the pub?" I open my mouth to respond, almost forgetting my purpose with all the Krist-illy-gate happenings, but he continues. "Did I see you kiss Clyde?"

My mouth gapes. "What?" *Has he lost his mind?*

"Did you. Kiss Clyde?" He slows as if I'm not quick on the intake.

"Are you kidding me? How would you notice anything being you were all wrapped up in Kristy Moseley?"

"Were you jealous?" he asks, as a seductive grin slowly graces his lips. "That's it. You are jealous." His smile grows salacious and pleased, but I snap.

"I won't be squeezed out of Sadie's life if you take a wife."

That smile instantly disappears. "What?" He's so loud I turn my head to the side, no longer able to face him. He tightens his grip on our linked fingers and pulls our collective hands under my chin. "What on earth made you think I'd take a wife?"

"You're with Kristy. I've heard the rumors." I can't even use the word dating for what they might be doing.

"You've heard rumors, huh?" Billy chuckles. "And you always believe what you hear, right?"

"No, but—"

"I'm a real ladies' man, one-hit wonder, right? You *saw* me, remember?" His laughter turns sardonic, his tone bitter, and I concentrate on his lips, trying to ignore the press of his firm thighs against the upper part of mine. *Is he hard?* I can't even go there in my head. It's been so long, and he's so close to the promise land. I was dating Chad before I decided to move to Blue Ridge, and he decided he wouldn't move with me. That was three years ago. Since then, the bookstore has been my lover, but it's been a lonely substitute.

"I saw what I saw. And yes, that's what I've heard," I snap back as if it's an insult. "And I won't be pushed out of Sadie's life when you take a woman as a partner."

"A woman as a partner?" he repeats, the chuckle slowly dying. "I'm not square dancing, darlin', and who do you think I'd be taking as a partner, anyway?"

I ignore the sarcasm and continue. "Sadie can't have a revolving door of women in her life. She'll need stability, continuity, and not some passing through, one-night stand floozy."

Billy leans his upper half away from me as he returns our joined hands to the brick, but his lower half digs deeper against me. If he slips a little lower, the loose material of my skirt would easily give, and he'd be exposed to my current condition. Heat radiates between my thighs with an unquenchable thirst for friction. *What is wrong with me?* This is Billy Harrington, manwhore galore.

"Are you done yet?" he snips, narrowing his eyes on me. My chest heaves. The women. The one-nighters. The fear for Sadie.

"I won't let another woman push me out of Sadie's life."

His eyes shift from narrowed to etched with something I can't interpret, but the expression of his hardened jaw relaxes.

"You aren't going anywhere. You're Sadie's aunt."

"It's more than that," I offer, bracing to hand him my feelings. "She's everything to me. I'm practically a second mother, and I won't lose her."

As Billy continues to stare at me, he gingerly lessens the pressure of his lower body on mine.

"You aren't going to lose her."

"I'm all she has," I interject, and my voice cracks. The emphasis is a combination of me being all she has and her being everything to me. I can't lose her. I can't lose another person from my life.

"Sadie has me now, too." His tone softens, lowering as his eyes watch my lips.

"But she doesn't. You haven't called her, and you must have the results. You must *know* by now that you are her dad."

"I've been busy," he mutters.

"That's not an excuse. That's what you say to someone like Kristy, not your daughter."

Billy's eyes snap up to mine.

"I've been looking for the right time."

"There isn't a right time, Billy. The time is now. Any time. That girl lost her mother. She found out she has a father who works across the street from where she lives. She needs you."

Billy tips his head back, his eyes drifting up the building as if he can see Sadie above us in the apartment.

"You need to step up, William." I've lost my steam and don't even say his name with my typical demeaning irritation. My tone saddens as I address him. *Sadie needs him.* She won't admit it, but her growing silence and dark mood prove what she isn't saying. She thinks he's rejecting her.

"Okay, Roxie." I typically don't like how he shortens my name because the nickname is reserved for those closest to me. I especially don't like the way he emphasizes it—pausing on the rocks and exaggerating the e-sound—but he's lost his bluster as well, and the way he exhales over my abbreviated name makes me shiver. The tremble draws his eyes back to my face. "I don't have her number, but I'll stop over tomorrow and sort it all out."

"Don't give me empty promises," I state. "And don't give Sadie false hope. If you really want to be her dad, you have to be more than a name on a certificate or a contact on her caller ID. Otherwise, you really are a sperm donor, and she doesn't need anything from you."

I'm not convinced Sadie can go on without Billy now that she knows who he is and where he lives, and I have a sneaky suspicion Billy might just need Sadie in his life as well.

"I'm not just a sperm donor," he grits, his tone returning to the Billy I'm more familiar with. The one who irritates me whenever he speaks.

"Fine. Prove it."

The gleam to those earthy-rich eyes returns. "Game on, Roxanne." With my full name rolled from his throat, another shiver ripples up my spine, and my thighs clench against his.

"Now, we have other questions to be answered. You still didn't tell me if I *saw* what *I think I saw*. You kissed Clyde outside the pub."

"It was only on the cheek. He was being a gentleman." I don't know why I answer him or even justify the action because it's none of Billy's damn business. "Why? Were *you* jealous?" I retort, throwing the question back to him. His nostrils flare, but he doesn't answer.

"Like this kind of kiss?" He lowers quickly to my upper cheek, close to my ear, giving me a whisper of a peck. I can't speak. I'm so stunned by the motion I can't find words. He slowly pulls back, dragging his nose tenderly along my skin to the corner of my mouth. He draws back only enough for a wisp of space between our lips.

"Or was it more like this?" He shifts his head to the other side of my face and kisses the opposite corner of my lips. My breath hitches, and my lips part. I've never had a corner-lip kiss before, and it's terribly sweet and disturbingly sexy.

"More like the first one," I choke out, my voice husky and rough. Billy tips back, allowing more space between us, but his eyes linger on my lips.

"Doing the gentlemanly thing," he whispers. He steps back and releases my hands. I'm strangely chilled without his warmth, and my fingers tingle, wanting to reach for him and follow his retreat. Instead, I squeeze them as if restoring feeling and lower both hands to my sides. Billy turns to his side and juts out his elbow. "Allow me to walk you home."

Too surprised by the sudden shift in him and flabbergasted by his suggestion, I wordlessly press off the wall and loop my hand through the crook of his arm. It's only a few steps, and I've walked this direction a million times in three years. I'm perfectly safe in Blue Ridge, and I don't need an escort, so I'm stumped as to why I'm playing along with him.

We haven't gone two feet before Billy mutters, "Fuck it. I'm no gentleman." I'm pressed back to the wall with his hands on either side of my head, and his mouth crashes into mine.

His lips are soft but demanding, tugging and teasing mine as he moves my head the slightest bit to deepen his attention. His tongue licks the seam of mine, and I open without thought, drawing him into me. Billy's body returns to pressing me to the wall, but there's no threat or menace like earlier, and my thoughts drift again. If he'd only lower his hips a bit, my legs could spread, and his thick thigh could press right there…but I'm distracted by his mouth on mine.

I'm kissing Billy Harrington.

The thought makes my heart race and my stomach triple flip.

Good God can Billy Harrington kiss, *and he's kissing me.*

My mind slowly catches up to reality.

I'm kissing Billy Harrington!

What the hell am I doing?

I use all my strength to push on Billy's shoulders, forcing him off me.

"What were you thinking?" I snap, as I realize a moment too late what he was doing.

Billy Harrington was kissing me.

"I was…"

"Kissing me," I clarify, only my tongue hangs out of my mouth, and it sounds like I've said *icking e*. The back of my hand dramatically swipes across my lips as if to scrub off the kiss. He'd just kissed Kristy Moseley with those lips of his. Those delicious, devious, sensuous lips. I stick out my tongue and swipe down the length several times with my index finger, scrubbing, scrubbing, scrubbing.

Oh my God, he kissed me after kissing her.

And I let him.

"What are you doing?" he groans, and my eyes leap to his, which are full of puzzling hesitation.

"You just kissed me after kissing Kristy." I drag my knuckles over my lips again, disgusted with myself for giving in to the tender yet demanding direction of his mouth on mine.

His eyes widen in horror and then narrow to slits.

"That's what you think?" he questions, his voice gravelly and low. "Jesus, Roxanne, you can be such a…" He stops himself and scrubs a hand down his face, resting his palm under his chin against his throat. My eyes leap to the scruff on his jaw. The same soft scruff my fingers long to touch. The same soft scruff that just tickled my chin.

He says nothing else but turns on his heels and begins to cross the street, jaywalking on the diagonal to reach the other side. My heart hammers in my chest, and my hands lower to press into the brick at my back, steadying me.

He kissed Kristy Moseley before me, right?

I watch his retreat, my shoulders slowly lowering, and my stomach settling from all the double backhand springs inside.

I watch as Billy spits into the street before reaching the curb, lifting his hand to his face, and dramatically swiping at his mouth, then flicking his wrist as if to rid his palm of something sticky and gross.

A kiss from me.

Chapter 10
Kiss and Seek

[Billy]

Why the fuck did I have to kiss her?

Have to? my head clarifies.

Had to, my dick responds.

First, that Clyde takes her out of the pub before I know what she's doing in there, and then I see them through the front window. She tips up on her toes because Clyde is tall, and she kisses him.

In front of my pub.

In front of me.

The second Clyde returns, I've finally extracted myself from Kristy, ignoring her pleas for another night together—big mistake happening the first time—and I'm brushing past Clyde for the front entrance with a muttered, "I'll be back."

I cross the street with long strides, racing up behind her before she can reach her stairs and then…

Although I knew I'd scare her a little, those eyes snapped to mine, and when our fingers linked in my grasp, I just had to have answers.

Why did she kiss Clyde?

In typical Roxanne form, she sidetracks and reroutes and accuses me of marriage and other women and just…dammit that woman. I reach for the large handle of the pub door and yank the thing open. The swell of loud country music and the blare of sports games on the TVs fill my head but do nothing to stop my racing heart or the throb in my jeans. I'm sporting a major boner as I cross through the bar. I should have adjusted myself, but this isn't going down without something to relieve it.

I ignore every greeting and a few smacks on the back as I rush to my office. Then I slam the door, throw the lock, and fall against the barrier. Both hands cover my face, and I swipe down my cheeks.

What the fuck have you done this time? my brain screams.

Why didn't you let me out? my dick weeps.

Fucking Roxanne McAllister and her fucking delicious lips which kissed me back for a moment there. She opened for me with a sweet sigh and an eager tongue. Her hips rolled forward, begging my thigh to separate hers, and my fingers twitched to grip those hips, forcing her to ride my leg. But I couldn't release her face. Her skin is so soft, my thumb stroked over her cheeks as I moved her mouth with mine.

My fingers brush hastily over my lips, and I toss my hands to my thighs.

Goddammit.

I'm still stiff as a pine tree, and it's only getting worse, the longer I think about her lips mixing with mine.

Then I consider the things she said.

Not going to be pushed out of Sadie's life.

Need to step up for Sadie.

Kissed Kristy before her.

I did not fucking kiss Kristy. What does she take me for? But I know the answer. She thinks I'm a player, and I have no evidence to prove her wrong. My history corroborates the truth, and Sadie is exhibit A that I've slept around.

My shoulders slump against the door, and my head falls forward.

Sadie.

Roxanne wasn't wrong there either. I should have called. I should have gone to see her. This is all new to me, but like Roxanne reminded me the other day, it's new to Sadie. She's a kid, and she's been through a ton of changes lately, and while my mother likes to say kids are resilient, I don't know how well I'd be if everything were piled on at once like that.

Poor baby, my heart whimpers, and I clutch at my tee, uncertain where the sentiment came from. I immediately vow to do better by her. I'm the adult, so I need to make the first move. It's not like I was waiting for Sadie to come to me. I don't expect her to lead me through this parenting thing and tell me what to do, after all, but I do need some guidance. I think about Roxanne's comment—she purchased some new books on fathering—only I'd never have the patience to read, and the struggle to make it through a whole book would be torture.

Why'd I admit I had dyslexia the other night? I saw the pity in Roxanne's face like I'm some moron who isn't smart. I wasn't diagnosed until right before I dropped out of college. By then, I'd developed a system to get by. It wasn't always correct, but it worked for me. I did end up working manual labor in my dad's brewery, which was fine, but I wanted something more for me. I didn't want to lug the beer but collect the Benjamins. When Rachel and I divorced, it was the perfect time to open my own business. I took some classes and got some tutoring to develop strategies for business reading. Invoices. Numbers. Accounting. Numbers aren't as difficult for me as letters.

I press off the door and head for the bathroom, a plan forming, but first I have something I need to take care of.

+ + +

The next afternoon, I write my digits on a Post-it and stalk across the damn street. Again. I'm all worked up and ready to slap the note on Roxanne's desk and give a little speech, but my fury is instantly deflated upon seeing Grace Eton.

"Where's Roxanne?" I ask a little too aggressively.

"She had to go to the high school. Something for Sadie." Grace gives me a hesitant, pinched smile, and I know she knows my secret. *I'm Sadie's father.*

"Did something happen? Is Sadie okay?" My pre-anger-at-Roxanne has settled into post-concern-for-Sadie.

Grace shrugs. "I'm sure she'll be fine. There's just a lot going on for her." Grace keeps her eyes on me like she's trying to tell me something, but I can't read her.

Sheepishly, I meet Grace's eyes, and ask, "Should I go to the school, too?" I don't know why I ask other than knowing Grace is the mother of five handful boys. She'd be a good source on parenting.

"Are you ready to tell everyone who Sadie is?"

Who Sadie is? The question flutters before me, and it takes a second to realize the deeper context.

Who Sadie is…to me.

I haven't told anyone minus Jordan and Clyde, and Roxanne has obviously told Grace. Who else did she tell? How many nosy Nellys know my business?

"I…I think Sadie and I need some time to figure out things before I tell everyone." Grace's once sympathizing smile morphs into a controlled grimace.

"I see. Well, you need to do what's best for you," she tells me in a rather mothering voice. I nod to agree and hand her the paper with my number. "Can you give this to Sadie? I don't have her number, and I'd like her to call me."

Grace twists her lips, thinking as she stares at the paper, and then takes it from me. "Sure. I'll pass this on to Sadie because I'm sure you' busy later working at the pub to cross the street and get her number yourself."

Grace is exactly right. I work late afternoons and evenings. The pub is my baby and my life. I nod again, almost surprised by how well Grace understands me. Why can't Roxanne be so understanding?

"Thanks." I double-tap my fingers on the edge of the check-out counter and smile one last time at Grace before exiting the building.

As I'm crossing back to the pub, Grace's words roll through my thoughts. *Tell everyone. Too busy. Do it myself.* I stop in the middle of the street, and an oncoming car blares its horn as it approaches. Holding up a hand in apology, I continue walking and realize I'm misinterpreting the credit I thought Grace gave me. She actually understands me better than I think. I'm messing this all up again. *Dammit.*

Chapter 11
Mistakes and Mishaps

[Roxanne]

"I'm certain you understand an altercation of this type is not permissible in our school, Ms. McAllister." Clarence Steinmetz looks down his nose at me. Of course, I understand. Bullying of any type is not allowed—*not permissible*—but can't he see Sadie's hurting? Was she really bullying another student, or were they having a conflict that needs resolution like the rest of her life?

"I understand, Mr. Steinmetz. I'm sure it won't happen again, and Sadie's sorry. She's just struggling with the adjustment."

Her mother's death. Moving here. An absentee father.

Is that what Billy is? Then, I think of his eyes and the way he peered up at the building before…*before*…and the questioning expression on his face, like he wants to do the right thing but doesn't know how.

Just as Sadie wants to fit in here but doesn't know how either. It's been an adjustment for her, as I said, to move to a smaller town where everyone knows one another. The kids have all grown up together, and Sadie is like a shiny new toy, one dressed in head-to-toe black with midnight hair covering her face. She reminds me of Violet from *The Incredibles*, a Disney movie about a family with superpowers, which she loved as a child. Is that what she wants—a superpower to disappear? Does she want the ability to put a forcefield around herself?

"If it's okay with you, I'd like to take Sadie home with me and give her the rest of the day to think about her actions."

"I think that's an excellent idea, Ms. McAllister." Clarence leans back in his chair, eyeing me over the ridge of his glasses. I don't miss the dip of his gaze or the way it travels down my body. *What's he looking at?* I wonder but ignore the stare. I'm about to stand when he speaks again.

"Might I ask, is there any additional family support?" The principal holds up a paper, skims the page, and glances back at me. "I know about her mother, but there's no father listed, and you're her guardian."

Is there a question in that statement somewhere?

"Is there some other issue? Something I'm missing here?" I question.

"It's only that, well, Sadie mentioned how her family runs this town, and she can do as she pleases while she's here. It's a strange comment coming from someone new to the community."

There's still a lingering unasked question, but he won't get an answer from me. An implication of running this town means only one name—Harrington. The mayor is one. The brewery that employs quite a few townspeople is another.

"I'll speak with Sadie," I assure him, standing to express my wish to leave. It's strange that even as an adult, I feel like I'm the one in trouble in this office.

"You do that, and if there's anything you need, here's my card. You can call me. For anything." My brows pinch as I take the card. Isn't that what I was doing here? Seeking help and compassion for Sadie, because that's what I need. That's what *she* needs.

I exit the principal's office and wave at the secretary. Sadie sits in a seat across from the empty cubical desk of a second secretary.

"Let's go," I whisper to Sadie, disappointment ringing in my tone. Even if I did ask for some sympathy from the school on Sadie's behalf, I won't disguise how upset I am at this situation.

"I'm leaving?" Her brows disappear under her dark hair which she has pulled forward over her face.

"For today." I press through the door, expecting her to follow me into the hall. She does, keeping pace with me as I walk as quickly as I can to get out of this building.

"Am I suspended?"

"Would it matter?" I snap. When Sadie lived near Atlanta, her mother wanted her to get into the most prestigious schools. She pushed Sadie to work hard, study harder, and learn all the things. Sadie rose to that challenge, but it wore on her. She didn't get to do anything extra, like be a kid. Sure, she had extracurricular activities, but everything involved practice. Piano. Karate.

"Yes." The softly spoken word stops me in my tracks, and I turn on Sadie in the middle of the hallway.

"Really? Because this isn't the Sadie I know. Picking on another girl because of her clothes, calling her a name, and threatening her." My eyes have a will of their own as I take in Sadie's appearance. The same could have easily happened to her.

"And what's this about saying your family runs this town? Acting like you're superior to the rest of the kids and can get away with something like casting stones."

"I didn't throw anything," she mutters.

"You know what I mean, Sadie Wilhelmina," I say in an exasperated tone and a little too loudly as my arms flail out to my sides and then slap my thighs. I hitch my crossbody purse on my shoulder although it doesn't need adjusting and glare at my niece. Where did the sweet girl go? Why is she hiding?

"She started it," Sadie whines. Her voice reminds me of when my sister and I would fight, putting blame on each other rather than admitting who did what first.

"Sadie," I groan.

"She said I looked like Violet from *The Incredibles* and maybe I should disappear like her as well."

My stomach flips as I considered the same thing. Not the disappearing part, but the overall appearance of Sadie.

"Well, you do look like Violet. I thought that might be the look you were going for." I try to soften my tone, teasing her with the truth while trying not to insult her. "You can look like whoever you want, honey. But I am worried. Are you trying to disappear?"

Sadie has mentioned to me how the kids are different here. In some ways, she might be right. It's more in-your-face community than what she's used to, but it's another reason I moved back here. I was tired of being just another face in a sea of people in a big city. Sadie looks off at something on the wall and swallows. "That's what Billy wants. Me to disappear."

Heart. Ripped. Out.

"Baby, I don't think that's true. He's just…he's struggling like you. He doesn't know what to do or how. It's confusing for a man like him." Really, it'd be confusing for any man to suddenly have a kid show up, a kid you didn't know you had.

Sadie huffs, proving she doesn't understand, and I shouldn't be defending Billy. She has her own issues.

"Do you need to collect your backpack or anything?" I ask, and Sadie shrugs her shoulder, emphasizing the pack already hanging on her back. "Oh. Okay. Let's go."

We walk in silence to the car, but everything still weighs on my mind. We settle into my Honda Civic and head back toward Main Street when I finally ask, "Did you tell the other kids you were Billy's daughter?"

Sadie's head lowers, and her hair curtains her face. She simply shakes her head, and her hair sways.

"Do you want to tell the other kids? Would that…I don't know…help somehow?"

"It doesn't matter," Sadie groans, laying her head back and staring out the passenger window. We continue the short drive without another word and pull into the alley behind the second block of Main Street where the bookshop sits on the corner. As I near the private parking space, I see the broad body of someone sitting on the stairs leading up to my apartment. Sadie's eyes remain trained on the wooden staircase and the outline of the man we can see through the risers.

"Did you call him?" Sadie whispers. I shake my head in response although she isn't looking at me, and I'm thinking the same unspoken question.

What is Billy doing here?

Sadie and I exit the car and slowly approach him. Billy doesn't stand from his seat on the stairs.

"Hey." His voice croaks as his eyes find mine and then quickly drift to Sadie. "You okay?"

Sadie shrugs. If she wants to escape him by running up these steps, she's going to have to climb over him because he doesn't look like he's moving anytime soon.

"Did you get in trouble?" He's keeping his eyes on Sadie although she isn't meeting his. Sadie shrugs again. Billy waits out the silence, and Sadie finally speaks.

"What's it matter?"

"Sadie," I hiss, rolling my eyes to the heavens.

"I got in trouble a lot when I was in school. Whaddya do?"

"Why is it that *I* did something?"

Billy chuckles. "Yeah, it was never my fault either."

I fight the smile wanting to form on my lips. He's sweet with her and looks kind of cute sitting on my steps, fidgeting with his fingers on his thighs.

"Why don't you tell me what happened anyway?"

I'm expecting Sadie to snap at him, give him another snarky comment, but to my surprise, she doesn't. She explains.

"Heather told me I look like Violet from *The Incredibles* and I should disappear like her."

Billy nods. "Heather? As in we only wear pink on Wednesdays?" I think he's mixing up his chick flicks, but I'm impressed he even knows the comment. "And what did you say?"

"I told her she dressed like a slut and maybe she should go fuck herself."

Oh, my God. "Sadie!" I hadn't gotten all those details from the principal.

Billy chuckles, and I try to spear him with my ire, but he lowers his eyes to the ground and slips his elbows to his thighs. Why is this such a sexy pose for a man? And why can't I hold my anger at him?

"Well, maybe she is one."

"William!" I shriek. This isn't a joke, and it isn't appropriate.

"Heather who?" he asks Sadie, nodding as if trying to suppress his laughter.

"Heather Quinton."

Billy sits up straighter, fighting back another chuckle. "Well, see, the apple might not fall far from the tree."

"William," I hiss, narrowing my eyes at him and snagging his attention this time. Heather Quinton is the daughter of Hestia Quinton, who wears the unfortunate nickname of town slut. Rumor has it she's broken up a marriage or two. I don't know if that's true, though. Personally, I feel sorry for her. So, she sleeps around. *You do too*, I want to remind him. *Pot meet kettle.* And how dare he judge her, considering he has the same reputation.

Maybe she's the one he had against the wall.

Oh, God, brain, stop thinking.

"Okay," Billy says, rubbing his hands down his thighs. "You probably shouldn't have called her that name, but she shouldn't have said anything to you either." He stares at Sadie a second, as if he has more to say, but there's a question in his expression. Whatever it is, he doesn't ask, though, and silence falls around us.

"Why don't you tell him what else you said?" I interject, pushing the issue I see as most relevant. Sadie turns on me, stabbing me with a glare similar to the one my sister would give me when she was upset with me.

"What else did she say?" Billy asks me, and I look over at him. I shouldn't get involved, although I just poked the sixteen-year-old bear. I nod in her direction, and Billy turns back to Sadie. "What did you say?" he questions her, and I smile despite the seriousness of this conversation.

"It doesn't matter," Sadie says. She attempts to rush past Billy up the staircase, only there isn't enough space between his body and the railing. Billy's quick to grab her wrist, stopping her in place next to him. His eyes focus on his thick fingers around her thin wrist, and I wonder what he's thinking. Sadie's staring at the place he's holding as well, and a strange heaviness falls around us.

"Tell me what else you said." His voice isn't demanding although his command holds authority.

"I said my family rules this town, and I can say what I want to say."

Billy's head shoots up to Sadie's, and for a moment, I think he's fighting another chuckle, but he stays focused on her face.

"Sadie, I'm not going to lie and say being a Harrington isn't a big deal. I love my family, but we aren't anything special other than to each other. I'm assuming you know your uncle—" Billy pauses and swallows hard. "—he runs this town as mayor, but that doesn't mean anything to me. He's still just my kid brother."

Sadie doesn't say anything, and I'm not certain the impact of what Billy's trying to impart is making sense to her. She can't be throwing out the name. Then again, when will he tell his family? Does he want her to disappear? The question instantly comes to mind, and I chastise myself for thinking such a thing.

"As for being a Harrington, well, I'd like to tell my family first before announcing to the whole town who you are. Do you understand me?"

Sadie nods, but the pinch in her face suggests she might not. She tugs at her arm, and Billy releases her. She stampedes the remaining steps, thundering up the wood, and Billy turns to watch her retreat. When she enters my apartment and shuts the door, he turns back to me.

"I expected her to slam it like Mati." He chuckles without humor. "She's got a little fire in her like my sister."

It's a sweet comparison. I'm younger than the youngest Harrington by a few years, so I don't know her well, but she and her brother work together at the pub. If appearances could speak, I'd say they seem rather close as siblings.

"What are you doing here?" I wonder aloud. Billy presses off the step and towers over me before taking them down to the sidewalk.

"Thought I'd step it up, like you suggested." He smirks, and I hate to admit it's a darn enticing look on him. "Also, about last night—"

I wave a hand to dismiss any discussion and begin to apologize. I might have overacted, but he interrupts me.

"I'm sor—"

"I *overstepped*," he emphasizes, "and it won't ever happen again." With that, he hands me a piece of paper with a phone number and tips his head like a Southern gentleman missing his cowboy hat.

Chapter 12
The Best Things Come in Threes

[Billy]

"What is the meaning of this?" a female voice squawks through the phone.

"Who is this?" I respond although I have a good sense of who's calling me, and with that particular tone, it can only be one woman.

"It's Roxanne. And what's the meaning of these papers?"

I exhale through the phone. "I'm filing for custody."

The word tastes bitter on my tongue, and I feel a little sick from the formality, but Jordan recommended it. Silence that weighs like a ton of bricks on my chest follows my statement. I scrub at my sternum.

"Roxanne."

"How could you do this? This trumps my petition for guardianship." Her voice is so small, my heart falls to the pit of my stomach. I hear her swallow through the phone. *Is she crying?*

"I'm her *dad*. Her biological father." I use the legal jargon. "I have financial responsibilities toward this girl, and it's only fair. I can't expect you to bear the burden."

"Sadie isn't some girl, and she isn't a burden to me." Roxie sniffs.

"You're right. She isn't some girl. She's my daughter." The words taste foreign in my mouth, but I'll need to get used to them. "And I'm not saying she's a burden. I'm just saying it wouldn't be right to let you shoulder all the money stuff. I'm here to do the right thing."

"Do the right thing?" she mumbles, as if she isn't clear what those words mean. More silence ensues, and I'm ready to end this call. I don't want to hurt Roxanne, but I need to do what's best for Sadie, and Jordan assures me, as her biological parent, I'm the best thing for her.

"Couldn't we…can't we work something out? Like a legal mediator who helps us design a calendar of times and days and holidays, like shared custody or something. I've been looking into it."

I'm stumped. "You have?"

"I thought…well, I guess I should have discussed this with you, but I'd hoped we could work out a schedule, like a divorced couple with shared visitation, until Sadie gets to know you better."

The word divorce hits me almost as hard as custody. I already am divorced, and while I was grateful we didn't have children and were able to split everything rather amicably, I always wanted kids. I didn't realize how much until presented with one. This whole process seems so formal and rigid, sterile and legal, which isn't how I want things to be with Sadie. I want to get to know her, and I don't want to squeeze out Roxanne. She's an important link to who Sadie is, not to mention, it wouldn't win me any brownie points with my daughter to push away the only living relative from her mother's side. I just want to do what's best for everyone.

"What did you have in mind?"

"Well, I thought you could take Sadie out, get to know her better, or come to the apartment. Whatever seems most comfortable for both of you. Then we could decide on a regular schedule, like Tuesdays and Thursdays, and then every other weekend. We don't have to be rigid, just respectful. If something doesn't work for you, I can keep Sadie."

"What if it doesn't work for you?" I scoff, remembering what she thinks of me and how kissing her disgusted her.

"Please," she exaggerates. "The bookstore is my life. I'm always here." The sarcasm in her tone I recognize because I can relate. The pub is all I have despite my flirtatious nature and all the womanizing Roxanne *thinks* I do.

"Okay," I say, and a long pause follows, to the point I wonder if Roxanne has disappeared again.

"Okay what, William?" she asks although there's no bark in her question. She's like a timid dog, ready to pounce but pacing before defending itself.

"We can do it your way. *For now.*" I acquiesce because I don't think I can be alone with Sadie yet. I mean, I don't know her, and she doesn't know me. We could use Roxanne as our mediator, but I'll never admit to Roxie how appreciative I am of her suggestion.

"We can?" Her shriek is almost deafening, and I tug the phone away from my ear. With a chuckle, I return it to the side of my head, hearing her relieved laughter through the phone.

"I take it this makes you happy." My comment is snarky as I don't care to please her, but my chest constricts again with the sound. She has a nice laugh.

"You have no idea, William." She giggles deeper. "Thank you, thank you, thank you."

I like the sound of her gratitude even better, and a small grin curls my lips. I shouldn't care about her feelings, but apparently, it's pleasing me to please her.

+ + +

Roxanne and I map out a plan of visitations and daddy-dates, as she calls them, but the first few will be at her apartment. I have a strange sense Roxie wants to supervise Sadie and me, which is fine because we might need her interference. I've been trying to communicate with Sadie, finding myself stiff with each interaction but grateful for texting. A quick *have a good day* or *sleep well* fills my week, but I'm not in the practice, and after the first day I forget, Clyde suggests I set reminders so I don't miss out.

"Daily communication is important. Even a simple text in the morning can be like a hug from an absent parent," he tells me, and I stare at my big friend.

"How do you know these things?"

He shrugs. "I read."

Right. Lots of words.

If Roxie wants to admonish me for the time I forgot, she keeps it to herself when Thursday arrives and I'm at her place for dinner and a movie. I'm expecting it to be a night of chick flicks full of cheesy lines and mushy romance, so I'm surprised when Sadie selects *Deadpool* starring Ryan Reynolds. Roxanne is animated as she says, "Oh, I've never watched this movie before."

Sadie grins and meets my eyes, which I take as a show of solidarity, but I'm a little nervous. I have seen this movie.

"Are we sure this is appropriate?"

Roxanne's startled expression makes me chuckle. "You're worried about appropriateness?"

"Okay, you asked for it." I shrug, settling on the couch. It's an oversized three-cushion sofa with an extension at one end, like a built-in ottoman. Sadie's curled up in the corner, forcing me to sit between Roxie and her. It's almost as if they have their spot—that sort of undesignated seat on a couch where you always sit. It reminds me of being a kid in a house full of mostly boys and the back den which we called the trophy room. Each of us had our place of preference and whether you were sitting there or not, you claimed it once you entered the room. I remember one particular time I wanted my seat back and James wouldn't relinquish it. The memory makes me miss my older brother.

The movie begins in all its graphic glory, and then Ryan Reynolds meets the girl.

Oh, shit. How could I forget this part?

"I'm going to go make some popcorn," Sadie says, hopping off the couch, and I'm relieved because Wade and Vanessa are about to have a sex montage. The kiss begins, and I want to hide behind my hands like a frightened child watching a horror film. This is bad. *So bad.* It's a calendar year of sex, graphically displayed by a variety of positions. Wall sex. Missionary. Doggy style. My heart races, and I'm hyperaware of Roxanne beside me. From the corner of my eye, I see her hand travel to her throat, and my mouth waters. She strokes a finger to the dip between her collarbone, and I shift on my cushion with the need to adjust myself. I sit forward instead and place my elbows on my thighs, which is almost as painful. I'm stiff as a tent pole and trying to disguise it from Sadie, who waltzes into the room at the timely end of the scene.

"My, that Ryan Reynolds is hot," Roxie states, and I roll my neck to glance at her over my shoulder.

"I knew you'd like it," Sadie simmers, and I turn back for her. My eyes pinch as she devilishly smiles at me. *Oh, this kid.*

"Aunt Roxie, we need to find you someone like him."

Roxie's nervous giggle makes me shake my head, and I return my eyes to the screen.

"What do you know about guys like him?" I ask.

To which Sadie says, "Plenty."

"What?" Roxie and I say in unison.

"I just mean, I've dated boys."

"I don't want to hear this," I mutter.

"You'll have to get used to these things, *Dad.*" The mockery in her tone should upset me, and in some ways, it makes my insides flip flop, but a strange warmth fills me as well. Will she call me dad one day, or will I remain this nameless man? She currently doesn't address me even as Billy.

"You can tell your…" Roxanne falters on what to call me as well. "Or me, anything, honey."

My attention turns back to Roxie. *What?* I am not listening to my daughter talk to me about dates or sex, especially not sex, and absolutely, definitely not about sex like what Roxanne and I witnessed in the movie. Roxie's eyes widen at me as if she read my thoughts and she's responding with an you-will-listen-to-anything look.

I shake my head again. I don't know that I'll survive fatherhood.

+ + +

"You're spending an awful lot of time over there," Clyde comments, motioning his head across the street.

"Where you spendin' your time?" My oldest brother Giant sits across the bar from us. His stature fits his name as he's a big guy, thus the nickname Giant when his real name is George. He runs our family's brewery, taking over from our father who ran it when our pap died. Giant bears the name of generations of George Harringtons, and I don't wish for the pressure he's under. I have my own concerns.

I'm not bartending, just managing this evening. More like hanging out as the more time I spend over at Roxie's with Sadie, the more I don't like being home alone.

"Nowhere," I grumble, giving the stink-eye to Clyde to keep his mouth shut. It's been two weeks of shared visits. It isn't that I don't want to tell my family about Sadie; it's just that I'm waiting for the right time. I need to get through Oktoberfest, which includes my brother because we only distribute Giant Beer that night. Our fall blend was released a month ago with great success, and we have a winter ale coming out in time for the holidays. Thanksgiving has been my target date. That's the day I plan to tell my family about Sadie and introduce her and Roxanne to the Harrington clan. Well, I mainly mean Sadie, but it's strange to separate the two in my head. They're a package deal, and it makes me wonder how Sadie was with her mother.

Roxanne has hinted that Trixie was tough on Sadie, forcing her to make the grades and practice for everything. She sounded strict, and it makes me wonder how a motorcycle fit into her life. Maybe she had an alter ego, desperate for the wayward girl she once was before she became a mother. I'm also curious how I would have been as a father, actually raising Sadie from the ground up instead of jumping in mid-shift.

"You seem preoccupied," Giant states, and I glance back at my brother.

"You look the same." Giant nods and glances down at his phone. "What's going on with you?"

"I'm…I'm bringing a woman to Oktoberfest."

My hands slip from the counter at my back. "What?" I chuckle. My brother is practically a hermit. He spends more time than me at work, and when he isn't working, he disappears up the mountain to the cabin Pap left him. I haven't seen him date or heard of any commitment other than a semi-regular visit to a girl outside of town, which sounds semi-pathetic to me, but I don't judge. He married his high school sweetheart like I did, only his ended with a sadder fate. Cancer sucks. Clara was awesome.

"So, who is she?" I step toward the bar and rest my arms on the top, leveling my gaze at my oldest sibling. "This must be serious if you're introducing her to the family during Oktoberfest."

Giant's dark eyes gaze down at his beer, but he wears a shit-eating grin. He shrugs noncommittally.

"But you like her," I tease, like the teenager inside me.

"I do." His smile grows, and it's almost infectious, although I don't want the love-bug disease he's caught. Love. *Ew.*

"Why?" The question comes out harsher than I intend, but I'm also curious. I've been spending so much time with Roxanne and Sadie, I've gotten to the point I actually enjoy Roxie. *A little bit.* Sort of. After her rejection of my kiss and her accusation of seeing me having sex against a wall, there's been no discussion of anything ever happening or happening again.

You're the one who told her it wouldn't, I remind myself.

"I like the way she looks at me," Giant answers without thinking about it. "And I like how she laughs." His eyes sparkle like a kid finding something shiny and invaluable, and I realize I want that feeling as well, but I can't admit this to my brother as he's borderline gushing.

"You're a sap," I tease.

"Pour me over pancakes," he says. "I won't lose her for anything."

I'm startled by the words. *I won't lose her for anything.* Those are some strong emotions, and I instantly think of Sadie. It isn't the same thing as Giant loving a lady, but a reminder I don't want to lose Sadie. I just found her. This makes me think of Roxanne. We aren't parents in the conventional means, but Sadie needs both of us, and so far, Roxie's plans for visits are working out, which means I can't lose Roxanne either.

"Wow," I mutter in response. Giant winks at me and picks up his phone.

"Hey, Cricket…" He's walking away before I can make a comment about her name sounding like an insect.

+ + +

On the Thursday before Oktoberfest, I don't make it to see Sadie. It isn't that I forgot, but I forgot. I was so tied up in last-minute arrangements with the tent service, the rentals, the temporary bars, and just everything else that before I knew it, it was almost eleven.

Shit.

Sadie doesn't answer me when I send a text, and I assume it's because she's in bed. But she's also a teenager, and sometimes they stay up late. I don't typically contact Roxie, preferring to keep all communication with Sadie. Confirming dinners. Assuring her I look forward to our time together. Tonight, I slipped up, so I call Roxanne, whose number I have for emergency purposes.

"I fucked up," I say immediately. It's something my father once said works best with women. Admit your mistake before they can call you out on anything, and you're forgiven.

"You didn't even call her, William."

Okay, unless you are Roxanne McAllister, and then the stick up your ass chokes you.

"It got late. I was working."

Her silence tells me that's not a good enough excuse except it's the truth.

"Who was she?" The bitterness in Roxie's tone could be construed for jealousy, if there was someone to be jealous of. Instead, I'm pissed at the accusation.

"She's a full-body mistress. Frothy and refreshing as she glides down my throat."

"You pig," she hisses.

"Yeah, well, *oink, oink* because I'm telling the truth. Oktoberfest is this weekend, which you know, and I'm working on all the last-minute details. It's been hard enough since our band cancelled a week ago but thank God we have a replacement. But then there's the tent company and the—" I abruptly stop. Why am I telling her all these things? "Never mind."

"What do you mean never mind? What else do you need to do for your party?"

Thankfully, Roxie dropped her permit request shortly after the paternity test. I'm surprised she's asked about my *party*, but find I want to talk, maybe vent a little bit about my frustration. This will be one of our biggest years yet, and I just want it all to be perfect. Historically, our financial statements support this is more than a party but profitable for us, and I tell Roxanne all of this for some reason.

"I'm always trying to prove to my dad how important BRMP is to me, but also how I'm not a total fuckup."

"Just a little one, occasionally." She laughs as she teases.

"Nothing little about me," I proudly state, then realize it might sound a bit wrong. Roxanne purrs through the phone, and fuck, if that's not a turn-on.

"Is she really mad at me?" I let out a deep exhale as I swipe a hand down my face. I'm lying on my bed, staring up at the ceiling and considering how quiet my place is. I like hanging out at Roxie's although it's small for three people.

"Yeah." Roxie pauses a moment as if contemplating something. "Deep down, I think she's scared you don't want her. I mean, you haven't introduced her to your family and without that comes some uncertainty."

"What does she want to know? What can I do to make her understand I do want her?" Because the truth is, I want to get to know my daughter. I want to be a decent dad. Maybe better than I feel my father treated me. But a part of me feels like my questions go deeper than Sadie. What does Roxie want from me? What can I do to make her see that I don't want to break up our little party of three? I like our threesome, which is not something I thought I'd ever say about a woman who drives me crazy and a daughter I don't know. I *want* Roxanne to like me.

"You're trying, and I think that's the most important thing. Just don't give up on her no matter how tough she gets, okay? You're bound to make mistakes. I make mistakes all the time like thinking spaghetti was a favorite of hers until she finally told me she doesn't like it that much."

I chuckle. "Can I tell you a secret? I don't like it either."

"Then why did you eat it when you came for dinner that first night?" Laughter fills her voice.

"I wanted to impress both of you." I hear Roxie gasp—*crap*—so I try to cover my tracks. "I didn't want to be rude."

"You don't need to impress me, William." Her tone softens my name. It's not so edgy and condescending, and I swallow before I admit, "I want you to stop thinking I'm a manslut."

Roxie laughs again, and my stomach flips a little. It's a nice sound from her.

"I don't think you're a manslut."

"You do." I inhale. Exhale. "And I don't like it because it's not true. I don't know what you think you saw, but it wasn't me. Not like that, not outside against the wall of my building. Give me a little credit, Roxanne. Please."

I hate the whine to my voice, *the plea*. I don't care what others think, but for some reason, I don't want Roxie thinking these things of me, especially as I'm trying to build something with Sadie. Silence fills the line for a second.

"You're doing a good job, Billy. With Sadie." The use of my name in a softer and more tender tone widens my eyes in surprise, and then I smile. It's a start.

"I'm sorry I didn't show up or even call her."

"It's okay. Well, not really, but I understand. She will, too."

"I sent her a text, but she didn't answer me."

"She's probably reading." Roxanne chuckles, and I like the sound too much. Strangely, I feel so much better now that I've spoken with her, unleashed my frustration with the fest, fears about my father, and even my irritation at her opinion of me.

I just want Roxanne to accept me for who I am and not who she thinks I am.

And I want my father to accept me as a successful son.

It makes me think of Sadie, but she has nothing to prove to me. I already accept her as mine.

"Yeah. Lots of words," I joke. Silence falls between us again, and I realize I could just lie here listening to Roxie breathe, which is weird and creepy but so comforting. I miss a woman in my bed for more than a few hours.

"Billy," she whispers.

"Huh?" I moan, drifting into a heaviness of relaxation.

"Time for sleep." I imagine her calling me *honey* or *baby* like she calls Sadie, and I lazily smile to myself.

"Okay," I mutter. "And Roxie? Thanks for listening to me tonight."

"Anytime, Billy," she says, and I'm certain she's forgotten who she's speaking to. "Good night."

"Good night."

Chapter 13
Oktoberfest

[Roxanne]

I almost hate to give Billy credit, but he knows how to throw an event, and this is a huge party.

Third Avenue is covered by a massive tent that I'm not sure is legal to place on a side street, but when your brother is the mayor, I suppose you get away with these things. It still stings that I moved my permit request to another date but after seeing this setup, I couldn't have competed. I'm hosting my own small-scale sales event during the following week leading up to Halloween and emphasizing the *boo* part of Booktober.

The fest is in full party mode with beer flowing and music thumping, and for the first time, I might enjoy myself being here if for no other reason than to watch Billy Harrington work his butt off. And unfortunately for me, I find my eyes wandering too often to his backside, which is snug in tight-fitting jeans. I hate that I'm attracted to him when I shouldn't be. He's barking orders and laughing uncontrollably, and his entire demeanor says, *I like to have a good time.* I wish I could be that easygoing, but I'm a little self-conscious as I mingle among community members who remember me as a teenager more than a businesswoman. I make small talk with many customers I recognize but excuse myself when I can and eventually find myself hanging near Grace.

As far as people go, I'd consider Grace one of my best friends in this town, even if she isn't from here originally. Her husband brought her to Blue Ridge on a visit, and she claims she fell in love with the place. When he died, she decided it would be the best place to raise five unruly boys without a father. She's counting on the saying it takes a village or, in her case, a ridge to raise her clan to good men. Grace and I don't have to chatter, so we remain near one another, smiling at townspeople we recognize and soaking up the atmosphere. Grace is simply happy to be among adults for a few hours.

A playlist of country hits played by a disc jockey, but rumor has it from Billy the musical entertainment will be a real treat. Unfortunately, Billy hasn't paid me much attention this evening other than a hand wave over a sea of people. A strange sensation tells me he doesn't want people to realize we share a connection since he still hasn't told anyone about Sadie, but I dismiss those thoughts, deciding he's just busy tonight. Clyde's the one who offered Grace and me our first beers. Somehow, we make our way to the back section of the tent and linger near the bar, where Giant Harrington pushes his way through the crowd with a girl by his side. I don't personally know Giant as I'm almost ten years younger than him, but everyone knows who he is, and he's another devastatingly handsome sight for the eyes, if you like men large and lumbersexual, which I do.

"This is Letty," he shouts to his bartending brother who immediately offers her a smile and wipes his hands on a rag before coming to our end of the bar. Billy reaches out for the woman who has sleek dark hair with a tall stature and an amazing body. I hate that I notice her physique, but Billy's embracing her and holding on a little longer than necessary. He mutters something to her that causes Giant to glare at him. When Billy pulls back, he claps his hands good naturedly and grins at his brother.

"I see how it is," he says. Letty laughs, and Billy's smile deepens. "What's your flavor, honey? I'll let you taste anything you like."

I hate the innuendo in Billy's voice, although it isn't as if I don't know he's a huge flirt. There's just something about witnessing it, especially after all the time we've spent together lately.

"William Forrest Harrington," Giant bellows in a warning only an older sibling can give.

Letty looks back and forth between the two men for a second. "I don't understand that one."

"What do you mean, love?" Billy questions, and with the use of the endearment, the conversation has my full attention even though I'm aware I'm eavesdropping.

"Roald Dahl," Letty explains, and Billy's eyes shoot to his brother.

"You told her the family secret?" Billy's taken aback, and then he mischievously grins again. "She really must be special."

It takes me a moment to realize what they are discussing, and I can't help but interject.

"Roald Dahl?" I question, looking at Billy with a tweaked eyebrow before glancing over at Letty. "Billy is the name of a character in a short story called *The Minpins* by Roald Dahl. It's a cautionary tale about not going into the woods." I pause for a moment, wondering what the connection is exactly between Roald Dahl and his name—what's the family secret? Then I make my own connection. *William Forrest.* "Seems appropriate."

Letty covers her lips with two fingers as if biting back a giggle. "Oh my," she says under her breath, and Giant tugs her to him, but her eyes remain fixed on me.

"What would you know about playing in the woods?" Billy mocks me, his voice sharp and not as playful as it's been with Letty or as easy as it's become with me over the past few weeks.

"More than you'd know about reading a book," I snap, instantly on edge again with this man. My response comes from his name connected to a fictional character, but then what I've implied hits me. Billy struggles with reading, and my retort suddenly feels like a low blow. Then again, Billy's being awful standoffish…and just awful.

"Oh, good one," Billy mocks, covering his heart with both hands. "Ouch, I'm hurt that I don't read."

"It's better than being anywhere near your wood," I bark, narrowing my eyes at him. If I had a momentary lapse of judgment, giving him some credit for working hard and playing harder or looking fine in those snug jeans, I take it all back. He's an ass.

"Go away," he stammers, shooing me to scurry along like a dismissed creature within those fictional woods, and I admit it hurts.

"With pleasure," I state, although the last thing I want to do is walk away because he's shooed me off. I'm upset and want to fight back but decide against it. I turn to Letty instead, and offer, "If you need a good book, come visit me."

"And if she needs a good wood, she can come to me," Billy adds, puffing up his chest as he bellows his comeback. Grace gasps beside me while Giant glares at his brother, and I remember we have witnesses to his harsh tone, his dismissal, and his innuendos. I turn and stalk away from the bar with Grace following me.

"He doesn't mean it," she whispers, but I'm too upset to believe her.

"He doesn't matter," I lie because the truth is, Billy's behavior sometimes does hurt, and I'm exceptionally susceptible to his lashing after all the time we've spent together lately because of Sadie.

Behave, for Sadie.

Within fifteen minutes of the altercation with Billy, he's introducing a band on the stage, and I'm starstruck. Lawson Colt of Colt45 was one of my teenage crushes. He eventually moved on to join his sister and form the band Kit Carrigan and the Chrome Teardrops. I forget all about Billy as Grace and I squeeze our way to the front of the crowd near the stage and cheer like teenagers when Lawson—now known as Tommy Carrigan—breaks into song. "Wait for Me" was one of those anthem songs that made me long for love as a pre-pubescent teen. As the haunting words flow over me in the rich, older voice of a man with chrome and midnight scruff and hair curling over his ears, I feel the same way I did some thirty years ago. Whoever I'm supposed to be waiting for, I hope he's still waiting for me. Then I shake the thought and laugh aloud to myself because I'm no longer waiting on him, whoever he was. I made my own way in life between Sadie and the bookstore. I'm comfortable where I am, even if occasionally lonely.

Before I know it, Clyde has brought Grace and me another beer. "Only take drinks from me tonight," he yells over the roar of the crowd singing along with Tommy and the band. Denton Chance is with him, and I recall the story of him leaving this town for fame and fortune. He definitely achieved it. He's just as mesmerizing strumming away on his guitar and singing backup to Lawson with his model good looks and edgier features. The final member of the band is Hank Paige, a slightly larger man with no loss of sexy silver on him like his band friends, and he's just as enthusiastically playing his drum kit.

Grace lifts her cup and takes a hardy drink of the amber liquid with a thick foam at the rim. I sip my second beer and realize the taste is growing on me. The mixture of spices and cloves gives this one a real autumn flavor, like fall in a plastic cup. I should serve this during the Booktober Sale the night we do first chapter readings until I realize why I like the flavor. It tastes like Billy smells.

I take another sip of the sharp flavor and smile as the band breaks into another song. Glancing over my shoulder, I curse myself for searching the rear of the tent where Billy is hoisting his sister up on the bar top, and then I follow her line of vision back to the stage. I vaguely remember some story of how Mati Harrington had been best friends with Denton Chance back in high school, but I was a few years younger than them and can't recall the details.

Speaking of high school, Cora Conrad makes her way next to me, and I bristle from her nearness. Cora's a blonde bombshell even as she pushes forty, but she's changed a bit over the last year since her divorce. Seems divorce becomes her because there's a glow about her tonight, but I don't let the luminescence fool me. Cora and I were in the same grade, and she made my high school years hell. Her family has status equal to the Harringtons and the Chances in Blue Ridge, but she stood out from the offspring of those other families as a single child who was just plain mean.

"My how you've changed," she addressed me almost three years ago when I opened the store, blatantly eyeing me up and down, noting the weight loss. Only she didn't say what people typically ask: *Have you lost weight?* No, Corabelle knew outright I had.

"That Tommy Carrigan was a young girl's wet dream back in the day," Cora states, turning to peer at me, her eyes rolling down my body once again. "We never could have obtained boys like him as teens, though, could we?"

I'm not certain what Cora's comment means, but I'm going with the assumption it has to do with the body shape I once had.

"I'm not certain *we* collectively are what you mean." If Cora's fishing for a compliment—a reminder of her beauty both then and now—she can forget it. I'm not about to boost the ego of a former bully.

"Oh, I just meant boys like him wouldn't have been interested in girls like us."

Maybe it's the memories in the music or the strength of the beer empowering me to turn on her. "What exactly does 'girls like us' mean, Cora, because there's no way you and I are in the same category, not even the same stratosphere."

Cora stares back at me wide-eyed with shock.

"Why, I didn't mean—" she squeaks, laying on her thickest Southern accent, despite the volume of the tune, but I interrupt her.

"Yes, you did, because you're always mean," I mock in my best Southern retort. "Cora, we aren't in high school, and I'm not that fat, quiet girl you loved to pick on, so whatever you're trying to imply, I'm over it. I don't need to worry about *not* getting the man of my dreams at thirteen or forty-one. I'm happy with me." I stand taller, and out of the corner of my eye, I feel someone watching us. I turn to find Billy with his hands on his hips, and Clyde standing slightly behind him.

"Cat fight," someone hisses near us, and Billy snaps out of his reverie.

"Ladies," Billy sweet-talks, "what's going on here?" Cora simpers by pouting her lips and batting her eyes as if she couldn't possibly be doing anything wrong. The flirt with Billy Harrington is so thick I could drink it like the beer in my cup, but that flavor would only be bitter. This reminds me of the flavor in my hand, and I guzzle a few gulps to calm my racing heart. I can't believe I stood up to Corabelle Conrad.

"I meant no offense, Roxanne," she states lacking apology and then turns to Billy. "Roxanne and I were just reliving our glory days, reminiscing about boy band crushes."

I'm about to tell Billy Cora is reminding me I was a heavy-set teen, but it's all so childish, I just don't mention it. Instead, I consider the woman his brother introduced to him and how Billy held her, like he was feeling her against him. Sleek. Pretty. Worldly looking. I can't compete with the women Billy hits on. I don't want to compete. There's no competition here.

It's all a reminder I'm never going to be what Billy wants in a woman, and I'm fine with that, just fine.

I turn away from him, ignoring Cora, and watch as Tommy introduces Gage Everly of Collision. Oh. My. Cougar heart. Speaking of thirteen, he's probably that many years younger than I am, but he's extremely good looking with chin-length chocolate hair and eyes as deep as candy. He opens his mouth to sing, and my panties melt almost as much as they did for Lawson.

"Hey," Billy shouts from my side, tugging at my arm to turn me to him. "I wanted to—"

"Let's dance," Clyde bellows over Billy, slipping an arm around my waist and reaching for Grace's hand. He tugs us both before the stage and breaks into the most awkward dance I've ever seen. I shouldn't laugh, but I can't help it when Clyde wiggles his brows and exaggerates his hips. He's got the white man's overbite going along with motorcycle handlebar motions. His large body is clearing space, and Grace and I laugh good naturedly at his display. He doesn't care that he's making a fool of himself in front of the stage and before the crowd, and it's a good reminder not to worry what others think, especially the likes of Corabelle Conrad...or Billy Harrington.

Chapter 14
Fired Up

[Billy]

Damn that Clyde, he's fired, I think as I stalk back to the bar. We're too busy for me not to tend tonight although I'm also trying to mingle and gauge what customers think of our newest blends. Giant has just as much riding on tonight as I do because word of mouth is still everything in business. Five-star reviews on food and drink apps could bring in new visitors, not to mention have people asking for the beer in liquor stores close to their homes.

I hate how Roxanne dismissed me.

I hate more so how I treated her.

Old habits die hard especially when it comes to that woman, and her comment about reading stung.

I've been keeping my eye on her all night, noticing she sticks to the periphery of the party. Her self-consciousness shows in the way she keeps brushing her hair behind her ear and looking down when people speak to her, but she doesn't see what I see. She's freaking gorgeous among this crowd. Those exotic gray eyes shift darker in the dim light and her hair glows with the mixture of varying whites. She's different from other women I've been attracted to in the past, and it's making her stand out even more in my eyes.

She'd been hanging by the bar, and I liked having her near even though I hadn't had a chance to really speak to her. I find silent comfort in her, like when she's hanging around when I'm with Sadie. She's pulling herself back, giving Sadie and me more space when I come over. I can't really help Sadie with her homework, but she tells me what she's learning, what she likes, and how she's a little more advanced than what they're teaching her in school. I bought her a new laptop and upgraded their internet, so Sadie has better access to research. Of course, Roxie admonished me for the gift.

"Don't be trying to buy her love."

"I'm not buying her love. I'm encouraging her to discover things on a deeper level."

That woman, I groan as I return behind the bar, looking up immediately to find her in the crowd. Why am I always searching her out?

Once the band began, and Denton Chance had his moment with my sister, Mati, I stalked after Roxanne, ready to apologize for how I behaved earlier. I'm snapping at her under the stress of the evening, and she doesn't deserve it, even if what she said about reading was a little mean. My eyes find Roxanne near Grace as Clyde dances like a fool in front of the stage. She's laughing at him—*or rather with him*—as he grabs her hand and twirls her under his arm. She looks like she's having a good time, and the jealousy strikes hard.

I pass out more beers and collect more tickets and return to the high of accomplishing my own thing for a few minutes until Clyde makes his way behind the bar, sweaty and chuckling.

"What are you playing at, man?" I snap, which instantly sobers Clyde's mood.

"What do you mean?"

"Dancing with Roxie when I was trying to talk to her." I hand two more cups to a waiting customer, nodding my thank you when they hand me a tip.

"Oh, was talking what you planned to do? I figured you were ready to tell her more about your wood and how she wasn't worthy." This snaps my attention to Clyde, and I overfill the cup I'm pouring.

"Dammit," I mutter, shaking beer from my fist and passing the fill to another customer. "What's that supposed to mean?"

"You're blind," Clyde states, stepping away to chug a cupful before he takes orders from customers a few paces down from me.

I have no idea what Clyde means, but my eyes scan the crowd, searching for Roxanne who's been approached by a member of Rebel's Edge, the local biker club where my older brother James is now second in command. It was difficult to watch him pull back from the family and lose himself in the club, although we know all the reasons. I'm ready to lose my shit, setting down a full cup without collecting drink tickets. I stalk to the end of the bar before Clyde catches my arm.

"He's got it," Clyde mutters, and I glance up to see my brother James intervening. At first, I think he's cutting the other guy off, until I see my brother cutting in and taking Roxanne in his arms.

Mothertrucker.

Of all my brothers, James and I get along the least. I'm actually closest to Mati in the family, and the thought makes me wonder for a brief second how Sadie feels about being an only child. As the third son, and middle child of five, I've definitely had my fantasies of being a single Harrington, but then again, I love my siblings, even if I want to pummel James at the moment, biker leader or not.

Clyde tugs at my arm, and I flick him off me, preparing to break through the crowd when Roxanne's eyes lift and meet mine. She looks uncertain, and I wonder if she's frightened of my brother. He turns at the same time and gives me a chin tip. Roxanne gazes back at my older brother and grins up at him. *Fuck*, I don't like that look. I'm not blind to the appearances of my siblings. James is the edgiest of us with his short, cropped silver hair and scraggly scruff. Some girls like that bad boy—or menacing man—look, and the thought of Roxie being attracted to that doesn't settle well with me.

"You've got customers," Clyde reminds me, which also reminds me I've lost my sister after she ran off during Denton's song.

Fuck, I'm too busy for all this drama tonight.

As the party winds on, the band closes out their set and the favor they did me by performing, although it had nothing to do with me and everything to do with Denton making a statement to my sister. Twenty-seven years. What a fucking long time to hold a woman in your heart. My eyes find Roxanne still hanging in the crowd, which surprises me. Grace remains, as well, and Alyce Wright, who my mother keeps trying to set Giant up with, is near them. Guess Mama got the message as Giant introduced Letty to the family tonight.

"Whatcha drinking?" I absentmindedly ask a customer until I glance up and find my brother James on the other side of the bar.

"House special." He snorts, knowing damn well the specialty is our family brew, the family he chose to walk away from. I pour him a cup, shaking my head to decline the drink ticket he offers me. "Got a second?"

"I'm busy as fuck," I snap, and his brows rise. I twist my neck, and mumble, "Hang on." I told myself a long time ago if James ever came back to the family I wouldn't judge, and I wouldn't turn him away if he asked anything of me. It's late, and the mania at the bar is settling. I serve another customer and come back to James.

He leans casually against the bar with his hip, his eyes scanning the room. "Saw the death glare you gave me over that woman." My eyes leap to the table where Roxie sits with Alyce and Grace. "Care to explain?"

"There's nothing to be said." I hate the denial in my voice, but I'm not ready to share who Roxie is to me. Hell, *I* don't even know who she is to me, and I definitely don't feel comfortable telling James about Sadie.

James turns to eye me, scanning my face like he's looking for something. He nods once.

"You know, if I had one second with Evie again…I wouldn't pass it up. Not for nothing. That's the look you were giving me."

"You don't know what you're talking about," I whine although I can't dismiss the first part. I know how James felt about Evie, and I understand what he's *not* saying. On the other hand, he knows nothing about Roxanne.

"I know more than you might think, little brother. Remember that."

"Is that a threat?"

James's brows pinch. "It's me telling you I still look out for everyone. I make it my business to know what's going on." His voice deepens, roughening to the point of caution. He takes a sip of his beer, resting an elbow on the bar as he looks out at the dwindling gathering. It's almost as if he isn't speaking to me with his back to me, but the words are registering. He knows…about Sadie.

"Want my advice?"

"Not really," I mutter, but knowing my brother, he'll offer it anyway. "Snap up that woman and don't let that kid out of your sight."

"I'm not interested," I defend. James shifts his body, anger brewing on his face.

"In the woman or the child?"

I swallow. I'm lying if I say neither. Sadie is really growing on me even though she's snarky and dark sometimes, and Roxanne, well, my eyes search for her in the corner again.

"That's what I thought." James chuckles, presses off the bar and walks to the corner where his brothers-in-arms remain. He has no right offering me brotherly advice when he chooses them over Giant, Charlie, and me, but then again, I heard what he said. He's still looking after us even if he isn't interacting with us. *Damn him.*

For the past hour, the music has been a mix of country songs, which means closing time is coming soon. We only have an extension on the city ordinance for noise until midnight. We've encouraged people to head inside to the bar, but surmising the amount of alcohol we've served, I know many people will be heading home to sleep off the start of a hangover or sleep with someone special tonight.

The next song begins, and I instantly recognize it.

"Hey, Clyde, be back in five," I state, walking around the bar as I speak and heading for Roxie. I've watched her dance with numerous men tonight, and now it's my turn. I approach the table, but her head lifts long before I get to her seat. She's watching me as my eyes lock on her. Damn, I love those eyes. The silver flints like the first spark of steel crashing together and making a flame.

"Miss Alyce." I dip my head as if I'm wearing a cowboy hat. "Miss Roxanne," I drag out her name.

"Billy." Alyce blushes, but her head turns to look at Roxie.

"May I have this dance?" I hold out my hand for Roxie who looks down at my open palm for a second. Her lips twist like she's fighting a smile, and I'm waiting for a snappy rejection from her until the tips of her fingers press into my warm hand. My fingers snap shut—*snap up that woman*—and I lead her to the dance floor. Only a few people linger as I spin Roxie and then draw her to my chest. I pull her close, closer than necessary for a dance, and slip an arm around her lower back. My other hand clutches hers and drags them between us, holding her hand near my racing heart.

The Lee Brice song "Rumors" drones on about a couple and the town wondering what's going on with them. My cheek lowers to rest near Roxie's, leaving my lips only a breath away from her ear. I sing the words, messing them up a bit.

"I can do what you want, baby, or you could kiss me here, and make it true…"

Roxanne pulls back, and those eyes light me up.

"Why would I kiss you, Billy Harrington?"

"Because you want to." I'm teasing her, but there's an unasked question in the words. Does she want to kiss me? She rejected me before, swiping at her tongue as if I'd given her a disease. Has she changed her mind, though? Her eyes draw down to my lips, telling me she might have second thoughts about that first kiss.

"You're so full of yourself," she admonishes, a chuckle in her tone. She's teasing me, and that's what I've discovered I like best about Roxie. She gives as good as she gets.

"I'm sorry about earlier," I admit. "I didn't mean to snap at you."

Roxie's eyes drop, and she glances over at the table where Alyce and Grace sat but are no longer present.

"It was a little unexpected," she says, her voice low.

"Nah, that's what we do, Roxie. We bicker." Her eyes come back to mine, softened and searching.

"Do we always have to fight in public?" Her question asks something deeper, and I have to admit things have been different in private when it's just the three of us. Roxanne and I still snip and scratch, but it's more in fun than a fight. Is she my little secret along with Sadie? *Thanksgiving.* That's the date I've set for when I'll tell my family. One more month and I'll be ready. "I guess, for a little bit longer."

Roxanne doesn't like that answer, and I feel her slump in my grasp. The song plays on, but Roxie no longer speaks to me. My cheek lowers back to her ear, and I close my eyes, letting the words in my head drift unspoken to her, adding my own version as a refrain.

Let's make the rumor true.

Chapter 15
Near Miss

[Roxanne]

He smells so good. I inhale at his neck and then catch myself, hoping he doesn't notice me sniffing him. He's a mix of man and the spicy clove scent in the beers I drank tonight. Too many beers. I'm woozy on my feet, but it might just be the way Billy is holding me. I'm pressed up close to him, melting into him. Hard chest. Firm abs. Large palms. His hand covers my lower back while the other presses mine against his heart, which is racing through his BRMP dress shirt. He's wearing an Oxford, rolled at the sleeves, displaying some serious arm porn. I lick my lips, my mouth watering to run my tongue up the vein exposed on his lower arm.

I hate that I'm having this reaction, especially to him, of all men, but he seemed so sincere in his apology. Then I think of his other words. *This is what we do.* We claw and scratch, only I'd like to do it in a manner where I'm drawing him closer and not pushing him away.

I've definitely had too much to drink tonight if these are my thoughts.

As the song ends, Billy still holds me, swaying in the silence before another song flips on. It's too fast for the slow pace he's set, and I chuckle when I say to him, "The song's over."

He purrs at my ear, and the shiver that runs down my spine is like the kiss of a summer rain. Refreshing. Sweet. Romantic. I pull back from where my head rests near his. I'm overthinking things. Billy Harrington is anything but romantic. He's rash and raw and flirtatious, and I'd be smart to remember these things. Only my head is fuzzy, and he smells so good, and he's holding me so close.

It's been too long since I've been with someone.

Billy doesn't fight me as I lean away from him, but as he releases me, I stumble.

"Whoa, darlin'." He's quick to reach out for my upper arms and right me. "I'm known to have that effect on women." He winks.

"I had too much to drink, I think." I'm not slurring my words, not that I notice, but things are catching up to me. "I think it's time I head home."

Billy's brows pinch, and he wears an expression of concern in his eyes. *He isn't concerned about you, Roxie. He's nice to you because of Sadie.*

"I'll walk you home."

I snort, unattractively. "There's no need. I live only a few feet from here." No joke. My apartment windows look down on this tent, which would be annoying except I'm certain I'll sleep like the dead once I hit my bed.

"I'm still walking you. It's the gentlemanly thing." He's mocking me, and I huff, but he's already looped my hand into the crook of his elbow, holding his warm fingers over my hand like a clamp, and leading me out of the tent.

If he wants rumors, he's about to set them in motion.

Billy guides me along the sidewalk to the back stairs of my building. He shifts to take my hand, and I follow him as we take the stairs. For a moment, I imagine us walking like a couple, entering my apartment and falling into each other, but the thought quickly passes when we reach the landing. I pause a second, and Billy steps back to lean against the railing.

"Can I ask you something?" His voice lowers.

"Sure." I turn to face him and lean against the screen door at my back. I feel like I'm on a first date, and it's the moment of should I kiss him good night or not. Only this is Billy Harrington.

"Who would be the man of your dreams? Was it really a rock star?"

I'm startled by the question and start to giggle until I realize he's serious.

I cough to clear the chuckle. "I just want a man who can love me for who I am, who can understand who I am." Chad didn't mind me being the manager of a major bookstore chain, but he wasn't interested in supporting my dream to be a business owner. He also tolerated Sadie but didn't love children.

"Where were you when we were younger?"

I glance away from him, realizing we're stretching toward a more serious topic. "I wasn't exactly the type of girl you'd notice when we were younger." I won't tell him about the weight. He's never acted like he remembers me as a kid, and I'd rather not jog his memory. "Besides, you went to school with my sister. We didn't go to high school at the same time."

Billy nods, and there's so much unspoken history between us. My sister had a major crush on him, but I know all about Rachel, his first wife, and how they were high school sweethearts. What I don't know is why they divorced, but rumor has it Billy had an affair. His flirtatious fame skyrocketed after Rachel, starting with my sister.

"Can I ask you a question?" I press off the door at my back and make a bold step toward him. With his backside leaning on the railing and his hands balancing on either side of his hips, he's sexy as hell. His eyes—the best feature on him—momentarily look nervous as I approach.

"Okay," he says, his voice lowering and rippling down my body. This time, it's more like a rain shower.

"Why haven't you ever hit on me like you hit on other women?"

"What?" His voice cracks like a teenager, and my hand strokes up his chest, curling around the collar at his neck. My eyes focus on the opening near his throat, and I want to slip my tongue—which feels thick in my mouth—in the little gap of his collarbone.

"Am I not attractive to you? Am I not good enough for you to bang against a brick wall?"

"Are you serious?" He chokes out.

"Just once, I want to be good enough for wall sex," I slur, and his eyes widen.

"Roxie, you're—"

"Why haven't you kissed me?"

"I did, remember? You didn't like it," he states, lifting a finger to scrape down his tongue, imitating me from that night.

"It's not that I didn't like it." My voice drops, and I swallow back the saliva building. "I just thought you had kissed someone else first."

"Well, I didn't," he defensively states, and I move on.

"You suggested I kiss you while we danced. Did you mean it, or where you just singing off-key with the wrong words?" He wasn't really singing poorly, and even though he botched the words, a rush ripped up my body at the suggestion. My stomach flip flops now. I can't believe I asked him these questions, and I can't believe how much I'm leaning on him. My breasts rest against his chest as my heart hammers in mine. The bulge in his jeans near my lower belly isn't low enough.

"How much have you had to drink tonight, darlin'?" His voice sounds like the way he flirted with Letty. Is he flirting with me? Does he want me like he wanted her?

I lean forward, ready to take what I want from him. *Kiss me*, my lips scream as my eyes focus on his mouth.

And then hands come to my shoulders and press me back.

"Wha—" I stammer as the reality slowly seeps in.

"I think I'll be a gentleman this time."

He's rejecting me. I'm throwing myself at him, and he still isn't interested. I'm mortified at my lack of seduction skills and the fact I can't even attract Billy Harrington, manwhore galore. He really isn't interested in someone like me. I step back, wrapping my arms around my middle. My stomach pitches, and my heart races faster than it should. Sweat trickles over my brow as I bend at the waist and heave all over his boots.

+ + +

I wake with a heaviness in my head and my heart. My tongue feels thick and swollen and dry as a hairy cat. I try to lick my teeth but feel a scratchy sensation in my throat. A sour taste fills my mouth.

Crap. I threw up.

My eyes whip open, and the room spins, so I quickly close them again. Even my lids feel heavy and then I realize there's a weight over my waist. My palm moves down the cool sheet before touching fingers draped over my stomach. I roll my head too quickly, forcing the room to whirl, and glance over my shoulder to find Billy behind me.

What?

I lift my head and discover I'm still wearing the dress I wore last night minus my cowboy boots. My toes wiggle, and I discover bare feet underneath mine. Billy isn't wearing his boots either.

Boots.

Oh God.

I puked all over his boots.

After that, the night goes hazy, but I obviously made it to my bed with Billy Harrington at my back.

"Billy," I whisper, feeling his forearm under my palm. His skin is warm, and he's deep in sleep, the arm heavy over my belly. My stomach flips, but I don't have anything left inside to release.

Good Lord, I drank too much last night.

Then what happened before I vomited returns to me.

Billy. My landing. Almost kissing him. Almost.

"Billy," I harshly whisper.

"Not yet, baby. I need to sleep a little longer," he mutters, nuzzling into my neck, but I'm certain he has no idea I'm the person he's nuzzling. He nudges forward, pressing the solid length of him against my backside.

"William," I hiss.

"Okay, darlin'. I can sleep-fuck." He rolls me to my back, then slips over me, forcing my legs apart and leaning down for my face without opening his eyes.

I place fingers over my closed lips. There's no way he's kissing me. My mouth feels like an animal died inside there, and my breath must be rank.

When Billy lowers, his lips meet my fingers, and his eyes spring open.

"Roxie," he mutters against my clamped digits. He lifts his head, eyes sleepy and dazed. "What time is it?"

I roll my head on the pillow and note the time on the bedside clock. "Five a.m."

Billy leaps off me and rushes to the window, tugging back the curtain. The street must be clean, but how long has he been here. My room isn't very large, and he turns back toward the bed, reaching for his phone on the nightstand. He quickly sends a text and then sets the phone back.

"What happened?" I ask as he stares down at the phone. My question is meant to ask why he's here, in my bed, next to me.

"You were sick." He scrubs two hands down his face and kneels on the edge of the mattress. "Look, I've only had about an hour of sleep. You mind if I crash here just a little longer to get my bearings?"

"Okay." My voice is hoarse as I watch him crawl back onto my bed and collapse on his stomach. His face is positioned away from me, and I roll on my side, facing away from him, only my head is full while my stomach is empty. My heart feels a little empty as well.

Chapter 16
Boo – Gotchou

[Roxanne]

"Aunt Roxie?" The tender concern in Sadie's voice rouses me from dozing on the couch. After Billy fell back to sleep, which happened rather quickly and was evident from his light snoring, I escaped my bedroom for the bathroom. I looked awful. Pale face. Bright red lips. Eyes too wide. Brushing my teeth made me feel only minimally better, and I changed into a longish T-shirt nightshirt. Pulling the afghan on the couch over my legs, I rested my head on the back cushions and promptly fell into a body-draining nap. I'd been thinking about Billy and losing Sadie and wishful dreaming we could somehow be together when Sadie roused me.

My lids blink in disorientation, and then I remember why I'm on the couch. *Billy's in my bedroom.*

"Sadie," I whisper, my voice still scratchy.

"Are you okay?" She helps herself to sit next to me on the cushions.

"Yeah, baby girl. I'm just not feeling well."

"You drank too much," she admonishes, a teasing lilt to her voice.

"How do you know that?" I wonder, although she knew I was going to the party.

"Billy helped you in the door." It's strange to hear her call him Billy, but she's not comfortable calling him her dad yet. She pauses for another moment, and my eyes close. The pressure in my head feels like a clamp. "Are you a couple now?"

"He...I...No, baby. We aren't together." Nothing happened. Literally. He rejected me. Is he even still here? I didn't hear him leave. "He only spent the night."

"I know what that means, you know." She giggles, throwing herself back against the cushions.

"It means he spent the night. He slept here and nothing else." Although I'm still puzzled why this happened. Why did he stay after rejecting me? Then again, I hate to think what might have happened had he started kissing me. *Oh God*, I internally groan and cover my forehead with a shaky palm.

"You know, it'd be okay to be a couple with him. Then I could be with both of you."

Uh-huh. "Oh, sweetheart. We aren't going to be separated, no matter what." I reach for her hand and pull it to my chest. "I love you forever." Tears well in my eyes. I'm tired. I'm hungover. And I don't want to think about losing her.

"Hey," Billy interjects quietly from the hallway. He leans against the wall with his hands slipped into his front pockets. He's wearing only a T-shirt, having removed his Oxford at some point.

"What time is it?" I ask, repeating his question to me earlier.

"It's seven," Sadie answers, surprising me that she's awake so early on a Sunday.

"I guess I should get going," Billy says without moving away from the wall.

"Is everything cleaned up outside?" I'm not intending to be snarky. I'm just curious. If he stayed with me for the remainder of the night, who took care of the party?

"Yeah, it's covered. But I'm gonna owe some favors." He removes a hand from his jeans and scrubs his throat, which scratches with the sound of his thicker stubble. He still looks delicious, standing sleepy and groggy in my hallway, and I hate how I notice this about him. "So I should probably…" He points over his shoulder with this thumb.

"Or you could stay for breakfast," Sadie offers.

"Sadie," I hush-whisper. The last thing Billy wants to do is spend the morning with us.

"How do you feel about pancakes?" Billy asks.

Oh God, I couldn't stomach pancakes, and I groan in response.

"Maybe eggs for Aunt Roxie. Do you know how to cook?" Sadie asks with a teasing voice. I notice she's forgiven him for not calling and missing out the other night. I also realize we've never been to Billy's house, and I wonder why. Well, Sadie hasn't. I shouldn't include myself in the invitation. My heart weighs heavy again when I consider Sadie may someday be at his house, and I'm the one who will need an invitation to see her.

"You okay, Aunt Roxie? You don't look so good."

"My boots are outside. Want me to grab them for you?" Billy teases. I smirk back at him but wince with the pain to my head. He chuckles, and then adds, "Breakfast is my specialty."

"I bet it is," I mumble to myself while Sadie hops off the couch to lead Billy to the kitchen. Making breakfast together is our thing, but I can see where Sadie needs to get used to doing it with someone else.

"Thanks for letting me sleep," Billy says, his hands now on the corner of the wall while his head rests against it. His slow grin does funny things to me, but maybe that's the residue of vomiting.

I wave a hand, dismissing him, and shrug.

"You didn't sleep okay? You moved out here." He nods toward the blanket covering my legs. I'm suddenly aware how short the nightshirt is underneath the blanket and how revealing it would be to stand before him.

"I didn't want to disturb you," I say, although it isn't true. When he laid back down, I felt his rejection again and didn't want to stay on the bed with him.

"Huh." Billy double taps his hands on the wall and disappears down my hallway.

Huh is right, buddy. What are you doing here?

I finally drag myself to the kitchen after finding a pair of yoga pants to slip under my short tee. Sadie's giggles and Billy's smiles make me feel like an intruder in my own home. They work in symmetry in my small space, falling into a rhythm while they discuss baking breakfast foods. My heart pinches, knowing this might be Sadie's future. Sundays…without me. I should be used to it. Sadie isn't my child, and I've lived without her easy presence for three years, but when she was a child, this was our routine. I'd let my sister sleep and make a big breakfast with Sadie.

"Coffee?" Billy asks over his shoulder. I hadn't even noticed he noticed me standing in the doorway.

"That would be a dream," I say, and Billy stops, pausing with the batter-filled cup over the electric griddle but not pouring it. Did he ask me something about a dream last night? I'm so fuzzy on the details once we walked up the stairs, but not fuzzy enough to remember I threw myself at him and he rejected me.

"Dreams coming true. That's me." Billy pats his chest with a loud thump, grins slowly at me, and then turns back for the griddle.

Give me that coffee. Stat.

Billy does make me scrambled eggs and toast, and the whole experience of him cooking and me doing nothing in my own kitchen makes me uneasy. I'm on edge while we pass through the meal and feel drained once again after I eat.

"Seems Aunt Roxie needs more rest," Billy teases, leaning on the table.

"Except you cooked so she needs to clean. House rules." I have no idea what she means as I cook and clean every night, although Sadie does help me with the dishes most evenings.

"I think today we'll give Roxie a pass." Billy winks at me, and it's obvious this is some private joke between them. I feel even more like an outsider, and I just want to go to my room.

"Yeah, it seems beer and I aren't good company as I get older." I glance over at Sadie, a little embarrassed at admitting I'm hungover at forty-one.

"Beer and you are just fine as company. It's the overindulgence that gets you every time."

Again, I'm ready to retort with he should know, but I bite my lip and offer a tight smile. Billy's brows pinch in question, but I'm not about to get into it with him. He swipes his hands over his thighs and stands, picking up his plate and mine.

"I'll do it," I say.

"You need to go back to bed. I got it today."

"Just stack them. I'll do them later," I snap, losing my will to hold my tongue. This is what we do. We bicker, and I'm looking for a fight with him. Maybe it will restore my equilibrium.

Billy questions me again with softened eyes, but I glance away. I don't have the strength to read the whiskey color.

"Okay, I really need to check on what happened last night and the closing up of things."

Sadie gives him a short wave. "I have homework, so I'll see you later." Her voice hesitates, waiting on Billy to confirm he will see her again, and maybe even add when.

"See ya, kiddo." Then he does something he's never done before. He steps up to her and kisses her near the temple. Sadie blushes and turns on her heels for her room.

"That was sweet," I say, startled by the move.

"I can be, you know. Do the gentleman thing and all."

I think I'll be a gentleman tonight.

"Yeah…so…about last night. I'm really sorry…about…everything." The missed kiss. The puked-on boots. Spending the night.

"It happens," he says as if not fazed by anything. Women probably throw themselves at him all the time. I'm only surprised he passed up some willing opportunity last night to stay with me. Then again, it reaffirms what I've always known. He isn't interested in someone like me.

"I'll see my ladies later."

Not only do his words surprise me with the collective possessive, but then he startles me by stepping up and kissing my temple similar to how he kissed Sadie's. It does nothing to comfort me. Instead, it solidifies how he sees me. Although I'm too old to be a daughter to him, he considers me like a sister, and being the sister-friend is never a great thing.

+ + +

Monday begins my Halloween themed sale, *Book*tober, and I'm overwhelmingly busy, which is a good thing. It doesn't provide me time to reflect on the missed kiss with Billy or the plaguing question of why he stayed the night. He's come to visit Sadie, now joining us three nights a week for dinner, but I'm in such a rush, working double shifts with Grace, that I hardly have time to chat with him. He's grown very comfortable with visiting my apartment, and I note again he hasn't invited Sadie to his place.

My bookstore has an old library table near the front where I can watch kids who hang out work on homework. Sadie hasn't been part of those crowds, and I worry about her making friends here. She hasn't mentioned anyone other than the classmates causing trouble during class.

In addition, there's a cozy corner in the back where I have a loveseat and an overstuffed chair for those who want to linger and read in quiet. It's a tight fit in the corner for my First Chapter Fridays, but I don't want to move the book night to another location. The point is to bring readers into the store and discuss books.

However, Billy's presence at my home has the rumors circulating as we convene the Friday after his Oktoberfest.

"So, a certain someone has been seen frequenting the upper stairs of this place," Cora Conrad simpers, eyeing the rest of the other ladies present tonight. Alyce Wright, an English teacher at the high school and assistant girls' volleyball coach to Mati Harrington, is present, along with Hetty Miller, owner of the floral shop down the street. Penelope Stryder, the owner of Pearl's next door, two newbies, and Cora, who's really been on my nerves this week, are also in attendance.

"I don't know what you're talking about," I say, keeping my eyes on the book before me, flipping pages well past chapter one in my haste to avoid this topic.

"I'll give everyone a hint. He's tall. Silver on top and dark on the bottom. Oh my, that sounds scandalous, and I think he works right—"

"Alyce, why don't you begin this month?" I interject, cutting off Cora who's craning her neck like she can see through some nonexistent window behind my head and peer across the street.

"I'd be happy to," Alyce replies, giving me a wink, which I appreciate, and she begins to read a new MC book about a woman returning to her small town after a broken marriage and meeting a man she never meant to love. It sounds similar to our community with Rebel's Edge outside of town, and I notice Cora grow more uncomfortable with each passage.

"I think it sounds wonderful," Hetty says when Alyce finishes.

"I think it sounds impossible," Cora mutters, her eyes focused on the cover of the book in her hands.

"I think it all sounds like a bunch of romantic hullabaloo," a masculine voice interjects, and we all look up to see Billy Harrington in his Friday finest—jeans and a BRMP tee. "The real thing can do better than that." His smoky-brown eyes land on mine, and a slow, cocky grin grows. I have no idea what he means, but if he's implying he's the real thing and can fulfill fantasies, I'm certain he isn't wrong. I've been dreaming of him all week.

"Thought you ladies might like a little sample with your reading hour."

A few ladies break into a wave of snickers, and Billy clarifies his innuendo by holding up two growlers of craft beer. Did he bring us his fall blend?

"I'd love one." Alyce smiles appreciatively, and I stand for my office.

"I'll see if I have any plastic cups." I pass Billy and enter my office, needing a moment to ponder his presence.

"Roxie," he addresses me from behind, startling me, and I jump before spinning to face him.

"William." I draw in a breath, the sound of his name ragged on my lips. "That was sweet of you. I've always wanted to do a pairing of your beer with books."

"Really?" His brows rise, but his expression looks sheepish. "My sister had the same idea for a while as well, but I wouldn't let her." His lips clamp shut after he speaks as if he's said too much, and I take a moment to digest what he's said.

"You wouldn't let her?" I question. He looks away from me, and I form my own assumptions. "Because you don't like me."

His face returns to me, and his brows rise even higher, wrinkling his forehead. "It's not that I don't like you, Roxie." He steps forward, filling my personal space, and I try to step back but bump into my desk. Everything in my shop feels too small tonight, and I can't get enough air, especially with him standing so close before me. "Not dislike." His voice lowers, and he brushes back my hair, his eyes following the motion as he curls his fingers around my ear and then pauses on my neck. His thumb reaches for the corner of my lip. The corner he kissed that first night.

The corner that's never been kissed like that.

His eyes leap up, and I swallow.

"I said that out loud, didn't I?"

"Like how, Roxie?" His thumb strokes over the curl of my mouth, rubbing back and forth on the edge.

"I've never had a corner-lip kiss." I exhale with the admission, a cross between relief and embarrassment. Billy's lip crooks again, and another cocky grin appears.

"I'm happy to be your first." The statement is filled with suggestion, only the ship of my virginity sailed long ago. Still, there are many firsts I haven't had. Positions. Locations. This man.

What am I thinking?

My hands lift to push him away, only my fingers dig into the shoulders of his tee as if tugging him to me.

"You've been so busy this week." His eyes scan my face but eventually land on my mouth. "We haven't had a chance to talk about last weekend."

"Life of a small business owner," I jest, hoping he'll understand. "Although you're hardly small business in this town." He doesn't fall for the compliment or allow me to divert us. I'm expecting a retort of *how big he is* when he only whispers my name, and the brush of air crosses my lips.

"I apologized," I stammer as if that clarifies everything.

"For puking on my boots." He chuckles, watching his finger trace over the lower curve of my mouth. "But do you remember apologizing for nearly kissing me?"

"Why would I try to kiss you?" I stammer defensively against what I did try to do. Billy purrs in response.

"You also told me a few other things that night."

Panic settles in quickly. What could I have said to him? Oh, God, there are so many things. My stomach flips, and my shoulders fall.

Your eyes are beautiful.

You are an incredibly sexy man.

I'm attracted to you more than I should be.

"You told me you'd never had a man take care of you like I did."

I pause, blinking up at him. "What?" I choke. We didn't do anything. I'd have known, right? I would have felt something, aftereffects or…Billy wouldn't do that. He wouldn't take advantage of someone in my condition.

"You were so sick, and I held back your hair. Then I brushed your teeth for you and washed off your face."

Oh. "You did?" How could I not remember these things?

"I led you to bed, and you kept apologizing, telling me you didn't mean to kiss me, and it would never happen again."

Oh God, but it's true. I wouldn't ever offer myself up to him again, but then I feel the warmth of his fingers against my neck while his thumb continues to rub my lip, and I'm a mess even lower. I'd throw myself at him in a heartbeat if I knew he wouldn't reject me again.

"Then you told me you could fall in love with me."

I gasp. If I said that, it was the worst attempt at a seduction in the history of seductions. On the other hand, I would never admit to him how I could fall in love with him under better conditions. My eyes freeze on his face. I don't think I even blink. "I did not say that."

"I guess you'll never know." The corner of his lip curls even deeper while he continues to watch his thumb outlining my lips.

I decide ignorance is bliss and continue to pretend I didn't do what he said. "Why would I want to kiss you?" I adamantly defend, returning to the first offense.

"Me thinks she doth protest too much." One brow tweaks.

"I don't," I state, although I'm unsteady as I speak, and my eyes continue to drift to his lips.

"Oh, but you do."

"Why would I want to kiss you?" I repeat as if I'm looking for an answer. The one where he tells me he wants to kiss me.

"Because you know it might be the best kiss of your life," he teases.

"You are so full of it," I snap, our eyes locking. Fine. I can play his game. "Kissing you would mean nothing."

"I guess we'll never know," he mocks, and I take the challenge. I lean into him, clamping my lips over his. My first thought is he won't escape me again. My second is I can't believe I've thrown myself at him *again*, and my final thought is, I hate when he's right.

Our mouths move like they were meant to be pressed together. His hand cups the back of my neck, holding me in place as he quickly takes control of the moment, no longer allowing me to lead but him to command. He wants my lips, my tongue, my breath, and he's stealing it all from me. And I'm giving it to him like the fool I am.

The desk edge bites into the back of my thighs as my full body presses against the wood. I'm leaning back when I realize where this could lead, but like I challenged of him, this will mean nothing. I press at his shoulders, not as forcefully as that first time but enough to signal I'm done. Billy pulls back reluctantly, stealing another quick tug before meeting my eyes. His brow arches in question.

"See? Nothing," I lie as my stomach flutters and my palms sweat. A beat races at my core. My voice betrays me. I'd keep kissing him if I didn't think he gave in to prove his point, and he proves mine with his next words.

"Kissing is my specialty, darlin', and I know that was the best yet."

The brakes on this moment screech to a halt.

"Because you've kissed a lot of women." It's more a reminder to myself of his history than a question asking for an answer.

"That I have," he teases, but the words are like a slap of reality. My hands push at his shoulders, and he has the decency to step back, giving us some space. Shock fills his face. "I didn't mean—"

"You don't need to explain," I snap. He's had a lot of practice to perfect his craft while I'm relatively inexperienced compared to his done-it list, and compared to my first attempt, this goes down as the second worst seduction.

Billy scrubs a hand up his throat like he does and pauses under his chin.

"You still think I'm a total manwhore, don't you?"

"Well, you just admitted it," I say. We stand in a very precarious position, further justifying my thoughts, and not for the first time do I realize the real Billy Harrington and the fantasy of him are two different things.

"You know what, Roxie? You're a piece of work," he huffs, slapping a hand on his thigh and then turning for the door. He throws his hands up next. "I don't know why I try with you."

He takes two steps and spins back to me. "And for the record. It's *not* that I'm *not* attracted to you, Roxanne. I think you're fucking stunning and worthy of wall sex, but when you open that mouth...I just...*dammit*...I just can't..."

Then he actually turns away and leaves me stumped for words.

Chapter 17
Cat Got Her Tongue

[Billy]

I cannot take her tongue, I think as I exit the back door of her store and return to the pub. I mean, I took her tongue and those lips. I want a few other body parts of hers, too, because the feel of her under my hands from the other night won't leave my damn head. I didn't take advantage of her. Didn't grope a feel or experiment, but just having my hand on her hip and then slipping it forward to wrap my arm over her middle, something clicked inside me. I held her to my chest, possessively holding her as if I didn't want to let her go, couldn't let her go.

I could love you, Billy Harrington, and that would be the worst thing I could do.

That sharp tongue of hers—so help me God—I meant what I said. I don't know why I try. I'm busting my balls to get to know Sadie and learn about Roxie at the same time, and I tried to do the right thing the other night by being a gentleman and not kissing her when all I wanted was to ravish that willing mouth. The same mouth that spewed on my boots and calls me a manwhore. Then I held her all night, although honestly, that wasn't a conscious choice. I told myself I'd only lie down next to her and keep her on her side, so she didn't vomit in her sleep, but as my arm wrapped over her and her fingers unconsciously brushed my arm, I was too comfortable. More comfortable than I'd been in a long time. *Click-click, like the turn of a lock.*

I don't really cuddle. I'm not opposed to it, but I haven't held someone other than my ex-wife. It felt awkward after random sex. Do I hold her all night when I don't want to? Or do I hold her for a few minutes? But for how long? I was like Billy Crystal in that movie *When Harry met Sally*. How long was too long?

With Roxanne, it ended up being all night, and it didn't feel long enough. Then she let me crawl back into her bed, but when I reached for her, she was gone. It was a strange feeling. The emptiness. I'm the one who always leaves. I'll never allow myself to be left again. I'll always be the first to exit, but I wasn't in a rush that night, or in the early morning, or even later when Sadie asked me to stay for breakfast. I was relieved she asked as I didn't want to beg to hang out, but I was close. Too close. I had to cut out of there when I started envisioning myself being there all day.

Roxie's been so busy this week she's hardly had time for Sadie, let alone me, and I didn't like the feeling—the feeling of her ignoring me. I didn't intend to confront her this evening. I was going to bring over the beer, hoping it might encourage the ladies to visit the bar afterward.

Oh, who am I kidding? I was hoping Roxie would visit the pub, only it's been another strikeout.

Her mouth. It wants mine. The way her tongue peeks out and she nibbles at the tender skin of her lower lip, she wants me. I thought I'd bring over the beer, hang out a bit, and then…

What, Billy? What did you have planned? Taking her over her desk while the ladies wait outside? Not a bad thought but also not logical. I keep fucking everything up when it comes to this woman.

After entering the Blue Ridge Microbrewery & Pub, I slip behind the bar through the hinged service entrance and let the piece slam back into place as I stalk toward the taps. I'd snap someone's head off for that behavior with the counter, but I'm not thinking straight. I'm headed straight for a beer. I pull back the tap and give myself a hearty pour. Then I drink the entire tallboy in one swallow.

"Didn't go as planned?" Clyde teases beside me. He saw me leave with two large growlers, and without asking, his assumption of where I went can't be denied. I continue to swallow, not acknowledging him. When I finish with a loud *ah*, I answer.

"Nothing with that woman ever does."

"What happened this time?" Clyde chuckles.

"She accused me of being a manwhore."

Clyde's brows rise. "Did she say that?"

"No, I said I've kissed lots of women and—"

Clyde's raised paw stops me. "And somehow you think that statement convinces her otherwise?" His expression turns stern, almost reprimanding. What is the deal with Clyde and Roxanne?

"Well, it's true, but I was hoping to impress her with my kissing expertise." I'm filling the glass again while I listen to myself, and the words sink to the pit of my stomach.

"And I'm sure that statement did the trick," Clyde mumbles. I lift the glass and begin drinking again. What does he know about women? "A woman likes to feel special, one of a kind."

Did I ask my question out loud, or is he suddenly into mind reading? I don't stop to ask. I just continue guzzling down the crisp taste of our house specialty. It's the head on this brew that makes it so good, and I chug it to keep the flavor consistent.

Let me give you a taste of my head, I like to joke as I pour for a flirtatious female customer.

"A woman wants to be wooed." Clyde's still rambling.

"She wants my *wood*," I mutter, removing the empty glass from my lips and reaching for the tap again.

"Not your wood, nimrod. *Wooed*, like wined and dined. When's the last time you took a woman on a date and not your office for a quickie?"

I don't take women to my office. That's my sacred space at the pub. But I can't answer his question about a date. I haven't dated in years. The only time I take with a woman is the time it takes to…

"You sound like a goddamn woman, Clyde. How do you know so much about this shit?"

"I read," he states proudly, standing to his full height and puffing out his chest. I shake my head. Well, that explains it.

You don't touch a book, William. You read it. You enjoy it. And you'll never read mine.

"Yeah, well, there's a reason I don't read," I mumble. Too many words, like those that hurt.

Chapter 18

Floored

[Roxanne]

By standing near the front counter, I see him coming before he even enters the store. I'm fixing a display on the side counter when his body appears in my periphery. I turn and watch as Billy crosses the street, holding up a hand to stop an oncoming car in order to reach my side of the road. My eyes remain fixed on him as he yanks open the front door that sits at an angle to the corner, and then he struts up to the counter, only he doesn't stop to speak to me. He rounds it, takes the step up to the platform, and reaches for my wrist.

"William," I snap as he tugs me forward. He looks both ways as if crossing a street, which is ironic, considering he charged right across the legitimate road outside and continues to drag me down the main aisle of my store.

"Got any customers in here?" he asks as he leads me toward the back, and I hustle to keep pace with him.

"No," I answer too quickly. It's Monday afternoon. Several businesses are closed on Monday, allowing themselves a break from the weekend visitors, but I like to remain open. I consider it my business day. Inventory checks. Restocking. Basic accounting. "But what are you doing?"

He tugs at my wrist in a way that I spin to face him, backing me up between travel books and writing manuals. His other hand comes for the nape of my neck, and he responds, "The ungentlemanly thing."

His mouth crushes against mine. It's a battle of wills for a moment. Mine is under surprise attack. His is out for total control. Eventually, we find common ground, and then we lower for it. His mouth is taking mine as if I'm the air he needs to breathe, and the pressure of his kiss is dragging me to the floor, literally. He lowers to his knees, bringing me with him, refusing to remove his mouth while keeping his grip on the back of my neck. Dammit. I hate when he's right. He is the best kisser I've ever experienced. This, of course, reminds me of the other night, and how he reminded me he's kissed many.

"Billy," I mutter against his mouth as my knees hit the hardwood. We kneel while kissing.

"No talking," he states against my mouth and continues to devour me. I'm leaning back at his insistence, and the next thing I know, I'm on my back with Billy's knee between my thighs. *Oh God, this is crazy.* I'm not thinking about how unsanitary it might be on the hardwood flooring, or the fact we are on the floor in my place of business. All I can concentrate on is Billy Harrington over me and his mouth against mine.

"Billy, slow down," I whimper. He's going to eat me alive if he keeps going at this pace, and I'm not complaining, but something isn't right. He's too adamant for this kiss. Too determined. He pulls back but only enough. I can still feel his breath brushing my lips. His forehead rests against mine. "What's wrong?"

His eyes close, and he rolls his forehead gently over mine as my hands reach for the scruff of his jaw.

"So many things," he says. I swallow the sting. Am I one of the things wrong in his life? Is it Sadie? Is it all too much? Before I can ask my questions, his mouth returns to mine. "Just keep kissing me."

I'm lost to his lips for another few seconds, allowing him to take what he needs from me as I feel equally desperate to receive what he's giving. His mouth on mine. Hands on me. His knee between my thighs. Without thought, I rock against the broad curve against my core, the friction like a spark to forgotten flint. My sex clenches. It won't be enough. I want to rub my entire body against his. The sound of a high-pitched ping filters to my ears.

"I hear bells," I mutter against his mouth.

He chuckles against my lips. "That's a new one," he teases. We continue to kiss a second before his words register. It's another reminder he's been with so many, and I push at his shoulders.

"Dammit, Billy, why do you have to ruin everything?" The question stops him short, and he pulls back slowly as a scratchy feminine voice calls out my name.

"Miss McAllister, are you here?" Her voice is a little grating, and I recognize it immediately. A sharp tapping on the hardwood floor tells me she's walking down the main aisle at a rhythmic pace. Before Billy and I can untangle ourselves, she speaks again. "Oh goodness, what's going on here?"

Billy draws back, keeping his eyes on mine. He opens his mouth to speak when our interrupter continues. "Billy Harrington, is that you? What are you doing to that poor girl?"

"Mrs. Pritchard," Billy mutters, the name soft as his brows pinch while he speaks to me. "She has to be like a hundred years old." He shakes his head and then speaks louder in explanation. "She fell, and I'm helping her up."

With catlike reflexes, he springs to his feet, while simultaneously tugging down my skirt which has ridden up as I undulated against his knee. He bends at the waist, offering me both his hands. I'd prefer the floor open me up and swallow me as I've just been caught by one of my best customers rutting against Billy Harrington.

"Goodness, honey, are you okay?" the older woman asks of me.

"I'm fine, Mrs. Pritchard. Just slipped." *In judgment,* I don't add as I speak to the ceiling, blinking up at the bright lights. "It was nothing."

There's a hitch of breath, and I lift my head to see Billy's eyes widen. Does he think I mean this is nothing? That kissing him was nothing, like I told him the other night? In my current predicament, it's obvious it was very much something. I was working myself to an orgasm against his knee, not to mention his mouth is a sin I want to repeat.

I raise my hands for Billy's, and he tugs me upward. Once standing, I break free of one hand, swiping at my backside, while Billy grips the other hand as if he's afraid to release me.

"Are you sure you're okay?" Billy asks, an eyebrow rising. "Maybe you should go upstairs and lie down for a little bit." His voice lilts, teasing me.

I shake my head. "No, no. I'm good. What can I help you with today, Mrs. Pritchard?"

"I'm here for the final book in that series you recommended to me." Her Victorian aura prevents her from stating aloud the title she means, and her eyes shift to Billy. "You know which one."

"Of course. I'll grab it for you." Then I pause, my hand still in Billy's. "Could you give me just a second, though?"

"Sure, honey. You take a moment to recover yourself." Mrs. Pritchard steps out of the aisle and heads for the back where the comfy seats are tucked in the corner.

Billy and I remain hidden between the shelves, listening to the tap of Mrs. Pritchard's cane as it grows less predominant, the farther she moves away from us.

"I'll give you something to grab…"

"I didn't mean…"

We speak at the same time, and I blush. I lick my lips and Billy moans, stepping up to me. "You do that thing where only your tongue peeks out, and it drives me crazy."

"You drive me crazy," I mumble, but I'm giggling like a schoolgirl as heat rushes my face.

"This isn't finished," Billy states, his voice raspy and rugged. "I'm not done with you."

A thrill should not be coursing through my body at the sound of those words, but I'm like a live wire, humming with energy and itching for a power surge.

"And this"—he points back and forth between us—"is not nothing." With a quick kiss to my temple, he leaves the aisle, and I collapse to my side, allowing the shelves to hold me up.

What the hell just happened?

My fingers trace my swollen lips, which smile of their own volition. Remembering Mrs. Pritchard is waiting, I press off the shelves and turn the corner.

"Mrs. Pritchard?!" I hadn't heard her return down the main aisle. She shakes her head with a knowing smirk.

"Who knew bookstores were so dangerous? You should have your floors examined."

Or my head. What was I doing on the floor with Billy anyway? Adding myself to his list of women is what I'm doing, and I hate that my body doesn't care. My head, it's starting to catch up with what happened.

"It's okay, dear. A good tousle never hurt anyone." She winks at me, and I nervously laugh. This is the schoolteacher who allowed Billy to cheat in class. "Now could you help me with my book, please?"

I nod as I consider the romance section. I keep a generous stock although many independent booksellers don't. Romance makes up eighty percent of all fiction sales, and the locals love a little romantic scandal. I pull the book from the shelf for Mrs. Pritchard although I'm certain she could have found the title herself.

"Here you go," I say, handing over the distinctly covered book with a gray mask. For a former schoolteacher, I'd have assumed she'd read more intellectual works, but there's nothing wrong with a little sexual fantasy. Sex against the bookshelves has been one of mine. My mind drifts to Billy and where things could have led had we not been interrupted. I suppose an almost-orgasm-inducing kiss on the floor between the shelves is close enough. I blush with the thought.

"How did you know that was Billy Harrington?" I ask, curious as Mrs. Pritchard hadn't seen his face at first.

"I'd recognize that backside anywhere."

"Mrs. Pritchard!" I shriek, believing she means the firm globes I haven't had my hands on yet.

"I spanked that hide more than once for his misbehavior in my classroom." She chuckles. "But if I had known of spankings like this." She shakes the book at me. "I might have reconsidered."

I don't know whether to be appalled at her admission or titter with giggles at her raunchy sense of teacher-student infatuation. I take a second to glance at the book she holds in her hand. If she had only recommended books like *that* to Billy Harrington, he might have loved to read. Then again, he seems like a practical man—meaning he'd prefer to practice the activities in that novel rather than read about them.

Me, too, I internally sigh. Only, the one person I want to practice with is Billy, and he's already practiced with half the women in this town.

+ + +

True to his word, Billy returns just before closing time, like a minute before I'm ready to approach the door and turn the lock deciding it's been a day of torture. *Will he return? Will he not?* Metaphorical daisy petals litter my floor.

He enters, pulls the toggle for the open sign to click off, and leans his back against the glass. "I'm back," he warns in a quiet teasing voice, and I giggle with nerves. "Lights?" He tips his chin, and I turn for the panel of switches behind me. I flick most of them off, minus one column of low-lit bulbs leading to my office. There's a switch in the back hallway for the final overhead lights. As I lead the way to my office, my heart racing with nerves, two hands cover my shoulders and shift me between bookshelves once again. It's almost déjà vu except we are in the final row.

"Why here?" I ask instead of the question I should be asking, which is *what are you doing?*

"I want to finish what we started, where we started."

"Maybe this isn't such a good idea. We should think of Sadie." I place a hand on his chest and feel his heart racing through his shirt.

"What about Sadie?" His brows pinch as he leans forward and kisses the corner of my lips. My eyes close at the tenderness.

"This…" I point back and forth between us. "This could get messy."

"It won't. Player, remember?" He pats his chest, and my heart clenches a bit, but he's right. We don't need to define emotions or label ourselves. "We keep it casual. Nothing complicated."

"We have to assure we remain a united front." I add to his conditions. "For Sadie."

"Oh, I want our fronts to unite."

With those words, his hand cups the back of my neck, and his mouth presses over mine with a little less force and a little more care than earlier. I'm instantly lost to his lips, spiraling downward once again as he slowly lowers us to the floor.

"I'm going to kiss you until you realize there's something between us." That sounds like a definition when he just declared us casual, but I'm too wrapped up with his mouth and his hands coasting over my body. I moan into his mouth as his knee spreads my thighs, returning us to the position from earlier. My skirt rides up to the top of my legs as Billy nudges forward, pressing into the heat of my center. He breaks the kiss a moment and glances at our position.

"Red, again?" he questions, and my brows pinch. "The first night I had dinner with you, you told me you were wearing red underwear. Is it a matching set?" His eyes draw up to my breasts which are covered in a red T-shirt to go with the fall motif skirt I'm wearing. His hand comes to the hem of my tee and lifts, holding the material so he can gape inside. A smile crosses his lips. "Yep." The bra and undies match. What can I say? I like coordinating undergarments. Apparently, he approves as well, but he doesn't reach for a heavy breast, aching with the desire to be caressed. He returns to kissing me until I'm moving my hips and rubbing myself against his knee again, the thickness causing a friction that sets butterflies to flight in my lower belly.

I'm so close, but I just can't get over the edge, and Billy's hand moves down my hip, tugging upward the last bits of material from my skirt. His fingers slip under the elastic at my hip and slide torturously down the inside of my underwear, skimming the backs of his fingers over my skin. I'm conscious of the puffy bulge at my hip bone. I'm not the heavier woman I was. I'm a healthier woman, but I'm still not all smooth and tight. I break the kiss, but Billy doesn't complain. His eyes watch his hidden fingers until he slips between my legs and meets slickness.

"Darlin'." His eyes leap up to my face, surprised by the heat, and I blush. "Can't be *nothing* if you're this wet." His pretty eyes sparkle. He's damn pleased with how I'm responding to him, and there's no denying it. I can't deny it. I won't deny…*oh.* A thick finger enters me, and my back bows off the floor.

"That's it, love," he says, and my insides flutter at the endearment. My hips rock as his finger draws a too-quick orgasm. That's it? *That was too fast*, I want to yell. My body has betrayed me with a few strokes of his finger, and I'd scream if I wasn't worried Sadie would hear me upstairs. The thought is an instant buzzkill, and then a soft ping tingles from the front of the store.

"Bells," I whisper, my voice lost as I'm still suppressing the shout.

"Again, darlin'?" He chuckles, but I grip his wrist and tug his fingers from me. I rush to sit upward as I hear the sound a second time. My head tilts toward the front of the store, and I glance in that direction although I can't see anything from the floor.

"No, the front door," I whisper, returning my eyes to him. "Did you lock it?" Did I hear the click of metal when he entered, or was I too enthralled by his return?

"Of course, I locked it." He pauses. "I think."

"The bells are my front door," I hush-whisper, suddenly concerned someone is inside the store with us. Billy rocks back on his ankles and then stands. He disappears from the aisle while I straighten my clothing and help myself up. This is mortifying. I've just had a too-fast orgasm on my bookstore floor, and we've been interrupted *again.*

"Oh fuck," Billy grumbles as I hastily approach the entrance to find the cash register drawer open and empty. Billy turns to me, wide-eyed and concerned. "You've been robbed, Roxie."

Chapter 19
Book 'em

[Billy]

The expression of horror on Roxanne's face is not the look I was hoping for moments after giving her an orgasm. She came so quickly, but that only meant there was more to come, every pun intended. Only now, her bookstore being robbed is a bigger buzzkill than Mrs. Pritchard's interruption earlier.

"We need to call the sheriff," I say to Roxie who hasn't moved. Her eyes remain wide, staring at the open drawer, empty of cash. She has one of those old-fashioned registers with keys like a typewriter.

"Roxie?" She hasn't responded, and I approach her. When my hand touches her upper arm, she flinches. Dull eyes glance at my face, but I don't think she's registering me.

"I've been robbed," she whispers. I reach for her again, not allowing her to pull away from me. She's shaking, and I tug her to me. Wrapping my arms around her, I hold her to my chest while her arms dangle at her sides.

"Hold onto me, darlin'." She needs something to grasp, to pull herself together.

"Who would do this?" She pulls back, but I don't release her.

"I don't know, baby, but let's call the sheriff. We don't want to waste time as it just happened." I should have run outside to see if I noticed anyone sprinting down the block or driving off, but I didn't think that quickly, and I didn't want to leave Roxie alone.

I dial 911 and get Vikki Stunner on the line. Yes, that's her real name, but it's not a label for her appearance although she's a decent looking woman.

"9-1-1. How can I help you?"

I proceed to explain how BookEnds has been robbed, and the sheriff is dispatched.

"Billy Harrington, is that you?" *Oh boy*. I hadn't identified myself when I called. I don't need to be wasting time with conversations. We need a sheriff here stat.

"Yes, ma'am," I answer.

"Don't you ma'am me. I'm younger than you, remember?" Vikki starts. "I haven't seen you lately. Been spending a lot of time at that bookstore?"

I recognize a fishing expedition when I hear one, and I'm not about to take the bait.

"Jerry told me you've been over there quite a bit."

I want to tell Vikki her husband should spend more time at home, minding his own business than minding mine, but I don't, mainly because I like Jerry. He's a regular, and regulars are good for business. Second, I don't mention it because I'm relieved Jerry married Vikki after she hit on me one too many times years ago.

"You should come to dinner some night." I'm still holding Roxie in my arms while this conversation continues, and I feel the weight of Roxie's eyes on me. She doesn't miss the seductive attempt through the phone, and I cringe. I have no interest in Vikki, married or not, but especially married. Married women are definitely not of interest to me.

"Thanks for the invitation, Vikki, but I'll need to pass presently. Can you tell me when June will be here?"

June Barne is the first female sheriff of our community, and even though her last name reminds me of a purple dinosaur, she's one tough cookie. In her uniform, she's a badass, but I remember her from my high school days. She was almost as much of a troublemaker as I was. June lives by rules now, but she walks a fine line along those rules, knowing where the straight and narrow grows hazy. Fortunately for me, June and I haven't crossed any lines over the years.

Vikki gives me an ETA of June's arrival, and I thank her, ending the call.

"Where's Sadie?" I ask, suddenly worried this wasn't random or only done downstairs. Roxie's eyes widen, and I race for the back of the store. Taking the steps two at a time, I rush through the door at the top marked private. I quickly cross the living room for Sadie's room but find her bed full, covers pulled up to the pillow. My fingers twitch to brush back her midnight hair which Roxie told me isn't her natural color. I want to stroke her peaceful cheek, but then again, she isn't here for me to wake her.

What the fuck?

After double-checking the locks on the back door, I return downstairs to find June asking Roxanne a few questions.

"So, you're saying, you were in the store when it happened, but you didn't hear anything?" June's brow pinches as she narrows her eyes at Roxie.

"No, I was…I was in the back." Roxie pauses as I approach, and I swipe a hand along her lower back. I mean it as comfort, but she stiffens, and I instantly drop my hand. Unfortunately, June doesn't miss the touch.

"And you're the one who called 9-1-1?" June nods at me.

"I did. I was in the store with Roxie when it happened."

June's brows rise, her smooth forehead furrowing. Her hair is pulled back into the most severe bun I've ever seen, tightly tugging her skin near her temples.

"And where were you located in the store?" she questions.

"I was in the back as well."

"Your exact position?" June questions, and I swallow. *She isn't serious, right?*

"Between the shelves," Roxie clarifies. "The last row."

"I see," June draws out. "You were both in the back, and what exactly were you doing that you couldn't hear anything other than bells?" Her lip crooks up, fighting a smile, and I'm ready to tell her it's none of her business when I realize it's important to explain Roxie and I were busy, which is why we didn't see anything.

"We were…"

"Shelving a book in a place I couldn't reach," Roxanne blurts. "Billy is very handy."

I choke, and June's smile grows a little broader. "So I've been told." *Dammit.* Why can't she move along in her questioning?

"Yes, well, because we were in the back, I didn't see or hear anyone breaking in." Roxie's voice begins to tremble, and my hand clenches and unclenches, wanting to reach for her again.

"Well, no one broke in, it appears," June states rather formally. "There's no forced entry."

Roxanne's head turns to me. "Didn't you lock the door?"

"It wasn't locked?" I'm peering at June as I speak, hesitant in my confidence. I can't recall hearing the lock click into place as I was fixated on Roxie. Her shy grin when I entered. The rush of heat along her neck. The way her eyes latched onto mine. All I could think about was getting her between the shelves and having a do-over of what wasn't done earlier.

June glances back and forth between Roxie and myself with one brow arched. Her smile wavers. "The door wasn't locked when I walked in. Did you unlock it, expecting me?"

"I haven't moved," Roxie states.

"I went through the back and up the stairs to check on Roxie's niece." The words draw Roxie's attention, and she turns on me with a scowl. I hold my face still, hoping not to give away what I discovered up there or rather who I *didn't* see.

"You have a niece?" June asks.

"She's newly moved in with me," Roxanne clarifies, and June makes a note on her tablet.

"Can you tell me a little bit about her?"

Roxie explains details, like Sadie's name, age, and the circumstances of her moving to Blue Ridge. Thankfully, she leaves out my involvement. It isn't relevant.

June nods, no longer teasing either of us with the information she received. "I've heard of your girl." Roxanne bristles beside me and stands taller. June's addressing me as she speaks, and for a second, I think she knows my secret. *My girl.* She knows Sadie is my daughter.

"Heard she's a little troublemaker up at the high school."

"Now, wait a minute..." I begin, but Roxie steps forward, her hands fisting at her side.

"She's had a lot of things happen at once. More than any child should have to bear. Her mother died. She moved here. She discovered…" Roxie pauses as she looks at me, but I shake my head, just a slight twitch, and her face hardens. "She needs some compassion, and she isn't getting it from the other kids."

This is the first I've heard these things. I mean, I knew there were issues up at the school, but this sounds a little more serious than just a conflict or two.

"Does sound like she's had it rough," June sympathizes. "But I can't deny this looks like an inside job, and as the two of you seem to be each other's alibi, I'd like to question Sadie, if I may."

"She's sleeping," I interject, turning to Roxie for approval of this defense, but I've lost Roxanne. She's stepped a foot away from me, putting some distance between us.

"I can assure you my niece would never do such a thing as steal from me." Roxie's voice trembles again with conviction and anger. The sheriff deputy is Butch Marshall, and his radio crackles from where he stands by the front door. He tugs the receiver up to his mouth.

"Barne," he addresses his superior. "We have a possible break-in at Hetty's Flower Shop down the street. An alarm is going off."

June slaps the tablet cover closed and gives Butch permission to follow up. Then she turns narrowed eyes on Roxanne.

"Doesn't your niece work there?"

Chapter 20
Denial. It's More Than a River Wide.

[Roxanne]

I refuse to believe Sadie robbed me or the floral shop a block away. Sadie would have no need to steal money. I give her everything she needs, and she's a responsible girl. At sixteen, she wanted a job and instead of working for me, which she said would feel like she was taking more money from me, she got a job from Hetty down the street. I love fresh flowers, and I've befriended her as I try to buy a bouquet a week to adorn the front counter. Greenery adds a certain element to any space, but I digress because I don't want to think Sadie could possibly be a thief. Robbery? Breaking and entering? I just don't believe it.

I hate the fact doubt is festering as I climb the stairs to my apartment with leaden feet. Billy left at the same time as June, offering to walk her out and wait while I locked the store behind him. He turned back for a second, his eyes worrisome and focused on me, but I can't give anymore thought to Billy.

I stand in the middle of my entry and turn in a slow circle within my store. Everything checked out. Nothing else removed. Still, I feel violated in a way I've never felt before. Stripped, naked, and grimy. My hands rub up and down each arm as I hold myself. I push away thoughts of Billy, remembering how we were on the floor. I don't want to equate the two experiences in my head, but they merge, and I shiver with an additional sensation of violation.

I'm not accusing Billy of anything. I willingly went down to that floor and let him enter my underwear, but…nothing's going the way it should with him, which means nothing should be happening with him, of all people, and now I feel dirty about what we did. I need to get my head together. I need to make Sadie my focus.

I enter my apartment, caution filtering around me.

There was no forced entry.

I'm safe here, in my home. *Sadie's safe as well*, I tell myself as I enter her room. She's laying under the covers, the yellow quilt pulled over her shoulder. She faces the wall, and while I don't want to disturb her, I need to touch her. I need to assure myself she's here, and she's okay. I brush back her midnight hair, finding sweat at her temples. She's very warm under my knuckles, which skim the side of her cheek. My hand instinctively cups over her forehead. Is she feverish? She feels clammy. Is she sick? My hand pulls back, and I tuck the quilt tighter over her shoulder as I stare down at her.

Heard she's a troublemaker up at the high school.

This isn't Sadie. She doesn't cause trouble. She follows the rules as her mother instilled in her. Schedules. Timelines. Structure. These were the ideals my sister embedded into Sadie. That's not to say she didn't have a slight rebellious streak, and Theresa allowed that freak flag to fly on occasion with me, but once I returned Sadie, it was all back to business. My sister's greatest fear was Sadie would be like her—a wild child, who made a mistake one night to fulfill a fantasy—and end up derailed.

Sadie's been derailed anyway, and her black mood with matching hair and nails is further evidence of the rebel inside who has been longing to be released. She isn't a troublemaker. She's troubled, and I don't know how to reach her.

I turn from the edge of her bed and stumble over something as I try to exit her room.

"Dammit, Sadie," I mutter, thinking she needs to pick up her things, especially her gym shoes which lay right inside her door.

A soft knock comes to the back door as I exit her room and my heart leaps. I'm suddenly so jumpy. Hesitantly, I stalk through the kitchen and grab a knife from the holder on the counter. Nearing the door in the darkened room, I slowly slide two blinds apart to see a man looming against the window. I'm ready to scream when a hand comes to the window, and I hear a muffled voice on the other side of the glass. Pressing his face to the window, I see it's Billy.

"What the heck?" I snap, unlocking the door and tugging it open with enough force the blinds rattle against the door.

"I just wanted to check on you," he states, forcing himself into the apartment.

"I just saw you," I remind him, my voice rising as well as my temper.

"I know, but I'm unsettled by how things went."

"You mean, how I was robbed?"

"I mean how things happened on the floor."

We stare at one another. I don't want to say what happened is forgotten because it's not, but it's also the furthest thing on my mind in the present.

"Why are you holding that knife?" Billy hisses, and my head lowers, eyes finding the knife still in my hand.

"You scared the crap out of me."

Billy's brows arch. "Are you scared? Are you afraid to be here?"

I'm not. Not really, but a part of me can't shake that feeling of being violated, and I don't want to be alone. Billy steps up to me, his hand coming to the back of my neck.

"Let me stay. I'll make sure nothing happens to you." The plea in his voice along with the promise does strange things to me, and I agree without a thought. It feels a little wrong, but him touching me also feels so right. It's just what I need.

Billy takes off his boots and then quietly follows me to my room.

"Sadie okay?" he whispers as we enter my bedroom.

"Yeah. She's asleep." I don't bother to tell him my concerns for her health. Billy nods and then curls onto my bed, lying on his side.

"Go do what you need to do before bed," he states, and I stare down at him, feeling strange about his position and soft command. It sounds so…domestic, and I don't dare dream of such things with him. Entering the bathroom located off the hall, I brush my teeth, change into my nightshirt, and comb out my hair. When I return to my room, I slowly sit before Billy and then match his position, my back to his front.

A hand coasts up my spine while his body lowers, scooting his knees underneath mine and forcing me to tug them upward. My nightshirt shifts, and a warm hand rubs over my thigh.

"What are you doing?" I whisper, not accusing him but curious. My shirt lifts higher until my underwear is exposed, and then his mouth sucks at the middle of my back. Open mouth kisses travel down my spine to the base and the edge of my panties.

"You're safe," he says between suction. "I'm here," he tells me, and I want to believe he means so much more. My eyes close as I give into the soothing sensation of his mouth working over my skin, along my skeleton. He remains in the same general area of my body. Moving to my waist and nipping at my hip. His hand continues to stroke over my thigh. Eventually, he palms over one covered cheek, and I still.

"You're okay," he reminds me. "Nothing's going to happen to you. Or Sadie." The comment relaxes me, and I fall back under his spell. His soothing kisses. His stroking palm. Then he slips his finger under the band at my leg and curls along the elastic until he comes in contact with an area he's so recently discovered.

"I don't like how we did things downstairs," he says, and I still once again, afraid he means me and my too-quick reaction.

"I want to take my time with you, Roxanne. You're that type of woman." He leans over my hip and sucks at the tender skin. His fingers slip through wet creases within my panties. "And while I'd take you against a brick wall if that's what you really want, I think I'd prefer to have you in a bed like this."

A finger slips into me, deliberate and direct, and I hum under his touch. He's not frantic or frenzied like we were on the floor but taking his time to delve in and draw back, and I fall deeper into him. His touch. His kisses. A second finger joins the first, and he takes his time to slip forward and back, drawing out the pleasure he's created. I separate my knees a bit, holding them apart to allow him better access to me, and he groans against my back.

"You're so wet, Roxie, just as I knew you would be."

Knew I would be? Has he thought about me? Has he considered what it'd be like to be with me? I don't ask. I just feel.

"Billy." I hiss, his name a soft cry, and his fingers increase their pace.

"I want to taste you, Roxie. Let my mouth do as my fingers are." I shift, and he sits up, tucking his fingers in the waistband and lowering my underwear. I'm not wearing the sexiest pair as this was the last thing I expected to happen tonight. Then again, I never expected to kiss him or be robbed either.

"Stay with me," he says, almost sensing I've traveled back to the bookstore below. "We're up here. Together."

Together. Billy Harrington and me. It's surreal. A fantasy, and I suddenly understand how my sister must have felt all those years ago. This is what she wanted. Him like this with her.

Billy lowers his head and kisses just below my belly button. His tongue comes forward and circles the area, and I chuckle as it tickles.

"There's my darlin'," he mutters against my skin as he drags his nose over the coarse mound of hair and then lowers it between my slick folds. My legs spread of their own volition and then his hands force them farther apart. His tongue comes out like it did at my belly button, and he drags it around my most central part before slipping forward, and I break apart. My back arches. My fingers comb into his hair. My knees lift as his tongue does things to me I've never had done before. Delicious and dangerous, all the things I thought Billy Harrington would be like. He's sweet while insatiable, lapping at me, licking me until I'm so wet I feel myself dripping.

"Billy," I warn, knowing this time will be different. It wouldn't be that rush that surprised me on the bookstore floor, but a lingering wave of release, rolling down to my toes and spreading to my belly. I curl upward, my head lifting as I bite my lip to hold back the scream. He's relentless as the orgasm lingers and his tongue moves in earnest, flicking over the nub and then slipping back into me. I've hardly come down from the first when a second threatens.

"Billy," I hiss, his name draining the last of my oxygen as my breath catches, and I instantly come a second time.

"Holy shit," I mutter as I fall back to my pillow, my body more relaxed than it's been in years. My head lulls to the side, and I stare off at the window a moment. Billy kisses my inner thigh and then sits up, wiping a hand over his lips.

"How was that for distraction?" he teases, and I want to retort something witty and sharp, but I have nothing. He took it all from me. He took my stress and my orgasm, and unfortunately, I think my heart's going as well. Casual and uncomplicated he said earlier, but it's already getting complicated for me.

+ + +

The next morning, Billy's gone, having snuck out sometime during the night. Sadie acts like she can't wait to leave for school while I want to tell her about the break-in and warn her about being diligent of her surroundings. While I wasn't personally attacked, I worry about Sadie's safety.

"Maybe this is why you should let me drive," she teases although she doesn't have her driver's license yet. She rides the school bus, which isn't the cool thing, she told me, but most kids ride it as they live spread out within the community. Sadie took driver's ed this summer, but she needs practice hours before she can get her permit. Unfortunately, I hardly drive anywhere in Blue Ridge. I live above my shop. I walk to Tom's Grocery when I need something. There isn't much opportunity to let Sadie drive, and an idea strikes me.

"William," I sternly say his name that afternoon when I call him. I'm all business. This call has nothing to do with the fact he touched me in ways I've never been touched. Or the fact I wanted him to hold me all night instead of leaving me in my empty bed still riddled with the shock of my business being robbed or the fact Billy went down on me and it's all I can think about.

With what we did, what *he* did to me, I should have returned the favor. I should have at least offered, but he curled up behind me after returning my underwear, pressed me to my side, and held onto me until I drifted off to sleep. Safe in his arms.

Nothing is going to happen to you. Or Sadie. I'm here.

"Roxie," he teases in return, his voice sultry and deep. "You're rather formal this afternoon." Am I? Isn't this how we are with one another? Isn't this casual like he suggested?

"I wanted to thank you for handling the sheriff last night and checking on Sadie." His concern for her is sweet. "Did you happen to notice if she looked sick last night?"

"Sick? Not exactly." He clears his throat. "Why? Is she sick today?"

"No. No, nothing's wrong." I pause, regaining my focus for the call. "She just felt warm, but she went to school. On that note, I have an idea. How would you feel about driving lessons?"

Billy chuckles. "Depends on what I'm driving."

My God he has a one-track mind, but so have I for most of the morning.

"I meant…giving Sadie lessons. She has her driver's permit, but she needs practice hours. I thought maybe you could drive her around the area or, rather, let her drive you around the area."

"Why can't you drive her?" Billy states without accusation, but I'm defensive when I answer.

"I thought it would be another way for you two to bond." I pause after I speak. Why am I trying to push Billy and Sadie together? In fact, I want to set some better boundaries for us. He can't just keep popping in like he does, unexpectedly showing up and then sticking around for dinner. We need a schedule, structure, like things used to be for Sadie.

"No, it's fine. I'd like to talk to Sadie about something anyway."

"Like what?" I immediately ask, curious.

"Nothing much. Father-daughter stuff."

My breath hitches. Billy could still seek custody of his daughter. He wants to be responsible for her in more ways than just a financial statement. What if he wants her to live with him? Will he make me see less of her? And then what if…and I'm back to considering him marrying someone. Sadie would have a stepmother. Not that there's anything wrong with stepmothers, but I just…I don't know what I just.

I've sought a child advocate for Sadie. Someone who knows her rights and can protect her. Sadie says she wants to remain living with me, and the advocate tries to assure me it's a possibility a judge might consider based on Sadie's age and circumstances. Sadie hardly knows Billy, and she's at an age where she can make her own decisions. I have no doubt she'll say she wants to stay with me, and Billy will be the one with a visitation schedule, if we get to that point. He promised we'd work it out. We just need to put it into better practice in our future.

I need to file an insurance claim for the robbery and change the locks for extra protection. For a moment, June Barne suggested Grace robbed the place, and I laughed. There isn't a criminal bone in Grace's body, and besides, I was able to provide an alibi for her. Grace had a date. Single mother of five, a date is a rare opportunity, one I strongly encouraged after Grace enjoyed herself so much at the Oktoberfest.

"What if he asks me about children?"

"Don't lie but don't offer details. This night should be about you. Stick to what you know."

"All I know are my kids." Grace chuckled but sadness touched her eyes. She wouldn't trade one moment with them, but she wouldn't mind a little adult time either.

I don't know why I was offering her dating advice. I didn't date. I had no advice to offer.

"It's fine," Billy says, breaking into my meandering thoughts. "I'd love to give Sadie driving time, but I'll have to come over around four. I have plans tonight."

"I…" I don't get to finish my thought when Billy hangs up. *What plans does he have?* Although it's none of my business. Popping in at four or even warning me he'll be coming over is an example of what I mean. Billy can't come and go as he pleases. It isn't fair to Sadie, and a small part of me realizes it isn't fair to me. *And what does he mean he has plans?*

If Billy Harrington needs to accommodate for his dates, he can leave us off his calendar.

Chapter 21
Lessons in Driving and Other Means of Navigation.

[Billy]

"I didn't steal the money from Aunt Roxie," Sadie whines, her eyes shifting to me.

"Keep your eyes on the road," I snap, tempted to reach for the steering wheel. These backroads are narrow, and once they shift into switchbacks, there's no shoulder, just a ditch. It isn't ideal for driving lessons, but this is where I learned, and a strange swelling in my chest happens as I realize I'm now teaching my daughter on these same roads.

What's also not ideal is discussing what I discovered last night.

"I checked on you, only you weren't in bed." I've already told Sadie my version of the break-in and what I discovered when I went to her room—she was missing.

"I already told you, it wasn't me."

"Then tell me where you were, and I'll drop it."

"I told you I was at Julianne's house."

I haven't heard of this mysterious Julianne who doesn't seem to have a last name. Not that I know all the who's who in Sadie's life, but I'm paying attention when she talks. I'm listening for the mention of others like Heather Quinton, the girl who keeps messing with Sadie by calling her Violet. If I didn't think it would stir up trouble, I'd march myself over to Hestia's house and tell her to keep her bitch daughter away from mine but approaching Hestia would be asking for it. I've already been there once, and it was one too many times. I was too easy for her tastes. Unmarried and uncomplicated, she likes a bit more challenge. It's quite sad. We have our own desperate housewife of Blue Ridge without her being someone's wife.

"So if I call this Julianne without a last name, and ask her if you were at her house, she'll tell me you were there?" Two thoughts occur to me simultaneously.

A friend covering for you as a teen is one of the oldest tricks in the book.

Accusing her and suggesting I call said friend makes me sound like my mother.

Dear God, I've become Elaina Harrington.

So if I call Griffin Duncan's mother to confirm you spent the night there last night, she's going to tell me you did? That woman could smell a lie frying the next county over, and she caught me half a dozen times trying to cook them up.

I decide to change tactics. "You know, if you did steal the money, you could tell me. Tell me why."

Sadie cranes her neck in my direction, swerving the truck with the movement.

"Eyes," I bark, and Sadie rights the tires before we veer into the ditch. My heart races in my chest. I'm clutching the seat belt near my throat.

"Do you need something? I can buy it for you. Just ask me. We can talk about it."

Sadie's eyes close for a second, and then she snaps them open before I speak. Her eyes shift sideways and back to the windshield. "I didn't steal the money." Her teeth clench, and I want to believe her. Deep down, I really want to trust she's telling the truth.

"Then tell me where you were."

She doesn't answer, but there's no lying about her absence. When I checked on her, she wasn't in her bed. Another old trick—making the bed with pillows to look slept in, although I don't know how Roxie could miss it.

Did Sadie look sick to you?

"Wherever you were, you were lucky to be back before Roxie came upstairs."

"Why? What happened?" Sadie's tone shifts to concern for her aunt, the one person I'd hope she doesn't lie to, yet she must.

"She was robbed, remember?" I state, reminding her of the reason for this awkward conversation. "Plus, she was shaken and worried about you. She thought you were sick."

Silence fills my truck as Sadie continues down the winding road.

"I used that trick a time or two myself. The old pillows lining the bed one."

"What?" Sadie doesn't dare look at me, but her fingers tighten on the wheel. "Why?"

I'm not about to tell my child the shenanigans I pulled, sneaking off to meet Rachel or catching rides with Mati when she snuck off with Denton a time or two. I need Sadie to know I'm concerned here. "I covered for you. Roxie doesn't know what I saw."

Sadie's head quickly turns in my direction, her mouth agape before she turns back to the road.

"I don't want to be lying to your aunt, though. It's not a good way to start a relationship."

"Are you and my aunt in a relationship?" she teases, her tone full of sarcasm.

"We're all in a relationship," I admit. "The three of us. But I don't want one based on secrets or deception. I think I've been deceived enough."

The truck falls quiet after that, and I feel a little bad. It isn't Sadie's fault I didn't know about her. I blame Trixie, and I've been damn near pissed off some nights thinking about all I've missed with my daughter. The thought hits me hard once again.

"Hey, up here, let's turn around. I know a place we should go." Then I grit my teeth as Sadie learns the art of a three-point turn.

+ + +

"Stick your butt out a little bit. Then run on your toes," I suggest, a smile filling my voice.

157

"I feel ridiculous," Sadie mutters, but she holds the ball upright before her, tiptoes to the line and then lowers to release it. The ball heads straight for the gutter. Again. "Dammit."

"Hey," I murmur. "Keep it clean."

Sadie turns to face me while her bowling ball disappears down the lane, glaring at me like how dare I make such a suggestion.

"I don't know why you're fucking looking at me like that," I say because I can't help myself. I also can't contain my laughter and neither does she. When Sadie laughs, her face lights up like motherfucking sunshine on the brightest day, and my chest does that strange gripping thing like I have indigestion. She's beautiful despite the darkness of her features.

"You're up," she says, walking toward me, and I head for the ball pit. When we pulled up before the neon-lit Bing-Bowl sign, Sadie stared at the dark, low building. Her arms hugged the steering wheel.

"I've never been bowling," she said, and I almost slipped off the passenger seat.

"Sacrilege," I stated with a grin because deep down I was thrilled to share a first with my girl.

My girl. My daughter.

Bing-Bowl is owned by one of the less involved Rebel's Edge members, although the joint is no less seedy looking. It's located outside of town by a few miles.

"Don't be telling your aunt I brought you here," I warned her before we entered.

"So much for a relationship with secrets," she jests, but I know Roxie might have a fit over the clientele. I've been here on several occasions, knowing no one is going to make a big deal of it. After all, I'm James Harrington's kid brother, and although most motorcycle clubs require you to separate from your blood family, the Rebels aren't one-percenters like that. James decided on his own to pull away from us.

Sadie takes a seat on the plastic bench, and I pick up my ball. Ironically, it's blue like my own balls have been since last night with Roxanne, but hot damn was she sweet once she gave in to me. The hum to her voice has been a silent soundtrack in my head all day, and every time I think of her, I have an issue. Her taste on my tongue lingered, and I want another swipe at her. I want more of her, and the thought hits me hard, but not as hard as I grow thinking about her. I need to get myself under control before I embarrass myself in front of my daughter.

However, Sadie isn't helping either as she keeps bring up the possibility of Roxanne and I dating. You like her, right? Of course, I like her. She's Sadie's aunt. But the lying liar who lies inside me knows it's more than that.

I do like Roxanne.

I like how she fights me, but I love when she gives in. Like last night.

And dammit, I have a problem again.

Baseball. Butterscotch. Bitter beer. Any thought to help me settle down.

"Hiya, Billy." A sugar-sweet voice says my name, and my spine shivers like someone scraped their nails down a chalkboard. Instead, hard-on softener. Slowly, I turn to face Kristy Moseley. *Shit.* "Been a long time, baby." She struggles to take the two steps down to the platform in her high heels and then shuffles awkwardly toward me. She shouldn't have those shoes on this wood floor, not to mention, she can hardly walk in the height, but I'm not about to reprimand her. I don't want anything to do with her and my eyes shift to Sadie, who's watching Kristy approach me with rapt attention.

Kristy reaches me and then reaches for me, her hand almost connecting with my chest, but I'm quick to catch her wrist.

"Whatcha up to this evening?" Kristy's voice rises, and I know she's been drinking. It's how we ended up together the first and only time. Drinking…and bowling.

"I'm bowling," I state the obvious, and my eyes drift to Sadie once again, who has crossed her arms over her chest and glares at the back of Kristy. Kristy turns to look over her shoulder, peering down at Sadie.

"Whatcha looking at, honey? He's too old for you."

"Don't insult me." Sadie smirks, and I see the expression of the girl when we first met, when she thought I was hitting on her, and I had no idea who she was. Funny how time has changed, and passed, and I wouldn't go back. Wouldn't go back to life without knowing Sadie.

I hold my breath, knowing what's about to come next from Sadie. *He's my dad.*

But something stops her, her mouth hanging open and her eyes widening as she looks at me. She doesn't say anything. An eyebrow tips, and I realize she's waiting for me to explain who she is.

"This is Roxanne's niece, Sadie." My heart races in my chest, and I watch as the expression on Sadie's face morphs from teasing to blank. *Why can't I say it?* Why can't I just introduce her? *She's my daughter,* my head screams, but I remind myself I'm waiting to tell my family first.

"Who's Roxanne?" Kristy turns back to me, and her eyes spark. Oh shit, I hate jealous women especially those who have nothing to be jealous of. Which isn't exactly true, because it's fucking adorable on Roxie that she's all hot and bothered about some mystery woman she thinks I took against a wall. But I mean, this woman, the Kristy kind, who I don't owe any explanation to.

"The owner of BookEnds. The bookstore across the street from the pub."

"You hate that woman." Kristy stammers in disbelief, and my eyes shoot over to Sadie, whose brows rise in question.

"I don't hate her." I speak to Sadie while I direct my answer to Kristy. Kristy cups my chin and turns my head to face her.

"Bookstore, you say? Heard you've been spending a lot of time over there lately." Kristy's drunk eyes narrow on me, but like I said, I don't owe her anything. I tug my face away from her and take a step back.

"If you'll excuse us, I'd like to get back to my date." I wink at Sadie as I approach the seat and sit. "You're up."

Sadie stands, brushing past Kristy in a way I've witnessed from my little sister—a defiant brush-off. She picks up her ball, which happens to be highlighter yellow, and steps up to the line. The ball heads straight down the middle with a little gusto and knocks down the first pin, which then takes down the rest of them. *Strike.*

"You did it!" I holler, giving a one hand clap. Sadie twirls on one foot, kicking out her other behind her, and then she takes a bow.

"Since when do you date teenagers?" Kristy snaps.

"It was a figure of speech, Kristy. I'm not dating a teenager." *She's my daughter.*

"Since when do you date period, Billy Harrington?" Kristy adds.

"Since he started dating my aunt Roxie. The bookstore owner."

Sweet Jesus. Sadie has no idea what she's saying or doing or the shitstorm she's brewing, but she looks even more pleased with herself than the strike she bowled.

"I don't believe it," Kristy mutters, her gaze on me while her arms cross over her voluptuous chest which I unfortunately know is fake.

"Oh, believe. Billy is practically living with us because he's over so much," Sadie interjects.

"What?" Kristy screeches.

Oh. *My. God.* This kid. She's stirring up the pot well and good now. I leap up from the seat and step between Sadie and Kristy, putting my back to Kristy.

"Sadie," I hiss. "Leave it." My eyes widen in warning, but there's a playful gleam to Sadie's eyes. She's enjoying this little display of female dominance and cat scratching.

"Well, I won't be seeing you around, Billy Harrington, so don't be looking for me," Kristy states, and I don't have to turn to know Kristy's attempting to stomp away without much success. Sadie covers her mouth to stifle a giggle.

"You're up…Billy," Sadie drawls, and for a moment, I almost thought she'd call me dad. Standing there with my heart racing, Sadie brushes past me, and I realize I might just want her to call me the label.

You don't deserve it, my head reminds me as I'm not acknowledging Sadie's relationship to me either.

I take my turn, watching my ball go too far to the left and only knock down a pin or two in the corner. As I return to the bench, a young guy dressed in black with matching midnight hair hanging into his eyes but shaved up the back walks past our seats.

"Hey, Sadie," he says, tipping his head at her as he continues past.

"Hi…Christian." Sadie shifts to follow his gait and lifts a hand too late for him to notice she waved. Suddenly, my blood boils, especially when Sadie turns back to the lane, and her cheeks are a deep pink.

"Who was that?" I can't contain the growl in my throat.

"That's Christian Grady."

Grady. *Grady.* Grady. How do I know that name?

"He's in my school. I mean, in my class. Well, he's in one of my classes. He's in my grade." Sadie giggles, then covers her mouth and closes her eyes. She sits up straighter and takes a deep breath. Then she stands for her turn. I don't even notice her bowl before she plops down next to me. I'm still concentrating on the Grady name.

"So, is that the type of woman you're interested in?" Sadie nods in the general direction of Kristy's exit. I don't need to turn to see if Kristy is still watching me. I can feel her eyes tossing daggers at the back of my head.

"If I was, you just" —*cockblocked me*—"buzzkilled it."

Sadie shakes her head as if she can read my thoughts. "So you like *her*?"

"Actually, she's not my type."

"Hiya Billy," Sadie mocks, and I laugh at the imitation. "That's not your type?" She assesses me a moment, taking in my dark jeans and the lighter denim shirt with pearl buttons. "Then what is your type?" *Oh boy, here we go again.*

"You know, that little stunt you pulled, saying I'm dating your aunt, that's gonna get around town from a woman like Kristy. It's called gossip." I tip up an eyebrow, and the "Rumors" song comes to mind. I'm not half as upset as I should be, though. It wouldn't feel wrong to have people thinking I'm with Roxanne, the bookstore owner.

"Rumors are going to spread anyway because you're at a seedy bowling alley with an underage kid." Sadie crooks up the edge of her lips. No one said she was stupid.

"You're my kid," I state without thought.

"Tell anybody that yet?" Sadie has me pinned, and the question bowls me over because she knows I haven't. My facial expression gives it away, and it must have been what she saw before she *didn't* expose me to Kristy.

"I want to tell my family first," I remind her, but Sadie tips her chin like she doesn't believe me. "Thanksgiving actually. I'd like to invite you and Roxie to dinner at my parents' house."

The words tumble out before I realize what I'm saying, and I watch as Sadie's face morphs from disbelief to concern. "Are you sure that will be a good time to expose us?"

It's not exposure. She isn't a dirty little secret. I just want to do the right thing at the right time and be surrounded by family. So my dad won't go apeshit. So my mom won't overreact. They can save their responses for the day after.

"It will be perfect." However, I already know it won't. I can already picture the disappointment on my father's face and the questioning glare from my mother. *How could something like this happen?* Elaina's voice grates through my thoughts although she doesn't want the semantics of sex.

How could you divorce that sweet girl? Did you fool around with someone else?

Always my fault.

They'll never accept that I didn't know about Sadie, and I'm just as upset that it took sixteen years and a few months to discover the truth myself.

"Have you asked Roxie?" Sadie questions, her voice dropping.

"I thought I'd ask you first. Want to come to Thanksgiving dinner and meet the rest of your family?"

Family, I watch the word silently form on Sadie's lip.

"Sure." She shrugs as she chews her lip.

"Now, I have a question. Who is he?" I tip my head back, insinuating the kid who walked past us. "Hi...Christian," I imitate her and add a giggle for emphasis. "Is he your type?"

Sadie smacks my shoulder. "Nooooo," she drags out, but her eyes search over my head. He's back there, and he better fucking notice her.

Wait.

Halt.

Rewind.

He better *not* fucking notice her. She's too young to date, and I don't want her dating any Christian Grady character. It sounds like that dude from those hot books made into movies and…

"Oh, hell no," I mutter aloud. "Bear Grady's son?" I twist in my seat to look over my shoulder, and sure enough, Bear Grady is sitting at the bar while his kid picks up a tray of drinks. He's way too young to serve alcohol, but this place doesn't exactly follow the rules, especially as his dad is the owner and a member of Rebel's Edge. "No way, Sadie. Roxie will freak out."

For a moment, I'm almost excited at the possibility, but then I turn back to Sadie, her face horrified.

"I mean, I don't think Roxie will approve." I lower my voice and tamper my enthusiasm because deep down inside, I'm the one disapproving. No dating. Not at sixteen. Not Christian Grady. Not any boy who will ever do anything to you like I've done to women. I shudder with the thought.

Oh God, I won't survive fatherhood.

Chapter 22
Panic and Other Modes of Anxiety

[Roxanne]

"Where the hell have you been?" I screech, standing from the kitchen table where I've been sitting for the last hour calling everyone I know who might know Sadie. Hospitals were next on my list as my thoughts raced to a car crash during her driving lesson.

Sadie looks up at Billy, who stands behind her, and he has the decency to look chagrined. It's been hours since he took her for a driving lesson, and neither one of them has answered their phones during that time.

"We lost track of time," Billy offers, but my eyes leap to Sadie.

"Are you okay? Did something happen?" I scan her body for evidence of anything amiss. I'm overreacting, especially when I see Billy's hand come to Sadie's shoulder.

"It was amazing," Sadie says to me, and the moment her face lights up, relief should wash through me. Instead, I'm filled with jealousy and additional anger.

"And neither of you thought to call and tell me about your amazing time? Or the fact it would take amazingly long? I thought you had plans," I snap at Billy, recalling my earlier thoughts of him having a date. Did he take Sadie to meet someone? Did he take her on a date with his date? Has he told someone about her, how he's her father?

"I was driving," Sadie says, lowering her voice and her eyes. "And I shouldn't be on the phone and driving, right?"

She's not telling me something. They couldn't have possibly driven for five fucking hours!

"Do you have homework?" I bark. Sadie's eyes narrow at me a moment.

"I'm going to take a shower." She turns to Billy. "Thank you for tonight."

She doesn't say for what before she stalks off down the hall to her room.

"What's this about?" Billy asks, stepping up to me and reaching for my shoulders, but I shrug him off.

"Five hours, William. Five. Hours. No call. If you wanted to take her on a date with your date, couldn't you have at least told me, so I'd be prepared for her not to come home. I mean, I made dinner." I wave at the meal still sitting on the stove. "And then, I closed the store, thinking you might have kidnapped her or worse, and I—"

"You what?" Billy barks, and then adds, "Lower your voice." His eyes drift to the hallway, and then he reaches for my shoulders once again.

"Don't touch me. If you just spent the evening with another woman, you do not get to touch me."

Billy's eyes widen in shock as his hands drop to his side. Then he brushes his palm up his throat and over the scruff on his chin.

"You're a piece of work, Roxie." He steps back, turns for the door, and then opens it.

"You do not get to walk away," I snap, taking a step after him. "I need an explanation."

Billy stops, turns back to me, and grabs my wrist, tugging me to the door. "I'm not arguing with you inside where Sadie can hear your crazy."

I willingly follow him, hit by the sudden coolness of the night. It's the middle of November, and the air smells of winter. I wrap my arms around myself.

"First of all..." I begin, but Billy turns to me, raising a finger in my face.

"First of all, I would never, *ever* kidnap Sadie. That's low, even for you, Roxanne. Of all the things to say to me, that's the worst accusation." Calling me by my full name pulls me up short, and I open my mouth to speak. He's right. Accusing him of kidnapping is overboard.

"Secondly, assuming I went on a date, *and took my kid*, is another low blow." This one I have to disagree with, and my mouth pops open again.

"And finally, I'll have you know, your niece in there played gossip fairy tonight and told one of the biggest mouths in this town that I'm dating you."

"She…" My mouth falls open and then clamps shut. *She what?*

"So before you accuse me of dating, let it be known, you and I are apparently dating. And since that's established, I'm going to assume…because assumptions seem to be your thing…that you're jealous I might have gone on a date that I didn't go on, and I fucking hate how that makes me feel a little smug and little like *hey, Billy, she might actually like you after all.*" He isn't actually wrong in his thought process. I do like him. And I'm all kinds of twisted up about that.

Billy stands straighter, removing his pointing finger from my face and crossing his arms. His eyes drift down my body and then widen. He shrugs off his jacket and slips it over my shoulders, pulling the front tight over my chest.

"Where's your coat?" he mutters, knowing he's the one who pulled me out here on the landing.

"Where have you been?"

Billy tilts his head to the side, and those bark-brown eyes sparkle. "What's this really about, darlin'?" The endearment makes my stomach flip, and I wish it would stop flipping every time he speaks to me in that tone.

"I…I thought something happened. To both of you. I envisioned an accident, and you were both…and she's all I have…and I can't lose her…" I hiccup, fighting back the sob. Suddenly, I'm in Billy's arms, my own crushed between us.

"Nothing happened, baby. We went bowling. I'm sorry you worried, and I'm sorry we didn't call. We were having so much fun, and I didn't think."

"You didn't think," I repeat, confirming my upset. Billy inhales a deep breath and then exhales, and I follow suit, drawing in the scent of him and blowing it back out to melt a little more against him.

"Hold onto me, Roxie," he murmurs near my ear, reminiscent of last night after the robbery. I slip my arms free of his jacket and slip them around his waist. He kisses my neck and then rubs his nose around the shell of my ear.

"Do you really think I'd kidnap her?" Billy whispers, not pulling back from me or allowing me to lean away.

"No. I'm sorry I said that. I'm…I'm a little worked up."

Billy chuckles against my skin, and he skims my ear again before kissing my jaw.

"Would you be jealous if I went on a date?"

"You said you didn't go on a date." Suddenly, I'm trying to tug out of his hold, but he holds me tighter.

"What is this obsession of yours with me and dates and women and brick walls?" He chuckles at the list, and my mouth pops open, but he continues.

"Let me be clear, *again*. I didn't go on a date. I don't *do* dates or multiple women and not some woman against a wall. Assumptions, Roxie. You're making them, a lot of them, about me, and it's getting tiresome."

"But your reputation…" My voice drifts as I realize what I'm saying, accusing him of having a bad reputation.

"People believe what they want to believe, but I'm being straight with you, so can we just temper the attitude down a bit. I'm not dating someone, marrying someone, or anything else with anyone else but you." He takes a deep breath. "Is there something more here I'm missing?"

I don't answer him—because how do I explain myself. My curiosity as to why I wasn't good enough for him sounds silly even to me. I'm more than enough, but still wonder why I was the only one he didn't hit on before, and if we're only in this position now because of Sadie.

"When I was married to Rachel, one of the issues we had was I didn't see the bigger picture, and she wasn't always honest with me." His voice drops quiet and sad. "And I don't want to ever be in that position again, where I'm not seeing what I should have seen, where I don't know someone's feelings."

I'm about to retort then why do you sleep around when it hits me— if he does sleep around, he doesn't have to understand someone's feelings. He can keep one night separate from something deeper, something emotional.

I still haven't responded, so he takes another deep breath, and says, "So for shits and giggles, let's say I did go on a date. Would you be jealous?"

Yes. "No. You can do what you want," I say, struggling in his arms again. Just because he did what he did to me last night and made me think of him as an us all day doesn't mean I have a right to him. It also means he doesn't have a right to me and my heart if he wants to sleep around.

"Really?" Billy pulls back and stares at my eyes. "Because I'd be jealous if you went on a date." He holds my gaze for a long minute, letting those words settle between us. Then he adds, "Sadie and I were talking while she drove, and once we'd gone far enough out of town, I didn't want to come back. She was opening up to me, and I didn't want to disrupt the moment."

I sigh, my shoulders falling. "I'm sorry I overreacted. I want you to get to know one another. It's important to spend time together. I just…I worried, and my mind went to the extreme. Billy, I can't lose anyone else important to me. There aren't many people left."

His eyes widen. "Are you saying I'm important to you?" The corner of his lip crooks upward, but when I don't answer, he adds, "You thought we were dead." His statement rings like a fact, concern filling his voice as he waits for confirmation of my wayward thoughts.

"I just…I can't lose Sadie. And the way her mother died." My breath heaves. I leave the unsaid hanging between us. "She's all I have, Billy. She's the only family I have left." I look up at him, pleading for him to understand. I'm essentially an orphan, like my niece, and I don't want to be alone. I don't want to be the one left behind

"She's not going anywhere. She's safe with me," Billy states, tugging me back to him. "And so are you. Quit this crazy notion of me dating or marrying or whatevering with other women. You're important to me." He pauses as his eyes widen, and he quickly clarifies. "Because of Sadie. You're just as important to her as she is to you. I would never separate the two of you."

I nod, a silent show of gratitude and relief.

"Now, let's get back to those plans you questioned me about. See, I was really hoping to spend more time kissing you." His voice drops, and his face lowers. His forehead coming to mine. "Maybe repeating a few things from last night and adding a few more things to the mix." He's teasing me with his suggestion.

"Is that your best pick-up line?" I ask, snuggling against him as my bare arms are cold. He slips my arms from his waist and tucks them back into his jacket, tugging the material to wrap around me.

"Is it working?" His arms return around my body as he leans against the railing of the landing. I stand between his spread thighs with my arms inside his warm jacket. It smells like him. Cloves and spice and everything manly nice. I shrug at his question, and he chuckles, the tension and seriousness gone for a second.

"Seeing as I'm officially dating you, according to my daughter, I'd say more kissing is a start."

"And how does it end?" I whisper, concerned that more kissing might lead to a point of no return, at least for me. He wants me to give up my notion of him being a player, but I'm struggling to let go of what I've seen even if I know I can't change the past.

"How do you want it to end?" Billy whispers, but I can't tell him I don't want it to end. Whatever we're doing, I don't want it to stop because that means it *will* end, and I don't think my heart can handle it. My body certainly doesn't want it to end. My engine is revving, ready to start the race, but not looking to speed across any finish line because once we do, once we stop, it's going to be crash and burn for me.

My thoughts scatter when his hand wraps around the nape of my neck and his mouth takes mine, slow and tender. He draws out the kiss, tugging at my bottom lip and quickly returning to full coverage. He moves over mine as he's meant to kiss me like this. As if this is the start and the finish all rolled into one. He pulls back after a lingering press.

"I'm sorry we worried you tonight. I'm sorry *I* made you worry." His head tips back, gazing up at the sky. "I understand a little of your concern. It's like I have opposite-fear or fear of missing out or something." He chuckles, realizing he isn't explaining himself well, and I smile up at him. His voice lowers again. "I've already missed out on so much of her life."

"You'll have the rest of her life, Billy. Theresa won't." It's difficult to say as well as accept, but the truth is, Theresa will never see Sadie graduate, go to college, fall in love, get married, work a job, or any other thing. While Billy missed the first sixteen years, he'll have the next fifty-six plus. Theresa will have nothing.

"I'm sorry she died," Billy whispers into the night. "But I'm angry with her. Angry that she never told me I'm a father to an amazing kid."

Amazing mutters through my head.

"So, you took her bowling?" I question to lighten the mood.

"She says she's never been. What kind of sacrilege is that? Who hasn't been bowling as a kid?"

"I've told you. Theresa had schedules and timelines, and fun wasn't on the list."

"You know, I hate to say it, Roxie, but Sadie sounds like she's better off with you."

My heart aches. I loved my sister. She was a wonderful mother in her own way, but Billy's sentiment has crossed my mind a time or two. *When has Sadie been a child?*

"Where is there a bowling alley near here?" I ask, hoping to bring the subject back to something simple. I haven't been bowling in years myself.

"Just outside of town. Bing-Bowl." Billy cringes as he says the name, and I somehow know it might not have been the most reputable place. "I don't want you to worry. She never left my sight."

"You can't watch her every second. I understand that. Besides, she's not a toddler. She's a teen."

"Speaking of going places," Billy starts, his knuckles scratching up his throat and his hand cupping under his chin. "I invited Sadie to Thanksgiving at my parents'. Sadie *and you.* A real Harrington tradition. It's going to be swell," he mocks. I'm surprised by the invitation, which includes me, and I realize this will be the moment. The big reveal.

"Don't you think you should introduce Sadie to your family without me? They'll have questions and…" She's family, and you'll want to show her off *to your family*.

"I don't think I can do it without you, Roxanne." The honesty in his voice nearly floors me. "I need you to be there for me. For her." He clarifies again, and my head tips.

"I'm not sure that's such a good idea," I whisper, my eyes lowering for the collar of his shirt. I don't want to intrude although I also don't want to spend the holiday alone. It will be Sadie's and my first without Theresa.

"It's going to be amazing," he whispers, his voice deepening as he lowers his face to mine, forcing me to look up at him. There's a gleam to his eye as though he's teasing me, and then I recall Sadie saying she had an amazing time with him tonight.

"Amazing, huh?"

"Amazing," he repeats, and then his lips come to mine, and suddenly, I'm not certain we're still talking about Thanksgiving being the amazing thing.

Chapter 23
Sisterly Love

[Billy]

"You're dating Roxanne McAllister?" my sister says as she enters my office for her locker.

"Not exactly, it's just—"

"I thought you hated that woman." She pauses for a breath. "Then again, hate is a rather strong word. You strongly disliked her." Mati places a hand on her hip. She might be smaller for a Harrington, but she's fierce, and her current body language imitates our mother, who is a force. "Is this one of those enemies-to-lovers things?"

"We aren't lovers," I choke.

"You aren't enemies," Mati corrects, hiking up a brow in question.

"No, we're…friends." It isn't exactly how I'd describe us. She feels like more than a friend to me. Do friends kiss? Maybe friends with benefits. But do friends think about the other all the time? Do friends count down the minutes until friends can see each other? Do friends' fingers twitch to touch wet folds again or do their tongues swell wanting another taste? "How did you hear such a thing, anyway?"

"When did this happen?" Mati asks, ignoring my question with her own. Her back is to me as she hangs her jacket in her locker and grabs her black waitress apron. Most of the waitstaff slip their order pad into a back pocket or memorize the order, but Mati likes the apron for her things.

Mati coaches the girls' high school volleyball team for our alma mater, and she's in the thick of state playoffs, which is a big deal for her. I've told her to take some time off, but she assures me she wants to work.

What am I going to do all day? Think about the playoffs? Work is a distraction, she told me.

I can think of other things more productive as mindful distractions. Roxanne comes to mind immediately.

"Mati." I swallow, my throat dry. "Can I tell you something?"

My sister looks up at me with eyes that match mine. "You okay?"

I lower to my desk chair, not even realizing I've been standing this whole time.

"I need to tell you something, but I need you to swear to secrecy, Matilda." Her brows rise at the use of her full name. She slips into the chair before my desk. "Not Cora. Not your boys. Not even Denton. No one."

Mati crosses over her chest with a big X and then twists her fingers near the corner of her lip and tosses an imaginary key over her shoulder.

"Do you remember Theresa McAllister?"

Mati's brows pinch. "I…I don't think so."

"Trixie," I explain. "She went to school with Rachel and me." I don't often speak my ex-wife's name. It isn't that it's difficult, only that it's been a long time, and Rachel is long gone from the area.

"Didn't she have a crush on you or something?"

"Yeah, something like that." *I've always thought you were so hot, Billy.* Words I haven't recalled in sixteen plus years come back to me. She was here for a girls' weekend. I was newly divorced, feeling the sting of what I'd learned about my wife. *Ex-wife.*

"She was Roxanne McAllister's older sister. *Was,*" I emphasize. "Trixie died a few months ago."

Mati nods. "Oh, that's sad." It is sad, and Mati's sympathetic because of her husband's death and the recent loss of Denton's mother. "But I don't understand what this has to do with Roxanne and you suddenly being friends."

"Trixie had a daughter."

Mati continues to look at me with wide brown eyes.

"And she lives with Roxanne now."

Mati curls her lips, understanding the connection.

"And the girl…is mine."

Mati's brow wrinkles.

"Mine as in *you are mine*?" Her fist rises in the air. "William, that's disgusting. How old is she?"

For fuck's sake. "For fuck's sake, why does everyone think I'm dating a child? She's *sixteen*." I raise my hand when Mati's mouth pops open. "And I mean, she's mine as in…I'm her father." Darth Vader's voice rings through my head, and I want to laugh except I don't find humor at the moment as I watch my sister's face morph from disgust to confusion and then shock.

"She's your daughter?" Mati's voice is rising. "You have a kid?"

"She's a teenager, and I—"

"Hey, boss. Just checking in and—" Clyde's voice interrupts.

"He has a kid," Mati states, turning to Clyde while gripping one armrest of the chair and pointing at me as if I can't see her. So much for keeping a secret under lock and key.

"Matilda Brooks Harrington." I take on the tone of my mother.

Mati turns back to me, blinking. "I'm sorry." She twists back to Clyde. "I'm sorry. I…"

"I know," Clyde says, hugging the doorjamb. His big body looks ridiculous the way he's holding the frame, and his dark eyes shift from business to thoughtful. "It's crazy, right? But amazing."

Good God. There's that word again. Instantly, I think of the way Roxanne was looking up at me as I stood on the landing at the top of her back stairs. I felt like a teenager at the end of a date when you don't want to say good night; you just want to stand at that moment and hold on forever. Her mouth against mine was *amazing*, although I didn't spend the night as I had hoped.

"Mati," I murmur her name, shaking my head.

"I'm sorry," she says, eyes still wide as she stares back at me, confused and dazed, but smiling. "I didn't mean to blurt it out."

"It's a good thing Clyde already knows."

"Does Mama know?"

I shake my head.

"Clyde knows before the family?" Mati twists to Clyde. "No offense, Clyde."

"None taken." He dips his head, gazing back at my sister.

"He was here when Sadie told me," I explain.

"Sadie." Mati mulls over the name. "Sadie Harrington." Her smile grows as she states her name.

"Sadie McAllister," I correct, and my heart drops a little bit. I wonder if she'll change her name now that she knows the truth. I don't suppose I have the right to ask her to change it, but I really like the sound of Sadie Harrington.

"McAllister," Mati drags out the name. "So this is why Roxanne and you... Are you dating her to get close to the girl?" Mati's voice shifts, demanding and determined. "William Forrest—"

"And I'm out," Clyde mutters, double tapping his hands on the doorjamb and disappearing down the hall.

"I am doing no such thing with Roxanne." My voice rises, defending myself at the offense as I glare at my sister. Have I made a mistake by telling her everything? I love my sister, and I'm closest with her when it comes to the emotional stuff. I thought she'd be a good one to test my announcement on, but this is going all kinds of wrong. "Is this what you think of me?"

Holy fuck, people really think I'm a player. I mean, I am, to some extent, and I don't care what people think, but people might be shocked to learn Kristy is the last woman I was with, and it was back in May. Not that it's really anyone's damn business. Note, it's November, though. That's six months of celibacy, which is a record for me.

"Billy." Mati softens her tone. "Why don't you start at the beginning?"

For the next half hour, I tell my sister everything. About Trixie and the one-night stand. The reasons it happened. Rachel. Meeting Sadie. And Roxanne.

"And then I just kissed her, and I don't know…" My voice drifts as I rub up my throat and pause on my chin. I stare off toward my office door.

"Yeah, I know." Mati's voice sounds dreamy, and I turn back to her, finding her eyes on me. "It's a nice feeling, isn't it?" After her husband's death, my sister was sad, really sad, and I understand because they'd been married for twenty-something years and then he died in a car accident. A deer in the road. Recalling Mati's sadness makes me think of Sadie. She doesn't mention her mother much. How is she dealing with her death? It isn't the same as losing a spouse, and I get that. The relationship is different, but it must be even harder when you're still a kid and it's your parent. Roxanne told me how she lost her mother at roughly the same age.

Mati's sappy tone comes from finding Denton and having a second chance at an old love, but Sadie isn't really in that position either. It's a different kind of love with parents. She's not going to get a second chance. Then something niggles in my chest, squeezing at me, and I grip my shirt, hoping to loosen the pressure. Am I her second chance? I'm not her mother, but I am her father, the one she's never known existed.

"And wow, about Rachel," Mati says, interrupting my thoughts.

"Yeah. Look, you've already proven keeping a secret is difficult," I tease, nodding toward the door where she blurted out about Sadie to Clyde. "So I'd really appreciate it if you didn't tell anyone about Rachel."

Mati's brow pinches. "How long have you been keeping that quiet?"

"Since the day she left."

"Billy." The softening of my name and sympathy in my sister's tone force my eyes to prickle and sting. I blow out a breath and don't respond. It felt good to tell someone.

"So Roxie, huh?"

"It's the damnedest thing." My own lips curl, imitating my sister's grin.

"I'm so happy for you. For Sadie and you. For Sadie, Roxie, and you," Mati adds.

"Well, it's nothing official," I state. Leaning forward, I place my arms on my desk and cup my fingers together.

"But it could be." Mati's brow tweaks, and I stare at her.

"What do you mean?"

"Oh Billy, you really aren't that dense, are you? All that screwing around knock a screw loose?" She stands, continuing to chuckle as she knocks on my desk. But I must be that dense because I don't understand what she means about the three of us.

Mati pauses at the door and then turns back to me. "I really am happy for you. I can't wait for Thanksgiving."

A mischievous gleam comes to her eyes despite her kind words. She knows Thanksgiving is going to be a shitshow when my parents learn everything.

Chapter 24
Break-ins and Broken Gratitude

[Roxanne]

There'd been another break-in down the street from BookEnds.

"I swear it wasn't me," Sadie tells me as her breaths came ragged, and her face is pink and sweaty.

"Then where have you been?" I scold, as Sadie hadn't been in the apartment when I came up the stairs. I'd never had reason to doubt her, but I'd also assumed she remained home when I took the closing shift for the shop. From her attire, a black fleece and leggings plus running shoes, it's apparent she hasn't been home, but she did not tell me she was going anywhere.

"I went…out. For a run." Her hesitation adds to my suspicion, and I don't like that I'm suspicious. Sheriff Barne wanted to interview Sadie earlier in the evening, and I intervened, saying she was upstairs doing her homework.

"You certain of that?" June interrogated me.

"I have no reason to doubt Sadie," I said, but I level a glare at my niece now that I know something. I put myself on the line for her, and she better come clean if she did something she shouldn't have done.

When I call Billy to tell him about what happened, I express my concerns. "Do you think this is a cry for help? Is she trying to get my attention?"

"There's no one more attentive to her than you," he teases, but I'm not certain it was me she sought attention from.

"I don't like this feeling of doubting her. She's always been a good kid. I want to think this is just some phase. There's so much happening all at once for her, and then with Thanksgiving…" My voice drifts.

"What about Thanksgiving?" he asks.

"I just don't know if it's such a good idea to introduce her then. The holiday will be difficult. It's the first one without her mom."

"And what she needs most is family to surround her," he argues. Yes, but family she doesn't know and knew nothing of her? Plus, I'm her family.

"Look, I've gotta go. We just got a shipment. Stop worrying. Leave that to me." He chuckles before saying goodbye.

That was on Monday. Today is the holiday, and Sadie woke up telling me she wasn't feeling well.

"I have my period and a headache," she says, her voice groggy from sleep. I understood her discomfort, but I worry it's an excuse to back out of the big reveal. I make her call Billy and explain herself, stressing over the dichotomy of wanting to protect her and allowing her to handle things on her own. I'd already given her another lecture about trust: how I wanted to trust her until she proved me wrong. It was the kind of statement I imagined Theresa saying to Sadie, but it'd didn't feel right coming from me.

I didn't have anything in preparation for a feast. Thanksgiving was typically a casual affair with my sister, my niece, and me. We'd make a big breakfast, watch the parade on television, and then play board games. It was a rare day my sister let her hair down and revealed a spark of who she used to be. She'd laugh. She'd cheat at the games. She'd tease. My heart pinches with my own memories of Theresa in the past few years, and I'm melancholy. I can only imagine how Sadie feels, so when she says she's going to take a nap, I search for an open grocery store, and then an open restaurant with delivery service. When I don't find either in Blue Ridge, I resort to a journey down to Elton at the base of the mountain and return prepared to start a new tradition.

"Sadie," I call out, keeping my tone cheerful despite my internal mood. "Come help me make dinner."

I've bought a small turkey, potatoes, boxed stuffing mix, and fresh corn. When Sadie, doesn't come to the kitchen, I listen for the shower, which I don't hear running and then stand outside her bedroom door.

"Sadie," I whisper, pressing open the barrier she keeps closed, and my heart begins to race before her room is fully exposed. The bed is made, the shades are drawn, and Sadie is gone.

When I reach the one-hour mark, I can hardly breathe from the panic inside my chest. My ribs are crushing my insides, and I can't take a deep breath. I call Billy repeatedly, but there's no answer. I send him texts in hopes Sadie went to the Harrington's after all. Maybe she felt better. Maybe she changed her mind. Maybe she wanted to go without me.

When Billy doesn't respond after another hour, I call Grace.

"I'm so sorry to interrupt your holiday, but I can't find Sadie." The words bring a rush of tears, and through sobbing breaths, I try to explain how Sadie didn't feel well, and we cancelled going to the Harrington's.

"You should have come here," Grace sweetly admonishes. "Neither of you should be alone." Grace understands grief, and it becomes clear I'm not processing the day well myself.

"But what do I do?" I cry. "I don't know anyone she'd be friends with. She never mentions kids from school other than the issues she's having. I hate to call Hetty as she's upset about the break-in and I think she questions Sadie's involvement."

"What about Billy?"

"I've tried, but there's no answer."

"Are you alone?" Grace asks with concern. "You shouldn't be alone."

"I don't want to leave in case she returns. She told me she runs sometimes at night, but it's the middle of the day, and it's been two hours. I just don't know what to think."

"Don't think the worst," Grace warns. "Let me call Clyde. Maybe he can come over."

"I don't want to interrupt anyone else's holiday."

"Don't you worry, although that's a natural instinct as a parent. I'll call back soon."

I'm ready to renounce Grace's words, reminding her I'm not Sadie's mother, but for all practical purposes, I am now.

Within another fifteen minutes, Butch Marshall and June Barne rap at my door.

"Heard your girl is missing," June addresses me, wearing a suspicious smirk on her face.

"I'm not certain what you're doing here, but if you've come to throw more slander on Sadie, I don't need it right now." I'm a hot mess as I'm certain my face is pale, and my cheeks are stained from tears. I haven't felt this empty since I got the news of my sister's death, and seeing these officers is a reminder of that moment.

Miss McAllister, we regret to inform you...

"Grace Eton gave us a call," Butch explains. I should have called the sheriff myself.

"Well, I apologize for interrupting your holiday," I snark, sarcasm not a pretty sound from me.

"Do you suspect foul play? Kidnapping? She's a minor, and we can run an Amber alert."

"Like a missing person?" The concept hits me hard, and I lower to the chair in my kitchen. My hands tremble as I reach for my forehead, pressing at the dull ache that's been present all day.

"Do you think she ran away?" June asks, and my eyes leap up to hers, expecting judgment but instead finding sympathy.

"I don't think so," I answer, but taste the hesitation in my mouth, the bitterness of disbelief on my tongue. Could she have run away? Where would she go?

"Let me ask a few questions while Butch sends out the alert." June sits across from me, firing formulaic questions about when I last saw Sadie, what was she wearing, how was she feeling, and is anything missing from her room.

"I didn't investigate. When I opened the bedroom door and found her gone, I waited. I wanted to give her the benefit of the doubt that she'd decided to go running or out for a walk and forgot to leave me a note."

Butch glances over at me from his standing position by the back door. He's been typing information into a tablet in his hands. Then he locks eyes with June a minute. The unspoken conversation makes me feel like I've done something wrong. I waited too long to act. I didn't follow an order I should have taken. I wasn't Sadie's mother. I didn't know these things.

"Okay, the alert is out. We'll start some calls into the bus station, and Butch will go over to the train depot." Blue Ridge is known for its scenic route ride. I know nothing about other train services. "We'll also send out an all-call to the other local sheriff's departments. You say about two hours?" June confirms, and I nod. "She couldn't have gotten too far."

"Unless she went into the woods," Butch adds, and June swivels to narrow her eyes at her partner.

"Not helping," she warns, and Butch apologizes. As he hangs his head, we hear the thunderous rumble of feet coming up the steps, and my heart leaps with hope. I'm standing up, ready to envelop Sadie in my arms and then wring her neck for making me worry, until I see Billy help himself through the door.

"Billy?" Butch questions as the door opens with enough force it hits Butch behind it.

"Billy," June repeats addressing him as she stands, but Billy ignores them both, stepping up to me.

"What happened?" His hands grip my shoulders, and I struggle under the relief of his touch.

"Sadie…" My voice wavers. "I think she ran away." I fall against Billy or maybe he draws me into his chest. I don't really notice other than the comfort I find in his arms. His hand cups the back of my head while the other presses at my lower back. I listen to him speaking to June, catching up on details.

"Shouldn't we be out looking for her?"

"Where would you look?" June questions, and Billy sags against me.

"Anywhere," he snaps. "Do something."

"Now, Billy, no need to address me with that tone. I don't see how any of this is your concer—"

"She's my daughter," he states, his voice cracking with the announcement. I pull back to look at him, surprised by the abrupt admission. He isn't looking at June or Butch, though, but down at me as he repeats with more conviction. "She's my daughter."

His hands cup my cheek as his eyes hold mine. "We'll find her, okay? I promise. We'll find her." Tears well in my eyes once more as he pulls me to him, wrapping both arms around me, securing me to him, and I only wish I was half as confident as he was.

+ + +

My small apartment overflows with people. June. Grace. Clyde. Billy. And I need a breather. I could step outside, but I long for the warmth of my bed. I just want a minute of solitude. My head is full. My heart empty, so I step into my room.

Grace has been telling me for the past hour that I need some rest. It's two a.m., and there's no chance I could sleep. I'm afraid to close my eyes, but hopeful this might all be a dream. A bad nightmare.

I'm so sorry, Theresa, I send out the silent prayer as I curl to my side, tucking up my legs and laying my head on my pillow. My eyes close, but I won't sleep. Within minutes, the door to my room opens and shuts. Shoes thump to the floor, and a body curls up behind me. Without opening my eyes, I know who it is, and he presses his face into the back of my neck while his hand comes to the side of my thigh. A deep inhalation fills me with the scent of him. Cloves and spice and male.

We don't speak for a long minute.

"I want to help. Tell me what to do." The fear in his voice does nothing to settle my nerves.

"I just don't know, Billy." My voice sounds weak even to me, and his forehead presses at the back of my head.

"I need to do something. How can I help you?" His voice strains as if he's asking more for himself than for me. What can he do to feel better that involves me?

Taking a deep breath, I whisper, "Just hold me."

"Hold on to me, baby," he mutters into my neck, and I spin, tucking my face into his chest. His strong arms slip over me, his fingers delving into my hair to hold my head against him. I squirm as if I could get close enough to him, as if I could crawl under his skin and he could keep me safe. My arms snake around his waist, and my hands flatten on his shoulder blades.

You're safe with me. I don't want to consider all the horrible things running through my head, so I clutch at him instead.

"I'm here," he mutters reassuring me. "We'll find her." I nod but can't speak as fresh tears slowly shed.

Chapter 25
Hard Facts and Soft Hearts

[Billy]

"They found her."

The statement jolts Roxie and I upright at the same time as Grace repeats the message. *Thank fuck.*

"She's in Atlanta."

"Atlanta?" Roxie croaks, brushing back her hair and looking sexy in her sleep-deprived appearance. I can't say we fell asleep, just held onto each other as tightly as we could. Maybe I dozed. I don't know, but I'm foggy, and I'm sporting a semi, which isn't appropriate, but I can't help it when I'm this close to Roxie. Since our night together and our back steps make-out under the stars, we haven't kissed again. I hate to admit how I often I think about kissing her.

"Okay," I groggily croak. "Where do we go?"

"They're holding her at a district precinct. Let me get the exact address," Grace offers.

"A police station?" Roxie questions.

"Yeah, something about a cemetery. Sheriff Barne can give you the details."

Roxie looks at me over her shoulder. "A cemetery." Her head lowers, and without thought, I kiss her shoulder.

"Let's go get our girl." I swing my legs off the bed, slipping back into my boots before extending a hand to Roxie. "I'll drive," I say, holding my breath, waiting for Roxie to argue with me, but she doesn't. For the first time, she looks a little lost as she stares back at my offered hand. "Roxie, darlin'?"

The endearment snaps her out of wherever her thoughts took her, and she scoots off the bed without my help. In minutes, we're on our way to Atlanta, which is an hour away.

+ + +

"What were you thinking?" Roxie begins the second we enter the precinct and find Sadie sitting on a bench in a busy hallway. Roxie's verbal assault isn't what I expected from her after all the tears and fear. "Do you know how worried we were?"

Sadie doesn't answer. Her head remains lowered, her midnight hair a curtain.

"Why don't we get out of here, and Sadie can tell us all about it on the ride home?" I suggest, but Roxie isn't finished, gripping her crossbody bag like it's a lifeline, and Sadie doesn't move.

"A cemetery. What were you doing in a cemetery?" Roxie's voice grows louder, and my head turns in her direction.

"Roxanne," I warn, feeling strangely like I understand Sadie's motive better than Roxie.

"Sadie?" Roxie drones, her voice lowering on the questioning purr of her niece's name.

"I wanted to visit Mom."

Roxanne gasps, but I release a breath, realizing my thoughts were correct. Roxie's the one who told me the holidays could be difficult, so I don't understand why she's overreacting. This makes sense to me for some reason.

"I thought you ran away." Roxanne exhales in frustration. "I had to call the sheriff. This does not look good with the suspicion of you and those break-ins. Running away makes it look like you had a motive to steal from me and Hetty. How did you get down here?"

I don't think now is the time or place to discuss these things, but Sadie's head finally lifts, her hair cascading back from her face, which is pale and tear-stained, not a trace of the dark makeup exists. It hits me how young she looks—how young she is. Despite the body of a young woman, she's still only sixteen, and Roxie needs to settle down.

"A friend brought me."

"What friend?" Roxie snaps as she'd already told the sheriff she didn't know of any friends. Maybe that's another issue for Sadie. She doesn't have anyone else in town but Roxie and me. Well, she would have opened the door to a large family if she had only come to dinner this evening, or was that yesterday?

As silence ensues, I turn to Roxie. "Are you finished yet?" Her mouth gapes when she looks over at me, hands still tugging at her bag strap and expression full of ire. I ignore her demeaning glare and turn to Sadie.

"Sadie," I interject. "Are you hurt?"

She shakes her head, acknowledging my question.

"Are you done here?"

Her brows pinch in question.

"Did you see what you needed to see in Atlanta? Do what you needed to do?"

Her head tips, and she slowly nods, her eyes welling with liquid as she looks at me. Something in me breaks, like that root-clenching sensation gripping my chest is now a twig snapping off a tree. I can't handle her tears.

With hands on my hips, I tilt my head, motioning Sadie to come to me. To my surprise, she slowly stands, bypasses Roxie, and walks into the arms I open to draw her into me. With hands covering her face, she burrows into my chest as I wrap my limbs around her and lower to kiss her head.

"It's time to go, okay?" I say to her, and she nods against me. When I look up, Roxie's stunned face includes a gaping mouth, and a flabbergasted expression.

"How am I the bad guy?" she mutters, and then her eyes close. "I sounded like Theresa." I hold out a hand for her, but she ignores it and brushes past Sadie and me. With an arm still over Sadie's shoulder, I escort her out of the police station.

My truck is silent for a while, and I can't take the quiet tension. Finally, I clear my throat.

"Ready to speak?" I ask, glancing over at Sadie, whose head rests on the back of the seat. In my truck, we sit three across on the bench seating. Sadie closes her eyes, and I shift my gaze to Roxie, who looks like she has plenty to say but won't. Her elbow rests on the passenger door, propping up her head.

"My dad used to have a rule. No questions asked for twenty-four hours. I can uphold that rule, but we have the time now." The last word lingers, hinting that this would be a good time to talk.

Roxie looks over at me, but I don't take my eyes off the road.

"Is this like a house rule?" Sadie mumbles, her eyes still closed, and I chuckle.

"Something like that, yes."

Sadie remains quiet, but I want answers, and I can't seem to abide by the rule I just mentioned.

"Let's start with where you go each night."

Roxie's head swings back in my direction, and I feel the weight of her eyes on me.

"I go running…to the cemetery."

It's my turn to side-eye Sadie. The cemetery is outside of town by a few miles. It's the resting place of my grandparents, Giant's wife, and Mati's husband. "Why?"

"It makes me feel closer to Mom."

I have all kinds of questions, but Sadie stretches her arms forward and surprises Roxie and myself by giving an explanation. "Mom's buried so far away, and I feel like if I go to the cemetery here, she might hear me, see me, find me somehow." Her head lowers, and her hair falling over her face a second before she brushes strands behind her ear. "That's weird, right?"

"Why didn't you say anything?" Roxie asks, her tone returning to her more normal cadence while addressing her niece.

"I moved to Blue Ridge, and it didn't hit me until I'd been here a while that I didn't have any way to talk to Mom."

My eyes finally met Roxie's over Sadie's bent head.

"So in missing your mom, you ran away to Atlanta?" Roxie questions.

"It's Thanksgiving. The local cemetery wasn't enough." Sadie's voice is so small, that cracked feeling returns, and I'm ready to turn this truck around and pitch a tent in the Atlanta cemetery if it makes Sadie happy. Roxie reaches her arm over Sadie's shoulder, and her niece falls against her.

"I'm sorry I made you worry," Sadie says, and Roxie closes her eyes as she shakes her head. All is forgiven when her lips press to the top of Sadie's head.

"How did you get to Atlanta?" I ask, the one question remaining this evening.

"Christian gave me a ride."

Roxie's expression shifts to puzzled, and I take a deep breath.

"Christian Grady?" I question. Then another thought occurs to me. "Tell me you didn't ride a motorcycle down here."

Sadie doesn't answer, and Roxie pulls her tighter as she moans, "Oh Sadie, no."

With how her mother died, I didn't think Sadie would ride a motorcycle unless she had some kind of death wish. I've heard about these things. Putting one's self in harm's way to prove she's immortal or in hopes of joining those deceased. My stomach feels sick.

We don't speak anymore, each of us with heavy thoughts filling our heads, and Sadie eventually dozes against Roxie. I struggle to keep my emotions in check as I think about the mortality of both Sadie and Roxie and realize that the most important people in my life are sitting in this truck. I blink at the blurring road before me as horrible visions fill my head, removing them from my life. The void they would leave if they disappeared hurts and curiously, I question why it's taken so long for me to find them.

+ + +

Sadie wasn't a baby, and I certainly couldn't carry her up the back stairs, so she had to walk like a drunken sailor, stumbling into her room and collapsing on her bed. I laughed as she fell face-first.

"When did things get so mixed up?" Roxie stated, staring down at her niece.

"I don't think anything's mixed up. She's just missing her mom."

Roxie turns sad eyes on me, glancing at me like she'd forgotten I was in the room with her. She looks lost herself, and I want nothing more than to hold her again. Reaching under my chin, I scrub at it.

"It's late or rather super early, so would you mind if I stayed? I can sleep on the couch...I just...I don't want to be apart from her." *From either of you.* I didn't know how to process my feelings, which seem to be slowly catching up to me now that we are back in Roxanne's apartment. The thought of losing them both still haunts me hard, and my leaden feet couldn't carry me out of this place without a fight.

"Sure," Roxie says, exhaling, and for a brief second, that release of air sounds like relief. Did she want me to stay as well? Maybe I could stay in her room and hold her like I want, but when she heads to a linen closet and pulls out sheets and a blanket, I learn my desire will not be met.

"It's been a long night," she says, her voice weak as she works the sheet over the cushions. Her hands shake, and I reach for her forearm, stilling her frenetic movement.

"I can do this," I say, not certain if I'm assuring her I can make up the couch or I can be a father. I didn't react the way Roxie wanted in the police station. Perhaps, I was supposed to rant and yell and accuse like she did, but I'd been on the receiving end of such negative attention a time or two, and I didn't want to do that to Sadie. She didn't deserve it. Not yet.

Roxie turns tired eyes on me and nods. She's hardly spoken to me since we picked up Sadie.

"Well, good night then," she whispers, sweeping back her hair and then leaving me with too many thoughts in her living room.

Chapter 26
Misgivings

[Roxanne]

When I finally hit the bed, I should have slept. It has been nearly eighteen hours of panic and fear, and my body should have crashed, only my thoughts refuse to let me be.

What if I'd lost her? Theresa would never forgive me. Even from the grave, my sister would haunt me with my irresponsibility and lenient ways, cursing me for being too soft, too kind, too unstructured. My sister used to be that way until motherhood. Is this what I'm turning into? I recall how my heart raced and I rushed the police department, frantic to find Sadie and tug her to me, but then lost my composure once I saw her. Relief overwhelmed me but so did frustration.

She missed her mother.

It made sense. I missed mine when she passed. I still do, and it strikes at the oddest times. I understood the loneliness, the abandonment, the hole in her heart, yet I went berserk, forgetting myself as I laid into her.

And then Billy. Damn him.

Are you done? he asked of me and then held out his arms like the good parent. Good cop. Bad cop. I am not going to compete with him. I am not going to let him get off so easily. Parenting takes a united front. I've heard horror stories of dads who are always gifting items, taking expensive trips, and allowing kids anything while moms must play the other side of the coin: offering what kids need versus want, providing opportunity versus fancy vacations, and regulating manners. The separation in our roles weighs between us.

"Roxie?"

Go away, I want to snap, but I didn't. I lay there, my eyes closed, hoping he'll think I'm sleeping.

"Roxie, are you sleeping, or are you faking it, so I'll go away?"

I hate how he can read me.

"What do you want, William?" The barrier of his given name provides the formality I need to restore the balance between us. Forget the tender kisses. Forget the mind-blowing orgasm. Forget the small sweet gestures of his continued presence. He's gotten too close to me lately, and it's messing with my head. *And my heart.*

"I want to sleep with you." The quiet tone of his voice and the hesitant statement turn me from my side to look up at him over my shoulder. "I just…I want to hold you." He pauses, scratching under his chin like he does. "Tonight scared me a little bit."

I sit up, surprised by his admission. He appeared so rational. Driving to the police station, wrapping Sadie in his arms, and then diplomatically asking her questions in his truck, he was calm and collected while I was losing my cool, brewing like a pot of tea.

"You seemed so unaffected," I state, drawing my knees up to my chest. I'm wearing a mid-thigh flannel nightshirt, but the blankets cover me. Billy's sweater is no longer on his chest, and his T-shirt clings to his midsection. He's solid from what I know of him. With my eyes on his abdomen, he crawls up the bed next to me, making himself at home on his back. He tucks a hand behind his head, but the other slips around my backside, tugging at my hip. I lower to rest in the nook he's made for me.

"I was dying a little inside. That was intense," he admits. He twists his neck, so his lips brush my forehead. Something I'm noting about Billy is his need for physical contact when things turn tough. It happened earlier when he showed up along with the local sheriff. When he climbed behind me on my bed and held me, like he couldn't get me close enough. When he doesn't know what else to do in a situation, he offers up himself.

"I'm not sure what I'd do if I lost her now." He swallows, the movement of his throat near my forehead. He clears it, and continues, "I just found out I have her. My daughter. I don't want to go back to a time without her."

We should talk about the future. What's going to happen moving forward as we can't change the past. But not tonight. For now, I'm relieved Sadie is home and safe. She needs some additional support outside Billy and me, and we should talk about that option as well. But again, not tonight. Tonight, I need to relieve Billy of his worries, assure him that Sadie and I aren't going anywhere just like he's tried to assure me he has the same thought. We're a unit. Nothing will separate us. Nothing will separate the three of us.

My hand falls to his chest, flattening to coast the plains of his pecs. His nipples stand erect under the tight tee, and I pause with a fingertip on the short nub. Then I circle it. He sucks in a breath, his abs drawing tight. His hand still cups my shoulder, and I skim lower, my palm covering the slight bumps and bulges of muscle above his waistline. He's fit and firm, and I wonder what else is that way on him. My eyes drift lower, the evidence of his arousal present under his zipper. I pause, but my fingers twitch to discover him, distract myself from all other thoughts.

"Roxie." His voice croaks. "Whatcha doing?"

My eyes close, afraid he's read my mind, and I swallow the tightening in my throat when I admit, "I'm thinking about touching you. Comforting you."

His hand moves from behind his head, cupping my chin and tipping it so I look up at him.

"Comfort me however you please."

Before I can respond, his hand covers my cheek, and he's guiding my mouth to meet his. Our lips start slowly as his body shifts, pressing us front to front while we lie on our sides. Within seconds, the kiss deepens, and his body leans mine back, covering half of me as a leg slips over my thighs and his hand travels to a covered breast.

"You're fucking perfect," he mutters as he watches his hand cover me.

"I had a breast reduction," I quietly state. His head pops up, his eyes wide.

"Why?"

"I was…heavier when I was younger, and they were too large, almost annoying. I had them reduced a few years back."

Billy looks down at my chest and then curls up to his knees. He throws back the cover and lifts my nightshirt, fulling exposing me to him.

Staring at my chest, he speaks to them. "I'm sorry babies. She didn't mean it."

With a giggle, I reach out to push him away. "You're so immature," I say until his mouth latches onto me, and I fall back to the mattress. The warm cavern of his mouth takes as much of me in while his hand palms the remaining globe. He massages as his tongue laps around my nipple and then sucks at the stiff nub. My back arches, forcing me into his mouth.

"That feels so good," I whisper, uncertain when my comforting him turned into him turning me on. My hands slip into his hair, scrubbing over his head as he moves to the other breast and returns his attention in a similar manner. Licking while squeezing. Sucking and nipping the sharp peak. He pulls off with a pop and stares down at them once more before lowering to my midsection, kissing my skin as his hand travels faster than his mouth and slips into my underwear.

"Billy," I groan as tonight was supposed to be about him, not me. But when his fingers enter me on a rush, two at once, I forget all thoughts, arching once again. My thighs separate, and my mouth seeks his. He's driving me mad, working those digits in a manner my body responds to instantly. I don't want to come so quickly, but I can't seem to help myself. He's at the forefront of my daily fantasies, and it's easy to reach the edge when he's touching me.

"You come so quick." He isn't teasing me, just stating a fact.

"You do that to me," I admit, embarrassed by the truth. A smile breaks across his mouth.

"Only means more to come," he flirts, and I roll my eyes until his thumb flicks the sensitive nub and my eyes roll for a new reason. He knows how to play my body, and I don't want to think of all the practice he's had.

"How long's it been, Roxie?" he asks without finishing the full question.

"Three years," I admit. Three long, lonely years with only fingers and an occasional steamy book as my lover.

"No wonder it's so quick, darlin'. But I'll make up for lost time." He shifts, tugging my underwear off my legs and tossing them to the floor. Lowering his face, he's a man on a mission as his arms hold him over me, but then his face disappears between my thighs. Only his tongue touches me first, splitting me open and diving into my depths.

Sweet Jesus.

"You're delicious, darlin'." He parts me and enters me, and the thickness of the muscle in his mouth brings me to the edge again. My fingers comb into his hair, and my knees separate but lift.

"Billy," I warn as my hips begin to rock, rolling upward to draw him deeper into me with his tongue. He licks faster, his tongue curling, and the pressure along with the wetness stimulates another release. I bite the inside of my cheek to hold back the scream, remembering Sadie is down the hall dead asleep.

"Fuck, Roxie. I want inside you." He presses upward, tugging his T-shirt over his head and fumbles with the belt in his jeans. Quickly, he's unzipping and shimming down the denim to his knees. Then he pats his pockets and searches the nightstand for something.

"My wallet. I left it locked in the truck. I don't have a condom." He stares down at me, his eyes hesitant but pleading.

Do I want this? Can I do this? He's a player, and I know these things about him, but right now, I need him as much as he seems to need me. I want to be close to him, as close as I can be. I reach forward, my fingers wiggling.

"I swear on all things—on Sadie, my mother and the pub—that I'm clean. I haven't been with anyone in six months and never go without a condom. Not since Rachel." That was a long time ago. Sixteen years actually. I dismiss this awkward conversation, struggling with the inner turmoil, but my body is winning out.

"Just pull out or—" I don't finish as he tugs his legs out of his pants and boxers collectively and tosses the material to the floor. His lower half comes between my open legs, and he drags himself through the slickness he made on my swollen folds.

"I don't have to enter you," he says, watching where he rubs his head against my wet skin, and I whimper at the anticipation. "We can just play." His voice turns playful as he strokes himself against folds and stops at the precious nub. The seeping tip of him presses against me and then he drags himself upward.

"Uh," I groan, the sensation too much.

"Can I draw another one out of you?" he teases, working himself against my core, just outside of me, flirting with my clit enough to make me wild. My head rolls on the pillow. My fingers clutch at the sheets. He's rocking his hips forward but not entering me. Instead, his thickness rubs along my seam, coating him in wetness, allowing him to slip and slide, and make my legs shake with the possibility. I want him inside me.

"Billy," I hiss, begging for relief. He rushes into me with a firm thrust, and my head lifts from the pillow. My hands reach for his backside, the area I've often noted as hard and perfect but never knew how exquisite he was until I held those tight globes in my hand, forcing him to remain deep inside me.

"Darlin'," he warns with strained tension in his voice. He pulls back once and then slams forward again, and I break. My legs stiffen, and my back curls. My fingers dig into his ass as I clench around him, holding him as deep as I can and as tight as I can grip because I don't want to lose this connection. I don't want to lose him.

My head falls back to the pillow while he begins to move in earnest. Holding himself over me with the pillars of his arms, he thrusts forward, tapping at something inside me while I lay there replete and unworthy of this worship he's paying me. He mutters words like perfect and stunning, and how he never knew it would be like this, and then he quickly pulls out of me. Gripping himself, he squeezes his thickness, and warm liquid hits my hot skin near my pelvis. His ball sac presses against my wet folds while he relieves himself on my lower belly, and my head rolls to the side on my pillow.

Eventually, he collapses over me, his hand coming to my nape and tugging me so my mouth meets his. His kiss is nearly as intense as what we just did, and our rapid breathing gets in the way. When he pulls back, he doesn't look at me but places his face at my neck.

"Roxie," he whispers, and a million questions linger in my name.

"Billy," I state, equally as confused by the wonder of his body with mine and what this means for us both because casual just got complicated.

+ + +

The day after Thanksgiving isn't my busiest day as most people head to the outskirts of town for the faulty sales and false promotions of the larger chain stores. I'm looking forward to Small Business Saturday when people will shop local. I'm relieved the day won't be busy as I'm exhausted when I wake. I need more sleep. Real sleep, not Billy under my head, heartbeat racing in my ear sleep.

Surprisingly, I slept until noon, startled when I realize Billy is still in my bed minus most of his clothes and nestled up close to me under my blankets. The sensation confuses me as the reality of what we did last night settles in. I could get too comfortable accepting Billy Harrington in my bed. Briefly, I wonder how others feel when Billy visits and then leaves theirs.

We've kissed. We've touched, but I have no idea how many others are still on Billy's bedside list. It's difficult to imagine his availability with all the time he spends with Sadie and myself, but still…he owns a bar, works late nights, and hasn't come to my bed in the wee hours of the morning until this morning. Whose bed does he grace each evening? It's difficult to believe he heads home alone every night.

"Where are you going?" he mutters, his arm around my waist even as I sit up, attempting to slip from my bed.

"I need to work." It's true, I do. Grace and I decided on reduced hours for the day due to the holiday as well as Sadie's unplanned disappearance. It will be good to head to the bookstore. I need something to occupy my mind for a little bit as I struggle with my thoughts of what I did with Billy.

"What time is it?" he mumbles, not making any effort to rouse.

"Time to wake up. Need to sell the books."

His eyes flip open, and his head rolls on the pillow. His pupils dance around the room, taking in my small space and the dull light coming through the blinds. It must be gloomy outside. With a hand scrubbing down his face, he sits up next to me and then looks at me.

His hair sticks up a bit. His scruff a day fuller. His lips roll, and I wonder if he's worried about morning breath. I am. Then he brushes his lips over my covered shoulder and twists to the opposite side of my bed.

Huh.

Not exactly a heartwarming greeting for what we did last night, but I remind myself—casual. I assume this is how it goes. He grabs his pants from the floor while I stand. I need to pee. I need a shower, but something stops me from leaving the room as he hops once, tugging his pants up his legs and then turns in my direction as he buttons them closed. I don't know why I'm watching him. I don't know why my heart is clenching and my stomach wobbling and my eyes threaten to tear.

Then he looks up at me, like he's looking through me, and my mind recalls his confusion a moment ago. He's wondering what he's doing here. Perhaps he's wondering what we did, and why, and can't believe he did it with me.

I can't believe I told him about the breast reduction or that I'd once been fat.

"Is this how it usually goes?" I begin, shutting off the butterflies in my belly at the sight of him tugging on his T-shirt. I didn't explore his skin near enough last night, and now it's over. This can't become a thing. We can't be using each other to right our spirit when Sadie throws us for a loop.

"Meaning?" he asks, a little bite to his retort.

"Sneaking out at noon. Makes it rather obvious, though."

"What's obvious?" His hands slip into his pants, straightening his pockets and then he pulls them out to swipe through his hair. Good lawd, it's a sin how good he looks in the morning, all messed up like he spent the night between my thighs, and I…

Goodness. My hand floats up to my throat, and I clear it.

"I mean, with your…friends…I don't suppose noon is…unless you have nooners… and…" Billy's staring at me, his mouth agape with his hands on his hips. My voice drifts. I don't even know what I'm saying or why I'm speaking. I need to get dressed and get downstairs.

"Just what do you think happened here last night?" He nods toward the bed.

"We had sex. No big deal, right?" I shrug, but my heart crashes within my chest as I don't feel half as cavalier as I'm trying to sound.

"Nooners," he repeats with an irritated snort like the crack of a whip. He bitterly chuckles.

"Yeah, like afternoon delight," I clarify. Maybe that's when he sleeps with others. *Before* he goes to work, *before* he comes to see Sadie, before he has dinner with us and hangs out and takes her bowling and watches movies and…

His fingers clench at his sides as he stands to his full height.

"What happened here was *not* my reputation," he says quietly.

I stare at him, but he doesn't look up at me.

"You know, Roxie. You can be a real piece of work sometimes." He shakes his head. "Not that it matters, but last night, you ruined me for all others." The deepness of his voice along with the sharp tone is almost a slap of awakening.

"*May,*" he emphasizes, reminding me what he told me about his recent sexual history. "One night with the wrong woman. And you think I'm having nooners, afternoon delights, and any other list of nefarious acts with random women."

"Nefarious," I snort.

"Yeah, even the dumbass pub owner knows a big word or two." He sighs. "Why can't you let it go?" He scrubs up his chin and holds his jaw.

"You're breaking me here, Roxie." He pauses again. "But as for last night, thanks for clarifying. Lesson learned."

He tugs at the blankets fallen from his side of the bed, poorly straightening them in his anger and then stalks past me.

I slowly spin as my bedroom door closes, and I hear him greet Sadie in the hallway, his voice tight as he attempts to be chipper. "Hey." His irritation is poorly contained while I'm left wondering where I went wrong. I'm trying to play it casual like him.

I ruined him for all others. I'm breaking him. He must be wrong. He's breaking me as I watch him walk away.

Then I reflect on what he's said. May. One night. Wrong woman.

Am I the one wrong…about him?

Chapter 27

Introducing . . . My Daughter

[Billy]

"Hey," I greet Sadie who stands just outside Roxanne's bedroom door. Did she hear us fighting? Did she hear what her aunt said to me? *Jesus,* Roxie's words can hurt. I shake my head and turn for the living room where I left my boots, socks, and winter jacket. I don't bother with the sheets, spread but unused, on the couch, and I also don't feel like giving Sadie an explanation for walking out of her aunt's room.

No big deal.

Yeah, right, but this is complicated, and I don't do complicated. I like carefree and easy. Sleep where I will; fuck who I want.

Only that's not really how I feel. Not this time. And my eyes look up to find Sadie watching me, and I realize it's so much more complex than that.

"Fuck," I mutter, scrubbing two hands down my face and then returning for my boot to snap the shoelace as I tugged too tight.

"She didn't mean it," Sadie says, leaning on the corner of the wall marking the start of the hallway. "Whatever she said to upset you, she didn't mean it."

I sit up straighter, my brows furrowing as I look at my daughter. If she didn't hear what Roxanne said, then how does she know what her aunt means?

"I scared her last night. She's probably taking it out on you. My mother used to do that same thing to Aunt Roxie. She'd be upset with something I did but blame Roxanne for it."

I nod, but in my mind, this is a little different.

"Yeah, well, Roxie isn't your mother, and I'm not her sister." I stand, brushing my hands down my jeans. "I'm your dad." Her breath hitches as her eyes widen and her forehead wrinkles. "And as you skipped out on Thanksgiving dinner and meeting my family, I'll be here tomorrow night at five. You'll be meeting everyone then."

I'm not allowing any excuses this time. Stepping toward her, I intend to slip past her, but then I stop. "No running away this time." I reach out for her, cupping her neck and pressing a kiss to her temple, reminding myself I'm grateful she's safe and home.

I move forward, making my way for the kitchen, noting the sound of the shower as I pass the bathroom. Thank goodness. I can't face Roxanne.

"Can Aunt Roxie come, too?" Sadie asks. I didn't hear her following me, and I halt, spinning around to face her as we enter the kitchen.

Presently, I don't really want Roxie there. Forgive me if I'm in the wrong, but what she said hurts. I meant what I said: she's breaking me. I had my heart ripped out by Rachel some seventeen years ago, but this…this makes that chest-clenching tightness burrow sharply into my sternum.

"Fine," I grit.

No big deal. If this is how Roxie wants to play it, I can play. *Keep it casual.*

"Also, I…uhm…I need to tell you something." Sadie looks over her shoulder down the hall, listening for the shower before she speaks. "I'm not proud to say this, but…"

My face turns white, and her fingers clutch the back of a kitchen chair.

"Out with it, Sadie." Her name drones from my lips, echoing through the room. Her eyes close.

"I didn't steal the money, but I might know who did. He didn't mean to do it. He was doing it for me." She pauses. "That sounds wrong. He was just trying to help. I didn't have the money, and…"

"Christian?" I hiss. *Christian Grady?* "You are not to see him again."

"What?" she shrieks. "You can't tell me who I can and can't see."

"Yes, I can because I'm your father." I hate how I sound like my own father, but my chest puffs.

Sadie remains silent. Her cheeks shade an embarrassed pink color, and as she has no response to my directive, I let myself out.

+ + +

Poor Clyde. He listens to me say fuck about twenty-five times and then curse women of all ages before I settle into telling him what happened.

Sadie ran away.

Sadie's friend—I choke on the word—*stole money.*

Sadie is meeting my family.

I leave out the list of infractions against Roxie. She isn't worth my thoughts, which is a lie I repeat to myself over and over to steel my heart. I feel strange after what we did, but more so after what she said, dismissing it so casually. I didn't lie when I told her that she was breaking me. I like her. I thought she liked me, finally. I feel connected to her in a way I've never felt connected to another woman. Rachel was different. She was my best friend, and we might be the poster couple for why friends shouldn't marry, but it was more than that. And Roxie means more to me.

As I told her, what happened last night was not my reputation. Fine, I admit I've done the slam, bam, thank you, ma'am, and I'm always the one to leave long before daylight. I'll always be the first to go, but last night, I lingered because I wanted to stay. I wanted to continue the cocoon we wrapped around one another, falling into each other like we did.

Damn, she comes quickly, but after the first one, it's long and lazy and so fucking sweet. Then, when she came around me, I was the quick one. I can't believe I left the condoms in my truck, but I never thought, not in a million years, that Roxie would hold onto me like that. Her hands. Her mouth. Her pussy. She clutched at me like she didn't want me to leave her, and I didn't want to go anywhere but right where we were with me buried inside her.

Then she had to open her damn mouth this morning and brush it all off like it was nothing. *No big deal.* Well, it was a big deal to me because, despite my reputation, I do have a heart and not just a dick. It hurt to lose Rachel, and it hurts to feel like I'm losing Roxie. All the women between weren't close enough for this kind of feeling. First and last, that's how I see these two women, only Roxie seems to disagree with me. No shocker there.

"You know," Clyde begins, interrupting my rambling thoughts. "The second you tell kids they can't do something, like date someone, that's the person they want most."

I stare at Clyde and his unsolicited fatherly wisdom.

"Clyde, when did you become an expert on being a dad?" My sarcastic tone makes my friend flinch.

"I'm not. I'm an expert on being a son, and as soon as my dad told me no, I wanted to do whatever it was twice as much. Didn't you?" He tips a brow at me. *Point taken.*

"Shit," I mutter. "I'm really messing this up."

Clyde sighs and then chuckles. "They don't come with a manual like bartending or business owning." My hand scrubs down my face at his comment. "But you're doing fine, Billy. I mean, you seem really invested. You go over there all the time. You've taken her places, and you were obviously concerned when she went missing."

"What about this stealing issue? Roxie's going to flip, and Hetty…I just feel guilty." The flower shop is at the other end of the block. Her business does well, but any type of theft feels like an assault.

"You'll figure something out," Clyde assures me, but I stare at him, hopeful he'll have a solution. "*Okay,*" he stresses, rubbing his hands on his jeans. He could use some new clothes as his zipper is popping open a bit. "How about giving her a job here? Making her pay off the money. That should teach her. You'll get to spend time with her, and you can introduce her to people as your daughter on your terms. Or turf, however, you want to see it."

"Yeah, okay. This is good, this might…" I glare at Clyde. "Wait a minute. You mean announce to everyone she's my kid." *Whoa, whoa,*

whoa. I already blurted it to June Barne and Butch Marshall, and I'm waiting for them to blast it to the community, although there should be some confidentiality law in question there, right? I need to tell my parents before I tell the town, and then I remember I'm having dinner tomorrow night with my folks, even if my mother doesn't know it yet.

"Okay, this could still work," I tell Clyde who slowly smiles with pride at his suggestion, and I'm still wondering how he got to be so good at dad advice when he doesn't have children.

+ + +

When I arrive at Elaina and George Harrington's home, aka my parents, with two women in tow, my mother is the first to comment while my dad just lifts a questioning brow. Roxanne remained quiet and distant in the truck while Sadie's eyes shifted back and forth between the two of us. She's worn extra black tonight, reminding me of the girl in *Beetlejuice*. Black lace dress. Black hair, lips, nails.

"When William told me he was bringing two ladies to dinner, I had no idea you'd both be so beautiful," my mother gushes, not even flinching at the darkness of Sadie's appearance. Roxanne, on the hand, looks her typical naturalist self with a long, flowing skirt and a T-shirt with some kind of denim blazer over it. The three of us appear as mismatched as they come as I wear a dress shirt with dark pants.

For years after Giant's wife died, my mother tried to set him up with every available woman within a fifty-mile radius. She never attempted setups with me, thinking I made my own bed to lose Rachel.

"Or so young," my father states, stepping out of his stupor and leaning in to give Roxie a cheek kiss. "Roxanne, lovely to see you." As the largest industry in the area—Giant Beer Company—my father makes it a point to know all the other business owners within the community. When my brother became mayor, my father was on board with his ideas to bring tourism to our town to improve the economy. My father saw tourism as an indirect boost for the brewery. However, he's never recognized my contribution to the brewery through serving and promoting the family beer for over fifteen years in my pub. He also doesn't know how I assist Giant on the sly with brew craft.

"And this must be your little sister," George Jr. flirts as he cups Sadie's shoulders. She looks at me, but Roxanne quickly saves us all by saying, "This is Sadie. She's my niece."

"I heard about your sister," my mother addresses Roxanne and then gazes at Sadie. "I'm so very sorry." I don't know how my mother knows these details other than her busybody nature.

"Well, let's not stand here. Come in, come in. Dinner is almost ready." My mother leads the ladies, as she referred to them, toward the living room while my father hangs back and walks with me.

"William, what are you up to?" he mutters because it always has to be something with me. He has no idea of the truth in his concern. As I cross into the more formal room which holds our large family better than other spaces in my childhood home, I see my brother Charlie and his daughter, Lucy, are present.

"Uncle Billy," Lucy yells, running for me like she's still five instead of ten and getting bigger every day.

"How's my girl?" I tease, catching her under her arms and then pretending it's a struggle to lift her because she's grown so big. My eyes glance up to find Sadie watching me with my niece, and I realize I've said something wrong. Lucy isn't my girl. Sadie is…or she should be. And at this moment, I realize again how I've missed out on a time in Sadie's life when she was young and innocent like a nine-year-old can be.

Further greetings occur as Charlie recognizes Roxanne, and she introduces Sadie again as her niece.

My daughter, whispers through my head, and I swallow as I realize I don't know how I will tell my family. I only planned to get Roxie and Sadie to the house. From there, I didn't know how to break the news.

Within minutes of drinks being dispersed, Mother announces dinner is ready. She didn't bat an eye when I requested dinner for this evening so close to Thanksgiving. She lives for these moments. Making meals. Entertaining. Bringing us all back into the house. Even tomorrow, which is a Sunday, she'll be feeding whoever shows up for morning brunch, which has turned into Mati and Denton on the regular, along with his grandmother, Magnolia.

We've hardly taken our seats at the dining room table which casually holds up to ten when my father speaks.

"So William, how is the bar?" my father questions, and Roxanne smirks. Yes, my father calls me by my full name most of the time in the same manner as Roxie, which is one reason I hate it when she does. The patronizing, condescending tone elongates my name with his disappointment in me.

"The pub," I correct him, "had record sales with Oktoberfest. We're on point for the holidays, especially with the seasonal brews."

"Giant works hard," my father states, and I cringe, nodding and pursing my lips. He has no idea who works harder.

"He sure does," I respond sarcastically, noticing Roxanne watching me from across the table. I'd love to glare back at her, tell her the truth, and watch her reaction. The intensity of those prying steel eyes tries to read me. Yep, I have another secret from my father. *No big deal*, I want to snap, but the sympathy in her gaze holds my tongue as does present company.

"Sadie, how do you like Blue Ridge?" Charlie asks, ever the peacemaker and trying to shift the attention at the table. He'd wink at me in silent solidarity if his focus wasn't aimed at Sadie, ever the politician. *Look them in the eye. Make them like you.*

"It's been…different."

Afraid she'd say she hated it, I release a breath I didn't know I was holding. *Different*, I can work with; hatred, I can't.

"What do you like best?" Charlie asks, and my airways clog again.

"You have a nice cemetery."

Sweet Jesus.

"And a decent bowling alley."

Charlie swings his head in my direction, holding my eyes a second. I feel my mother's glare on the side of my face, but I refuse to look at her. I can only imagine the chagrin on my father. It's no secret the only bowling alley is run by Rebel's Edge, the biker club James belongs to and owned by the infamous Bear Grady.

"Well, yes. Those are interesting places," Charlie says, lying as he smiles back at Roxanne's niece.

My daughter.

"And what don't you like about Blue Ridge?"

"The high school. Kids are jerks."

Lucy's head pops up, and my mother's fork hangs in midair. Charlie glances at me again as Roxanne clears her throat and then in a hushed tone, admonishes Sadie by stating her name.

"I see," Charlie says although I'm sure he doesn't.

"They don't know what to think of me," Sadie begins. "I'm from a big city. I use big words. I like to read, and I dress like this." She waves a hand at her attire. "Flannel doesn't come in solid black."

Roxie shakes her head, and I've lost my appetite, setting my fork to rest on my plate.

"Maybe they think you look like Violet from *The Incredibles*," Lucy interjects, sweet and innocent and complimentary. My eyes meet Charlie's across the table and then shift to Roxie's. "Violet is beautiful, and she can make herself invisible. Who doesn't want a superpower?"

"I want a superpower," my mother interjects, trying to save this conversation. "I'd love to time travel."

"That's because you watch that show with the guy in a skirt and the woman who walked through stones," my father mutters.

"*Outlander*?" Roxanne cheerfully questions, and thankfully, the subject shifts from Sadie.

As dinner ends, the bomb needs to be dropped before coffee is served and my mother's famous pumpkin pie is passed. I swallow, rubbing my hands down my thighs, noticing Roxanne watching me. She shakes her head in warning, but this is how I do things.

How I told them I was dropping out of college.

How I told them I was divorcing Rachel.

How I told them I was opening the pub.

"Momma. Dad. I have something to tell you." Charlie reaches for Lucy's ears, mockingly covering them.

"Is this a good time for this?" My younger brother's eyes narrow on mine, and it occurs to me he knows what I'm about to say.

"Sadie is more than Roxanne's niece. She's someone special to me."

My mother's breath catches, the gasp so loud the chandelier quakes. My father's deep brows lower. "She's a little young for you, son."

"Gross," Sadie groans. "I'm his daughter."

The words hang in the air.

She's my daughter.

I wasn't the one to announce it to them.

"Surprise. I'm a dad." The enthusiasm is lost and lacking in my voice, but I attempt cheerful, adding jazzy hands to emphasize the announcement.

Silence follows. We can hear the grandfather clock in the main hallway tick-tocking.

Tick-tock. Tick-tock.

"How did this happen?" Dad asks.

"When did this happen?" Mother questions.

"If she's Uncle Billy's daughter, that means she's my cousin," Lucy states, clarifying the relationship. She fondly stares at my daughter with wide blue eyes, blinking as tears fill them. "I have a cousin. A girl cousin close to my age. I'm almost a teenager. You are a teenager. We can be friends." Her hands clasp before her like she's received the greatest of gifts, and I agree with the excitement on her sweet face. Sadie is a present, even if my mother and father are still flabbergasted by the announcement.

"Explain yourself, William," my father interjects. My eyes meet Roxanne's for some reason, and then I turn to him.

"It was after Rachel. We were…over and…Theresa McAllister was in town for a girls' reunion with some other women from our high school class."

"Have you learned nothing about protection?" My father snorts in disgust as he's the one who'd slip condoms into the trophy room, hidden behind remote controls and game consoles in the top left drawer.

"Dad," Charlie admonishes, his eyes shooting to Lucy.

"I know what a condom is," Lucy says, and Sadie laughs, then covers her mouth in an attempt to stop.

"I don't even want to know how you know," Charlie remarks.

"Television," Lucy clarifies, but my mother clears her throat.

"So, Sadie…how old are you?"

"Sixteen," Sadie answers, looking over at my mother. Sadie's trying to hold her head high, but if I know anything about my mother, it's that she can make you wither with a simple look. Only Sadie is staring back at my mother like she'd burn her, and I remember that scathing glare from when she first told me she was my child.

"You have your father's eyes," my mother states, shocking me.

"She what?"

"The shape matches Roxanne's, but the coloring, the look, I'd recognize one of my own anywhere." I don't know what my mother means or what she sees, and I turn to Sadie who sits at my right.

"I just don't understand how this happened," my dad questions. "You know better. You know to wrap it up."

"Dad," Charlie pointedly calls his name, side-eyeing Lucy.

"George," my mother scolds.

"I'm sorry. I just…this is too much. Excuse me." He stands, placing his napkin over his plate, and leaves the room, sizzling a hole in my heart at his dismissal, but the puzzled hurt on Sadie's face sets that hole aflame.

Pushing back her chair, she states, "I think I'll—"

"Want to see my room? I live in the house next door." Lucy stands as quickly as Sadie and circles the table, taking Sadie's hand. Sadie tries to tug free, but Lucy holds tight before leading Sadie toward the kitchen, which offers a back door and a path directly to Charlie's estate—the official mayor's home.

Charlie stands next. "I'll keep my eye on them. Take your time, Billy. Roxanne." He nods to Roxie and walks to the end of the table. Leaning to kiss our mother's cheek, he pats her shoulder in sympathy before exiting.

"I certainly know how to clear a room," I tease, reaching for my beer and downing the rest. "I think I'll take a minute as well." With that, I stand and leave Roxanne to my mother.

Chapter 28
Motherly Advice

[Roxanne]

Elaina Harrington is an intimidating woman with her perfect coiffed hairstyle and her form-fitting dress, appropriate for her age and making her look stunning. She's a true Southern belle, but I don't care about any of this because I'm pissed.

"How about more wine?" she asks, standing to clear her plate and reaching for Billy's. I follow with mine and Charlie's, but once I reach the kitchen, she makes no attempt to return to the dining room. She pours into fresh glasses from a bottle on the counter.

"George has always been hardest on him." She shakes her head and curls her fingers into the thick necklace near her collar. She smiles weakly without looking at me. "It can be hard to be a Harrington."

I nod with a grimace and take a sip of wine. It's difficult being anyone, so rejection from parents isn't acceptable to me. And because I can't hold my tongue, I'm about to say as such to the matriarch of the family when she continues.

"We were so disappointed when he divorced. Marriage is work, and Billy lacks ethics. Plus, Rachel was perfect for him. Kept him on his toes." She pauses to sip her wine. *Work, ethic.* Has she not been to his business? Has she not seen what he's done with the pub, for the community, for tourism?

"We've taught our children marriage is sacred. A vow before God of loyalty and respect." There's a warning somewhere in what she says. I've heard the rumors. He stepped out on his wife with another woman. Perhaps she thinks Theresa was the woman, the one whom Billy cheated with.

"Sadie is sixteen. Billy was divorced when he was with Theresa." I defend both my sister and Billy. She nods, and I add. "My sister never married."

Elaina blinks as if caught in thought. "Yes, your sister. So tell me about Sadie's mother."

"She was strict." I hate that it's the first thing I offer. "She was smart and witty, but she lost her easygoing nature when she became a mother. She worried. She always worried about Sadie, wanted her to do well in life. Sadie was an A-plus student in all honors classes. She studied hard, played piano, and practiced karate. All that's gone now that she's here with me. I don't have a piano, and I couldn't find a karate studio. I'm afraid she's struggling in school and not making friends." I leave out the questionable connection to a kid named Christian Grady and the possibility that Sadie stole from local businesses in town. I sigh. "I think it might be time to seek help for Sadie."

Elaina's head pops up, eyeing me before she nods with a weak smile. "Are you her guardian?"

"Things were pending until Sadie found Billy."

"Sadie found Billy?"

It isn't my story to tell, but as Sadie isn't here to explain and I feel the need to defend my niece's innocence, I break into a monologue of explanation. What Sadie didn't know. What I didn't know Sadie did know. And then how Sadie introduced herself to Billy.

"Well, I imagine that was quite a shock." She chuckles softly. "And I'll make no assumptions about your sister. As women, we all have our reasons for what we do, why we handle situations a certain way, whether it seems fair or right to an outsider."

The statement of female solidarity surprises me, and my shoulders relax. She isn't judging my sister. There'd be no point as Theresa is dead. She can't be questioned. She can't be reprimanded. The choices were made, and we move forward from there.

"So therapy," Elaina states, and I cringe at the hesitation in her voice, not to mention I haven't spoken with Billy about my thoughts. Not that I always value his opinion, but I'm trying to be respectful that he might have a say in Sadie's well-being.

The other night still haunts me. What we did with one another and then his dismissal of it so quickly the morning after. I want to apologize if I said something wrong, but I haven't found the time. Tonight came up without warning, and it's been just short of a shitshow.

"Yes, *possibly*," I try to retract.

"I can recommend someone who deals with grief. Both my daughter, Matilda, and my son Giant went through this. I'll get her number for you," she says but doesn't move. "I have a piano." It's an odd statement until I realize what she's offering. An olive branch in the form of eighty-eight musical keys.

"Thank you."

She smiles, a more genuine grin, and I note Elaina might not be as tough inside as she looks on the outside. Seems vaguely similar to her son, Billy. "Maybe I should find Sadie." It might be best if we leave and let the Harringtons process what they've learned. The problem is we came with Billy, and he disappeared.

"I'll call over to Charlie's house and have Lucy bring her back." She winks at me, a twinkle in her eye for her grandchild. "Instead, maybe you should find Billy." Her voice shifts, dropping a little quieter. "He needs someone like you. Try upstairs. Curve around the bannister and his old room will face you." I have no idea what she means about needing me, but I take her suggestion and climb the stairs to the second floor.

+ + +

The Harrington home is large, but the second floor is tight. The hallway is more a square with a plethora of doors, and I curve around the bannister as Elaina mentioned. The room I face is the only one with a door that's closed. I knock but don't wait for a response. Turning the knob, I find a large, older male on his back across a twin bed, clearly too small for him. His feet rest on the floor, and he tosses a baseball into the air, catching it as it falls back to him. A desk lamp dimly illuminates the room.

"Billy." He catches the ball with two hands, holds it over his chest and takes a deep breath as he closes his eyes. Then returns to tossing it in the air like a moody child.

"I can't deal with you right now, Roxanne." He doesn't look at me but continues to toss and catch, toss and catch.

"I'm sorry they weren't immediately receptive," I begin, ignoring his statement as I close the door behind me. "Think about when you learned the truth. Weren't you in shock? They just need time to process."

He pauses, holding the ball in one hand when I finish.

"Don't defend them, Roxie." Surprisingly, I feel better that he's returned to the abbreviation of my name. If I can rouse him, poke him enough, he might open up to me. Then again, my heart aches at the sadness on his face and the dull, lacking expression in those eyes of his. His eyes. Sadie's eyes. I hadn't seen it until Elaina pointed it out. They match perfectly in color, and there's no denying she's his.

"I'm not defending them." I exhale, hands coming to my hips. "I'm on your side here. But I also need to think of Sadie. It will crush her if they reject her."

Billy sits up, catching the ball as it plummets back to him, before it knocks him in the head.

"I'm only thinking of Sadie as well. Did you see my dad's reaction? He couldn't even look at her. And then, my mother's comment. She has my eyes. I mean, what the fuck?"

"Well, she does," I admit. He stares at me a minute, the brown tone near walnut versus rich bark in color. He falls back on the bed and resumes his mindless tossing.

"Roxanne, go home."

"Well, that'd be difficult as you drove us here." Irritation is evident in my voice. He halts pitching again and covers his arm over his eyes. I step up to him, slipping my feet between his which rest apart as his legs are spread while he lays on his back.

"Billy…I…I'm sorry for what I said the other morning. I didn't mean to imply—"

He sits up so fast, I stop. His face could collide with my breasts if he wasn't looking up at me, his face earnest. "You're so…mean sometimes."

"I'm sorry. You bring it out of me," I tease as I reach for his cheeks, the feel of that stubble under my palms is like a live wire direct to a body part pulsing and wet when it shouldn't be. I want to comfort him. I want to tell him this will all work out. His family will accept Sadie, and maybe it will help his relationship with them, but I don't say anything. I just hold his face, stroking my thumbs over his jaw and staring at those soulful eyes. His hands cup the back of my thighs, pressing upward just under my backside, and I lower to kiss him.

The intention was to be soft, tender, and sympathizing, but Billy crushes my lips. With anger and frustration written on them, he instantly takes control. His fingers dig into the back of my thighs as his mouth opens, his tongue rushing forward to tangle with mine. Not a drop of delicacy is in this kiss, and I easily fall into it, loving it. His knees come between mine, and the next thing I know, I'm straddling his thighs. Then he falls back, keeping our mouths attached as he draws me over him. His hands come to my hips, positioning my lower half to rest over the length growing harder underneath me. Fistfuls of my skirt get readjusted until it's only my underwear against his denim. I'm wet and worried I'll leave a mark, but I moan into his aggressive lips, enjoying the mouth-spar.

"Billy," I mutter against his mouth after he moves me, and I drag over his thickness. "Billy, this isn't a good idea. Not here."

"No one misses me," he mutters. "With this full skirt, I could unzip and slip into you. No one would know the difference." It's crass but a little thrilling to consider. Then it hits me. He's hurting. He's hurting, and this is what he does. He seeks a distraction through physical connection.

"Billy," I groan, pressing at his shoulders and removing my mouth from his, pushing myself upward as best as I can, but still distracted by the thick presence of him wedged against the heat of me.

"Fuck," he moans, closing his eyes and pushing his fingertips into my hip bone, forcing me to rock over him.

"Not here," I whisper. "Not like this."

His eyes open, and the color shimmers, dancing gold and brown and a hint of green. "But you want me, right? You can feel me, feel how much I want you?" The question is desperation, not passion, and I sympathize, but I'm not giving in. Not like this, I said, and I mean it.

"Billy. Stop." He stills, his hands releasing my hips and falling disinterested to the outside of my knees. He rolls his head to the side, gazing off at something on his teenage walls. I lower, boxing him in with my arms on either side of his shoulders. My hair falls forward. "Tell me about Rachel."

His eyes blink shut. "I'm not doing this with you, Roxanne." My full name is the lash of a whip, but I take the sting.

"I want to understand what happened between you two. It's not my business, but I want to know all the same. I want to understand you better." Because like it or not, he is Sadie's father, and I should know him. Because like it or not, my feelings for him are strong.

"My mother said something, didn't she?" He still doesn't look at me.

"She might have suggested her disappointment and something about the disloyalty of sacred vows."

He shakes his head. "And you believe her. Everyone knows it's my fault." He looks up at me, defiantly. The one who covers his feelings with a playful mask. I stare down at him a moment, us seated in this precarious position.

"I don't believe *you*. I don't believe it's your fault."

His eyes widen only a touch and then narrow, assessing me. "I'm not telling you anything."

"Okay." I sit back, still resting over him, my center balanced on the swell of him still evident and hard.

"Fuck," he groans, scrubbing both hands down his face, the stubble scratching under his palms. "Do you know how sexy you look right now, with the glow of the light behind you and your hair. *Shit*. I feel like I can't deny you anything in this position."

I stare back at him, stunned beyond words. "What?"

"You're so stunning, Roxie."

If he's attempting to butter me up in hopes to butter my biscuit, it might work with those pretty words. No one calls me stunning, least of all him. Then I recall he did once, in the heat of a disagreement in my office. Stunning is one of those words on a whole different level than beautiful or pretty.

"That's sweet of you," I say, tucking hair behind my ear.

"I'm not being sweet. I'm being honest. I can hardly look at you without wanting to take you to the floor and devour you."

What? "What?"

"Roxanne, has it ever occurred to you that the reason we fight is because we're attracted to each other?"

Well, I know I'm attracted to him, but… "You're attracted to me?"

"From the first moment I met you. Even though you called the cops on me."

I stare down at him, flabbergasted. "But you…you always mock me."

"Flirt."

"Tease me."

"Sexual frustration."

"No," I gasp. "You don't even like me."

He presses upward, the evidence of his attraction pressing into me. "I very much like you, Roxanne."

He sits up again, and I almost fall back, but he catches me with two hands on my ass. He squeezes the globes as his eyes peer up at me, devilish and mischievous. "Admit that you like me, and I'll tell you everything."

"I like you," I mutter, and the playful gleam returns to his eyes. What's with this man? He seems so desperate to be liked. Is he desperate for love as well? I don't get it. I hadn't seen it, but his player reputation is a cover-up for something deeper. Acceptance. He wants people to like him. He wants me to like him.

"You're a bad boy, Billy Harrington," I tease, clapping his cheeks between my palms.

"And you might love it." He smiles. I shake my head as his mouth crushes mine again. He kisses me hard but not as suggestive, not as desperate. More hunger, more devour, and more plea to give in to him. I feel myself fall forward, him tugging me down over him once again. My chest rests on his as I catch myself with my hands on the bed. The kiss only lasts another second before he stops, and I pull back, peering down at him, just as his bedroom door opens.

Chapter 29
Caught in The Act

[Billy]

"William?"

"Dad," I choke, my eyes holding Roxie's whose are wide and mortified glaring down at me. *Kill me*, they say before she closes them and then she shifts. Only I have a problem, and I don't want her to move. My hand comes to her hip, keeping her in place. I'm certain she's left a wet smudge on my pants, and my dick is so hard there's no mistaking what she's done to me.

What is she doing to me?

I like you. She admits it, and I feel like the kid who found the golden ticket in a chocolate bar. She apologized for what she said the other morning and then said she didn't believe things were my fault. *What does she know?* I internally snarked before accepting she sounded sincere.

"I can come back," my dad mutters, but he doesn't move, and I feel like a teenager all over again. Actually, James was the one caught in the house with plenty of women; Dolores Chance, our neighbor most often.

"I think I'll just…" Roxie sits back, again attempting to move, but it forces her heated center one hundred percent over me, and while my dad's interruption should be a buzzkill, I haven't softened. I want this woman. I want her comfort. I want her warmth, but most of all, I want her heart.

Could she love me?

Fuck, my mind screams as I scrub a hand over my face before sitting up and letting Roxie slide off my lap.

She chuckles hesitantly. "This is so embarrassing, sir." She addresses my father, swiping back her long hair—wild and white curtaining her face as she leaned over me. Illuminated in the dim light, she looked otherworldly, and I want to enter that world…within her.

"It happens," my dad states, lessening his tone a bit as he opens the door wider, suggesting she leave. I don't want her to go. I want to hold her in my arms as a shield against the onslaught of attack from my father. *Billy fucks up again.* Huzzah! Party of one.

Roxanne doesn't look back at me as she excuses herself, and my father leans on the door jamb as she exits.

"So, you're a father," my dad begins, once Roxanne heads for the stairs.

"I am." The obvious has already been said, so I wait, knowing disappointment is coming from him.

"Now what?"

"I had a paternity test." My father waits for more explanation, but I promised Roxanne we'd work it out. Only Jordan's been pressuring me. I don't need guardianship, he says. I'm Sadie's father, but I should seek residential custody. Sadie should live with me. I'm opposed, it's just what I have arranged with Roxanne's seems to be working. Financially, though, Jordan says we need things in writing. A formal agreement of responsibility, which just seems cold to me. I'll take responsibility for my child however she needs it.

"I want Sadie to live with me," I blurt, although I haven't settled the decision with Roxanne. It's something I haven't been able to bring up yet. I don't want to rip Sadie from Roxie, which is one of Roxanne's fears, but I also want my turn at parenting. I want my child in my home.

"And what do you know about raising a teenage daughter?"

"What did you know before Mati?" I sass back. Mati is the baby girl of four brothers. I have no doubt she was a different kind of handful than us boys, but she's also daddy's princess.

"I'd already been a father. I had some practice."

"Fine, then before Giant?" I question.

"Let's not split hairs," my dad snaps back.

"Then what should we split? You're here to tell me I've eff-ed up…*again*…and remind me of all the things I didn't do well before. College. Rachel. But you don't see what's right in front of you. The pub and the amazing success it's had for the past fifteen years. *Fifteen.* And now, I have a daughter, who I've missed out on for sixteen. I don't want to miss any more time with her."

George Harrington Jr. falls silent for a moment, weighing his words or calculating them, I'm not certain.

"Where did you ever get the idea we weren't proud of the pub?"

"Because you've never said it," I shriek, exasperated with the man I admired and hated a little growing up. I wasn't going to conform. I wasn't going to fit in the puzzle, but then again, neither did James. He just walked away.

"William, I'm proud of all my children. That includes you even if I don't agree with all your life choices."

Life choices. I snort. He means Rachel and what he thinks he knows. And now, possibly Sadie.

"What's with Roxanne?" He nods toward the bed, and my face would have heated in embarrassment if I wasn't already steaming mad, slowly trying to decode his words.

"We were just fooling around." As soon as I say it, the words taste bitter, the label incorrect. I need to stop fooling myself. I like her a lot. I *care* about her. And I want to fuck her again.

Shit.

"This is playing with fire, William. She's your daughter's aunt. She has temporary guardianship. If things go south, she could ruin you in a character testimony." I don't know how my dad knows such things, but I know enough to realize Sadie has a say in things. She'd have the final say in where she lives, if I push, but I don't want to push her.

I wonder what she'll say. Who would she choose? Is it a choice?

"That won't happen," I huff, defending Roxanne's opinion of me. We might not be on solid ground, but we're getting there. I'm not in a rush. She isn't a one-night stand to me, so I can take my time. I know she runs hot and cold with me, and adding physical trysts blurs some lines, but I don't need a firm definition of us. As long as we stay a united front for Sadie, as she suggested, we'll be okay. I believe that.

"Are you…dating? In a relationship?" The awkward questions make me laugh a bit bitterly.

"No, Dad. It's complicated." How very social media of me, and I don't social media other than to market the pub.

"It seems like it." He pauses a second, looking down at his polished shoes. My dad is a powerful man who can dress up or down and still have an aura about him that says he's someone accomplished. I don't know that I'll ever feel that way. "I'm going to head back downstairs. I have a new granddaughter to meet."

My brows rise at the sudden spark of enthusiasm in my father's voice. Does he mean it? Will he give Sadie a chance? I stand and follow his retreat. If I ever had fantasies about taking a girl in that room, they've all been washed away by Roxanne on top of me.

Dammit. I can't think of these things right now, and I instantly stop once I descend the stairs and reach the edge of the living room. My daughter is playing the piano with my mother. My father stands to the side of Momma, hand coming to her shoulder, and she reaches up to quickly pat it before returning her fingers to the instrument which was a wedding present from her mother to her. The younger Harrington generation wasn't very accomplished as musicians, so it startles me to see Sadie's nimble fingers racing over the keys. My eyes wander the room for Roxanne who stands on the opposite side, listening with an expression I can't read, and worry even if I could interpret it, it wouldn't be good.

+ + +

Eventually, I drive Roxie and Sadie home, relief hitting me hard once we leave my childhood one.

Well, at least that's over.

As we pull into the parking lot behind the bookstore, the familiar feeling I always have when I leave the girls behind fills my chest. I don't want to go home alone. Actually, I'd like to bring them to my house just outside of town.

Why haven't I done that yet?

As I park, the truck idles, and Roxie reaches for the handle.

"Monday at three thirty," I say as I nod to Sadie.

"See you then," she says, slipping out after her aunt. "Thanks for dinner. It was…interesting."

I chuckle at her sarcastic gratitude. "Just trying to keep it…interesting." Then I add, "Hey Roxie, can you stay a minute?"

Sadie pauses, looking up at her aunt, and something silent passes between them. I decide it's a girl thing, and I look away, glancing over the steering wheel while I wait. Sadie's legs rush up the back steps, and Roxie climbs back into my truck.

"What's up?" she says all casual, like she wasn't just dry-humping me when my dad walked into my old bedroom.

"I wanted to check in about Sadie. Did she tell you she'd be working for me?"

"What? When?"

"Monday. At three thirty." After Sadie told me about her possible connection to the bookstore and the flower shop robberies, I decide to anonymously cover the damages for each of the businesses. There wasn't physical vandalism as much as property violation, loss of petty cash, and a level of distrust. Roxie's struggling to understand Sadie. Hetty might not forgive. Talking to Clyde made it clear I need Sadie to pay in some way for what she's done, even if only an accomplice to the thefts, and I need to start introducing her to the community with a title. "I'm going to start telling everyone who she is to me."

Roxie looks over at me and arches one brow, so I clarify although she doesn't need the clarification. "My daughter."

She slowly smiles. "That's awesome, William."

Oh Lord, here comes the formality again.

"Well, Roxie…" I drag out her nickname. "I was also wondering if I might have the pleasure of your company for dinner this week. Just us."

Her head shoots upward. "Like a date?"

Sure. "Yeah, sure, a date."

Her mouth falls open, and I'm waiting for her to exclaim, *I thought you didn't date.* She isn't wrong. It's just dinner, but we can call it whatever she wishes. Date as a label works for me. Instead, her mouth clamps shut.

"It doesn't have to be fancy." I pause. "On second thought, yes, let's make it fancy. The Patio." It's a steak place in an old house near the municipal buildings. "Dress up." I eye her full skirt. She has this boho chic look, as my sister calls it, no matter the occasion. Full skirts. Tall or short boots. T-shirts. Necklaces and bracelets. I like it all on her. I'd like it better off. "Let's say Friday night."

"I'm not sure I should leave Sadie alone." We both know what she means. The concern she'll run is real.

"Maybe she can spend the night at Charlie's. Lucy's just a little enthusiastic she has a cousin closer to her age." I smile when I think of my niece.

"Nine and sixteen is a big difference, but yes, she did seem very receptive to Sadie." *Versus my mother, my father…*

"I don't really want to talk about tonight yet," I say, looking back through the dark windshield.

"I understand."

Does she? As I turn back to her, she might be the only one who can understand.

"But I do want to apologize for my father walking in on us. Don't be embarrassed."

She waves a dismissive hand. "It happens."

"Really? How often have you been caught on top of someone in their teenage bedroom?" I tease.

"Oh, you know…a million times." She's mocking me, trying to make light of something I'm certain bothered her.

"My dad won't give it a second thought. He's used to it."

Her head turns to me.

"Not from me," I defend. "From James," I clarify, noting the glare of those silvery eyes. Damn, I want to kiss her. Slide her over to me on this seat and then lay her back.

"Friday night? Say yes."

"Okay," she answers, sweeping hair behind her ear. *Damn, I want to kiss her*. I want to feel her under me.

She reaches for the door handle, but I reach for her forearm. "I'm sorry again about my room." I don't just mean my dad, though. I mean the fact we were interrupted.

"Sure, I'm almost having an orgasm, on your childhood bed, and you think I shouldn't be embarrassed."

"You were close?" I smile sheepishly. I never want to leave her unsatisfied, and I tug at her arm, forcing her to lean toward me.

"Weren't you?" She cringes after asking as though she's afraid of the answer.

"Fuck yeah. I was about to come undone in my pants, and I haven't done that since I was a kid in that room."

I lean forward and cup the nape of her neck, drawing her to me to take her mouth, allowing my lips to savor her before stretching my tongue forward and breaching the seam of her lips. She gasps at the intrusion, and I tug her closer to me. Her body presses against mine as best she can as we sit side-by-side on this seat, and then she snakes her arms around my neck. Our mouths move, but I want more.

"So you were close," I tease against her lips. "Let me finish you."

"Billy," she groans, her mouth meeting mine with eager vigor.

"Climb on my lap again." I press at her hips, moving her over me.

"Sadie's upstairs. She's waiting on me," Roxie says, but her mouth continues to kiss me, not making any effort to release me.

"I promise it won't take long," I tease, knowing how quickly she comes, and with such ease under my fingertips. Her legs straddle my lap, and I reach for the lever to set the bench seat as far back as it will go.

"People can see us through the window," she states, pulling back, but I quickly follow, keeping our lips attached for another second.

"The windows are fogging." It's a natural screen. My hands skate up her thighs, massaging the muscle before hiking up her skirt and searching for skin underneath. As my fingers find her underwear, she's as damp as she was over me on the bed. I slip two fingers inside the material and rush into her heat. She stills over me.

"Damn, woman. You are so wet." I growl as I lean up for her mouth again. My fingers move, my hips rock, imitating what I want to do to her.

"Billy," she groans over my mouth as her hips undulate, holding my fingers deep within her.

"I want inside you again," I mutter, and she stills.

"Here?" she whispers, and I appreciate her hesitation. It's sweet and a bit daring, and I wouldn't give up this position if someone paid me.

"Right here, darlin'." I press her back only enough to reach for my glove compartment and search for a condom. Tugging the foil packet forward, I set it on the seat and return my fingers to her, keeping her satiated while she fumbles with my belt buckle and unzips my zipper. I'm coming out of my skin, eager to enter her. The truck's overheating with the engine still running and the heat blaring, but I'll burn in hell in order to get her over me. She scrambles back enough to tug her underwear off from under her skirt, and I roll on the condom, my fingers shaking with anticipation.

Holding myself upright, I guide her back to my thighs and then press the tip at her entrance. We can hardly see with her skirt over my wrist and all our clothes still on, and for a moment, I realize this isn't how it should be with Roxanne. It should be in a bed where it's soft and warm and I can take my time, but her wet core presses over me, and I move my hand, allowing her to sheath me within her. She falls over me, swallowing me into her, and we both gasp.

"Damn, you feel so good, Roxie." My hips buck, and her hand goes to the ceiling. The other holds the back of the seat as she moves in eager undulations, riding me. My hand comes to her hip, aiding her movements as I thrust upward, and she rocks over me.

"I just need—"

My hand slips under her skin, blindly finding her clit with my thumb, and she breaks as she does. Her mouth falls open, and her body stills, but her channel clenches around me, setting me off. I thrust upward, absorbing the friction, and find my own release, pulsing deep within her.

"Fuck," I growl as my fingers dig into her hip and my eyes close, the jetting off within her like an endless stream. Thank goodness for the condom. Eventually, I settle, and when my eyes open, I find Roxie watching me. A small smile graces my lips.

"So…Friday?" I tease before releasing her from my lap.

"Is that a scheduled booty call?" she mocks.

"Nope, it's a date."

Chapter 30
Questions

[Roxanne]

Sadie working for Billy means he won't come to dinner as often as he did because *his daughter* will already be at his place of employment, where they serve food and can spend time together. These are the little things I'll need to get used to as time passes. Sadie will spend more time with him, and him alone. And I'll be back to who I was before her presence in my life every day. Alone myself.

Sadie's apprehension the first afternoon is real, and while I want to stay away, told myself they needed space, I decide to break one of my unwritten rules and eat at the pub, hoping it will give Sadie silent support.

I'm here for you.

Clyde comes to my table even though he's the bartender and not a waiter. "What can I get you to drink?"

"I'll just have a Moscato, please."

He smiles and then helps himself to the seat opposite me. "Come to see how it goes?" He tips a brow and lowers his head. "When you spy on someone, you should really be incognito."

Poor Clyde. He reads too many adult comic books. Rapping his thick knuckles on the tabletop, he excuses himself to get my drink.

I'm not spying. Well, okay, maybe a little bit, but Sadie doesn't notice me as Billy walks her around the room, showing her the ropes. He also introduces her to enough people that the crowd takes the news and spreads it to the rest.

"Billy Harrington has a daughter?"

"That the girl?"

"Who's the mother?"

Ah, Theresa. This isn't how she saw it happening. Then again, she hoped Sadie would never know. *When the time is right*, my sister would say. I guess this is the time, and I watch Sadie move about the room looking up to Billy for reassurance with each order or maybe it's the introductions. Whatever he's saying, she slowly grins as he puts his hands on her shoulders when he talks to his customers.

She can't legally serve alcohol or be in the bar past a certain hour, but a short three-to-seven shift a few nights a week won't hurt. Maybe she'll stop running to the cemetery.

Clyde returns with my wine, and I slowly sip while I peruse the menu.

"Hello. My name's Sadie, I'm his daughter. Can I take your order, or do you need another minute? I recommend the pub burger. It's delicious."

Sadie's face glows as she announces everything, her tone a little brighter than the melancholy teen she's become. Her dark hair is pulled back in a ponytail, accentuating the paleness of her skin, but the makeup around her eyes is a little less thick and her mouth holds a deep red color instead of black.

Billy stands behind her, shaking his head with a smirk on his lips.

"Wow," I say. I'm not certain she took a breath in her introduction. She exhales, and Billy chuckles. "Since it comes as a recommendation, one pub burger please with fries."

Sadie writes on an order pad and then taps the pen to click. "Got it. I'll go put the order in." She walks off, and Billy slips into the booth for a second.

"That isn't really how she's introducing herself around the bar," he says as something in my face must ask for clarification. "She's amazing, though."

Amazing.

He's beaming himself, and his eyes spark with pride. This could have all gone poorly, but whatever he's doing, she's accepting. He doesn't seem as anxious as I thought he would. These are good signs, good for Sadie.

"She's excited to be here," I say, although she acted sour about it before three p.m. She wouldn't tell me how working for him came to be, especially as she's declined working at the bookstore.

"So Friday…" He smiles sheepishly back at me. "Charlie offered to have Sadie over. Pizza movie night or something like that." Billy rolls his eyes like Charlie is a dull man. "My mother wants both the girls to come to the house instead. She mentioned Sadie practicing piano."

As the evening ended at the Harringtons, Elaina invited Sadie to play her piano anytime and then made me promise Sadie would visit twice a week. As I hesitated, saying we'd need to coordinate with my work schedule, Billy volunteered to bring Sadie to his mother's home, and Elaina even offered to pick Sadie up from school, all to which Sadie said, "You know, *Dad*, if you bought me a car, I could drive myself."

She doesn't have her license yet, and she only calls Billy dad when she's sarcastic. A pregnant pause lingered before George Jr. chuckled. He said Sadie sounded just like Mati at that age, and Elaina hugged her.

Sadie's assimilation into being a Harrington is happening a little too fast for me.

"That's fine," I find myself saying, although the pit of my stomach disagrees.

"You okay?" Billy asks, his forehead furrowing before we notice Sadie following another waitstaff person to a table.

"Yeah." I sigh. *It's going to be okay, right?* I tell myself this affirmation several times each day, assuring myself Billy Harrington means what he says. We will continue to work it out. He wants to recognize Sadie as his, and he'll step up in all areas of need. We have yet to discuss a therapist. We have a lot of things we need to discuss, but he interrupts my thoughts with a question.

"You aren't going to cancel Friday, are you?" His smile turns seductive, and I recall what we did in the front seat of his truck.

"Oh no, I'll be there for our *date*."

Over the past day, I've decided it will not be a booty call. We will go out to dinner like adults. We will discuss Sadie without her being in the other room. We will work out details for the future. Perhaps it won't be a romantic date, but it'll still be a date all the same.

"Our date," he teases and then winks, adjusting a knit cap on his head. He looks like an older skateboarder…and a troublemaker.

+ + +

Come Friday, I don't know how to dress for our date. He said to dress up, but I don't have anything nicer than my everyday clothes, which qualify as mix and match material. A shopping trip might have been in order, but I didn't have the time, and with nerves in my belly, I decide Billy gets what he gets with me.

Within one week of Sadie working at the Pub, plus piano time with Elaina, I feel her slipping away from me. Grace tried to affirm this is the life of a teenager. *Always so busy*, she said. But the unease won't rest.

She's loving the job at the pub, meeting people who don't care about her age or her status.

She's the boss's kid, they tease her, but she says they don't mean it. *They've all been so nice.*

The connection has even helped her attitude improve a little. However, I'm giving the excitement of employment time to settle. I haven't given up the idea of a therapist. Elaina offered me a number, and I made Sadie an appointment for next week.

"Am I babysitting?" Sadie asks as she lies on my bed while I fidget with an earring.

"No, Charlie just thought it would be nice for you to get to know Lucy, and I think Elaina wants to spend more time with her granddaughters." It feels foreign to say the word. My own mother never got to meet Sadie. Sadie never knew my mother, and the thought makes me sad. They would have loved one another, and perhaps Theresa wouldn't have been so hard had our mother still been here when Sadie was born.

"Should I call her Grandma?" Sadie asks, and my heart pinches.

"I think you can call her whatever you're comfortable with." Mrs. Harrington does seem rather formal, and Elaina seems improper, but as she doesn't call Billy dad, I think calling his mother by the title grandmother might hurt a bit.

"All of this is just a ruse so you and Billy can go on a date," Sadie says, surprising me.

"It's just dinner," I clarify, putting in an earring, the string of bracelets on my wrist clattering together as I lift my arm, and I catch Sadie's eye in the mirror.

"But you like him, right? You like each other?" Sadie hesitates, and I'm overwhelmed with how complicated my relationship with Billy has become.

"Sure, we like each other," I assure her. *United front,* I tell Billy all the time.

"But I mean, you *like each other* like each other?" she repeats, wanting more of an explanation, and I wish I had answers for her other than *it's complicated.* "Do you think you could love him?"

"Oh Sadie." My eyes leap up to hers in the reflective glass. "Would that be weird for you? Your father and your aunt? Not to mention, no one can predict love. It just happens, and I'm not certain Billy's a love kind of man." He seems sensitive and passionate, but love? I think he gave his heart to Rachel and whatever happened with her, she kept it when she left.

"But it could happen," Sadie continues. "You could fall in love, move in together, and I could live happily ever after with both of you."

Oh boy.

"Is that what you want? To live with both of us?" I hesitate. "I know it doesn't seem ideal to go between homes, but I don't think Billy and I could ever live together. We'd kill each other." I humorlessly laugh at the thought. "Besides, he has a house, and I have this apartment. I like my place." I look around my small room. It isn't as grand as the Harrington house, but it's still my home. Not to mention, neither Sadie nor I have been to Billy's place. It's like it's some big secret man cave.

"I'm overdressed," I mumble to myself in hopes to change the subject. Swiping my long, silvery hair behind my shoulders, I then nervously smooth my hands down my black dress. Snug at the bodice, it hangs fuller from the waist down to just above my knees. The sleeves are long, and I worry I look like I'm attending a funeral instead of a night out. This dress is almost too formal for just dinner, but the dark material contrasts with my eyes, making them stand out. I sigh. *I'm overthinking this.*

Could you fall in love with him?

The question is not that strange to ask as I feel like I'm already falling.

"He's going to love it," Sadie says, standing behind me, and I take her in through the reflection. She's almost as tall as I am, willowy and thin with that jet-black hair and those Harrington eyes. I see it more and more since Elaina mentioned it. Sadie's a beautiful girl if only those eyes didn't still glimmer with sadness. "He's going to love you."

"*Sadie,*" I drone.

"What? I'm sixteen. I know these things."

I want to ask her what she knows about love, but I remember all the crushes I had when I was her age and all the boys I thought I loved.

"Maybe I should stay home," I interject. I've hardly seen her all week. "*We* could order pizza and watch a movie."

"No," Sadie says a little too forcefully. "I mean…I think Billy's really looking forward to this."

Is he? Has he said something? What does she know? The questions curl around my tongue, but I refuse to ask like a teenager. I hate to admit it, but I've been looking forward to it myself. The last date I had was with Chad before I moved to Blue Ridge three long years ago. I'm not complaining. The bookstore is my life, but still.

A knock on the door stills us both. Nerves ripple through my belly again, but Sadie gives me a reassuring smile through the mirror.

"He's going to love you," she sing-songs as she rushes around me to answer the door for Billy.

I follow Sadie, and my breath catches when I see Billy. He's wearing a blue blazer over a light denim shirt and dark jeans. He looks *amazing*. Sadie and I each grab our jackets, and as Billy holds the door for us to leave, he stops me with a hand on my forearm. The smell of him overwhelms me. Cloves and spice and my mouth waters for a sip of him.

"Hey," he says sheepishly as if he didn't already greet me.

"Hey, yourself." I smile and then he leans in and corner kisses my lip.

"I'm excited about tonight." His eyes dance, and I'm ready to skip the formality of dinner and get to later, whatever later might bring.

I'm in over my head here because for all my denial of the possibility of loving Billy Harrington with Sadie, my heart knows the truth. I'm already head over heels for him. Back against the wall, heart at my feet, willing to give him everything if I could only be assured that he wants me. If I could feel like this is more than casual.

We drop Sadie off at the Harrington home and then head to The Patio, a famous steakhouse, and the only fancy restaurant in the area. It's an old Victorian home converted on the lower level into dining areas. It's private and quiet and dark. Billy and I have a small table in the back corner of what I assume was once a parlor. He knows the owner and jokes with the waitress who used to work for him.

"Tell Braxton I want the best steak he has, especially as he stole you from me."

For some reason, the teasing tone in his statement unsettles me, and I sip my wine while they continue to banter. As the pretty woman with reddish hair and bright blue eyes saunters away, Billy looks at me.

"What?"

"Always a flirt," I mock, trying hard to swallow the acid in my throat. He shakes his head and crosses his arms on the edge of the table.

"Roxanne." He exhales my name in frustration, but it also sounds like plea. "Am I at dinner with her?"

"No."

"Then can we call a truce for one night? No, Billy is a player cracks. No, one-hit-wonder comments. Just you and me tonight. That's it." The plea settles to a near whine, begging me, and I swallow.

"I'm sorry. Yes. Yes, let's just enjoy each other."

His bark-colored eyes spark with the candlelight at that comment, and a salacious grin curls his lips I'm growing too familiar with. "That's what I'm hoping. Enjoying each other."

The innuendo is evident, but I chuckle.

"So I wanted to talk to you about a few things regarding Sadie. I was thinking—"

Billy holds up a hand, and I halt speaking. "I'm going to make us sound like an old married couple, but can we please not talk about the kid tonight either? No Sadie conversation. Just us. I want to know more about you, Roxanne. What makes you tick? Where have you been for sixteen years? What do you want next in life?"

I'm floored by the rejection of Sadie-talk but equally surprised at his questions. Brushing my hair over one ear, I glance down at my plate. How long has it been since I've talked about myself? I wouldn't know where to start.

"Okay," I draw out. I have so much to say about Sadie, but I hold back.

"Tell me about you before you came back here. Love interests. Things you did with friends. Anything. Everything." He laughs as he lifts his beer and takes a sip. It's almost comical how he's drinking *his* beer in this other establishment, preferring the robust hops of his heritage to anything else.

I nod and begin with things I consider factual—college, employment with the big chain bookstore, and then the dream to have my own place. I mention how I missed Blue Ridge after we moved and how sad I was at the loss of my mother, which feels strangely similar to Sadie's situation. I don't mention Theresa or Sadie, though. I stick to only me. Friends. Travel. And then Chad.

"We were together for five years, and I thought he might be it. Not in a conventional way. He never asked me to marry him." I shrug, dismissing my disappointment that he hadn't proposed. "I just thought we'd be this forever couple. Content and satisfied where we were at."

Billy's engaged expression sobers a bit, and he nods like he understands, but his brows pinch like he has a question he wants to ask but doesn't as I continue.

"When I mentioned the bookstore, he always blew it off like it was just a pipe dream and never a reality. A fantasy for someday."

Billy nods again, his lips pursing in agreement.

"Then when I told him I wanted to move to Blue Ridge and open a store here, he told me to follow my heart, but he wouldn't come with me. His heart was no longer mine."

"He said that?" Billy asks astonished, brows rising.

"Not in so many words, but pretty close."

Do what you want, Chad said with a shrug, nonchalant and complacent, like my leaving or staying meant nothing to him one way or the other.

"Here's the thing. I don't think people should settle, and I had. I didn't want to be content or mildly satisfied, but live my best life, and that meant moving here. Walking away from Sadie was difficult, but Sadie also wasn't mine to keep. She is my niece. *My sister's daughter* as Theresa would remind me if I stepped too far out of line with her." I'd settled here as well. I was content to be the aunt when I really wanted my own daughter. I shrug again, fearing I've said too much. "I needed to do something for me. Something that made me *happy*."

Billy stares at me before slowly sitting back in his seat. His eyes focus on my face, taking me in, and I wonder what he sees. He's called me stunning, but he hasn't commented on my dress tonight other than to say I look nice. I don't need his approval, but I appreciate it all the same.

"It's strange how much I think you get me without knowing everything about me."

What?

"I wanted the pub because I wanted something for myself as well. While it meant proving something to my parents and even Rachel, deep down, I needed to prove to me that I was good enough. I could do this…thing…for me, be successful on my terms, and in the end, be happy."

I smile. I do understand. I don't know why he'd need to prove anything to his ex-wife or his family, but I get it.

Silently, I wonder if that's where all the women come into play. Was he trying to prove something to himself there as well?

"I'm sorry it didn't work out with Chad, but he's a fool. And it isn't love if you can't accept each other's dreams."

Is he speaking from experience? Did Rachel reject his dream?

"So you lived with Chad, huh? And what was that like?"

I tilt my head, wondering what he means. People live together all the time outside of marriage.

"Would you ever consider living with a man again?"

"Like roommates?" I scoff, laughing at the thought.

"Something like that, sure. I guess." His expression shifts. Does he really mean as roommates or perhaps he means in another manner? Either way, I don't understand why he even asks, but I'm quick to answer.

"I don't think I could do it again, not without a promise of more." My head lowers as I feel awkward having this conversation with him, but it's a good reminder we aren't anything more than…friends. We aren't romantically involved. We've had sex. It's how Billy does things. "With the store and now Sadie, my life is pretty full, though." The words fall short. I'm missing a sliver of something deeper, and I know what it is, but I won't be sharing that reality with Billy.

"Yeah, I know what you mean. Sadie. The pub. I'm good." He doesn't sound convinced either, leaving me wonder what sliver is missing for him.

Our dinner arrives, and he *oohs* and *aahs* over the steak, moving our conversation out of serious-zone to carefree-casual. Dinner ends on a more rambunctious tone as Billy can't believe I'm not a fan of any particular sport.

"Baseball?"

I shake my head.

"Football? Georgia State?"

Nope. Another shake.

"Oh my God, are you human? Everyone loves a sport. Something. Hiking. Walking, even." He laughs more as I continue to twist my head side to side. "Then how the hell do you stay in such good shape?"

I stare at him. "You think I'm in shape?" I choke a little on the laughter coming from my throat.

"Yes." He drags out the word and widens his eyes, glaring back at me.

"I get winded going up the back stairs," I tease.

"Well, I know one sport you're good at..." His suggestive tone softens, and I stare back at him, anticipating his next word, and then he mouths it to me. *Sex.*

Just because he's triple-crowned or World Series'd or whatever in the activity doesn't mean I have.

"Are you serious?" My voice squeaks as it rises, drawing the attention of a couple seated near us. I lean forward as if I can hide myself behind my wine glass, and I lower to a whisper. "You can't be serious."

"I'm very serious." He wiggles his brows, which makes me laugh again, and then he lifts his arm for the bill. He isn't answering me, and the lack of response leaves me anxious. Is this what he expects? I'm not opposed, but it seems so obvious. Who sleeps with a man on the first date? Oh, right, I've already slept with him, so is this just a formality? Why am I thinking all these things?

Could you love him?

I'm overthinking all of it.

Billy pays and leads me out of the restaurant with a hand on my lower back before helping me into his truck. I don't normally wear heels, and I struggle with the running board.

"Whoa," Billy warns. "Don't tell me you drank too much?" There's real concern on his face when I look up at him and assure him I merely slipped.

Once situated in his truck, he rounds to the driver's side and hops in. He sits for a second, not pressing the automatic ignition. Slowly, he turns to me. "I don't want to take you home yet. I'd suggest a drink at the pub, but I don't want to take you there, either. I want to be alone, but I don't want to imply anything despite my teasing at dinner. If it's okay with you, I'd like to take you to my place."

His house.

He told us a while back how he purchased an older home and fixed it up, taking his time to do each room himself.

"It's been a labor of love," he admits as he pulls up before it. The rustic clapboard is a dark color, like most homes in the area. Immediately upon entering, we stand in a living-dining room combination with a thick, rustic brown leather couch and matching chair plus a large wooden coffee table on small wheels. The furniture might be too big for the space, but it's comfortable. Inviting. He takes my coat and hangs it on a hook by the front door, and I marvel at how it looks as though it belongs on this peg with the inhabitant of this house.

The ceilings are tall, and the walls are a soft gray. It's very minimalist and clean, which surprises me a little. Billy leads me to a kitchen only a little bigger than mine but with state-of-the-art appliances in stainless steel and light pine cabinetry. It's surprisingly fresh for a single guy, homey even when I expected something more mountain-man from him. We round a staircase, and he leads me upward to a casual loft area with a sofa and a television set.

"This is where I spend most of my time." It's strange to imagine him here as I've seen him so often in my place. Two bedrooms and a bathroom are the other rooms upstairs. He leads me back to the first floor, and we turn right through a wide opening off the living room at the base of the steps. Looking over my shoulder, I note a sliding door closes off the space to the living room, and then I turn back to the room. A lush bed fills the space with thick log pegs for the four legs. On the other side of the bed is a patio door, and Billy motions me toward it.

"This is my favorite place." He flips a switch, and an enclosed porch comes into view. It's all screens, but he opens the door and steps outside. "It's cold but would you like to sit here for a bit? I can light the pit."

A cedar loveseat lacking cushions and two rocking chairs surround a firepit. It's probably not safe to light it inside the covered porch, so I shake my head to the fire.

"I can make hot chocolate." He hangs his head, hesitant with the suggestion, and I smile despite myself.

"I'd like that."

When his head pops up, his expression is like a child given a present. He steps forward and kisses my cheek. "Be right back." Quickly, he returns and hands me a heavy quilt to wrap around myself. Sitting on a rocking chair, I absorb the peaceful quiet of a cold winter's night. It's so dark. Without the streetlights of town, I can't see a thing outside the screen panels. A string of small white bulbs decorates the ceiling, giving the enclosed area an outdoorsy feel, like a springtime party.

I wonder how many women he's entertained here, and I hate the thought of being one of several.

He returns with two thick mugs, whip cream peeking over the top.

"No marshmallows?" I tease.

"Not a fan."

"Really?"

"Bad experience as a child."

"Another drinking story?" I tweak a brow as I blow at the steaming mug. His eyes narrow in on my lips, pursed as I release the air.

"More like a holiday mishap. I tend to overindulge in things and one too many Peeps later, a rainbow of them…shall we say…revisited the Easter table."

I laugh. "Oh my."

"Yeah." He smiles as he sips his hot chocolate and a white dot forms on his nose.

"You have something…" I point at my own cold nose and twirl my finger around it. A thick fingertip swipes at the spot, and then he places said finger in his mouth, sucking off the sweet whipped cream. I watch, his finger lingering between those warm lips, and I swallow hard.

As his finger recedes, we fall silent, surrounded by the lack of noise. "It's very peaceful here."

He nods. "It gets kind of quiet. It's one reason I hang out at the pub so much. I like the noise. But I also like having a place where nobody knows my business. This is my space for when I need to wind down."

Again, I wonder how many women have wound him up here. With the porch off the bedroom, it's like a mini getaway attached to the rest of the home. It's romantic.

"I know we said no talk of Sadie, but I'd like to start bringing her here. She can have one of the bedrooms upstairs, and the loft gives her extra space to have friends over. Honestly, I might need to get used to her in my space." He pauses, twisting his lips. "I'm not good at sharing."

"Might make it difficult to bring people home." I chuckle, dismissing the edge to my voice. Sadie here. Other women here. He's thinking of the future with her and without me.

Billy sets his mug on the wood planks of the deck and rocks forward in the chair he's been sitting in. His elbows come to his thighs. He's removed his blazer and rolled up his sleeves. More arm porn for me, but his tone turns serious.

"I don't bring people here. My family. Clyde. Guy friends. Not women." His glare is pointed as he looks at me. He stands abruptly and enters his room, leaving the porch door open for me to follow.

I set down my mug, follow him, and close the door behind me. The cool air leaves a chill in the room but so does his distance, standing to face a fireplace at the end of his bed. His back remains to me.

"You can't let it go, can you?" he whispers. "My *reputation.*"

Stepping forward, tugging the quilt tighter around my shoulders, I pause near his back.

"I just want to understand. Not the rumors, but the why. Why so many women? Why an affair?"

"It was her, not me," he says, his voice quiet and low. "Rachel. She had the affair, not me."

My breath hitches, and I stare at his broad shoulders, the weight he's carried allowing people to think it was him.

"Then why—"

The question cuts off as he spins to face me. "People believe what they want to believe, and it was just easier to let them. It was easier than admitting my wife had an affair *on me*…with another woman."

My breath catches again, eyes widening in surprise.

"That's right. Rachel Hollycock didn't like cock, especially her own husband's."

"Billy," I whisper. It can't be true. They were high school sweethearts. They were the golden couple. People aspired to be them. Treated them like they were royalty.

"She experimented in college. I thought it was a phase. She thought it was a phase. Things were different twenty-five years ago."

We've entered a new millennium. Being homosexual isn't a stigma, but even as young as twenty-five years in the past, it had been.

"Rachel met *her* on an airplane on a trip to Florida. When she arrived, she called me to say she was never coming back. Found herself and her true love." His head remains lower, his hands slipped into his pockets. "When we divorced, she paid me a settlement. The chick she fell in love with was loaded, and Rachel wanted it to remain a secret. I signed a fucking NDA to keep quiet." He swipes a hand through his hair. "She'd been my best friend. I'd lost my virginity to her. I was willing to accept anything about her. I didn't want to take the money, but the other woman insisted." He exhales, looking to the side.

"So you lied to save face for her."

His head shoots back to me. "I lied to save myself. God forgive me, but I was embarrassed. Not that she's gay, I didn't care about that, but I was upset I didn't know. I thought she was just holding out on me when we were younger, and then thought she didn't like sex or maybe just didn't like sex *with me* when we were married. Honestly, all of it was true. She wasn't being *true* to herself and couldn't enjoy what we did." He exhales, turning his head away from me one more time. "It's silly, but at first, I was ashamed of myself. Ashamed I wasn't enough. And whether it was a man or a woman, I was humiliated she cheated on me. I felt betrayed because I loved her despite everything, and she left me. She ran away to be with her."

The pressure of their image landed on his shoulders, and it's clear to me he didn't know how to handle the reality of their situation. It's also becoming clear that Billy Harrington loves hard, so when he lost her, he took it equally as hard and didn't know how to recover. He covered for her, taking on this reputation to disguise his hurt. His devotion to Sadie makes sense to me. When he loves, he loves. But when he hurts, he aches. I don't want him to ache.

"People thought what they wanted, and I didn't deny it. It wasn't anyone's damn business. Hell, sleeping around perpetuated the gossip."

He swipes another hand through his hair and stares at me. "I know...*I slept around*," he emphasizes like a confession. "I wanted to prove to myself I was a man. Okay? A worthy man. If not to my wife, who couldn't help herself, then at least to someone else. The whole thing messed with my head."

I sympathize. I can see he cared for Rachel, and he wanted to be open to her situation, her reality, but there were ramifications for him.

"Billy, there isn't a woman in this town who doubts your masculinity." He's a vision of virility, broad in stature with the dark beard and graying hair. His flirty personality and overall aura of sexuality screams he's all male. But he's more than the sexual persona. He's a man with deep feelings, ones he's guarded to admit so he isn't hurt again.

"I doubted myself. She was the only woman I'd been with. I didn't have any other gauge until I..." He drifts off. *Until he slept with others.* A growing need to prove himself.

"I already told you the last time was May and before that was probably close to February." He sighs, the weight of his admission still wrapped around him. Swiping one more hand through his hair, he pauses with his hand cupped around the back of his neck, defeated. "I'd appreciate if you didn't tell anyone about this. No one in my family knows the truth, except for Mati, and that was just recently."

"About not sleeping with anyone since May?" I question, and he finally looks at me, seeing I'm teasing in hopes to break some of the tension.

"About Rachel," he mutters.

"I won't tell a soul, Billy."

We stare at one another for a long minute, the room finally restored to some heat. I release the quilt I've been holding with clenched hands at my chest and set it on his bed.

"Is it weird that it feels good to finally tell someone?" he asks, and I look up at him as I shake my head.

"That's a lot of pressure to carry."

He scrubs his knuckles up under his chin and his eyes shift. "Yeah, well, that certainly put a damper on the evening, though. I don't know where all that came from."

I do. I'd pushed him to the edge, and when I consider it, I'm surprised he told me, but his honesty makes me feel special—important to him—like I can fully trust him. We're going to work things out with Sadie. Maybe we'll even work out as well.

"I guess I should take you home." He interjects, his eyes still avoiding mine.

Is that what he really wants? Because he looks a little lost and a lot alone. All that proving to himself can wear a man down. Who builds him up?

I want to build him up. I want to be that support for him.

"You're turning into a great father," I say, stepping toward him. His eyes widen when he finally looks at me. "You've stepped up from the start." His brows crease, the skin puckering between them.

"And I think you're an incredible businessman." His forehead furrows. "You've done so much for the community, and I know you donate a portion of your profits each month to the school." His eyes widen. Yeah, I heard it through the grapevine of gossip how Billy Harrington gives money to the special education department.

"I don't want some kid with dyslexia to feel like a failure," he whispers to justify his cause. I smile but ignore the comment.

"And I don't think you should have any concerns about proving your manhood." I'm in his space, and his nostrils flare. "You have beautiful eyes. Strong hands. An incredible body." I lower my hand to grab one of his, pressing our palms together. "Irresistible lips." His eyes slowly lower to mine, blushing at my compliment. "Rachel had to be who she was, but she didn't need to break you."

He nods once, rolling his lips inward. My hand lifts his hand, placing it just above my left breast. My heart races. This man has been a dysfunctional and frustrating crush of mine since the moment I met him, and the moment of truth lays before me.

"Any woman would be proud to be with you, Billy Harrington." And then I admit all that I shouldn't. "I would be."

Chapter 31
Sex With Socks On

[Billy]

I would be.

Does she mean it? Would she be proud to be with me, really be…with me? Or is she just trying to ease my ego? I went a little serious on her this evening. I don't know where the confession came from other than her accusing me of bringing women here. I haven't done that. This is my haven because I knew I'd need one. I need a place to detox from the parties and women and the upkeep of the façade. I *was* a player, proving to myself I could play and proving to the community what they already thought—it must have been *him.*

It was always Billy's fault.

Roxanne stands before me, too close, too potent, and once again, that need to prove myself rears. I cup her face and then slip both hands behind her neck, lacing my fingers together. I don't draw her against me but just hold onto her, like a man clutching at a buoy before he's about to drown.

Her hands coast up my chest and fingers curl into the collar of my shirt, giving it a tug. I lower as she tips up, and she kisses me. Soft. Sweet. Sexy. Her mouth is a guilty pleasure, and I open, allowing her to give me more.

Hold onto me, the kiss screams because I want her. All of her, like I haven't wanted anyone, not even Rachel. Over time, I accepted Rachel never fully gave herself to me. Not in the way I thought lovers should. However, Roxanne is before me, warm and willing, and my hands unclasp, brushing down her body to pull her closer to me. She shivers against me.

"Cold?" I mutter against her lips, knowing it's quite possibly not the air temperature making her tremble.

"A little." She laughs. She's right. With the door open for a few minutes plus the time spent outside, she's chilled.

"I'd like to warm you," I tease.

"I'd like you to warm me."

I pull back to look down at her and see those gray eyes sparkling like polished silver.

"Would this be a first?"

I've already admitted I haven't brought anyone to my home. I'm on the verge of telling her I saved her for last. She's who I've wanted for a while and just didn't see it behind the bickering. She'll be the first and last woman to enter this bed because she's it for me.

Instead, I ignore the question, and say, "If you're chilly, let's get you under the covers." Her eyes question the shift to my voice, but she nods. I spin her so I can unzip her dress. The material hugs her breasts while flaring out at the hips, accentuating her curves. She looks gorgeous, but I don't think I've complimented her yet in it.

"You look beautiful in this dress, but I'd love to see you out of it," I whisper as I tug down the zipper and suck at her neck. Her head tips as I nip a particular spot, and she purrs. Then I bite the juncture, and her knees give. An arm at her waist catches her, and while I don't want to rush, I do want her clothing off. I press at the edges of the dress, exposing her back and slipping it over her shoulders. She lets it slide to the floor and then turns to face me. Long legs in knee-high boots. Black lacy underwear and matching bra.

"You're fucking stunning." My finger traces the hardly contained swell above her bra. A breast reduction, she told me. She's still voluptuous and a vision of naughty with her wild silver hair, so much skin on display, plus those boots. If I thought I could get away with it, I'd ask her to leave them on. Instead, I guide her to sit on the edge of the bed and unzip them, taking my time to remove the leather. Inside, are bright yellow socks with rubber ducks on them.

"What the hell?" I laugh, and she covers her face with both hands.

"I knew my feet would be cold."

I continue to laugh, the spell of my seduction slightly broken as I remove the other boot but allow the socks to remain.

"You're going to have sex with me with my socks on?" she chides.

"Who said anything about sex?" I tease, tugging my shirt from my pants and then pulling both undershirt and dress shirt over my head. Her breath catches at the sight of me. I work hard at my abs, but I don't shave my chest. Wild curls dance over my skin there, and her hands lift instantly for them. Her fingertips scratch through the coarse hair like they do on my chin.

Damn, that feels good.

Her hands drag lower, and she helps herself to my belt and then unzips my pants. Before I know it, Roxanne has taken control, and I'm in her mouth, wet and eager, as she sucks at me with unleashed enthusiasm. Her cheeks hollow, and the suction increases, tugging and stroking the length of me with her tongue.

"Roxie," I breathe. I'm losing control, but I need to regain it. I need to keep proving myself. I press at her shoulders, pushing her back to release me. "Roxie, darlin'."

The endearment stills her, and she unlatches after a final long drag down my dick.

Damn.

"Get under the covers," I tell her as I bend to step out of my boxers and pants, kicking off my shoes as I do.

"These sheets are toasty," she mutters, pulling them up to her neck. She looks innocent and goofy in my bed, like a little kid trying to warm up before sleep. Somehow, she also looks right in the light gray flannel and thick charcoal duvet under her chin. I slip under the sheets myself and pull her to me.

"Roxie," I whisper, still feeling a little unraveled at how things are progressing.

"William," she teases. There hasn't been the mad rush to disrobe or the hasty groping of my typical sexcapades. No dash for the mattress or a quick jump to the finish line. My hands take their time outlining her body as she heats under the sheets. My hands coast her arms. Fingers trickle along her collarbone. I curl around her neck. The rightness of her in my bed is overwhelming.

Her hands lower for me once again, and though I appreciate her eagerness, I want to take my time with her. Strangely, I feel like this might be the only night I get. I grip her wrists, halting her fingers from curling around my dick.

"Let me explore a little first. I want to read you."

She stares at me.

"*You don't touch a book, William. You read it. You enjoy.*" I imitate her voice and her words to me from weeks ago, and her brows lift. "You're a book I want to touch and read and enjoy over and over again."

She huffs at the reminder. She said I'd never read her. I'd never discover the fine lines of her face. I'd never uncover her breasts or her backside as I do removing her bra and then her lacy underwear. I'd never devour the unwritten words in her sighs or purrs, the ones she gives me as my hands roam over all her skin. And then my lips follow, kissing, sucking, and nipping. Her neck. Her shoulder. Her inner wrist. I nibble her fingers and her nipples and then the middle of her belly. I lower, the covers a tent over us, and I read between the folds of her.

"Billy," she groans as my fingers draw around her before my tongue dips into her. Her hips respond with a slow thrust before dropping back to the mattress. I hold her in place, but she undulates minutely beneath my palm on her hip bone, making love to my tongue as it delves into her.

She bends her knees, opening, spreading, and allowing me in. Her body slowly dances against my face, and the soft stroke of a sock-covered foot swipes up my lower back. I'd laugh at the strangeness, only it feels too right. With the bed tent keeping us under darkness and warmth, I'd have sex with this woman every night, socks on and all.

She doesn't come quickly like when I simply touch her but allows me to draw it out of her, letting it roll in a slow wave. Her head turns to the side. Her fingers delve into my hair. Her mouth opens on a deep sigh. She is so beautiful when she opens for me like this and comes.

Once she settles from the high, she purrs, "My turn."

"You already had a turn," I tease, climbing back up her body, licking a path as I proceed north on her. I circle a nipple again and then suck at her neck.

"It wasn't enough," she whispers, and my chest aches. The clutching of roots, digging deeper and deeper, gripping me.

It's never going to be enough.

Holding myself in my fist, I stroke my tip through her soaked folds. She's so wet from the combination of her and my mouth, and I want to slip in, thrust forward, and rush to fill her, but I won't. I spilled on her belly that first night when I should have taken more care with her. Roxie is different. She's so much more to me.

"Condom?" I question, not withdrawing from the slow drag through her heat, but letting her coat me completely. Damn, she feels so good like this, but it isn't smart, not responsible. I know we did it the first time without one, but I don't want any doubts. No concerns over my history. "I've laid it all out for you."

"I know you did," she replies, taking a deep breath. "And I have an IUD." Her fingers stroke over my temples. "You have nothing to prove to me. I already know you're a good man."

Shit. This makes me want to be a better man. She smiles weakly, and I want to assure her. She's the only one I want. Her fingers reach around me, tugging up sheets and blankets, restoring the fortress of warmth around us.

"You're sure about this?" I ask. I'm not even certain what I'm asking. *About us? Here? Now? The future?* I don't want any doubts. I also don't want to turn back, feeling as if we've already gone too far, but something in her eyes makes me hesitate.

"I'm not certain of anything," she admits. "But I want you."

We should talk about that uncertainty. *Does she not feel how much I want her?* My heart races. My fingers tremble. I'll never be close enough even once I've entered her. I want all of her.

But I'm too wound up to talk, so I position myself and then take my time entering her. I'm not certain I've been this cautious, this reserved, but I want to worship her, savor every second. Every ripple. Every ridge.

I want to feel her surround me, and I easily slide home, filling her. Then I still. I need a minute. With those sparkling silver eyes, intense and questioning, this moment seems like so much more. She's important to me, and I want her to feel it. I was right when I teased her. *Who said anything about sex?* This isn't sex. It has never been just sex with her.

I pull back, and her eyes roll closed. Rushing forward, I stress. "Open for me."

Her lids lift, and she watches my face as I retreat once again. Her hands are already on my shoulder blades, but it isn't enough. I thrust forward and groan near her ear, "Hold onto me."

Her fingertips massage into my back and then lower to my ass, squeezing the tense globes as I set a controlled rhythm, dragging out the motions to fill her and repeat. In and out. In and out. It's as if we're dancing, and I never want the music to stop.

There's a rumor going 'round…

No more rumors. Only truths. I want all of Roxanne.

"Billy," she moans, her head lifting, her fingers digging into my ass, attempting to hold me in place as though she wants me to fill her, she wants me to stay inside her, she wants me. Her leg rises higher against my side, and I slip an arm under her knee, opening her even more to me. Still taking my time, I increase the tempo. Her body begs for more, and my body needs to up the beat.

"I love my name on your lips," I stammer, thrusting faster. "I love your lips on my dick."

Her breath catches, and I move faster.

My name is a soft plea to give her everything.

"I love how deep I am inside you. I love how you hold onto me."

Billy becomes a strangled cry of relief and release as she unfolds around me. I take in her face. Lids lowered, teeth digging into her lip. I'd kiss her except she looks so fucking beautiful, and I implode, stilling all but my dick which jolts inside her, spilling into her depths.

I collapse, crushing her only momentarily before rolling to my side and dragging her with me.

"I thought you weren't going to have sex with me with my socks on," she teases, nuzzling into my neck.

"I didn't have sex with you, Roxanne. I made love to you."

And before she can speak, I lift her chin and kiss her.

+ + +

I wake to the soft murmur of her voice outside the room.

"Are you sure?" She attempts to remain quiet, and without hearing an answer to her question, I assume she's on the phone. I reach to the floor for my boxers and slip them on under the sheets. It's still warm from the heat of us together, but her side is cooling. I don't like the sensation. I don't want the night to end.

"Okay, well, tell Elaina that's very generous of her." I pause at the doorway to my room, looking past the stairs to Roxanne wrapped in the quilt I gave her earlier. She's sitting on my leather couch, feet tucked up in the blanket. The rightness of her sitting there fills me again as I watch her speak.

"Okay, baby. We'll see you tomorrow. I mean, me. I'll come get you in the morning." Her eyes close, and a shaky hand comes to her forehead. I step forward, and her head twists in my direction. "Night, Sadie."

She clicks off the phone and sets it on the coffee table. "I just wanted to check in with her."

"What time is it?"

"It's close to midnight."

I nod, scratching at my chin. "I guess I fell asleep," I sheepishly admit. After kissing her and begging her to promise she wouldn't speak, I just held her as she held me. Arms wrapped around one another, she slid to her back, and I followed, my head resting in the crook of her arm. Her bare breasts are distracting but not as distracting as her fingers massaging through my hair. I closed my eyes and gave in to her touch.

"You did, but it's okay. You must have been tired. Anyway, your mother asked Sadie to spend the night. I guess Lucy is staying there as well, and they are enjoying some girl time. Your dad's at the pub."

I huff. As much as my father has always been uncertain of my decision, he financially supports it by sitting on a stool most evenings.

"Sounds good. Is that okay with you?"

Roxie shrugs. "It's Sadie's decision."

"You doing okay? A lot is happening kind of quick. I knew my mother would easily cave, welcoming Sadie into the fold. It might be one reason I prolonged introducing her. I didn't want to have to share her with all of them." I chuckle half-heartedly. *Or you*, I should add. I don't want to share Roxie yet, but I hold my tongue.

"This is what Sadie needs. A family. A big one. It's something she's never had, nor did Theresa or I. Speaking of, I want to discuss therapy with you."

"Therapy for me?" I raise a brow, my arms folding over my bare chest. I'm standing in only my boxer briefs. Her eyes fixate on my pecs before shaking her head.

"No, William. Not for you. For Sadie."

"Why? What's wrong?" My arms fall, and I step forward, lowering to the sturdy coffee table before Roxie. She gives me one of her scathing looks.

"A lot of things *have* happened rather quickly," she repeats my words, eyes narrowed.

Oh, right. "Sure. I think my mother mentioned something about a grief counselor." Momma has good intentions, only I didn't want to push.

Roxie still gives me this look like I'm dense.

"You know, I find it cute how you hate me sometimes," I tease, reaching for what I suspect is her knee, tucked up under the quilt.

"I don't hate you," she states, sounding a little unconvincing.

"Then what *do* you do me?"

She laughs hesitantly. "I thought I just did do you."

I laugh, a deep bark as I slip to my knees on the hardwood before her. I push at the coffee table with my feet, forcing it to move as it's on wheels. My hands slide under the blanket for her ankles, and my knuckles brush the back of her thighs.

"Speaking of doing…whatcha wearing under there?"

"Do you know how creepy that sounds?" She laughs, but excitement fills her voice.

"Let me see." I peek under the quilt to discover she's naked other than my T-shirt, and I swallow hard. "Roxanne, is your naked ass on that quilt?"

She wiggles her hips. "And if it is?"

I tug her ankles forward, forcing her to drop her knees and dangle her legs off my couch. "Then I need to see." Only I don't look. I let my hands explore under the covers while she holds it pinned at her chest with a fist. My fingers quickly find her bare thighs, climb higher, and then press between them. She spreads.

"Someone's eager," I tease, but her eyes spear me in a warning. Touch or else. "And if I don't touch you?" I flirt, responding to her glare.

"Then I'll take matters into my own hands." I freeze at her words. "Like I often do."

"Sweet Jesus," I mutter. "Show me."

She gasps, but I pause, curling my palms over her thighs and spreading them wider. The top of her is still covered but her knees move the quilt, allowing me a peep show of her center. Fingers come into view near a patch of dark curls, and I watch.

"I can't believe I'm doing this," she whispers, but I'm too mesmerized to speak as two collective fingers dip lower. Her head tilts back. Her lids close, and I can't believe she's showing me this either, giving this to me. Watching her touch herself feels forbidden and intimate at the same time. A gift, and I realize what she's doing. She's proving herself to me.

"Stop," I command, and she does. Her head snaps up, and her fingers retract. I reach for her wrist and draw her hand to me. Opening my lips, I suck at the digits just touching her. My free hand roams forward, brushing over the swollen clit, ripe and ready for taking me again. My finger enters her quickly, and her head falls back. Her fingers remain in my mouth, allowing me to lick them clean while I add another finger to my attention to her lower lips. Her legs spread wider, and she sighs.

"You're so bad, Billy," she cries, and I work faster, delving deeper.

"Yes, but you love me."

Her breath hitches as does mine, and we both still. I should retract my fingers and my words, but I don't. I press on, hoping to distract her, hoping to erase what I've put out there. She told me once she could love me. *Could she still?*

She comes as I wish, and I reach around her for her backside, tugging her to the edge of the cushions. I hike her leg over my shoulder and lean up over her. Open. Satiated. Willing. I shove down my boxers, stroking the naked tip over her folds as I did earlier, stiff and weeping to enter her bare. I continue to tease, moving in a way she coats my length.

"Tell me you want it and I'll do anything you ask, but I want all the words. I want all your thoughts." *I want your heart.*

"My thoughts?" she snarks, her eyes widening and then quickly lowering. "You can't handle my thoughts, William."

"Meaning?" I snap, comfortable sparring with her in this sexy position. I'm back in control. The rightness sensation when I made love to her was beginning to freak me out. Our eyes meet in the battle of wills I so love about her. She's holding back from me. I sense it, but I'm also fool enough to ignore it because I want what she's offering at this moment. *Her.*

"It means…just fuck me, Billy." Her voice softens, a mix of lust and confusion. She wants me. I know she does, and perhaps it puzzles her. It certainly snuck up on me, but I'm all in now. There's no turning away from her, no turning away from giving her what she wants.

Could she love me?

"Time's wasting, William." Her voice mocks my name, but she's teasing me. Her hand lowers to her inner thigh again. She's a vision, all glistening and skin. Her fingers move toward her center, but I swipe at her hand, batting it away.

"For me," I cry like a spoiled child. "I want…" *to love you, be with you, hold you*. Guiding myself to her entrance, I allow only the tip before her hips tilt, and then I rush forward. She lets out a gasp, and I still, holding inside her. *Hell yes*. This is wild and reckless and a little dangerous, and everything I want from her.

I draw back and then ram into her, hammering at her as her breasts jiggle and her breath hitches in a thrusting rhythm. I turn my head to suck at her calf resting over my shoulder. This is insane and incredible, and I'm never going to get enough of her. My hands balance me over her hips. Her channel clutches at me, and the base of my spine warns me.

"Roxie. I…it's gonna be huge." I can't last. Her warmth. Her wetness. Her saucy stare. I still and explode, silver stars dancing before me. My dick juts, spilling into her. I jolt again, and her eyes watch my face. A knowing smile greets me as she bites the corner of her lip.

"I…" *I love you*, I almost blurt.

Where is that coming from?

From the sex, William. You just had sex with this woman on your couch—this woman who stole your heart—and it's messing with your head.

Chapter 32
Wall Sex Woes

[Roxanne]

While Billy sleeps late, I'm awake early. Our internal clocks are set different as we discussed last night after round two. He's a night owl, and I'm an early bird. I help myself to coffee and sit on the leather couch once again. I'm wearing his T-shirt with the quilt draped over me just like the night before. I might steal this quilt.

He trusted me last night with some heavy secrets, and I don't take that lightly. I've been holding the secret of Sadie's paternity for sixteen years. By not only accepting his honesty, I wanted him to know I trust him. I trust him to do right by Sadie *and me*.

I made love to you.

Does he love me?

Is that the direction we're headed?

He's had a lot on his plate over the years.

Rachel Hollycock liked women more than Billy Harrington? He sounded like a faithful, passionate lover to her, and she cheated on him.

I'm trying to prove myself.

He has nothing to prove. Son. Husband. Father. Man. I want the charade to stop with me. Aware of the truth, I see how much it hurts each time I mention his past indiscretions, and I promise myself to do better. Trust. It's been a difficult thing to give in regard to Sadie, but I also need to trust in myself.

He is not his reputation.

He made love to me last night.

He is more than something casual.

"Morning," he says, standing just inside his room, his hair rumpled. He's wearing plaid pajama pants and an oversized Georgia State sweatshirt. He's dressed like a teenage girl, and I chuckle.

"What?"

"You're ruining the fantasy," I tease.

"What fantasy is that?"

"One where you walk around only in your boxer briefs." He looks down at the sweatshirt, tugging it forward by the hem.

"Yeah, well, it's cold, and someone keeps stealing my quilt."

Ha. He's been willingly giving it to me.

"I can share," I tease, flipping over a tiny corner.

"Don't overdo it," he mocks, his voice a little rougher this morning. There's a strange vibe rolling off him, but I dismiss it for early morning. *The morning after.* Has he not spent the night with a woman in the past? Does he typically steal off once they finish? I hate that my thoughts return to these things.

He's here with you, I remind myself.

"And my fantasy is seeing you wear those black boots again and only your lacy underwear."

My mouth falls open, and he rubs his hand down his front, adjusting the tent pitching in his pants. "Maybe we should have some breakfast first. How do you feel about pancakes?"

He seems confused. He doesn't know what to do with me in his home this morning. Pancakes are his specialty with Sadie, and it touches me a little that he's willing to share the experience with only me, but I can't shake the weirdness coming from him. Speaking of Sadie…

"Maybe we should go get Sadie. Or maybe you should take me home and I'll pick her up. She probably shouldn't know I spent the night with you."

"Why not?" he snaps.

"Because she's only sixteen. That's not a very good example to set, if I go out for dinner with some guy and don't return until the morning after."

"Some guy?" Billy barks. "Got a list of them?"

What the hell?

"No," I snap, irritated and hurt. He already knows I haven't dated or been with anyone for three years.

He takes a deep breath and rubs up his chin with his knuckles. "I need coffee," he mumbles, shaking his head and stalking off for his kitchen.

Well, good morning to you too, Mr. Grumpy.

While the fantasy of him in only his boxers isn't dead, I wouldn't be upset with him wearing only those pajama bottoms hugging his backside, accentuating the firmness with each movement of his legs.

This gives me an idea.

+ + +

Making my way to the kitchen as quietly as I can, Billy has his back to me, flipping pancakes on the stove. He's removed his sweatshirt but remains in the plaid bottoms. His backside is so fine it's a crime, and I take a deep breath, clear my throat, and then lean on the opening between the dining room and the kitchen.

Billy stills, spatula in hand. "Look," he starts without turning to me. "I'm sorry. I guess I'm just crabby when it's so early, and I haven't had any cof—"

His words halt as he turns to face me. Spatula still in hand, raised slightly and outward. He looks like a hot pastry chef minus the pastries.

"Roxie," he breathes.

"Was this the fantasy?" I stand before him in the knee-high boots and his tee. My fingers twist in the cotton material, not feeling nearly as brave as I did a moment ago. He gulps, eyes wide on me. "I just wanted one more time," I whisper. One more time before we need to go back to thinking about Sadie and her future and what that means for both of us.

His eyes appraise me until he squints. "Whatcha got under there?"

I shake my head once.

Exhaling, he sets the spatula on the island and turns off the stove. The look in his eyes almost frightens me. It's so direct and intense and focused. It matches my feelings for him. Direct. Intense. Focused. I want us to continue like we did last night. This relationship has grown more than casual and crossed the line to complicated.

For some reason, I twist and walk quickly away from him, despite the high-heeled boots and the lack of underwear. Billy chases, and I squeal. He easily catches up to me just inside his bedroom and pins me to the wall.

"You tease," he groans at my ear, flattening my chest to the plaster. Outlined through the thinness of his pajama pants, he protrudes into my backside, barely covered by the length of his T-shirt. His hand slips over the curve of my ass and then under. He continues forward until two fingers impale me. I cry out, and he stills.

"Is this what you want?"

I want you. The words remain in my throat. My hand slapping on the wall is my only response. I want everything from him. This is more than his body and casual sex. I want *his* thoughts. His heart. His soul.

I made love to you.

But does he love me?

Or is he using pretty words to dress up what we are doing?

"Fuck, Roxie. Do you have any idea what you do to me?" I don't. I only know what he's doing to me. He's marking himself on my heart, and I won't be able to walk away easily. I can't stay in the casual zone. I won't be able to just stay friends, a united front before Sadie, if this all goes sour.

I haven't answered him, his fingers distracting me as they slide back and forth where I'm wet and ready for him. Behind me, he struggles to lower his pajama pants with one hand. He isn't wearing boxer briefs underneath the flannel. His foot kicks at my heels, forcing me to spread my feet.

"Tell me how you feel?"

"I…" I can't think. His fingers and then the length of him, warm and thick against my backside, mean I can't string together any words. Billy stills. A strange shift occurs that I can't read as he holds out for an answer I haven't given him yet.

Then he bites my shoulder—*hard.* "Forget it," he mutters into my skin as his fingers return to their thrusting.

"You wanted it to be you against a wall?" His voice turns bitter.

My mind races to what I saw years ago. Him. Her. A brick wall. "Yes."

"You want me to fuck you like I fuck the rest."

What?

Why is he saying this? Why is he comparing me? What is he doing to me? My heart clenches, but my body gives in to him. Does he not see it's so much more than sex against a wall I want from him? I want to be the woman who makes him lose his mind but gain his heart. This isn't some joke to me.

"I always knew I'd get you to beg, Roxie." He bitterly chuckles, but I don't find the humor. I smack at the wall, my cheek pressed against it.

"Screw you, William," I mumble without any bark or bite, just defeat. Screw him for making me feel like this, wanton and begging for more. Screw him for telling me we'd keep it easygoing and then making it complicated with pretty words. Screw him for making me feel like I could fall in love with him and making me fall apart over him.

"Screw me? Is that what you want? Is that what you want to call it?"

He slams into me, hitching me upward a bit, and I'm thankful for the heeled boots, helping me balance. A bit rough at this angle, Billy holds my hips, thrusting inward as I arch back, drawing him deeper in a different manner.

I should stop him. I feel us unraveling, but I allow us to continue in this position in hopes it will keep us together.

My palms slip down the wall, struggling for anything to hold me in place as Billy hammers into me, deeper, faster, harder.

"Hold on," he growls. I'm out of control. I squeeze, and I clench. I grip him. I want to get there, but I just can't. I feel myself slipping from him because I want him to want me more than anyone else.

I don't want to be just some woman against a wall.

"Shit," he grunts before he stills, and I feel the telltale signs of him inside me, pulsing, jerking, releasing. I sigh against the wall, frustrated with how close I am, but also how disconnected I suddenly feel from him. This isn't how I thought it would be.

He quickly withdraws from me and then to my utter surprise, he slaps me on the ass. I spin to face him, horrified with the smack and what it's doing to my libido while my head is discombobulated and my heart squeezes like a vise grip.

"Thanks. That was fun."

My mouth falls open as I stare at him. His eyes.

I can't read him.

I can't read myself.

How much I want him. How afraid I am of losing him. How afraid I am he just lumped me with all the rest. Afraid we'll walk out his door, and it will still be something casual. But I can't it. Not like this.

Deep inside, he's a good man—caring and loyal. He's a *good* father, and that's attractive. He's an excellent lover, and that's just dangerous.

My emotions are running faster than my heart.

I want him to accept me. I want him to tell me I'm enough—not because of Sadie—but because we feel something for each other.

"Why do I feel like you're pulling away from me?" I whisper, my voice hoarse as I fight the shock of what he did, what he said.

Thanks, that was fun.

My body stills. My back stiffens. The cursed wall is the only thing holding me up from collapsing under the weight of my emotions this morning. What started out as a seduction has left me feeling slimy and incomplete.

"Aren't you doing the same thing?" he questions, crossing his arms. He's already hiked up his pants, and I'm still standing before him, more exposed than naked.

"I'm not." I swallow a sudden lump in my throat. *Is this over?* I don't want us to end. I want us to move forward. Last night, he was so sweet and honest, but today…today, I just feel this overwhelming sense of uncertainty.

Thanks. That was fun.

That ass slap. That cavalier comment. It's too casual for me.

God, I can hate him sometimes while still thinking he's amazing. I'm too raw to think straight, and I don't even know where the next words out of my mouth come from. *Poke the bear.*

"Not a brick wall," I snark, slapping my hand at the plaster. "But a wall nonetheless."

His mouth gapes. Those brown eyes widen before shuttering, and then he straightens. "Well, I try my best to satisfy."

Oh no, he didn't.

He did not carelessly dismiss what happened. Yet haven't I done the same thing?

Why did I do this?

Why did he?

Thanks. That was fun.

"Say you didn't mean it? Say it was more than wall sex?" I whisper, my heart hammering in my chest, trying to recover us. Not the us that prods and pokes but the us whose bodies connect so easily.

But he says nothing.

He's already given me all his pretty words last night.

I made love to you.

I was a first in his bed.

Perhaps the reality of those things hit him this morning, or maybe he never meant them. It's like the light of day brought new awareness. We aren't poking at one another like we do. This is different than that.

"We should go get Sadie," he says, stepping back from me, and I realize as he walks away that I fell for all of it. His sweet words. His tender touches. I fell for him.

And I've been played by the player.

Chapter 33
Family Shouldn't Be The Enemy

[Billy]

She was going to say goodbye. I felt it when she didn't answer my question. When she couldn't tell me how she felt after I'd tried to be so honest with her last night. She was pulling away, and I promised myself I'd never be left again.

Or maybe she really did want it like all the rest. *Ride the Billy Harrington express.* One stop only.

Damn wall sex.

But it wasn't that simple. Nothing was that simple.

We drove in silence to Mountain Spring Lane, the famous lane with only three antebellum homes. Roxanne wanted to go home first, but I told her this was easier. I could pick up Sadie, drop them both off, and then walk away without a scratch. Only that continual clawing sensation, the roots of a tree growing inside me, is now gouging out my heart.

Why was I such an ass?

When we arrive at my parents' house, Roxie keeps her arms wrapped around herself, tugging her jacket tight over her dress. It's obvious she's still wearing the same clothes as last night, and this might be the worst walk of shame anyone ever had.

After the night we had, and the way I opened up to her, she could have clung to me instead of making me feel like the whole night was just her wanting something she'd never had.

Wall sex, I huff to myself.

What's the big fucking deal? It wasn't me she thought she saw, but she wanted it like she wants a piece of me. Not my heart but a part of me others have taken.

And I find myself falling in love with her when she doesn't feel the same way.

We enter the house to a gaggle of female laughter. Sadie is surrounded by the women of my family. My mother; Mati; my nephew's wife, Maggie; and my other nephew's new fiancée, Hollister. Lucy and Sadie join the mix. We just need Giant's daughters, and the circle of women would be complete. I turn to Roxanne, finding her staring at the family tradition. Eyes suddenly hollow as she takes in the mess of ingredients and the cheerful faces.

"It's our annual Christmas cookie-making day," Lucy announces.

Shit. I recognize the look of someone on the outside looking in. I know that look because it's been me so many times, watching my dad praise Giant or dote on Mati. His pride in Charlie as the mayor and even his sadness at the loss of James.

I reach for her, but she shifts away from me.

"So how was your night?" my mother asks, her eyes moving from mine to Roxanne's and back. Her perfectly arched eyebrow arches in question with a hint of concern.

"We had fun," I say, knocking my elbow on Roxanne's arm, and she smiles a pinched grin.

Thanks. That was fun.

I'm such an ass.

"Sadie, we should go. I need to work today." It's the first Roxie's mentioned the bookstore, but I can read an excuse when I hear one. She wants to get out of here.

"Can I stay?" Sadie turns her head from her aunt to my mother, who smiles back at her, and my heart warms at how willingly my mother has pulled Sadie into the family. This is what I want. Sadie accepted. I turn back to Roxanne.

Why can't Roxie accept me?

"I can give her a ride home later," I suggest, but Roxanne ignores me.

"I'll bring her to the bookstore when we finish," Mati offers, and I look up to find my sister's eyes narrowing on me with the classic *What did you do now, Billy?* glare.

Yep, it's always me. My fault.

"I don't want to impose," Roxanne says to Mati, drawing my sister's attention back to her, and Mati smiles, the pinched grin matching Roxie's.

"It's no imposition."

We stand another moment in awkward silence, the tension vibrating off us when Jordan walks into the kitchen.

"Hey man, I didn't know you were joining us today." He pats me on the back as he passes me for the fridge. Retrieving a few beers, he steps up to his wife, kisses her cheek, and says something in her ear.

Why can't I have that? Why can't I find a woman who looks at me like I've hung the moon?

Because you walk away, my heart whispers.

Because you're afraid to put it all out there again, my brain says.

Both are correct, and I glance back at Roxanne. Her eyes shift to the floor. "I really need to go." She swallows before closing her eyes, and my heart pinches.

This is bad. Really bad.

"Remember you have those court interviews this week," Jordan states as he walks toward me again, and everything in the room stops. My mother's hands freeze. Mati's head shoots up. Sadie stills without looking at me.

And Roxanne speaks. "Excuse me?"

My eyes close. It's just gone from bad to worse.

"I forgot," I say, opening my eyes and then turning to Roxanne. "I forgot." I reach for her, but her movement away from me is more pronounced, obvious to the entire room.

"Forgot?" she groans.

I feel Jordan watching me, and I want to punch him. He's pressed for this legal stuff when I've told him Roxie and I would work it out. As a man of the law, he didn't like that answer, and he set up a series of interviews with child services to discuss Sadie's options.

"It isn't what you think," I say, without knowing what she thinks.

"You said we'd work it out," she whispers, her eyes shifting to my family. My mother is trying to round everyone out of the room, but the damage is already done.

"We *can* work it out. I mean that. This is just a formality. It's a way to discuss the best interest of Sadie."

Roxanne glares at me. "Last night, you told me we couldn't talk about Sadie."

Jordan slips from the kitchen, disappearing down the hallway at my back.

"Last night, I said a lot of things."

Roxanne glares at me, the familiar daggers of years of poking at one another. Only these are the flames of someone ready to torch me in my mother's kitchen. Her anger runs steel-fire hot.

"Like making love to me, and I was the first in your bed," she mutters.

"Well, I saved the best for last, Roxanne." Her full name is bitter on my tongue. "That's what you wanted, right? A piece of Billy Harrington like all the rest. I think I've proven a wall, and you work well together."

I don't see her hand before it connects with my face, the smack of skin resounding throughout the room.

"What's going on here?" The rough voice of my father behind me makes my blood run cold. Roxanne looks over my shoulder and then lowers her eyes, which are filled with tears.

"I didn't mean…" I step forward, hands reaching for her. *Oh God, I've made a mess of this.*

"I think you've said enough," Roxanne says under her breath. "You've proven yourself, William. I trusted you to do the right thing by me and worse than anything is this betrayal with Sadie. You promised me. You *promised*." Her head shakes, and although I can't see her face, the tears fall to her jacket, dots of liquid spilling like rain. "The only piece of you I wanted was your heart."

"William." My father steps forward.

"Dad, please stay out of this," I snap, but Roxanne speaks over me.

"If I could trouble you, Mr. Harrington. I need a ride home." My father slips an arm around Roxanne and leads her down the hall to the front door while I'm left standing in the kitchen with my heart at my feet, knowing I've just made the worst blunder of my life.

She's walking away from me, and it's only because I pushed her to go.

+ + +

"You dumbass. Isn't there some attorney-client confidentiality rule you just broke?" I lay into my nephew as I stalk into the trophy room where Jordan and Jaxson, my nephews, and my brother Charlie watch the Georgia State football game.

"What happened?" Charlie asks, and I feel myself being dissected by the eyes in the room.

"I just assumed she knew. You spend all your time with her," Jordan says, defending himself.

"Never make assumptions when it comes to women," I state.

"So, what happened?" Charlie asks again.

"Jordan announced to the kitchen the interviews with child services." I scratch against my neck and then rest my hand on my chin. "I hadn't told Roxie yet."

You said we'd work it out.

I did say that, and like I told her, this was all a formality.

"On purpose?" Charlie questions, his eyes narrowing at me from his seat on the old couch.

"I honestly forgot. We went out last night, and I didn't want to discuss Sadie. I just…" What did I want? To enjoy her. To be just us. To make love to her. My eyes close a second.

"Does she have a lawyer?" Charlie inquires.

"Someone in Atlanta was pursing guardianship and custody after Theresa passed away, but I don't know if she retained that person." *Because you told her you'd work it out.*

"And she stopped that process, correct?" Charlie continues. "Obviously, she knows you had the paternity test and filed to update Sadie's birth certificate, but haven't you told her about proceeding for full guardianship?"

My eyes narrow at my brother. "I hadn't exactly decided."

"What do you mean, you hadn't decided? You're her father," Charlie admonishes.

"Yeah, but Roxie. They're so close. Sadie and I are getting closer, but she's still closest with her aunt." I didn't want to hurt Sadie. I didn't want to hurt Roxie. I didn't *mean* to hurt her, but I know that I have.

"Custody battles can be tricky sometimes, and you two have a unique situation," Jordan adds.

"We aren't in a battle," I scoff.

"Are you sure?" Jordan asks, reminding me of the altercation in the kitchen.

This is my fault.

"Roxie and I are a united front for Sadie."

"But what are you with each other?" Charlie asks, and I fall into a vacant chair, my hands covering my face.

The only piece of you I wanted was your heart.

"I don't know," I whisper, my eyes lowering to the floor. I fucked this up.

"What about living arrangements? Have you even asked Sadie if she wants to live with you?" Jordan asks.

"Why don't you just have Roxie and Sadie live with you? Problem solved." This comes from my nephew Jaxson who's been living with his baby momma and finally proposed to her at Thanksgiving *after* they had the baby. It was all backward.

I straighten with the thought.

Everything with Roxanne has been unconventional. Sadie is her sister's daughter *with me*. It can't get more backward than that, yet I want Roxie in my life. I want all of her.

Then why the hell did you push her away? my heart screams.

I don't know. I just don't. I panicked.

Could I live with Roxie? I hinted at it last night, and she mentioned she'd never live with another man without a promise. Could I marry Roxie? The idea seems absurd, but I can't say I haven't considered it.

You promised. Her voice rings in my head.

She'll never believe me. She'll never trust me again.

"Yeah, I guess I should ask Sadie what she thinks," I say to no one in particular, but Charlie is watching me.

"And what about Roxanne? What does she think?"

The only piece of you I wanted was your heart.

I told her my history with Rachel and gave her my justification for my actions after the divorce. I opened up to her, and instead of running, she came closer, accepting my need to prove myself. Only, it didn't feel like I was proving anything to her. She told me what she thought of me as a father, a business owner, a donor, a man.

Any woman would be honored to be with you.

She even sympathized about Rachel, saying it wasn't right to break my heart.

And then this morning, I broke hers while she broke mine.

I hate myself.

"Roxie wants Sadie to stay with her. She's the only family Roxie has left." The words taste like acid as Roxie told me her most vulnerable concerns, and now she thinks I've betrayed her. She thinks I want to separate them, but it's the furthest thing from my thoughts. I want Roxie to feel like my family can be her family. *I* can be her family.

"You're in deep, aren't you, man?" Jaxson says to me, and I feel Jordan's eyes on the side of my head. "You love her, but you fucked it up, didn't you?"

How does my twenty-seven-year-old nephew know this stuff?

I shake my head, lowering my face. I'm a disappointment…to myself. She trusted me.

"Roxie could be a game changer for you," Jordan warns, offering advice as my attorney, but he has no idea of the truth in those words. She already changed the game. I want her. I want Sadie *and her*.

Chapter 34
Disillusioned by Disappointment

[Roxanne]

"So how was your date?" Grace asks me. We have extended hours through the holiday season, and she's offered to stay late this Saturday. Tourism is up as people want the quaint and the quiet of a small town to draw them into the festive spirit. Blue Ridge is pretty with the streetlamps and mini white lights in the trees. Every storefront holds a wreath or plaid bow on its door, greeting customers.

I'm thankful for Grace's presence as I've been distracted all afternoon. At some point, Sadie returned to the apartment, texting me to say she was upstairs. Mr. Harrington did not drive me home after all. Mati did, and I was grateful for her silence after telling me she loved her brother, but she knew he could be a jerk sometimes.

"It was…" What did Billy call our night together? *I made love to you.*

Fun. Insightful. Hurtful. Before the wall sex, I might have said earth-shattering and a game changer. I suppose even after wall sex, it was game changing. "He lied to me."

"What happened?" Grace stares at me, but I don't look up from the stack of books I need to re-shelve.

"He played me, Grace. I thought we were maybe starting something…something different, special even, but he played me. He told me we could work things out about Sadie, and all along, he had plans to seek full custody. He used me to get her."

I forgot. The words ring through my head. How do you forget such a thing?

"He…wouldn't separate you from Sadie," Grace tries to assure me, but even she sounds skeptical.

"I don't think it's a matter of separating us. Just establishing his rights as her father." I swallow the bitterness in my throat. Not that he isn't her father, but that he never told me he planned to go this route. "He has court or something this week."

Grace continues to stare and then reaches out for my hand. "Are you sure it isn't a misunderstanding?"

"What's to misunderstand? He's her father, right? And I'm just a woman he had sex with. He used me to get close to his daughter." Tears well again, and I rapidly blink.

"Oh, honey, I don't believe that. *You* don't believe that."

My head snaps up, and I finally look at her. "Grace, I wanted to believe a lot of things about him. Believe that he meant what he said when he promised he wouldn't file, and we would work it out. Those were his words, and like a damn fool, I believed him. And then I fell for his charm." *I made love to you.* The tears fall harder, and I cover my forehead with a hand. "He's a player, and I was played."

What did I expect? I'd been upset for years that he hadn't shown any interest in me, and now I feel like the interest was only because of Sadie. I was a means to get close to his daughter, and now he is.

"Was he bad?" Grace's voice lowers as she holds two fingers a few inches apart. She's trying to ease the tension.

A sad, weak smile curls my lips, and I shake my head. "He was…fine." My face pinkens. It's not even close to how he was or how I felt.

"Do you mean fiiiiine?" She wiggles her brows. For a woman without a sex life, she's still spunky. Sure, Billy Harrington is fine in the elongated emphasis. His body is incredible with smooth plains and little valleys. And his appendage…phew, I want to tug at my collar and fan myself, but he is more than just sex on a stick—or I thought he was. He opened up to me. He told me about his history.

I made love to you.

Love? No, I'm not certain Billy is capable of it after Rachel. We are physically attracted to each other, and my body betrays me when I think of his.

The way he touched me. The way he kissed me. The way he entered me.

"I'll just be one of many," I state flippantly as I pick up the stack of books.

"You don't mean that," Grace states, surprise in her tone. "I don't believe he feels that way."

"It shouldn't matter, right? Billy and I have danced around each other for years. Sadie's the only reason we came together, and I made a mistake." I swallow over the word. "I let things go too far and got in over my head." *And my heart.* "And now, I just need to deal with the aftermath. I won't lose Sadie to him. Not like this."

"Roxanne, I think you just need to talk to him. This just doesn't feel right to me. I've seen him around you. He lights up when he looks at you, and he seeks you out. He's…totally into you…and it's not just because of Sadie." I don't know how Grace can see such a thing. She doesn't even recognize that Clyde's always looking at her like she's something sweet.

I hitch the stack of books into my hands and tip my head. "I'm going to shelve these." I don't want to keep talking about Billy. I'm numb to him. Now, if only my heart would get the memo.

+ + +

I'm exhausted, and after a long shower with more tears, I curl into my bed. I'm holding a book, but I'm not reading the words as my thoughts race. A soft knock comes to my bedroom door, and I shift as Sadie enters.

"Hey," I whisper, my voice hoarse from crying.

"Hey." Sadie enters and then crawls up on the bed next to me. She lays on her side, her head on the opposite pillow. Her eyes search my face. "Why do boys have to suck?"

I bitterly chuckle. "I don't know, but they don't grow out of it."

"Think that's why Mom never married?" The question surprises me, and I shift against my own pillow.

"I think she just never found the one she thought was right for her and you." My sister didn't date much. I'm certain she had nights of commitment-less sex with acquaintances, but no one she ever brought home to Sadie.

"And you haven't ever found the one either?" she asks. Sadie knows about my long-term relationship with Chad, and there were many questions at thirteen when we broke up, and I moved. It seemed easier to explain how people fall out of love than how people make a decision to fall in love.

"I haven't met the one for me either." Billy could have been him. He checks all the boxes with regard to Sadie, but the boxes are slowly unchecking for me.

Sadie weakly smiles at me. "What did Billy do?"

I don't want to turn Sadie against her father, so I need to tread cautiously.

"Billy just wants to be involved in your life," I begin. Not mine. Only hers. "As he should be. I didn't know about the interviews he has scheduled." I fault our child services advocate in this matter and can't contact anyone until Monday, which is frustrating. "Did you know Billy was seeking custody?"

Sadie shakes her head. "He's asked me if I thought I could ever live with him."

I hold my breath, waiting for her answer. "I wouldn't be opposed, but I don't want to leave you. I don't see why things can't stay as they are."

I reach out for her, brushing back strands of black hair. "I agree, but Billy is your father, and he has more right to you than I do in the court of law."

Sadie stares at me a long minute while I continue to stroke her hair. "But you like him, right? I mean, you went on a date last night." Her eyes tell me she has more to add, knows more than she should.

"I…made a mistake, Sadie. An error in judgment on my part." *I trusted him.* With me. "But that's between Billy and me and has nothing to do with you."

"But you were fighting about me this morning," she states, and I close my eyes. The whole scene comes back to me, and I'm so embarrassed. I'll never be able to face the Harrington clan again.

"Sadie, I don't think it was so much about you as it was that we both said things we shouldn't have said, and then he didn't tell me about the interviews."

"After you left, he told me they would be nothing more than a bunch of questions. I can say what I want and express my opinion."

I smile weakly at her. "I won't let anything separate us, Sadie. You're my family. I love you."

"I love you, too. But they're my family, also." Her words are like a slap, although I know she isn't wrong. "Can't you talk to him? Work something out."

Ah, his famous words to me.

"I think we're past speaking to each other. It might be best to just let the courts handle things between Billy and me for you, honey." I swallow the lump in my throat. This is just how I didn't want things to go. I didn't want her to feel like she was in a tug-of-war.

"Please. For me. Just talk to him. Hear him out."

Why? Does she know something I don't?

"I'll think about it," I say, and I hate that I'm lying to her because I won't.

I have nothing to say to Billy Harrington.

Chapter 35
The Hole Deepens

[Billy]

"Looking for someone?" Giant asks me, catching my eyes traveling to the side window of the pub.

"Nah." I pull my eyes away from the glass for the hundredth time.

"Huh," he huffs.

"What's *huh* mean?"

Giant smiles, shaking his head. He's been less grumpy now that he has Letty in his life. She lives in Chicago, though, and I don't know how he does the long-distance relationship thing. For now, I know he has his reasons, but still. I'd want my woman daily, *if I wanted a woman*, which I don't.

My eyes drift to the window once again.

"That's what *huh* means." He lifts his beer and points the stein in my direction. I've been caught.

"What's going on?" He nods toward the glass. "I don't think your wandering eyes are looking for your daughter. But you don't like Roxanne if I remember correctly." His lips slowly turn upward like he knows something else.

"I don't. I didn't. I...I don't know." My shoulders sag. I messed up so badly this morning, and all I want to do is turn back time and crawl under the bedsheet tent and bury myself inside her. I need a do-over. "We've been seeing a lot of each other."

"Dating is hard," Giant agrees.

"We aren't dating," I snap. I don't know what we're doing, and at this point, I don't even think we're *doing* anything ever again.

"You just said you were seeing each other."

"You're seeing someone?" My attention turns to the Minnie Mouse voice squeaking to my right.

"Kris*ty*," I grit. Usually, I do a duck and cover when I see her coming, but I'd been so focused on the window I hadn't noticed her arrival.

"Billy Harrington, did I just hear you're *dating* someone?"

"Me?" I choke. "You know I don't date, honey." I wink at her and catch the eye of my brother. His face hardens as he watches me.

"Well, that's what you've been telling me for months. You still like doing other things, right, sugar?" She's leaning over the bar, pressing her fake tits together, making them swell enough they might pop out her low-cut T-shirt. It's too cool outside for such a shirt, but I know what she's playing at and what she's insinuating.

"I sure do. I'm always up for a good time." I smile, but my teeth clench. A hand hits my shoulder hard and holds. I look over at Clyde, who's watching me almost as intently as my brother. The words taste acidic on my tongue, and then something catches in my periphery.

"Billy Harrington, you've been avoiding me." Kristy interjects into my upset.

"I don't know what you're talking about," I mock, knowing full well what she means.

"It's been months."

Nearly six, but who's counting.

"I've missed you," she pouts, and I might throw up a little in my own mouth. There's nothing for Kristy to miss. It was one night and too many drinks.

"I heard you have a daughter." She lowers her voice like it's top secret information. "I didn't know you wanted to be a family man." Stars fill her eyes. *Oh, hell no.*

"I didn't," I say, finding another statement burning my tongue. Once upon a time, I figured Rachel and I would have kids eventually, but she'd been holding out on me for so long, or so I thought, and I thought children might never happen. I later learned she hadn't wanted children in the conventional manner, and she'd been on the pill our entire marriage.

"It's okay with me. I find daddies sexy."

Something was so wrong in Kristy's statement, and I stare back at her while she leans against the bar.

"I have something to do in my office," I state, dismissing myself and making a hasty exit from the main bar. I usually duck into the kitchen and take the stairs to my second-floor office that way, but for some reason, I head to the main stairwell leading to the party floor. Just as I open the door to the well, I hear the sharp sound of heels following me.

"Honey." I turn, attempting flirtation as a decoy. "You know you can't come into my office." It's the excuse I used when I led her to her car and took her in the back seat like some pubescent teen. It's my policy with any woman, except Roxie. She's been in there on a few occasions.

Roxanne is the exception to everything.

"But you've been avoiding me for so long, and you seem so stressed lately." She sidles up to me, slipping her arms over my shoulders. My skin crawls, and I circle her wrists, drawing her hands off me. Her fingers drag down my chest until I step back, holding her at arm's length.

"I'm not stressed," I say with a little too much force. "I'm just busy." I'm not about to go into the details of embracing my new responsibility and learning about my daughter while fucking up the first relationship I've had in years. Kristy isn't the person to share such things with. Roxie is. My chest aches.

"You could be busy with me," she pathetically flirts, attempting to step into me as the door to the stairwell opens.

"Dad, why is—" Her words stop as I look up. Sadie's eyes shift between me and Kristy and then fall to my hands around Kristy's wrists and her body leaning toward mine.

"I…" Sadie steps back, eyes wild as they move from Kristy to me. Shaking her head, she turns away from me, allowing the stairwell door to slam behind her. "Sadie," I call after her as she disappears into the Saturday night crowd. I glare at Clyde standing behind the bar as I pass. I've no doubt he let Sadie in the bar so late and then directed her to me.

"You're fired," I yell at him over the patrons.

"You're going to thank me," he yells back. As mature as I am, I flip him the bird over my shoulder as I pursue my daughter.

"Sadie!" I yell once outside as she crosses the street, and I pick up my pace. She's a runner, and she should consider track because she's fast. As she nears the back stairs to her apartment, she shifts around them and breaks into a full sprint along the back alley.

I follow her as best I can, but I'm short of breath and wheezing as I try to catch up to her, still yelling her name for a few blocks before she finally stops.

Holy shit, I fall forward, my hands clutching at my knees to get ahold of my breathing. If she breaks free again, I'll never be able to keep up, but I'll follow even if it gives me a damn heart attack.

"You're out of shape, old man."

"Jesus, you're fast. What's your time?"

She stares at me as I look up at her from my bent position. Her head tilts. "I don't know what you mean."

"You should think about track in the spring. Cross country maybe." I'm still huffing as I stand, the air cold around us, and she isn't wearing more than a lightweight pullover and leggings. "Where's your jacket?"

"Don't play father to me," she snaps, hands coming to her hips.

"I'm not playing anything," I bark.

"What were you doing with that woman?" she asks, like she's also a woman. A woman scorned.

"Kristy? She's nobody." Sadie's eyes narrow at me, so similar to the way her aunt does. "We..." *fooled around once.* "It was..." *only once.* Sweet Jesus, am I supposed to justify myself to my kid? I'm not about to tell her all the things I've done with women, which are all the things she better never do with a boy, or anything remotely male until she's like forty. I sigh in exasperation.

"Sadie, I..."

"Roxie is really upset."

My head lowers.

"She's mad at you," Sadie huffs.

"I know."

"I thought you two were getting along. I thought you liked each other."

"We do." I sigh. "As…friends."

"Friends?" she scoffs. "Do friends kiss? Do friends spend the night? Do friends look at each other all the time?"

"Sadie, it's…complicated." I exhale.

"It's called *liking* someone," she snaps, glaring at me. Hands still on her hip like she's lecturing me, and she is.

"Look, it's more—"

"You're right, it's more. You're in love with each other."

I stare back at her. "I was going to say more complicated than liking."

"Love is complicated."

I stare at her, really look at my daughter; her face flushed from running, mouth stern, eyes piercing. If she had lion-red hair, she'd be my sister at sixteen. I chuckle. "How did you get so wise?"

"I told you, I know a thing or two about dating."

"Yeah, well, I don't want to know your thing or two, and Roxanne and I aren't dating," I say, pointing back at her. It's the second time I've denied what Roxanne and I are doing, and it doesn't feel right to me.

Sadie drops her arms and fists her fingers.

"It's freezing out here. We should get you home. Besides, it's late." It has to be close to midnight.

"Why didn't you tell Aunt Roxie about the interviews?" Sadie's voice lowers, and I shake my head, disappointed in myself.

"I honestly forgot." I sigh. "When Jordan mentioned proceeding with custody, I wasn't certain I would. Roxie and I said we'd work something out, and I thought we were. I thought things were good."

Sadie tilts her head. "I thought so, too. Why does anything have to change?"

"It doesn't, but you're my daughter, and I want you to live with me." Her eyes widen, startled by the admission. I'm startled as well, as this is the first time I've spoken my feelings out loud. "I want you to live with me."

As Sadie stares at me, I continue. "Of course, you'll have a say in where you want to live. Reside. And I'll do what you want. I'll still see you all the time no matter what you decide." I honestly mean what I say. Sadie will probably request to remain with Roxie, the relative she knows best and who her mother wanted her to be with, and I'll follow whatever Sadie wishes, but I want her to know that I want her as well.

"Where you live changes nothing for me." I reach for her and shake her shoulders until I'm certain she understands. When she nods, I pull her into me for a deep hug. It's rare that I touch her. Rarer still that we've hugged, but when her arms come around me, my throat clogs. She's my daughter, and there can't be any greater feeling than holding your child, no matter what age.

When she pulls back, I keep my arm over her shoulder, tugging her into my side because it's freaking freezing out here.

"You need to fix this with Aunt Roxie," Sadie states. "I…I love you both, and I don't want her hurting because of you."

My heart skips a beat at the mention of loving me. I'm not certain she means it on a deeper level, but I take those three words and tuck them in my pocket.

"I didn't mean to hurt her," I say, lowering my voice. "I don't want her hurting either." I don't. I just don't know how to undo what I've done.

"What did you do?" Sadie asks, her voice reminiscent of Roxanne's when she entered my office nearly two months ago, chewing me out for my behavior toward Sadie after our first meeting.

"I said some things I didn't mean, and then I said more things I didn't mean."

God, I'm such an asshole.

"So say some new things to make her feel better."

"It's not that easy," I say to my daughter as I walk her back to her apartment.

"It's also not that complicated," Sadie states. "What's the worst that could happen?"

"She'll never speak to me again." I scoff.

"I think she's already there, so you have nothing left to lose," Sadie teases without humor. But she's wrong, I already feel like I've lost everything. If I don't have Roxanne, I don't have the *all* that I long for. Her and Sadie. "And most of all, say you're sorry."

I look forward as we walk, not certain how to do any of the things Sadie suggests. Talk to Roxie. Beg for forgiveness. Apologize.

"You can do this, Dad. I have faith in you."

The words stop me short, and I stumble as we walk.

I have faith in you.

She might be the first person who ever has, and I realize she might be the most important person who will, and I don't want to disappoint her.

Chapter 36
Case Closed

[Roxanne]

Billy exits the courtroom while I wait my turn. We interview separately with the court-appointed liaison. He looks as miserable as I feel, but I can't think about him. I need to think about Sadie. What's best for her? She'll interview next, and I'm not allowed in the room. Sadie has a child advocate assigned to her for her protection in the interview process.

When it's my turn, I note how cold, sterile, and impersonal I think the room is. The preliminaries are explained, and a series of questions are asked about my relationship with Sadie. I'm also asked a few questions about Theresa, and I try to be fair in my answers. She isn't present and can't defend herself, and I remind the interviewer that Theresa isn't on some sort of trial for her decision.

"Just establishing background and the relationship between Ms. McAllister and Mr. Harrington."

"There wasn't a relationship," I say. *Just sex*, I want to add, feeling a strange similarity to my circumstances with him. Pure, unadulterated passion and I miss him although I hate him.

As we near the end of our session, the liaison asks, "Is there any reason Billy Harrington shouldn't have Sadie living with him?"

My tongue thickens, and my mouth refuses to move. I don't have any objection other than my own emotional attachment to Sadie. Was she not listening? Did I not spell out for her all the things I've done? How involved I am with Sadie and always have been? How much I love her? These questions race through my mind as a hollow feeling knocks the wind from me.

It's over, isn't it?

"If someone were to come forward to discredit Mr. Harrington, would you find any justification in claims against his ability to parent?"

"I don't understand." I squint at her.

"If someone made a statement against Mr. Harrington's character, questioning his parenting ability, would you object?"

"Did that happen?"

"I'm not at liberty to say," she continues.

"So it did, didn't it?"

She holds her face still, guarded and firm. *Did something happen? Did someone come forward to discredit Billy?*

"Honestly," I begin, taking a deep breath as I straighten in my seat. "I can't find any reason Sadie shouldn't live with Billy. My feelings are selfish. I want her with me because she's *my* only family." I blink, eyes filling with traitorous tears as the truth slips forward. "But from the moment it sank in that Sadie was his daughter, Billy has made an effort to get to know her and be active in her life. He's been amazing with her. He has an odd work schedule, but he'd accommodate as needed."

"Do you see the pub as a deterrent? A possibility he might leave Sadie alone too often?"

"She's sixteen. She can be unsupervised for a while," I emphasize. "But no, I don't think he'd do that to her." And I didn't. If Sadie was at his home, he'd make sure he was present.

"And the possibility of dating?"

My brows pinch at the abrupt question. "Mr. Harrington doesn't date." He has said it himself. However, he hasn't subjected Sadie to anyone in the two months she's known he was her father. He admitted he doesn't bring women to his home. Strangely, it's the one thing I do believe about him, and I pause with the thought.

I went on a date with him.

I was at his home.

I was in his bed.

The interviewer wraps up by thanking me for my time. "The judge should rule quickly. Judge Bernard wants the case wrapped up before the holidays, and it's pretty straightforward."

I reach out for the interviewer's arm before she stands. "Do you think Sadie will stay with me?"

Her lips twist. "Honestly, ninety-nine percent of the time, it's the biological parent who wins these things. Despite the estrangement, he's stepped up, right? He's her father, but the final say comes down to Sadie. The judge will weigh her feelings and perspective. She's so close to eighteen, any decision would only be a rule for a few years."

Her dismissal of Sadie's age, as if two years is no time at all, doesn't settle well with me, but I nod, accepting her explanation as I stand. Billy has a right to Sadie despite the years I've spent with her and the love we share. The fact he shares direct DNA with her overrules everything else.

As we leave the room, I'm surprised to see Mr. Harrington, Billy's father, waiting outside the door.

"Mr. Harrington?" I step up to shake his hand, but he reaches for my shoulders and kisses my cheeks.

"Roxanne, lovely to see you again." He pulls back and smiles warmly.

"What are you doing here?"

"I'm next." He shrugs like it's no big deal, and I panic a little, knowing his opinion of his son and their history. Images of getting caught on Billy's lap on his bed flip to the forefront of my mind. Our position played into Billy's playboy reputation. I also slapped his son in front of him.

I shouldn't be concerned about who testifies in favor or against Billy, but panic strikes when I see his father. Billy's told me of their strained relationship.

"William," I snap into the phone when he answers on the first ring as I'm exiting the courthouse.

"Roxie," he groans, minus any irritation. He almost sounds relieved.

"Did you know your dad was going to the courthouse?"

"So?"

"He was there to testify after me."

"It's not a trial, Roxanne. No one's going to jail."

I pause before I enter my car, taken aback by the sharpness of his tone. I thought he might be concerned. It's his *dad*. The man he claims he's never pleased.

"I was trying to be helpful. I thought you might like to know."

"You're concerned about me?" His tone is sharp, and I yank open my car door with more force than necessary. As I slip into the cold vehicle, I sit with the phone pressed to my ear.

"It's your dad, Billy." I pause, deciding I'm making more of this than I should. "You know what, never mind. I have to go."

"Roxie, I—"

I click off the phone before I can hear anything else. Just hearing his voice made my heart ache again, but he was too curt. I toss the phone on the seat next to me and start the car as tears fill my eyes. Memories rush forward of losing my mother, my father, and my sister. And Sadie will be next. I'll be alone.

Chapter 37
Fathers and Sons

[Billy]

"What the fuck?" I hang up the phone and stare at my oldest brother as I slip the device into my back pocket.

"What's up?" We're standing inside the brewery in what we call the passion lab. It's a place where we experiment with ingredients and combinations and design the next flavors for our brew. Although it's the holidays, we need to be a season ahead, so we're working on summer stock, and by *we*, I mean me.

Yep, I have another little secret.

"Roxie called and said Dad is being interviewed regarding my case with Sadie."

Giant shrugs like this isn't a big deal.

"Giant, it's Dad. The judgmental prick. The one who thinks I fuck everything up."

"He doesn't think that." He unstoppers a growler and pours a sample we've been brewing for a bit. "Here."

Giant isn't a chemist. He's a businessman. While Dad knew all the classic recipes, passed down from generation to generation and perfected over time before craft brewing became legal in Georgia, Giant wasn't a master brewer. He accepted his position as head of company because the brewery needed more, and he needed a place to plant his feet after his medical discharge. He believed diversity was the way to grow, and he needed specialty flavors—limited selection promoting urgency.

That's where I come in.

Our grandfather used to bring me into this room and allow me to play with the ingredients. After a hard day under my father's demeanor and disappointment, Pap knew I needed to learn something for me— have my own secret success—and he decided this is where it would be. The passion lab.

I sip a swill from the sample, almost rinsing my mouth with the liquid, and then swallow, waiting on an aftertaste.

"Almost," I say, thinking the fermentation needs a bit longer.

"Dad won't say anything against you." Giant tries to assure me, pausing a minute as the expression on his typically stern face turns *sterner*. Is that even a word? I was the one who didn't do well with decoding words.

"What happened with Roxanne? The other night, you let her go and then went into the back with Kristy Moseley." There's a question he isn't asking. My brother's loyal to a fault, and he's never appreciated my ways. My *old* ways.

"Nothing happened with Kristy." I shake my head, getting tired of defending myself. So tired. I groan, scrubbing a hand down my face. "Everything is so fucked up."

"Look, I'm the last to dispense advice about love." My brows rise at my brother's use of the word. "But if you want Roxie, you need to chase. Run. Do not stop to collect two hundred dollars. Go after her."

I stare at my brother. "Who are you, and what have you done with Giant Harrington?"

He shakes his head, the corner of his lip curling upward. He nonchalantly shrugs, and I don't really need an answer. I know what's making my hard brother soft. His girl, Letty.

"I don't see you running," I poke the bear, although Giant has been traveling almost every other weekend to see his long-distance girlfriend.

"It's complicated, but the second it's not, I'll be chasing."

"Are you leaving the brewery?" I'd be shocked. This is our family legacy. This is his legacy. His name is on the bottle, for heaven's sake.

"Not if I can help it. It's complicated for now, but let's finish talking about you. What are you going to do?"

"I don't know." I huff, placing both hands on the edge of the table. "Sadie and Roxie are like a package deal. I want Sadie. She's my daughter, but Roxie"—I exhale—"I just want *her*."

Over the past few days, I've had time to reflect on my actions, accepting I did what I did because I misinterpreted her expression after wall sex. I pushed her away because I thought she was going to walk away. I had to be first, but I've missed her every second afterward. The habit of speaking to her every day, seeing her in some way, has become too easy, so routine, and I don't want to give it up. I wanted to add her in my bed nightly as part of that routine, but I've fucked it all up.

Giant chuckles. "Then what are you going to do about the mess you made?"

"Grovel. Beg. Apologize. The usual," I state, although none of those things are the usual for me. I don't chase. I walk away, and I'm finding it hard to figure out how and when to lay myself out to Roxanne, if she'll even listen to me.

"Is she scared?" Giant asks.

"Nothing scares Roxie." I snort.

Giant shakes his head. "Wanna bet? If you get Sadie, who does Roxie have left?"

My eyes narrow at my brother. "Meaning?"

"She doesn't have any other family, right? Without Sadie, she's—

"

"She's not losing Sadie."

"Isn't she?" His thick brows rise again. "If Sadie moves in with you, that leaves Roxie alone." Giant reaches for another growler, popping the top and pouring another sample. He slides the glass to me, but I haven't moved. My hands grip the edge of the table.

"I won't let her be alone. She has Sadie *and me*."

"Does she?" Giant tips his chin, noting I should drink. But nothing will taste good as acid fills my throat.

"Of course, she does."

"How does she know that? You conveniently forgot to tell her about the interviews. You flirted with Kristy. You know how the blasted rumors run in this town. I'm afraid to even ask what else you've done."

"Because it's always my fault," I snap.

Giant levels me with a glare. "Because in this case, it is. Have you reassured her of anything? Can she trust you?"

"Fuck you, Giant."

"What's going on here?" Our father's voice fills the room, and I chew on my lip as I hang my head. *Not this. Not now.* Another question is coming. What am I doing in this sacred room? I stand still, crossing my arms and resting my hip against the table. My head remains lowered, a cross between getting caught and an admission of guilt.

"You know this is where the magic happens," Giant states to our father cool and calm as if it's no big deal I'm standing in this private room within the brewery. George Jr.'s eyes are pinned on me, and all I see is his determination to make me speak. I rejected this business, walked away to run my own, and he never forgave me, calling me a quitter as I'd done with college and Rachel.

"I do know," my dad states, continuing to stare at me, emphasizing his awareness.

I unfold my arms and stiffen my back, preparing to leave. Giant and I won't be able to continue with Dad present.

"How was the courthouse?" Giant asks, and I freeze after my head pops up to him.

What's he playing at?

"Oh, you know, Bernard and I go way back," Dad states, dismissively waving a hand like it was routine to stop in and see the old judge.

I turn to face him. "What did you do?" The accusation catches in my throat, and I fight the chill running up my spine.

"I didn't do anything. He just wanted to talk to me."

"I don't need any favors," I stammer, the statement sarcastic. Did he try to pull strings against me? We glare at one another for a long minute until I'm the one to break. "I'll be a good father. I might not be perfect, but I'm still going to try."

I hate how I sound, weak and uncertain, exposing my fear that I won't be good enough, but I still want this. I want Sadie. And I want Roxie. A family. The new norm for me has slowly been developing when I didn't see it ever happening. Sadie, Roxie, and me. We are a family— *my* family—and even though we may be unconventional, the rightness is there. My heart stills. My lungs pause. And it hits me. I realize the thing I want most in my life, and I suddenly know what I need to do to get it.

"You don't have to be perfect. Trying is all any parent can do."

I snort, looking back at my father. "Right? Coming from the perfect parent, that's sage advice."

"You think I'm perfect?" Dad huffs. "I've failed higher than I can count, but the key to anything is to get back up and keeping move forward. You should know this."

"Because I'm a quitter."

"Because you always do it."

I freeze. *What is he saying?*

Surprising me again, he points at the table littered with growlers and samples. With a growl in his tone, he demands, "Tell me."

"I…" I glance from the table to my father and then over at Giant, whose hands brace on the wooden top. His head is lowered, his face a shadow. I turn back to my father. "You know, don't you?"

"You think I don't know what goes on in my business. I've known for years."

"Why didn't you say anything?" I question, glaring at him.

"Why didn't you?" he retorts. "Why didn't you tell me?"

I deeply inhale. For all my trouble in school, I was decent at chemistry, and I loved to experiment, especially with the family brew thanks to Pap. Despite my dyslexia, he taught me chemistry was full of formulas. Memorize those, and I'd never fail. And although I nearly failed out of college, I eventually shared what I could do with Giant. I got a license making me a professional after I'd been working in this brewery for years, playing around in the passion lab on the sly.

"I didn't want your disapproval."

"William, this is the second time in a month you've mentioned my disapproval. When did I give you that impression?"

I glare at him, ready to tick off all the ways, but then something occurs to me. "If you knew all along, why didn't *you* say something to me?"

"Perhaps for the same reason you didn't mention it to me. I wanted you to be proud of what you'd done and tell me."

"I am proud," I state, standing taller. I've helped this company in more ways than I've been recognized for as both master brewer and pub owner.

"And I'm proud of you," my dad says. "And I know you'll be an excellent father."

If I were ten, my knees might give out, and I'd collapse in disbelief on the spot. His eyes travel over the table, and I glance to the side, looking up at Giant, who is still silent but smiling despite his avoiding face.

"Well, carry on," Dad says, and he dismisses himself, leaving Giant and me alone again.

"You're a rat," I hiss at Giant, who shakes his head and finally looks up at me.

"I couldn't take all the credit, and like he said, there isn't anything he doesn't know about this company. Or you. He knows you're loyal to a fault. Look at what you've been doing for the brewery behind his back while running your own business. He isn't stupid, Billy."

"I never said he was." *I only thought he felt that way about me.*

"And he's right. You're going to be fine with Sadie. Raising girls is hard. I know what you're going through." Giant's wife died when his daughters were still teenagers. He hadn't been home long from his tours of duty when his wife passed. "I'm here if you need me. It will all work out."

"How can I be sure?" I ask because I've never been more uncertain of anything in my life. Sadie. Roxie. It feels like we're on the edge of imploding, and I don't want to lose either of them. I want them collectively. I want us *all* together.

"You can't be, man. You have to trust your head."

I snort, knowing that's what gets me in trouble sometimes.

"And your heart." Giant taps his large chest, and I want to laugh at his sentimentality, but my heart knows he isn't joking.

Chapter 38
Christmas Tree Apologies

[Roxanne]

"At the request of the minor, Sadie Wilhemina McAllister, the court awards custody to her biological father, William Forrest Harrington."

I stare in disbelief at the judge, and while this hasn't been a trial, I feel as if I've been sentenced to the heartache of all heartaches by having Sadie taken away from me. Deep down, I know Billy isn't stealing her. He won't prevent her from seeing me, but it all still feels like a betrayal, and I exit the courtroom numb to his voice calling after me.

I can't face Sadie. It's petty and mean and very unadult-like, but it hurts. While I don't fault her for her decision, the pain is too deep for me to bear. She decided to reside with Billy, and nothing I can do will reverse that decision. He is her biological father, and I've already been cautioned he'd win. Sadie isn't a competition, but still, Billy won. She's never truly been mine. She's my sister's daughter, but it hurts all the same.

"Whatever happens, nothing will change between us," I tried to assure her the night before the decision, but who was reassuring me? During the ruling, Sadie stayed out in the hallway with Elaina Harrington. The two have grown rather close in the past few weeks as, true to her word, Elaina allows Sadie to practice the piano at her home, and I've felt Sadie slipping further and further from me.

"I'm overreacting, right?" I say to Grace as I hide in my office, avoiding a sixteen-year-old child.

"You're human. It hurts that she picked him, but it's not really a choice. She's not choosing one over the other. Billy is her father. You can't change that or change the fact he didn't know. Cases like these never make sense to me, though. The best interest of the child is where the child already has a relationship."

"It was her request," I whine, taking another hardy drink of the wine I'd brought down from my apartment. "And I can't really blame her. I mean, nothing's wrong with Billy. He wants a relationship with her."

Grace's brows hitch, surprised by my defense of him.

"I just mean, he'll be a good father." I sigh, my shoulders falling.

"Why do you think she did it?" Grace asks.

"I have no idea." I look up at her sweet round face. "But I've definitely screwed up somewhere." Grace is raising five boys on her own, and I can't even raise one teenage girl who is self-sufficient and independent. That's the hardest part to accept. Sadie is smart and responsible, so why pick Billy?

"You didn't screw anything up. She's sixteen. They think they know everything at this age."

I snort without comfort from Grace's words.

"Maybe you should talk to Billy." She hesitates because she knows I won't.

I should ask Sadie why she chose him over me, but I don't want to come down on Sadie after she's been through so much. She needs Billy, but she also needs to know this isn't like picking out a movie. You don't get to change your mind halfway through the viewing. We won't see each other every day, which I thought she enjoyed. I was her daily hug, whether she wanted one or not. Life with Billy won't be the same.

Exhaling, I sit straighter, swirling the glass in my hand.

"It's not forever, right? In two years, she'll be eighteen." I'm trying to muster the positives the advocate tried to spew at me, but the mustering is hard. My heart hurts so much.

"Is this just about Sadie, or is there something more going on here?" Grace questions. She's noticed Billy hasn't paid any random visits to the bookstore or been to dinner in a while.

"There can't be anything more, right?" I shrug, but Grace's forehead furrows with concern. "It was already complicated."

"How do you think Billy is handling this? Think it's settled in for him?" Grace asks, not with compassion but curiosity. The court ordered

Sadie move in with Billy by January second, a non-government holiday date. That's less than ten days away.

"He must know what he's doing. He went through with this process despite promising me we could work it out. He's a liar." I lift my glass and swallow back my wine.

"You don't believe that," Grace says, but in some ways, I do. He fooled an entire community into thinking he cheated on his wife. He fooled me into believing he cared about me and my feelings. My chest aches as I consider his actions. He's been a good actor.

"I don't know what to believe anymore."

I stand, putting an end this conversation. I don't want to talk about Billy or Sadie anymore. I'm tired. Tired of worrying about others. I can't change the way Theresa handled things. I can't change how I feel about Billy. I can't change Sadie's decision.

I don't want to be mad, but I am angry.

I hug Grace, accepting her embrace in return.

"It will all work out," Grace states, leaning back, and I glance back at my friend. At one time, I believed in those words. Now, I find them to be the least trustful words I've ever heard.

+ + +

"We should get a tree," Sadie announces the night before Christmas Eve—Christmas Eve eve. I haven't been in the holiday spirit and keeping up the seasonal cheer in the store zaps me of all energy. This would be the first Christmas without Theresa, and Sadie will be at the Harrington's. My heart breaks in a new way. Theresa and Sadie were always my holiday plans, but the thought of having no one, not even Sadie for the day, just adds to my melancholy.

"Billy wants you to join us for Christmas," Sadie told me a few nights ago, but I snorted at the lie.

"I want you to be there," she stated. *"Or I can always stay here."* Her voice lost its luster at the suggestion, and I knew in her heart of hearts that she wanted to be with them. She'd already chosen them. It would be

a good distraction. Family. The excitement would drown out the absence of her mother, at least for a little bit.

"I'll have to think about it," I lied. Grace invited us to join her family. As a single mother of five, she wasn't going anywhere this holiday. Her late husband's parents were traveling to see his brother, and her sister lived in Michigan. *Just me and an overload of sugar and testosterone. Come join us*, she mocked, but her invitation was sincere.

"Go with Billy. It's fine. I'll see you Christmas Eve." I hesitated, hating how much the suggestion sounded like a couple splitting visits with a child.

"Definitely," she said, giving me a small smile as we sat across from one another at my kitchen as the new awkward silence grows around us.

"So a tree," Sadie interjects into my thoughts again as she stands in the living room.

"What?" I look up from the book open on my lap, but I haven't been reading.

"A Christmas tree. We could chop it down ourselves."

Umm... "Sure, why not?" I stand from my seat. As she rushes to her room, I reach for my phone, quickly searching for an open tree farm that allows us to chop our own.

A half hour later, Sadie and I wander through the lane of the Bernard Christmas Farm, which happens to be owned by the judge who decided Sadie's case. Technically, they close at six, but they allow visitors to wander for up to an hour after. We've made it just under the wire, but now the struggle begins—finding a tree and chopping it down ourselves.

My apartment isn't that large, but it does have tall ceilings. Still, we need to consider the width of a tree, so when we find one just right, we stare at the base. Sadie's been looking over her shoulder on occasion, and I'm wondering if she doesn't want anyone to see us. This is going to be comical.

"Here." I hand her the ax provided by the boy at the counter. Maybe she doesn't want him to see us. I noticed how pink she turned when we checked in at the front counter. "You go first."

Crouching, she's ready to give it the first whack when I place a hand on her shoulder. "Just don't miss and nick yourself," I tease.

"Thanks for the vote of confidence," she snarks before she takes her first swing. The ax hits the trunk but ricochets, and Sadie falls to the side. "Wow, is that hard."

She takes a few more cracks at it, putting a dent in the base but not making enough of a mark to knock it over.

"Let me have a swing." As Sadie stands, I reach for the ax. A saw would be easier, but as I lower for the base and take the first swing, I find the resounding crack invigorating. I sling again and again. Panting and sweating, I'm using the full force of my arm to hack at the sturdy trunk.

My thoughts drift to all my frustrations.

The damn holidays. The death of my sister. The ache for Billy.

"You trying to make mulch of that thing?"

The ax thuds as it collides with the solid trunk, and the blade sticks. *What the…?* I wiggle the ax free because I slowly rise and face Billy, standing with his hands in his winter jacket, watching me.

"What are you doing here?" I snap, and his eyes shift to Sadie.

"Sadie?" I question. *What is the meaning of this?* My eyes leap back to Billy, who is still watching me. He doesn't smile, but he fights a grin. I, however, am not happy. This moment is for us, Sadie and me. We don't need Billy.

"I was in the neighborhood," he lies, and I eyeball Sadie again. My hand curls harder on the ax handle.

"Here, let me finish it off." Billy reaches out for the ax, but I hold it back from him.

"This is a girls' night only," I mutter.

"I like girls," he teases, and I glare at him. "That's not what I meant," he states, his face growing serious.

"Isn't this fun? We're chopping down a tree. It's like a new family tradition." Sadie interjects, finding the tension between Billy and me thicker than the stubborn tree we were chopping.

Uh-oh.

"Why don't you put that thing down before you hurt someone?" Billy says, sidling up to me as I'm still holding the ax, primed like I might toss it at him. His hand grips my forearm. His other hand reaches for the ax handle. He's too close to me. The smell of him invades my senses—clove and spice and a hint of cinnamon.

"Roxanne." The whisper of my name makes me shudder, my body vibrating harder than the thump of the ax against wood. His eyes search mine, but I look away.

I hate you, I lie to myself. *How could you hurt me like this?* His cold fingers lift for my cheek, but I won't allow him to be tender, false, and sweet. I pull back just as Sadie bellows, "Timber."

The barely five-foot tree falls to the side. Sadie reaches for the lowest branches and begins to drag the tree down the lane. Billy steps back, and I gasp for air, not realizing I was holding my breath.

"I got it," Billy calls out, chasing Sadie.

"I have it, sir." A rugged young man in a construction jacket takes the tree from Sadie and begins walking forward with it. Sadie trots next to him, and the two head toward the check-out area. Billy stalks back to me.

"We need to talk."

"*We* have nothing to say. Everything is very clear to me now. You played me to get Sadie."

"Do you really think that, Roxie?"

"The only thing I think is you're a player. You've always been a player, and you played me. First with the custody and then with…with… my heart."

"You think I played your heart?" he snarks, sarcasm deep.

"Yes. The date." I wave my arms. "And making love." I twirl both hands as I blow out a breath, so I don't cry in my frustration at seeing him. I exhale and lower my hands, slapping them on my coat, which covers my thighs. "Excellent acting, William. The academy called and wants to know where to send the trophy."

"I wasn't acting," he states, stepping up to me. His voice is venomously low as he stands straighter, curling his hands to fists at his sides. We both breathe hard, puffs of air releasing from our noses in the cold air, mixing with each other's. "Everything I said, everything I did, I meant it."

"Oh, really? *You proved a wall and me work well together.*" I repeat his words with my own venom.

"Okay, fine, not everything." We glare at one another, and I'd laugh if I could find humor.

"Is there a checklist somewhere? I can't keep up. This statement means something. This statement doesn't." I snort. *He loves me. He loves me not.*

Billy's features turn angular, and his jaw tightens. "Roxanne, can we just call a truce, and you let me explain myself?" His eyes glow in the limited light like an angered animal.

"I don't trust you." The air swooshes out of me, along with the words. I hate how they leave an aftertaste on my tongue because I had wanted to trust him.

"Roxie," he says, his voice falling.

"It was just sex anyway, right, William? That's what you're good at," I add only as the traitorous tears start to fall because I couldn't keep it casual. I couldn't blow it off as cavalier and inconsequential. I'd given him my trust and my heart along with my body.

Billy's hand move so fast I don't have time to dodge him. He cups the back of my neck, not threatening me but holding me in place so I can only see him, focus on him.

"It was not just sex to me, Roxanne. I told you. I made love to you. And you're making it difficult to love you."

"Me?" I snap.

"You were pulling away from me." He swallows as his forehead comes to mine. "And I couldn't let you go. I couldn't let you be the first to leave."

"I could be the first in your bed but not the first to leave? Is this because you saved me for the last?" I mutter. He told me in his mother's kitchen that he saved me for last as he insulted me further about my ability with a wall.

His head pulls back, and he stares at me. "What do you mean?"

"You told me you saved me for last, after the wall…" I can't even finish the rest of my statement.

"First, of all, I don't understand this obsession you have. You never saw what you think you saw because it wasn't me. And I'm sorry you thought you were never worthy of wall sex or any other type of sex or position or label or whatever. I thought we were joking around like we always do that morning. I'm sorry for how I acted, but I'm not sorry for what we did. I wasn't fucking you, Roxanne. I was falling in love with you."

Billy stares at me for a long moment, letting the bomb drop, and my heart is suddenly in my throat. His eyes search mine before he takes a deep breath. "And secondly, my grandfather used to say it didn't matter who you loved first; it was the last who mattered. The last one holds your hand and your heart, warms your bed and your soul. That's the person who sticks. He didn't care who my grandmother loved first because he was her last, and that meant forever."

I stare back at him, the sweet sentiment filling me while my lungs struggle to work.

"That's what I want, Roxie. I want you to be the last woman I take to my bed because you're the first person I think of when I climb into that bed alone each night. I told you a few weeks back. You've broken me. I don't want to move forward without you, Roxanne."

The words are too much for me to process. I don't know what to say. I'm still raw and now confused. Our eyes hold each other's.

Could he mean it? Can I trust him?

He wants me. Forever? I just don't know that I can believe him so quickly, so easily, but I know one thing. Billy Harrington loves hard, and if he ever meant it toward me, nothing would hold him back. He'd be all in just as he was long ago with Rachel. Like he is now with a different kind of love toward Sadie.

I take too long to respond to him. I don't know *how* to respond to what he's just said. His hand squeezes my nape, and while his touch heats me, the rest of me shivers.

"It's cold out here. You should get your tree," he says, releasing me, which allows the chill to seep into my bones. I tremble with the loss of his heat, and then he turns on his heels and walks away. Staring at his back, I watch his shoulders slump forward, and his hands tuck in his pockets, and my heart feels like it's been hacked at like the base of the tree Sadie and I just chopped down. With heavy feet, I follow him, taking my time to keep the distance between us.

When we near the warming house and the check-out area for the tree, Billy walks up to Sadie and drags her to him for a kiss at her temple. He pauses and says something to her, and her eyes leap over to me. Her brows pinch, and her expression shifts. Sadness fills her face, which appeared to be brightening over the past few weeks. She'd been working with Billy and spending time with Elaina practicing the piano. She smiled more and wore less makeup. I thought the old Sadie was slowly re-emerging, but one look at me, and I see her face fall. The familiar melancholy returns.

And for once, I only have myself to blame.

Chapter 39
Christmas Confessions

[Roxanne]

"Why aren't you dressed?" Sadie says to me as she enters the kitchen midmorning on Christmas. We've already shared presents and made a big breakfast with festive music playing in the background. It's been a good morning, and I'm content with how things have gone.

I look down at my jeans and red sweatshirt, and then glance back at Sadie dressed in head-to-toe black again. Dress, Converse, choker necklace. However, her makeup is softer, and her eyes not so haunted. The Harringtons have been good for her.

"I am dressed," I say to her, examining her blank expression.

"Billy's going to be here soon to pick us up."

My shoulders fall, and I glance away from her before I speak. "I'm not going to the Harringtons for Christmas."

I hadn't planned to attend. She needed this time with them. When Sadie doesn't respond, I turn back to her. "This is a time for you to enjoy them. Celebrate. With your family." I try to keep my voice steady as I speak, encouraging her to embrace them when I'm having trouble embracing the future reality. Sadie will not live with me.

"You're my family, too, and I want you to be there," Sadie whines, and I have so many responses to her plea. Then why did she do this? Why did she ask for him? But being the adult I should be, I don't ask. She made a decision with her sixteen-year-old wisdom, and I plan to abide by it. There's no sense in arguing with her.

"I can't do it, Sadie. I'm sorry." Sadie's aware that Billy and I haven't spoken. Whatever he said to her at the Christmas tree farm, she hasn't mentioned any attempts to communicate with him again. It's like the two of them have a secret, and I'm the outsider looking in.

"Do you no longer like him?" Her voice squeaks, panicked.

"It isn't a matter of liking him or not. He's your father. We'll make the best of things because of it."

"But I thought you were falling in love with him."

My eyes momentarily close as I grip the back of the chair in my kitchen. "Sadie," I drone. We went over this a few weeks back. Things got too complicated and messed up, and it's best to let them be.

"Whatever I was feeling for him, I…I just… Sadie. I'm sorry. I don't want to play nice and pretend for his family. He apologized, and I accept that he didn't mean to hurt me, not like he did, but I don't know how to go back."

"You just do," she says, her voice rising in frustration and more panic. "If I could go back, I would. I can't. You can." It takes a minute for her words to sink in, the weight of her mother's loss hitting me.

"Sadie." The name is a plea and apology and frustration rolled into one.

"I thought it would work," she whispers. Her eyes close, and I stare at her.

Confused by her words, I ask, "What would work?"

"If I picked Billy, I thought we'd be together. All three of us could live together."

I stare at my niece, eyes unblinking as I try to process what she's said.

"You…you planned this?" I'm not accusing her but questioning. "Sadie, it doesn't work this way."

"I know. I just thought if I made the decision and picked Billy, you would follow. He'll let you live with us."

Oh my God. "Sadie." I state her name with exasperation and a chuckle without humor. "That's not how these things happen."

"But they could," she retorts.

"But they don't." We stare at one another, a standoff of wills.

A sharp rap on the backdoor startles us both, and I jump. Sadie walks around me and answers it, and I take a deep breath as I prepare to see Billy. Only, the breath I took catches, and I choke when I see him in dress pants and a nice shirt wearing a long camel-colored jacket and a scarf. He looks formal and serious and delicious.

"Hey," he says, stepping inside and ducking his head.

"Merry Christmas, Billy," I offer with a weak smile as I still struggle with what Sadie has done.

"Merry Christmas." His response comes with the surprise I've spoken to him. Then his eyes roam down my body, and heat crawls upward from his gaze. "Are you ready?"

"I'm…" I look back and forth between him and Sadie. "I'm not going."

His brows rise as he glances at Sadie. A quick eye-conversation ensues between them, and I feel like an intruder in my own home.

"I just need my bag," Sadie says and turns for the hall. Billy and I stand in awkward silence for a second before he clears his throat.

"I really hoped you'd come to my family's house for the holiday. I don't like you being alone." The corner of my mouth crooks a little in hopes to reassure him.

"I don't plan to be alone today. I have plans," I lie. My destination isn't conventional.

"Oh." His brows rise as he waits for more explanation, but I don't offer details.

"Can we talk for a second?"

"Sure." I pull out the kitchen chair, but Billy steps up to me.

"Maybe in your living room."

My brows pinch, but I turn and lead him down the short hall. Our tree is decorated with homemade ornaments, as getting a tree was a last-minute project. I stop near the evergreen, and Billy stalks up to me, standing so close I can smell him. Cloves and spice and a touch of bayberry today. He smells like a Christmas gift I'll never have.

"I'm really sorry about how things happened," he begins, but I hold up a hand.

"Sadie told me what she did."

His eyes widen, and then he scratches at his neck before resting a hand on his chin. "She told you her plan?"

My head tips, and for some reason, I'm skeptical whether the plan was solely Sadie's idea. "Did you put her up to this?"

Billy smiles, the grin a bit mischievous. "Nope. She came up with it all on her own." He shakes his head. "But I told her it wouldn't work."

"Why?"

"Why what?"

"Why wouldn't it work?"

"Because you haven't forgiven me yet, and maybe you never will. I'm struggling to forgive myself for pushing you away and wanting you back when I know you won't easily come." He steps forward, filling my space and lifting his hand for my neck. He holds and strokes at my nape. "I wanted you to hold onto me, and then I'm the one who pushed you away."

My breath catches as my heart skips.

"Roxanne, do you remember when you told me you'd never live with a man again without a promise?"

"Yes." I stare at him, eyes fixated on his as he ignores my question and asks his own.

Pulling something out of his pocket, he holds up the object with his fingers. "I was hoping you would come to my mother's house so I could give you this, but seeing as you have plans, I'd like to leave it with you instead. If you are ever ready to accept my promise to never, ever hurt you again like I did, I'll be right across the street waiting. Where I'm ready to promise you more."

My eyes drift to the square red box with a white bow on the top, and I'm wondering for only a second what's taking Sadie so long to return with her bag.

"What's this?"

"The promise you wanted before you could live with another man." He lifts the box higher until I reach for it. "I don't want to pressure you, but part of the plan was Sadie hoped you'd live with us. You and me and Sadie in one house. My house and I'd make it as much yours as you'd like."

My eyes fixate on the box, leap to his, and then return to the present. He can't possibly be asking me to marry him. That's not what he's saying, and I know he would never make such a jump from where we are. Hesitantly, I take the box from him and tip the lid. Inside is a silver band entwined with a silver band of chip diamonds. I stare at the item before looking up at Billy, whose eyes focus on the ring.

"I don't understand." I honestly don't know what he's asking or what this represents, but my heart screams for me to say yes to him. A thousand yeses.

"It's a promise ring. A promise to be true to you and faithful to Sadie. There are sixteen diamonds representing her age. The two bands are us, forever entwined together because of her. I'd never break you apart. *I* don't want to be apart from you. I want us to start over somehow, someway, when you're ready." His eyes slowly lift to mine. "I love you, Roxanne. I don't want to live without you."

My breath hitches. Words escape me, and I take too long to respond because Sadie finally enters the living room.

"I'm ready," she says, but I can't take my eyes off Billy, who isn't looking away from me.

"You don't need to answer right away," he finally says. "Think about it, Roxie. Take all the time you need, but there's room at my place for all of us. And room in my heart for only you." He steps forward and corner kisses my lip like he did that first night, lingering at the crease where they join and then slowly pulling away. "Merry Christmas, Roxanne."

I still don't speak, standing in the living room with the box in my hand and a ring of promises. I don't even blink, and then I see him step back as if waiting on an answer. Another step backward and his eyes haven't left mine. One more step and then he tips his chin and spins on his dress shoe heel. He walks to Sadie, who has been watching both of us.

"Ready, honey?"

"Ready, Dad." Her eyes observe me a second longer, and then she adds, "Are you sure you don't want to come with us?"

I'm not certain of anything at that moment, but my mouth finally opens as I watch father and daughter stand together.

"Go without me, baby. Merry Christmas."

+ + +

As I stand on the solid earth, packed down over the months, I stare at the minimal stone laid next to my mother's.

"Hey, Trixie," I say, eyes flooding with liquid, and her full name blurs. The dates disappear as well. My sister was only in her mid-forties. Too young to pass. Too soon to leave this earth.

"I messed up." I choke on the words and swallow the thickness in my throat. "I messed up so badly."

I sniff as I try to find the words to explain myself to my sister, hoping her spirit hears me.

"I thought she didn't choose me, but all she wants is a family."

Tears fall in earnest, and I swipe at my cheeks. "I thought I failed you, but you messed up, too. You were upset when you found out you were pregnant and so unsure of the future. You thought you could do it on your own, but you never did. I was there for you. You should have told him. It could have been more than a crush and just sex. He's so much more, Trixie, and you weren't fair to him."

I swallow as I sardonically chuckle. "I slept with him, too." I blink back the tears and stare up at the winter sky overhead. "I slept with him because I had a crush on him as well, but it has turned into so much more for me, and my heart feels like it's been ripped into a million pieces. I don't know what to do. He wants me to live with him. With both of them. He's a good man. Romantic. Loving. God, he loves so hard, Trixie. And he's directing that love at me."

I glance back at the grave where my sister eternally rests.

"I love him. I love them both. Thank you for trusting her with me."

Tears fall heavier as I confess to my dead sister how much I love the man she never knew and the daughter she's lost through no fault of her own.

I haven't been paying attention to Billy. Not the right attention. I've missed the signs he tried to hold up for me to read. The ones that screamed his vulnerability, yet he opened up to me. He didn't hold back. I'm the one who tried to play casual and misinterpreted everything about him.

He loves me, and he told me in all the little ways.

You're breaking me.

I don't think I can do this without you.

I made love to you.

I want you to be my last.

And then he gave me that heartfelt explanation from his grandfather. It doesn't matter who Billy had first, or how or where or why, because he has me last.

Forever.

And now I just need to prove it to him.

Chapter 40
Resolutions

[Billy]

"Boss, someone wants to see you," Clyde says, his big body filling the door to my office.

It's New Year's Eve, and the pub is packed. Both the main floor and the second-floor party room are full. It seems like every member of Blue Ridge has come out tonight to celebrate the beginning of a new year, but I'm taking a second for myself in my office. It's been a long evening, and there's still an hour to go before midnight.

Sadie spent Christmas with me and my family, but it wasn't the same without Roxanne. There was a hole in my heart that only she could fill. When I returned Sadie to the apartment, Roxie wasn't present. I should be grateful she didn't throw my gift back at me, but her eyes still spoke of uncertainty. She's never going to trust me again, and she also hasn't spoken to me since that day. I laid it all out for her and...*nothing*.

"Yeah, who wants to see me?"

"Some woman at the bar," Clyde says. His voice is a bit too tight and high with this announcement, almost like he's trying to contain a chuckle, but I don't find anything humorous about his statement.

"I have no interest in some random woman at the bar." I huff, scrubbing my knuckles up my neck. Roxie's the only woman I want.

"She said something about a noise complaint. The music's too loud and—"

"Are you shitting me?" I say, slapping my hand on the desk before standing. *What in tarnation?* "It's New Year's Eve. Who the hell complains about noise on New Year's? Who complains about the noise in general? We're a bar, and we..."

I pause as Clyde's smile grows, and my mouth falls agape as two hands cover his large bicep and push him aside.

"You're a bar, and you make a lot of noise over here."

"Roxanne?" I choke on her name.

"I want to file a complaint with the owner. Noise violation."

Those silver eyes sparkle like the confetti ready to explode at midnight, and I swipe a hand through my hair.

"A noise violation, huh?"

"I'll just…" Clyde points with both thumbs toward the hall and then offers me two thumbs-up as he steps back. He's such a goof. He reaches for the door and pulls it closed, leaving Roxie and me within my office.

"Yes, a noise violation," Roxie states, drawing me back to her.

"You know, complaining about loud music only proves you don't know how to have fun."

"I know," she says, surprising me. "I have other things to disprove as well." Her hand lifts for her throat and cups her neck. She's wearing a black dress with a velvet jacket in silver over it. The color enhances her eyes.

"Like what?" I ask, still standing behind my desk, my heart racing in my chest.

"Like I'm sorry. I thought you'd want to keep things casual, so I tried to do that, and I messed it all up."

"Roxie." My voice lowers. Her fingers tap along her throat, and my mouth waters to kiss her there.

"I couldn't keep it casual, so I pushed, maybe a little too hard. Lashing out is what we do, but I don't want to lash out any longer. You broke me by what happened with Sadie."

"I know. I'm sorry, I—"

"William," she interjects, holding up the hand from her throat, the back of it waving at me. "Let me speak."

She says something next, but I don't hear a word as my eyes are fixated on the silver gleam coming off her left ring finger.

"You're wearing the ring," I interject again, pointing a finger at her.

"That's what I'm trying to tell you," she snaps without much bite. I round the desk, stalking up before her. My eyes still fixated on her finger as she returns her hand to her throat. "I'm trying to say I'd like to take your promise and offer one of my own."

My head leaps up as my hands cup her upper arms. My mouth has gone dry.

"We need to talk, Billy. We need to talk about a few things, but I want to promise to pay better attention to the signs. To *read you* better. I want to promise that I will love you with my whole heart and all my being and—"

I don't let her continue as my mouth crashes into hers, wanting to swallow every word. I drink in the possibility of her promise. The hope she's saying yes to everything. Us. Sadie. The three of us together. I reach for the corner of her lips and kiss her in a way her mouth curls, and then I return to full coverage. Devouring the lower lip before licking against the seam, asking for her to let me in.

"You are trouble, Billy Harrington," she mutters against my mouth, and I pull back, hesitantly relinquishing her lips. I don't want to stop kissing. I want to keep kissing her until she accepts there's something between us. Something forever.

"But you love me," I tease, not expecting an answer.

"Yes, I do."

My brows rise, and my heart drops. *She...*

"I love you, Billy." Her voice softens as her hands come to my jaw, stroking my scruff. My eyes close, pinching under the relief that she's here. She's touching me. She's saying yes to me.

"I love you, too, Roxie. God, I love you," I say as my eyes open, and my mouth returns to hers for another breathtaking kiss before I pull back. I reach for her hand, stroking my thumb over the ring.

"I don't want to be just roommates," I say and then lower to kiss the back of her hand over the ring. Then turning it over, I press a kiss to her palm and a second on the inside of her ring finger. "I want us as forever-mates."

"Forever-mates?" She chuckles as she scrunches up her face. "Like roommates forever?"

"Like lovers forever. And best friends. And soul mates." I look at her face, holding her eyes with mine. "I want to marry you one day, Roxie. If you'll have me."

"I'll have you, Billy." Her lips curl into a deep smile. "Speaking of having you…" She tips up on her toes and takes my lips this time, her tongue pressing forward. Her body leans into me, but I want to be clear.

"So, this is a yes? You're moving in with me? You and Sadie. And it's not casual, and it's going to get complicated."

"So complicated, William," she teases, her voice lowering as she presses against me. "And yes, I'd like to move in with you and Sadie."

Another kiss ensues before I can't take it anymore.

"Fuck, I've missed you," I say as the kiss accelerates, and I'm stiff as a block of wood. "I want to slip inside you underneath this skirt." My hands come to her hips, rocking forward so she knows how I feel about her.

"What is it with you and my skirts?" she teases.

"It's like a little private tent over us, like a secret for only us."

"Only us," she whispers, and I lower my forehead to hers.

"I want to complicate things right here in my office," I admit to her, and she pulls back.

"Here? You said you never take women to your office."

I look at her hairline and brush back that silver-white hair before meeting her eyes. "No women. One woman. You."

"Does this mean desk sex?" she inquires, her voice a bit eager at the possibility, and my curious bookstore owner gives me a saucy look. I spin her so her backside hits the desk, and I lean toward her.

"Would you like that? Desk sex?"

"I want any kind of sex with you, William." Her voice softens on my full name as she flirts with me.

"Well, I don't just want sex with you, Roxie. I want to make love to you. In my bed. Against a wall. On a desk. I don't care as long as I'm inside you."

Her breath hitches, and her fingertips rub over my scruff again. "You should be a writer. You have a way with words."

"I prefer to be a reader."

"But you don't read," she reminds me.

"Yeah, but I want to read you, Roxie. Every page." I kiss her jaw. "And every corner." I kiss her lip in that spot that gets her. "And every fold."

"Billy," she hisses, and there's the sound I want to hear.

"Ready to beg me for it, Roxie?" I tease.

"Yes, William. Yes, I want you to give everything to me."

Like a firecracker, I'm off. Mouth on hers. Hand lifting skirt. My fingers can't get to her fast enough. As I slip past her underwear and into her warm depths, we both pause, and our eyes meet.

"I love you," she whispers.

"I love you," I say. "And I can't wait to take you home."

Her mouth curves. "How about you take me here first?" she says, and I don't want to disappoint her. I never want to disappoint her again, and I plan to make good on all my promises, including giving her what she wants on my desk.

Everything.

Our bodies lean back, and one of her legs lifts for my hips. Her hands clutch at my neck.

"Hold onto me, darlin'."

"I'm never letting go," she moans, and that's the kind of noise violation I want to hear.

Epilogue
February

[Billy]

I'm nervous when I shouldn't be nervous. My hands swipe down my jeans-covered thighs before I open the door for Roxanne and Sadie. Their items were moved in after the new year, and we've been working at building a life for three.

"Well," I say as I hold the door, watching my girls walk into the house. Our house.

"I passed," Sadie announces, holding up the driver's license in her hand. She beams, matching the photo on the identification. We discussed changing her name but conceded to hyphenating it, so she can keep her identity as a McAllister, but in my heart, she's all Harrington.

"I'm so proud of you," I say, pulling her in for a hug. I give them freely to her now, and she gives them back to me, which I know I shouldn't expect to always happen. She is a teenager, after all, so I take whatever she offers, and I stash it in my heart to hold it a little longer.

Roxie steps up to me next, offering a kiss herself, and I always find it a struggle to keep it chaste and clean in front of my child. Most days, I still want to ravish her from the moment her mouth touches mine. It's been so different being with her day in and day out, and although I don't compare Roxanne to Rachel, I see how different it can be. How different love can be.

We head to the kitchen, ready to make lunch when a knock comes on the door. Roxanne's head pops up. "I'll get it."

When she turns, she sheepishly looks at Sadie.

"Sadie, there's a boy here to see you."

Sadie's face turns bright red, and her hair falls forward as she looks at her feet, fighting a smile. She tucks a wedge of hair behind her ears and then steps out of the kitchen.

"This is a joke, right?" I stare at Roxie, who fights her own smile.

"He's cute," she teases, and I tip my head as if to look through the opening to the front entry. "Stop," she admonishes, pulling me behind the wall.

"Is it that Christian kid?" I hiss, and Roxanne's lips twist.

"Did you know he was the boy working at the Christmas tree farm?"

I actually did know. I got him the job to work off the money he stole so he could pay me back the money I paid out to cover what he'd done for Sadie.

"He's trouble," I warn, acting as if I can see through the wall into the living room where Sadie still stands by the front door with him.

"So are you," Roxanne teases, tugging at the collar of my shirt. "But under all that trouble might be a man with a soft heart." She brings my mouth to hers, and I fall into the kiss, forgetting for only a second that there's a boy speaking with my daughter in the front room.

"What do you think they're talking about?" I question, pulling back and leaning to the side as if I can hear them.

"Wall sex," Roxanne states, her tone serious until I look at her. Her silver eyes dance, and she bites the corner of her lip.

"That's not even funny," I retort, but I don't have any bark to my bite. "I think the troublemaker is you."

"Me?" She holds her hand to her chest. "I'm never trouble." But the smile she gives me tells me she is. She's still a pain in my ass somedays, and most days, I love it.

"I love your kind of trouble," I say, leaning toward her for another kiss.

"I love you," she says. It will never get old hearing her say those words to me, and she tells me every day. When I question what I'm doing as a father or wonder if I've proved myself with my father, she tells me she loves me, and I know I'm enough. Just me as I am.

"Ah-hem." Sadie clears her throat. She's used to this, often catching us kissing one another. At first, I found it strange she was upstairs whenever Roxanne and I buried ourselves in my bed. We've become rather creative with a teenager in the house. "Christian would like to take me out for hot chocolate, but I'd like to know if I can drive."

"You just got your license," I say, knowing the plan was a celebratory lunch and then bowling this afternoon.

"He's on his motorcycle."

"Here are the keys," Roxanne offers, leaning for the key hook near her head. She hands them to Sadie, who continues to smile. She's such a beautiful girl, and I'm surprised sometimes when I consider I made her. But it's been Theresa and Roxanne who molded her into the girl she is. The one conscious of her grades but still likes to have a little fun in life.

"Behave yourselves," Sadie warns us like we are the teenagers.

"We always do," I tease, and Sadie huffs with a roll of her eyes. "You behave yourself."

"It's only hot chocolate," she says, and I'm about to reply that it's never just hot chocolate, thinking back to the night I asked Roxanne on our first official date and brought her to my home. I knew that night everything would be different, and it was.

Roxanne covers my lips with two fingers, worried what I'll say next. She isn't wrong. My comment might have been too much for Sadie.

"Have fun," Roxanne says, smiling at her niece, and Sadie returns the grin before disappearing behind the wall. When we hear the front door open and close, I sag forward, resting my forehead on Roxanne's.

"I'm not going to survive fatherhood."

"I hope that's not true," she says, and I pull back, wondering what she means. My eyes narrow as my head tilts.

"What are you saying?"

"What if I were pregnant?"

My heart falls to my belly, and the chest-clenching sensation which hasn't been present for months returns. My knuckles run up my throat, scratching before my hand cups my chin. I'm forty-six. Roxanne is forty-one. Is this possible?

"Are you?"

"No." Her smile grows as my blood slowly begins to flow again.

"That wasn't even funny."

"It was kind of funny." She laughs.

"You nearly gave me a heart attack."

"Just wanted to poke the bear," she teases, still chuckling.

"I'll give you something to poke."

"Don't you mean, something to poke me?" Her voice remains playful. She slides out from her position between the wall and me and curls her body around the opening into the dining area. "We're all alone, William."

"Meaning?" I hitch a brow, understanding her implication before she even speaks. Her shirt comes over her head as she stands before me, and I lunge, but she takes off at a brisk pace, stalking through the dining room, then living room, and making a sharp right into our room.

Our room.

I catch her just inside the door and then reach back for the slider to close off the living room. We're alone, but I want to tuck us into the bed tent of sheets and bury myself in her, but first, I press her up against the wall.

"I love you," I tell her.

"I love you, and I was only joking about a pregnancy."

My hands slide over her bare belly, and I pause. "I'd never say no if you wanted to try." Roxanne knows I feel like I've missed out by not raising Sadie from the ground up, and I know Roxanne has always felt like she missed a part of herself, where she hoped to one day have a child of her own.

"I think Sadie is enough," Roxanne says, her hands swiping down my shirt and then tugging it up, so it slips over my head.

"You're enough," I remind her.

"So are you," she says before her mouth finds mine, and the way she kisses me is no joke.

Thank you for taking the time to read Silver Player.
Please consider writing a review on major sales channels where ebooks and paperbooks are sold.

Want a sip of Billy and Roxanne in the future?

SILVER PLAYER BONUS

Want to read the next Harrington brother to fall in love? *Silver Mayor* Opposites attract when single father, good guy Charlie Harrington encounters the new woman in town and wants to be a little bad with her.

Flip the page for a sample.

Read where the Harringtons were first introduced in *Second Chance*, Mati Harrington and Denton Chance's friends-to-lovers, second chance romance.

+ + +

A sip of *Silver Mayor*

Chapter 1
Put A Ring on It
[Janessa]

"What are you doing in here?"

My eyes leap up to the mirror over the dresser, meeting rich brown ones scowling back at me. The depth of his voice doesn't match his face. Smooth and handsome, almost pretty. With silver at his temples and a clean-shaven jaw, he's everything I left behind, and his question is a good one.

What am I doing in this town?

What am I doing in his house?

What am I doing in his room?

I stare back at him, my hand lowering to my belly. The fingers of my right struggle with the item on the left. I shouldn't be in here. I shouldn't have done this.

"Who are you?" he growls.

"I'm Jan," I say, struggling on the name. I should clarify with more detail, but I don't want to get my mother in trouble. With all she's sacrificed over the years, I don't want her to lose this job working for him. I don't need to ask who he is. I've heard of him.

Charlie Harrington, mayor of Blue Ridge, Georgia.

"I asked you a question. Do you not understand English?" His voice softens a little, trying not to insult me with the possibility but insulting me all the same. Just because my skin is darker than his, he's making assumptions I'm not American.

"I can speak English very well, thank you," I snap back at him, still tugging at my left finger with my right ones. I can't believe this is happening to me. It's what I get for being sidetracked.

Mama sent me over here so she could take care of something for my papa. I didn't want to be here, and my eyes wandered when I was supposed to be picking up the room. Make the bed. Straighten the pillows. Fresh towels. Toss the laundry in the washroom. I wasn't the housekeeper, and I didn't want to act like one. I didn't want my mother to be one either, but her entire life had been dedicated to cleaning up after others. It's what she did. She did it for me and my brother.

"You still haven't answered my question. I'm giving you to the count of ten before I call the police."

Dear Lord, he's acting like I'm a child, but I've done something childish. I couldn't help myself. I just wanted to know what it would look like but now I'm struggling to remove it. My right fingers tug as the knuckle of my left bunches.

"*One. Two.*"

The louder he counts, the more I sweat, and my ring finger swells. His voice isn't helping either. It's deep and rugged, clashing with the sharp suit and open-at-the-collar dress shirt. He wasn't supposed to be here. Mama said he left for work.

"*Three. Four.* What are you doing?"

My eyes lift back to the mirror, watching him stalk closer to me in the reflection. He's almost to my back but the aroma of him proceeds him. Manly and woodsy like this area. I didn't grow up in a place quite so lush with foliage and greenery. Texas was more dry dirt and barren. Dull brown.

His presence overshadows my childhood memories. His chest nearly presses into my back.

"*Five. Six.* I'm still waiting." He pauses and then his body language shifts. "Are you trying to steal something from me?" His voice elevates. His brows pinch, furrowing his smooth forehead and I glance up at him again through the mirror, but he's not looking at me. He's scanning the top of his dresser which is relatively clean for a man. He's not a bachelor. This I also know about him. He's a single father and he lives in this large house with his only child, Lucy. My mother is her nanny along with her other duties.

Thick hands come to my shoulders and he spins me to face him. My back collides with the tall bureau and I glance up at him, my eyes captivated by his. The brown isn't dull like desert sand, but earthy and rich like turned soil. His mouth curls downward as he continues to scowl at me.

"I wasn't stealing anything."

"Then what are you doing with your hands?" A brow tips again, the look almost playful, as if he has something more to say, something mischievous to add, but he stops himself.

Lowering my head, I lift my left hand and hold the back to him so he can see what I've done.

"It's stuck."

His eyes stare at my finger, focused on the gold ring with a large emerald and two smaller diamonds on either side of the gem. It's simple and beautiful, antique looking, and priceless, I imagine.

"Where did you get that?" His voice lowers, the rugged sound turning rough and menacing.

"I swear I wasn't stealing it. It was sitting in the dish." He has a small bowl with coins and such on the dresser and the ring sat inside with the collection of items. "I slipped it on." I exhale. "I shouldn't have slipped it on, and now I can't get it off."

With my right fingers, I tug once again, but my left knuckle is already red and raw from the aggressive effort I've put forth in attempts to remove the item.

"I should call the police," he states, and he's within his right. I can explain, but again, I don't want my mother in trouble. She says Charlie's a good boss, fair and kind, and I don't want to put any blame on her for this situation. I'm the one who slipped on the ring and I'm the one who can't get it off.

"Please don't. Just…Just let me get this off my hand and you'll never see me again." I'm good at being in the shadows. I've done it most of my adult life, married to a man who'd rather pretend I didn't exist, at least not exist with thoughts or intelligence.

Just stand there, Janessa. Look pretty.

Charlie grips my hand and I instantly react when I shouldn't. Something charged and prickly races up my arm and my heart skips a beat like it's been jump-started, although it's already racing.

Without words, he tugs me forward and I stumble after him. He drags me to the bathroom off his master bedroom and shoves my hand under the sink. Turning on the faucet with his free hand, the cold water almost hurts it's so cold. He reaches forward for the green bar of soap and works at my hand, coating it in a thin lather. More woodsy fragrance permeates the air around us.

He drops the bar in the sink and massages at my finger, but the ring isn't moving.

"I don't have time for this," he snaps under his breath and rinses my hand, working his fingers over mine to wash away the soap. Once satisfied I'm free of sudsy residue, he lifts my hand, droplets of water sliding down to my wrist and opens his mouth.

"What…"

Before I can finish my thought, my ring finger is inside the warm cavern between his cheeks. He closes his lips over the digit and his tongue circles around my finger. Within seconds, his teeth scrap the length of my finger. He pauses at the tip like he's pressing it with a kiss and then tugs my finger free like it offended him. Leaning forward as he lifts his other hand, he spits.

The ring falls into his palm and he stares at the sparkling emerald with the almost white diamonds on either side of it. I tug at my hand still held within his, but he doesn't release me. He glances up at me instead.

"This was my grandmother's," he states as if I asked which I didn't, but from the puzzled look on his face, I sense its value is more than something on a price tag.

"It's beautiful," I whisper, staring down at it, and then slowly my eyes lift, and we lock stares again. We're standing in his bathroom, a space clearly occupied by only a man. The scent of aftershave. The woodsy soap. The dark towel over the rod. His eyes aren't leaving my face but slowly his hold on my hand lessens. There's a question in those eyes. He wants to know more than who I am and what I'm doing in his room, but I won't give him answers. He's too similar to what I left behind, and I'll never go back to where I was, who I was.

Once I sense I'm free, I pull back my hand, turn for the door, and race for the hallway. He calls after me, but I take the stairs two at a time, hopping down them as if I'm a teen instead of a forty-something woman trying to escape a man's home, hoping to get away Scott-free from both his house and those rich, haunting eyes.

Continue reading: *Silver Mayor*

More by L.B. Dunbar

<u>Sterling Falls</u>
Small town. Big heart. Seven siblings muddling their way through love over 40.
Sterling Heat
Sterling Brick
Sterling Streak

Parentmoon
When the mother of the groom goes head-to-head with the single father of the bride.

<u>Holiday Hotties (Christmas novellas)</u>
Holiday novellas certain to heat the season.
Scrooge-ish
Naughty-ish

<u>Road Trips & Romance</u>
3 sisters. 3 destinations. A second chance at love over 40.
Hauling Ashe
Merging Wright
Rhode Trip

<u>Lakeside Cottage</u>
Four friends. Four summers. Shenanigans and love happen at the lake.
Living at 40
Loving at 40
Learning at 40
Letting Go at 40

<u>The Silver Foxes of Blue Ridge</u>
Small mountain town, silver foxes. Brothers seeking love over 40.
Silver Brewer
Silver Player
Silver Mayor
Silver Biker

<u>Sexy Silver Foxes</u>
When sexy silver foxes meet the feisty vixens of their dreams.

SILVER PLAYER

After Care
Midlife Crisis
Restored Dreams
Second Chance
Wine&Dine

Collision novellas
A spin-off from After Care – the younger set/rock stars
Collide
Caught

Rom-com standalone for the over 40
The Sex Education of M.E.

The Heart Collection
Small town, big hearts - stories of family and love.
Speak from the Heart
Read with your Heart
Look with your Heart
Fight from the Heart
View with your Heart

A Heart Collection Spin-off
The Heart Remembers

BOOKS IN OTHER AUTHOR WORLDS
Smartypants Romance (an imprint of Penny Reid)
Tales of the Winters sisters set in Green Valley.
Love in Due Time
Love in Deed
Love in a Pickle

The World of True North (an imprint of Sarina Bowen)
Welcome to Vermont! And the Busy Bean Café.
Cowboy
Studfinder

L.B. DUNBAR

THE EARLY YEARS
The Legendary Rock Star Series
A classic tale with a modern twist of rock star romance and suspense

Paradise Stories
MMA romance. Two brothers. One fight.

The Island Duet
Intrigue and suspense. The island knows what you've done.

Modern Descendants – writing as elda lore
Magical realism. Modern myths of Greek gods.

About the Author

www.lbdunbar.com

L.B. Dunbar loves sexy silver foxes, second chances, and small towns. If you enjoy older characters in your romance reads, including a hero with a little silver in his scruff and a heroine rediscovering her worth, then welcome to romance for those over 40. L.B. Dunbar's signature works include women and men in their prime taking another turn at love and happily ever after. She's a *USA TODAY* Bestseller as well as #1 Bestseller on Amazon in Later in Life Romance with her Lakeside Cottage and Road Trips & Romance series. L.B. lives in Chicago with her own sexy silver fox.

To get all the scoop about the self-proclaimed queen of silver fox romance, join her on Facebook at Loving L.B. or receive her monthly newsletter, Love Notes.

+ + +

Connect with L.B. Dunbar

 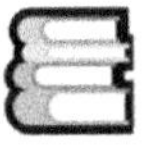